"WRITTEN WITH CONSIDERABLE THOUGHT AND COMPLEXITY."
—The New Orleans Times-Picayune

"Framing her story as a murder mystery, Woodward insightfully explores the greater mystery of family, the betrayals of love.... [Laura] is a character to care about as she copes with her grief, her mixed feelings about her mother and sister, what she perceives as her father's betrayal. Her boyfriend and her best friend both hurt and help her, but, in the end, she must call on her own resilience to face frightening revelations about those closest to her."

—The Orlando Sentinel

"Memorable characters distinguish this first novel by a New Orleans attorney who has as fine an ear for how people (make that Southern people) talk as she does for how lawyers—and eighteen-year-olds—think."

—Mademoiselle

"A poised whodunnit with a distinctly Southern flair... As much as [Laura] wants to believe Catherine guilty of the murders, her questions increasingly become doubts that ripple across the facts of the crime. But will those doubts lead to the real killer? The answers will surprise you."

—The Birmingham News

Books published by The Ballantine Publishing Group
are available at quantity discounts on bulk purchases
for premium, educational, fund-raising, and special
sales use. For details, please call 1-800-733-3000.

THE INDICTMENT

Margaret Woodward

IVY BOOKS • NEW YORK

Ivy Books
Published by Ballantine Books
Copyright © 1994 by Margaret Woodward

Originally published by G. P. Putnam's Sons in 1994 under the title *Still Waters*.

http://www.randomhouse.com

Library of Congress Catalog Card Number: 95-95319

ISBN 0-8041-1465-X

This edition published by arrangement with Putnam Publishing Group.

Manufactured in the United States of America

First Ballantine Books Edition: May 1996

10 9 8 7 6 5 4 3 2 1

ACKNOWLEDGMENTS

To do justice to my family, friends, and other helpmates, I would have to write a book-length acknowledgment. Instead, I offer my heartfelt thanks to all those who read, edited, advised, and encouraged.

Special thanks to my gentle editor, Carrie Feron; my persistent agent, Pam Ahearn; my mechanical advisor, Milton LeFebre; to Eino Friberg for his translation of *The Kalevala*; to Cathy St. John for typing and retyping; and to my informal editors: Chris and Avery Crounse, Steve Baker, Sally Draper, Sally Thomas, Amie Paul, Cheryl Suchors, Gregory Pechukas, Carol Baker, Beth Ryan, Lucie Cavaroc, and Vereen Woodward; and to the Iberville Point gang: Jo Harriet Strickler, Dot Waldrup, Karen Frazer, and Phyllis Potterfield.

For M. Truman Woodward, Jr.,
who wouldn't have liked this book
if anyone else had written it

PREFACE

Once in a blue moon the operator of the roller coaster at the county fair sends the train on a second run for free. Maybe he loses count, or maybe he acts out of malice toward his tight-fisted employers; but when it happened to Blake and me on that magical day last fall, we thought our infectious happiness had pushed the old man's hand forward on the lever. There we were, in the most public of public places, laughing and clinging to one another, believing that the best things in life are free and within reach, that even lost opportunities could be reclaimed. For example, childhood, an experience which I had missed but which Blake was determined to restore to me, as if he could stuff my head with a pink cloud of happy memories as easily as he poked tufts of cotton candy into my mouth. At the time, it seemed possible. Sugar-sticky fingers on the restraining bar. Mouth gaping into the down-sweep, a tendril of spun sugar windswept across my cheek. Childlike.

We were still breathless from the ride as we coasted to the platform, and when the train accelerated with a jolt, everyone screamed—even those who had hurtled downward in stoic silence. We screamed in delight and unpreparedness for the terrors ahead. A free ride. The thrill of being given what we could so easily have afforded but would not have dared to buy: another heart-stopping loop in the daylight.

This morning I awoke with a start, feeling the slight, lurching pressure of the seat back against my spine that says we are off again before we can catch our breath. I don't need my lawyer to interpret the sensation for me; the grand jury has emerged from its two weeks of secret deliberations to return an indictment against me.

Oh, Blake, without your arm to brace me in the turns, what is to keep me from flying out of the car?

1

THERE HAD BEEN days like this in every fall that Duck could remember, called "unseasonably" warm, although they were more customary for Alabama than the cool, crisp air elsewhere associated with October. What was different this year was the unrelenting grip of the summer. A two-fisted grip: heat, and oppressive humidity that pounded the heat into every pore. The wind that came up from the Gulf of Mexico was warm and dank like a dog's breath; people shut their windows against it, and the crickets could not be heard over the drone of air conditioners. The weather fore-casters had had nothing new to say since early May. Their pointers tapped excitedly at cartoon snowflakes in the Rockies and prodded tropical depressions in the Gulf in the barely contained hope of awakening them into full-blown hurricanes. But the cold fronts stopped dead at the northern state line and the big storms spun off to the east or west or crashed into some Caribbean island where the death toll caught only a moment's attention on the Alabama coast.

Duck lifted one thigh and then the other from the hot seat of the unairconditioned MTA bus. She had chosen a seat near the back, behind one of the few windows that opened. Her apricot silk shift, the most sophisticated dress in her wardrobe (when dry), was soaking wet against the plastic seat back. Another damp triangle above her breasts

3

had dyed the fabric a hideous orange. Her thick brown hair
had sprung into an unruly wedge of frizz.

Even through the gray film on the windows, she had to
squint against the glare and bustle of downtown. For two
months, she had hardly left the house, and she felt dazed
and disoriented, as if she had walked into the blinding sunlight after watching a long matinee, which was close to the
truth. On every window of the Spencers' big Victorian
house, the heavy draperies were drawn tight. Throughout
the new fall season, Duck and her brother Junior had sat
dully in the crepuscular glare of the television. They
watched sitcoms without laughing and game shows without
guessing at the answers.

Mother used to adjust the draperies daily, sometimes
hourly, to protect her interiors from the bleaching rays of
the sun. Mother devoted herself to those sorts of details. A
visitor swinging the heavy wrought-iron gate silently open
on its oiled hinges, padding over the herringbone quilting of
moss Mother had cultivated in the spaces between the
bricks of the front walk, and entering the foyer Mother had
painted teal blue, the color that best complemented her auburn hair, would sense at once, if only subconsciously,
Mother's exacting nature. But all of Mother's controls had
offered not the feeblest barrier against that most fundamental disorder, death. Mother had died five months ago, just
shy of her much-dreaded fortieth birthday. If that were not
lesson enough in powerlessness, death had claimed her
fifteen-year-old daughter Alexandra Spencer at the same
time.

Shoeboxes full of sympathy cards had promised Duck
that time would heal even this terrible hurt. Duck knew
most of the cards were homework assignments for her and
Alexandra's classmates. She could almost see the proper
format, the sample condolence on the blackboard. Yet she
clung to the fungible messages, carefully penned in so

many hands. *Time heals all wounds.* She had waited patiently, but healing had not come. Instead, her depression had deepened day after day. At first, she had only mourned for Mother and Alexandra abstractly. It was terrible, shocking that they were gone. But it was far worse, now, to miss them concretely, to have specific needs that they were not there to fill.

Today, for instance. If Alexandra were alive the trip to Catherine Liem's exhibit at the Galerie Maxine would have been a grand adventure. Maybe they would have worn Isadora Duncan scarves and rented a limousine. Or pretended to. Something to make the excursion bold, amusing, light-hearted. If Mother had accompanied them—and this was one of the rare occasions when she might have—she would have parked her Jaguar out front and strode in, demanding to see Ms. Liem's weavings. There would have been none of Duck's hesitation, secretiveness, or riding in abject discomfort on the bus.

Unfortunately, Mother and Alexandra were unavailable, and no substitutes were at hand. Most of Duck's friends, newly graduated, had left over the summer for college, including Duck's boyfriend, Rick. That left her home with her now detested father and her brother Junior. Though Junior would have been a willing companion, he had Down Syndrome, and while he functioned at a high level, art criticism was not within his capabilities.

Or Duck's, she feared. She was in a state of fuzzy-headed confusion. She had no bearings. Her sense of being anchored to a respected and privileged family had died along with Mother and Alexandra. Her father's flourishing architectural career had not protected the Spencers. Her mother's inherited wealth had not protected them. Mother's considerable fortune had passed to Duck, and she drew no comfort from it. None at all. She wanted her mother back. She wanted her sister.

Duck crouched miserably in her lurching seat, scarcely daring to look out. Her car was parked on Old Shell Road, in midtown. She felt conspicuous enough just going to the Galerie Maxine, without parking her red convertible out front, sporting its personalized license plate: DUCK. It was the name her sister Alexandra had coined when Duck, née Laura, was four years old and Alexandra was one and a half. Alexandra's plastic yellow duckie was her favorite toy, in or out of the tub. One winter night, Alexandra caught sight of Laura in her fleecy yellow footie pajamas; Alexandra clapped her hands and squealed "Duck!" (actually "Duh!") in delight. Their parents thought the incident was so cute, they preserved the nickname as a memento. And so a pattern was established: Alexandra would control her sister's life as well as her own.

Her name was the only unattractive thing Duck's mother had ever allowed her to wear, and from it she knew that Mother loved Alexandra best. The silly moniker no longer quacked at her, just as the mole on her cheek no longer pierced her with a sense of ugliness every time she spied it in the mirror. But it was there, a reminder. Once Duck had protested—only once, for Mother did not brook extended opposition. Mother reassured her, "You'll grow out of it."

"What about me?" Alexandra cried. "How do you grow out of a name like Alexandra?"

"You'll grow into it," Mother promised. But she hadn't had the chance.

This was the last day of the Catherine Liem exhibit, and unlike all the rest of Duck's plans, this trip could not be postponed. So Duck had relinquished the safe gloom of home and ventured to the first Mobile exhibit of Catherine Liem's work in almost two years. Although Liem was in her late twenties and relatively new to the art scene, her family connections, her money, and, Duck grudgingly admitted, her talent had quickly propelled her into international circles.

On the local scene, Liem was simultaneously putting on several displays: at Maxine's, in the courts, and in the news media. A made-for-TV life coming into full flower. Shipping magnate's granddaughter. Rock star's daughter. Precious charge of Elga, who had felicitously just published *Memoirs of a Nanny*. The media was shooting more angles on Liem's unfolding story than Hitchcock fixed on the shower scene in *Psycho*.

Duck missed the gallery stop on Dauphin Street because the crowd of schoolchildren in front of her were engaged in a friendly spitball war and popped in and out of their seats like popcorn exploded by the heat of the bus. When she finally escaped at Bienville Square, she tried negotiating the two blocks back with her eyes trained on the sidewalk, trying the childhood spell of achieving invisibility by seeing no one. It worked, but any thoughts she might have had about slipping inside Maxine's unnoticed were thwarted by the sign in the center of the locked glass door: PLEASE RING BELL. Duck's reflection in the front door was discouragingly bedraggled. Her long brown hair was a mess, her bangs had rolled up like a shade, and her dress was drying in a puckered sort of way. Worse, the small, curious crowd in which she'd hoped to get lost was nowhere to be seen. In fact the gallery was empty with the exception of Maxine, wearing a smile as big as a sorority house and rushing to admit her.

"Come in, come in," Maxine gushed. "I do hate keeping people out there, and in this heat. But things have been just too crimeful downtown lately and me here all alone." She took Duck firmly by the elbow, as if to prevent flight, and led her into the icy foyer. The blast of cold air mixed with embarrassment brought the blood pounding behind Duck's fair skin and set a pimple throbbing in the center of her forehead. It felt like a beacon of her youth and discomfort among the pricey weavings slung, draped, and dangling from the walls and ceiling of the gallery.

From the paper's half-page on the exhibit Duck had expected the weavings to be sinister. The article, headed "TANGLED WEBS OF MURDERESS ON DISPLAY AT MAXINE'S," had depicted a sharp-faced woman perched in front of what did indeed appear to be a hideous snare. Duck now realized that the woman in the photograph was Maxine, not the artist. And the "tangled webs," stark black and white in the photograph, had colorized into soft earth tones and glimmering metals, seeming more like the enchanted nets of Wynken, Blinken, and Nod.

Maxine was not one to let customers reflect silently. "It's been too quiet in here this afternoon. *Enough* of this quiet!" she shouted at the wall in a voice that sounded as if she had been shouting all day. "I can just tell you have an eye for beautiful things. And color! That yummy dress, I know you didn't buy it in this backwater town. New York, am I right?"

"London," Duck mumbled.

"Oh my God!" Maxine shrieked in her whiskey voice. "You *do* know the world! My favorite city on earth, and look over here, it's the *pièce de la* show." She strode to the back of the long gallery, Duck following uncertainly.

"London Wharves," she announced, with a grand gesture toward the weavings behind her. "Is that *it*?" she rasped. "Is that not *it*?"

Duck did not know what it was. Taken literally, it was a four-paneled weaving out of the rope and marine cable that were Catherine Liem's signature medium. Bottles, barrel rungs, seaweed, planks, and other assorted detritus were interwoven at odd angles that gave the weavings an oxymoronic three-dimensionality. In spite of herself, Duck was impressed by the rough harmony of the work and by the control that had bent these strange elements into something that transcended the medium Duck had associated solely with placemats and scarves.

Maxine caught her trying to squirrel a look at the price. "Twenty-two thousand dollars," Maxine volunteered, "and it's the only piece in the show that hasn't sold yet. My dear, they fell on these things like flies on honey the night of the opening. We had people who came in here just lurid with curiosity because of the press, but they were charmed, absolutely charmed by her work!"

"Who could afford to be so charmed?" Duck blurted out.

"Ha!" Maxine retorted. "Scandal is as good as an early death for a great artist. Me, I don't think they'll give her the electric chair. But even if they just lock her up for life, her career is probably finished . . . unless she can make a loom from her jail bars! Of course, I didn't have the slightest idea when I booked the show . . ."

Mercifully, a middle-aged couple rang the bell, and without another glance at Duck, Maxine trotted to the door and threw open her arms to these more promising callers.

Alone at last, Duck tried to focus on the weavings. There were fifteen of them, and circumnavigating the room at a point precisely opposite Maxine and the unfortunate couple, Duck was able to study them all. But though she strained to find some thread that would lead from the weavings to the heart of the artist, she found none.

She picked up a catalog at the front desk and half-waved her farewell to Maxine, who was cackling to her new captives, ". . . unless she can weave her jail bars!"

Duck let herself out quietly, feeling exhausted and defeated. She was no wiser about the woman who had killed her mother and sister, and who would undoubtedly have killed her too if she had been at home.

2

How often have I wished for empty time, free of commitments, to do solitary things like start a journal. Proof once again that one should be careful in making wishes.

And yet there is something liberating in having a thoroughly regimented schedule. Wake-up call, 6:30 a.m.; fifteen minutes to shower and dress; breakfast at 6:45; exercise at 7:30, and so on through the day. Papa could have designed the schedule, it is so like the one that regulated the early years of my life—without the poetry, the Greek, the violin, etc.

One of my earliest memories is of yearning for freedom. I must have been four or five, because I can remember craning to see out of the back window of the Lincoln, and even then, having the bottom part of the scene cut off because I was belted down tight. It was summertime and Bonard was driving in his short-sleeved livery. I don't know where we were going, but the route took us through a poor section of town with ditches instead of curbs and dusty front yards just big enough to hold a car on blocks.

And then on one of the corners we saw a group of children who had opened up a fire hydrant full force. The water gushed sideways a good twenty feet, and fifteen or twenty half-naked children jumped over, under, through, and against the torrent, their laughter spilling out as freely as the water. Bonard stopped, probably more concerned about his wax job than about the risk of striking one of the children.

The majesty of it! They weren't afraid of wasting water, of getting caught, of stepping on glass in their bare feet, of ruining their clothes, of missing their lessons—of anything. Oh, to be one of them, so free and so wonderfully wicked!

Bonard turned around in his seat to look out the rear window as he backed carefully down the length of the street. If he looked at me, I'm sure he saw the same sober-faced child that stares out of the few pictures in our scrapbook. But I watched those children as long as I could, and I fixed their joyous expressions in my mind. And while other little girls dressed up and played the part of princesses, I, the princess, dreamed that I was a barefoot black child in a wet T-shirt.

Perhaps some of those children are with me now in prison. Proving, yet again, that you have to be careful what you wish for.

3

DUCK ALWAYS entered the house through the back door now, preferring Bahalia's Scylla to the Charybdis of Mother's and Alexandra's ghosts in the dark front hallway. Bahalia, who had raised Duck and treated every encounter as another installment on her upbringing, started in before Duck could close the door behind her.

"Where you been, child?" the sonorous voice rumbled. The small woman leaned around a kitchen cabinet and eyed Duck's crinkled orange dress suspiciously. "Looks like your dress had some fun and you didn'."

"I went shopping."

"I'm not gonna say a thing," Bahalia said, a sure introduction to some uninvited advice. "Not a thing. Mmm-nnh," she repeated, pressing her thin lips even thinner and building to something big. Duck waited patiently, mesmerized by Bahalia's delicate craftsmanship with her heavy cleaver. The knife was as long as Bahalia's forearm and looked more dangerous to the cook than to the vegetables. Her bony elbows just cleared the tops of the counters, but she was deceptively strong. In her clawlike hands, the cleaver moved as fast as a hummingbird's wings, fluttering across rows of parsley, celery, garlic, green onions, and bell peppers, the essential minced ingredients of every one of Bahalia's dishes. Miraculously, the Spencers' meals had never been seasoned with her fingertips, which gripped the vegetables a constantly adjusted millimeter behind the flying blade.

"Nope, you axed me to keep out your room, so I'm keepin' out your room and out your business. Can't nobody else *fit* in that room anyway. You got room to go shoppin' though, I'll say that. Ain't one thing hangin' in that closet. All the clothes heaped up all over the chair, the bed, the flo', just waitin' for someone to put 'em on and go out lookin' like they slep' under a bridge las' night."

"Oh, c'mon, Bahalia, it's not that bad," Duck said, without conviction. "I'll clean it up soon."

"It's not like you got nothin' better to do, mopin' around here all day, goin' out shoppin' and comin' home in the same potato sack you lef' in." Bahalia gained speed as she tidied the greens into neat squares on the chopping counter. "You got to get moving with your life again. Your momma would roll over in her grave if she could see you hangdogging around all day long. And you gonna bring Alexandra jumpin' out the dirt to kick your butt into action."

Bahalia was the only one to mention their hallowed names in this house, which she did often, and with such rough irreverence that it jolted Duck every time.

Duck changed the subject. "I thought I'd take Junior to the Point tomorrow. Make a day of it."

"That sounds fine. You got the weather for a Fourth of July picnic. And in a minute you'll have the cole slaw and potato salad, too." Bahalia was tossing the greens into two ceramic bowls heaped with shredded cabbage and diced potatoes. Her method looked completely haphazard, without benefit of measuring cups or apparent attention; but she somehow achieved scientific precision in the consistency of her dishes. Duck had given up on trying to learn from Bahalia how to cook after the first lesson. She'd headed the blank first page of her notebook "Gumbo," a particular favorite of hers.

"Okay. What are the ingredients?" she asked, pen poised.

"First you gonna make your roux," Bahalia said.

"What's in it?"

"Some oil. Some flour."

"How much of each?" Duck asked.

"How much you gonna make? What kinda gumbo? What time of year you writing this for?"

"Bahalia, just help me get started here. I need to write *something* down."

"You already know how to write. I'm tryin' to teach you how to cook. Throw that book away so's you can learn somethin'."

Duck gave up. The concept of learning without written props was too foreign to engage her. Besides, in a kitchen run by her mother and Bahalia, there was already one cook too many. But since Mother's death, the family had had to fend for itself on Thursdays and Sundays, Bahalia's days off. Duck had scarcely been able to produce a peanut butter and jelly sandwich from the gourmet kitchen. And she would not accept her father's clumsy attempts at help.

Now Duck tried to concentrate on the two salads forming simultaneously before her.

"Is that what we're having for supper?"

"Nope. Eggplant casserole for supper. This here's for your picnic," Bahalia said.

"But I just told you about the picnic."

"Mmm. Have you told Junior yet? Maybe that'll take his mind off Miz Burke's tits," Bahalia chuckled.

"Oh, jeez, not again?" Duck asked.

"No, I think once was enough for the both of 'em."

Junior's newly awakening sexual interests were beyond his limited understanding. Last spring, after catching Junior ogling the discarded insertion diagram from her tampon box, Alexandra had unabashedly taken charge of his sex education. She used girlie magazines as texts and her teaching responsibilities as an opportunity for learning. "Wow, Junior, would you look at *that*," went a standard lesson, Alexandra's face pressed so close against the page Junior could scarcely see. Her sister must have never reached her planned chapter on sexual etiquette, Duck thought, which perhaps accounted for Junior's gaffe. Even Junior could not have been aroused by the eighty-one-year-old neighbor whose yard he had raked and mowed for five years. Though their father had once complimented Mrs. Burke on her "nicely turned ankle," he had been referring to the nylon leggings she wore rolled down to her feet summer and winter. There was nothing about the old lady's appearance that struck Duck as being sexy. However, her ample bosom, which hung just above the waist on her short frame, had moved Junior to proclaim, as they stuffed hedge clippings into a plastic bag, "I love your tits."

Duck could almost see Junior's cheerful and innocent delivery of this remark. They would probably have never learned of it from Mrs. Burke, who would have issued a polite and understanding demurral, except that her sister, Miss Tipton, whose hearing aid could detect impropriety at any distance, was sitting on the patio nearby, taking her afternoon tea.

"I knew something like this would happen," Miss Tipton cried, in her deaf voice, loud enough for Bahalia to hear next door. "That boy is dangerous, Eloise. He should be gelded. He should be gelded before it's too late!"

"Enough!" Eloise stopped her. "He's just a boy." She surveyed protectively Junior's muscular five-foot-nine-inch frame, now bowed a few inches by his shame at having provoked this confrontation. "If it weren't for all this talk about gelding, you might have some boys of your own, and then you'd understand."

"You mark my words," Miss Tipton said, jabbing her toast at her sister while retreating into the house, "that idiot's going to carve you up with the hedge-trimmers one of these days and I won't have time to say 'I told you so.' "

"Because I will have carved you up first!" Eloise shouted after her.

Mrs. Burke snatched an abandoned sandwich off her sister's plate and stuffed it into Junior's gawking mouth. Then she stuck out her tongue at the doorway into which her sister had disappeared.

Junior always reprimanded anyone he loved who misbehaved. "That wasn't nice," he said to Mrs. Burke, head hanging.

All afternoon Bahalia hooted to herself, "That wasn't nice!" and broke into fresh ripples of solitary laughter.

"Whatcha think, Bahalia?" Duck asked. "What are we going to do about Junior and girls and sex?"

Bahalia turned prim. "Eighteen years old you don't need to be worryin' about sex any more'n poor Junior."

"My father's had enough sex for the entire family," Duck said bitterly.

Bahalia thwocked a large spoonful of mayonnaise into each of the mixing bowls in front of her and began stirring with a vengeance, as if, by force of will and energy alone, she could blend the troubled Spencer family. "Don't you talk about your daddy that way." Her voice struck each word in time with the wooden spoon knocking against the edge of the bowl. "He always stood by his family, that's what's important."

"Not while he was lying with Catherine, he didn't."

"You not old enough to understand. Eighteen's too young for understandin' sex. That's how I got my fifth miserable child."

Duck knew Bahalia was changing the subject, and with a roll of her eyes she pursued the new tack. "I thought you had four kids. Besides, you love your kids, they're the pride of your life, you're always telling me."

"Four kids is the pride of my life. I got one miserable one who ain't my pride, and he ain't my child no more, neither."

"Bahalia, that's awful. What happened?"

"I always said you ought to throw the first one away and keep the rest," Bahalia said for the first time. "I ain't sayin' another word," she went on. And meant it.

Duck let it go. Bahalia's children made her nervous. Taneeka, the twenty-five-year-old resident, stopped by from time to time in the evenings. She would stand at the back door, waiting for her mother, melting into the darkness so that all that could be seen of her was her rumpled hospital greens and a spark of anger in her eyes. Her older brother Charles also came by, summoned by Mother to fix things in the house when they were broken. He was a genius with everything that had moving parts, but was so jittery himself that it was hard to see how he kept still long enough to work his magic. And his Rastafarian locks were unsettling to Duck, who fought so hard against her own hair's tendency to style itself the same way. Charles's Rasta look was an interesting mimicry of his father, Charlie Deed, who hailed from Jamaica but gave no sign of it except when he spoke in a lovely cadence. Duck had also met Bahalia's youngest boy, whom she knew only as "Dumplin'." Reluctant to address the eleven-year-old that way, Duck had not called him anything, nor had she found a way to talk to the quiet boy. There was also Brandon, who worked for Liem Enterprises. She could not draw up a mental picture of this middle son, though she vaguely remembered meeting him. She thought there was probably another daughter, too. Duck could not admit to Bahalia, who was like a mother to her, that she could not keep the Deed family straight.

"Anyway," Duck went on, "I wasn't talking about me and sex, and I sure wasn't talking about me and kids. I was talking about Junior and sex. I don't know if he understands the first thing about it and I can't help him."

"Good," Bahalia said and went on with her cooking.

Holding to the schedule fixed by Mother, dinner still began punctually at 6:00 p.m. every evening. Blake Spencer, Sr. returned at 5:55, allowing exactly enough time to toss his paper onto the couch, wash his hands, and take his seat at the head of the table. He thus avoided the awkward silence of his household before dinner, which was merely an aperitif for the awkward silence of his household during dinner and at every other time that he was present. He had always been quiet. Mother and Alexandra had dominated the table talk, leaving little room for the rest of them; and Blake, Sr. had been a good listener. Nowadays, though, Blake, Sr. was quiet in the cowering manner of a whipped dog.

Duck wordlessly sat down at her father's left. Mother's place to his right remained empty. Bahalia, balancing a salad bowl, rolls, and butter, teetered into Alexandra's former place and asked Junior's empty chair, "Where's my boy?"

Blake, Sr. pushed himself up from the table and went to the hall closet. "Son," he said softly into the coats, "this is no place for you to be. There's nothing for you to be afraid of in this house. Come on out to dinner." He led Junior by the hand out of the closet and to the table. Junior settled himself squirmishly, taking deep appreciative breaths of the open air.

"How long you been in there, child?" Bahalia scolded. "We gonna have to get us an alarm like the Murphys got in they pool, knock you out your skin when Junior falls into the closet."

Junior beamed at her. "Get one for my bike, too. I can be an ambulance."

"You a walkin' disaster already, boy. Eat this here. You

gonna outgrow that closet by Christmas. Then you'll have to move into Duck's. Got plenty room in there."

"Oh, Bahalia, please don't start up again," Duck pleaded.

"That's fine. You step in and help me hold up the conversation around this table, we can talk about anythin' you want."

Duck fell silent.

Junior fixed his eyes on the table and said to Duck, "Don't slouch."

She didn't answer him.

"Mebbe I oughta just pull the TV up to this spot and head on back to the kitchen," Bahalia said.

"Naw," said Junior, "the sports is over."

"Nobody even notice my beautiful pink fish," Bahalia whined. "We hadn't had one a them since the bake-off."

At that, Duck and her father smiled in spite of themselves, and Junior guffawed, remembering last year's competition between Mother and Bahalia for culinary supremacy.

Bahalia had thrown down the gauntlet. Glancing over Mother's shoulder while she was glazing carrots, Bahalia remarked, "You lettin' 'em go too long—you gonna get orange caramel."

"What!" Mother retorted. "You never touched a carrot except to boil it to a paste and pour the vitamins down the drain."

"Hmph! I can serve up any those raw dishes you fix, 'cept I don't want to poison the kids. Besides, it's only this month yours ain't overcooked. I never served 'em cinders yet—what you call it? 'Black Death'?"

"Blackened steak," Mother replied through pursed lips, as her carrots began to caramelize. "If you think you can outdo me, why don't you try your hand at my style, and I'll cook yours. We'll let the family decide whose cooking they like best."

Bahalia took the prize with her "Pinque Fish," raw salmon still wrapped in the plastic deli container, the whole thing encrusted sushilike in a shell of dyed-pink rice and bedecked with candied roses, under a cranberry glaze and a side sauce of pureed chrysanthemum buds in reduced salmon stock. "It's rurnt," the proud creator mock-sobbed, wiping tears of laughter from her cheeks, after she had rolled off the list of ingredients. "I wanted to use the pink oleanders for the sauce but Alexandra told me it might really kill you."

"Well," Mother declared, "I guess I won."

"Hol' on just a minute," protested Bahalia.

"They loved my swill," Mother claimed, pointing to the empty bundt pan that had held her bacon fat, mushroom soup, and rice casserole.

"That was *my* swill," argued Bahalia. "This here's your swill, this nouveau pink stuff. We weren't testin' the cook, we was testin' the cookin'."

"If you're going to change the rules, I demand a rematch," Mother said, to raucous applause. "This time next year, I'll make a meat loaf you can't stay in the house with." This was as close as Mother had ever come to "fraternizing with the servants," one of her many taboos.

Alexandra had promptly sent out formal invitations in her flawless calligraphy, and then died along with the event's sponsor.

Bahalia had since won the rematch, not by default but by demonstrating that she had had the versatility to mimic Mother's style in earnest all along. No sooner had she inherited the kitchen than she began to cook an eclectic mix of dishes every night. And about a month after the funeral, to the remaining Spencers' enormous relief, Bahalia had joined the family at the dining room table for dinners, saying, "This quiet in here is so loud I can't hear myself think in the kitchen."

4

There is no presumption of innocence here. Certainly not on the part of the guards, who have twice convicted all of us—first for our crimes and second for the further insult and expense to society of demanding trials. The prisoners presume guilt, too, but are infinitely forgiving, except of the woman on Block D who hammered her two-year-old twins to death. She is the only untouchable in a caste system I am just beginning to understand.

As luck would have it, I have landed once again in the Brahmin caste. My status derives from two things. First, the guards hate me for being rich and privileged on the outside. Probably the prisoners would have hated me for the same reasons, except that the guards beat them to it. The us-against-them spirit that prevails here compelled my fellow inmates to align with me against the guards.

Second, I am respected for the seriousness of the charges against me. Eudora's first question was not "What's your name?" but "Whatcha in for?" "A shooting incident," I confessed. "A shoootink in-see-dent," she said. "That's rich. You must have you a real good lawyer." I told her, "As a matter of fact, I do, but he didn't tell me what to say. He told me not to talk at all." "Yep," she said. "You gotcha a good one. So whatcha in for?" When I told her, she gave

21

me a freshly appraising look and said in an awed tone, "Wow, a double 6-2." For most of the women here, I've discovered, the criminal code is a second language, so when Eudora began introducing me as a Double 6-2, everyone understood I was charged with two capital murders. There is an unspoken rule against asking whether I committed the crimes, and an unspoken assumption that I did, which would be unaltered by denials. The us-against-them doctrine also applies to the outside world. Therefore, I am a heroine for having killed for love.

I get no respect for the things I value in myself. "You got a job?" Eudora asked next. I couldn't tell whether she had never read the papers, or was determined to gather her own information and form her own opinions. Either way, I loved her for it. "I'm an artist," I told her. She tried to keep her thoughts to herself, but an eyebrow lifted in silent condemnation (not of the murders but of my occupation—an effete occupation, the eyebrow seemed to say).

How to defend myself here? The barest house, the crudest hut, a yurt, a cave, an igloo ripples with light and shadow, color, pattern, texture. This cell is the only habitation I have ever entered that is stripped of all character. By design. White tile walls, suitable for disinfecting. Fluorescent light. Slab beds. Nondescript sink. Dark slot of window. Smooth cement floor. Sliding barred door. With a view. Onto an endless stretch of same, same, same cells. A house of mirrors nightmare.

Eudora watched my eye roving the walls for a pockmark, my fingers prodding the cement seams for a depression. Anything different. "You can't get out like that, hon." "I know," I said, studying the ceiling. "I'm trying to find a way to live here." The eyebrow again, quizzical. "This place is anti-art," I explained, "anti-life."

"Girl," Eudora said, "I am alive. You are alive."

Indeed.

5

DUCK HAD ALWAYS loved the short drive south from Mobile to the island. Outside of town, the hardwoods gave way to the graceful long-leaf pines that flourished in the sandy soil of the coast. Then the narrow road struck through the marshes, which stretched out for miles on either side. Gray-green grasses simulated a vast flat plain, but protected by a watery bottom, it was unbroken by fencepost or billboard. The occasional outposts, wooden shanties on stilts rebuilt as quickly and cheaply as the winds blew them down, advertised their offerings of Coke and bait not toward the highway but toward the canals cut civil-engineer straight through the marsh. Here and there egrets, startled by the car, pulled away from the roadside, flattening into flight with a few slow white flaps that seemed to defy aerodynamics. Further south, natural waterways opened up, plied by raggedy fishing boats slung about with perfect nets.

The open horizon and fish smell of the ocean cleared Duck's head. Junior was plugged into his Walkman, bobbing rhythmically, sometimes singing along in an eerily tuneless accompaniment. His voice, which had deepened the year before, now beat out a single high, flat note.

"What are you listening to?" Duck asked.

"I dunno." He handed her the plastic box in which the tape had come, with a jacket he was unable to read.

23

"Bunny Wailer. *Gumption*," Duck read. "I didn't know you like reggae."

Junior shrugged.

Iberville Point was at the end of the island. Their grandmother Mamoo, though expecting them, had made no preparations. "You're as welcome as the ocean breeze," she had told them time and again, "and you can blow in, unannounced, anytime, and find everything open to you." The windows and doors of the beach house were always flung wide. There was no air conditioning besides water and wind, and no need of any. The house had been built without locks thirty years before, and none had been installed since. Mamoo's late husband, Arthur Spencer, an accountant by trade and a carpenter only by avocation, had designed and built the place himself in two years of weekend work. It had withstood the worst hurricanes the Gulf could throw at this barrier island, storms that stripped the neighboring houses to their pilings and left an occasional toilet bowl or sodden armchair in the street. After a while, the owners of waterfront lots had begun bringing their architects around to study Arthur's unique design. He had built the house in two sections: one held the bedrooms, the other, connected by a breezeway, was a sixty-foot-long open space housing the kitchen, dining, and living areas. It faced into the wind like a catamaran's pontoons, riding on it instead of fighting against it. But even after Hurricane Frederick leveled everything else and made believers of them all, there was no mimicry. With the last catastrophic loss, the insurance companies refused to write any more policies on the island, and rebuilding of any design was discouraged; and so Mamoo and the shore birds effectively had the Point to themselves. It was a completely harmonious relationship.

Mamoo loosely described herself as "nondenominational"; but she confided in her family that the views of the Australian aborigine most closely resembled her own. And before she had ever studied the aboriginal culture, she had begun painting images that an aborigine might interpret as the "Dream Time" at the dawn of the world. The bold line drawings and the handmade dyes from plants and clay had come to Mamoo without training. Only the pelicans in place of emus, and the rats in place of wallabies, betrayed the cultural divergence. Mamoo's paintings trembled with the vibrancy of deeply felt, mysterious life forces.

They were not for sale. Mamoo had never yielded to the pressure of family, friends, or would-be agents to sell her work. But she produced steadily and gave generously. The paintings were prized by the friends who had received them, and in recent years, she'd donated one a year to the public broadcasting station's auction. Last year's work had fetched over $10,000.

Duck was fascinated by Mamoo's paintings. Literal-minded to the core, Duck would sit by her grandmother's side before a blank canvas, staring with her grandmother at the blue-green swells of the ocean, trying to draw upon it as Mamoo did and waiting for the ocean to be transposed onto the canvas. But Mamoo would pull from her imagination a gray and brown shrimp curled around a sandpiper that Duck could never see until they were there. If Junior asked about a particular animal, Mamoo would sketch it in extraordinary detail and accuracy, but these lifelike drawings were solely for Junior. Her paintings were more abstract, but somehow truer to life in their distortion. She had never done portraits. "Speciesism!" she spat. Yet she had done one painting of Junior that gave Duck gooseflesh. In it, Junior hunkered at the water's edge gazing down at his feet as a wave lapped at his toes. Although the face was almost featureless, it was unmistakably Junior, capturing his limitations of understanding and his tenuous contact with the great water, and making them symbolic of mankind's; but the sense of belonging and peace with the world that were peculiar to Junior were also there and imbued the painting with great hope.

As soon as they arrived at the Point, Junior bounded into the waves. His Walkman never left the car here; the waves pounded out all the rhythm he needed. He would stomp and romp in the shallow wash until called for lunch. Duck unloaded the picnic provisions into the kitchen and joined Mamoo on the catamaran's broad gulfside deck, where she was dabbing at a grouping of brown pelicans gliding just above the surface of water that imperceptibly merged into sky. Duck pecked at her grandmother's downy cheek, almost the only exposed skin. Mamoo wrapped herself against the sun as aggressively as the vacationers disrobed themselves. The result was translucent skin with wrinkles no deeper than a scratch on a polished wax surface. Mamoo's skin was shown off by a short, gamine haircut that could have been styled by Alexandra. But the similarities with Alexandra ended there. Mamoo's square-shaped face and full mouth had passed through her son, Blake, to Duck alone. Duck usually felt that Alexandra, who had inherited Mother's auburn-haired drop-dead beauty, had gotten the better end of the deal; but if she could age as timelessly as Mamoo, she might come to terms with her appearance.

"What are your plans for the trial?" Mamoo asked at once. Duck was always startled by her grandmother's directness. With Mother, it was the back end of a conversation that was important: the issue emerged from a carefully laid foundation, and if there were any question involved, the answer had been logically ordained before the question was posed. Mamoo, on the other hand, always came straight to whatever was on her mind, sometimes with breathtaking abruptness, and pursued it relentlessly, but tenderly. "It's only a week away, honey," she prodded.

"I know. I'm terrified." Duck collapsed into a nearby deck chair.

Mamoo immediately abandoned her painting, tossing her brush and its gob of cobalt-blue paint onto the deck at her feet, and pulled a chair up beside her granddaughter.

"You must be. I'm dreading it myself and I don't have any part to play in it. What do they want you to do?"

"The D.A. says he'll call me as the state's first witness," Duck said miserably. "He says 'all I have to do' is describe what I saw when I came home. A couple of his assistants have come to the house a couple of times to run through it with me. I get as far as opening the front door and I start to cry." Duck's throat began to tighten as the memory swept over her in an agonizing rush. She closed her eyes and only succeeded in sharpening the unbidden image of Mother's and Alexandra's bullet-torn bodies in the front hallway of their home. Newly dead, they looked as unlike themselves, as bereft of their spirits, as bloodstained stones. Duck could not remember them without being consumed with hatred for their killer, Catherine Liem. And one layer lower, a layer thinner than the film of sweat Duck imagined between the lovers' joined bodies, resided Duck's hatred for Catherine's lover, Duck's father, the once respected family man who had unwittingly driven his mistress to murder.

Duck willed away these dreadful images, drawing strength from the strong arms Mamoo had wrapped around her. She went on, through the last hiccuping sobs, "Joey Cristina says the prosecutors know I can't do it. They're just going to put me on to break down so the jury will get the 'human element' before they bring on the technical stuff from the police and coroner and forensic pathologist." Joey, one of her best friend Maria's four older brothers, was a deputy sheriff, and knew his way around criminal proceedings. He had reviewed with Duck the personalities and motivations of the participants, including their plans for her.

"Oh, Laura, that's horrible. Have you told that to your father or his lawyer?"

"What's the point of talking to Mr. Ernst? He listens, rocks back in his chair, and says, 'Don't you want to cooperate with the state's investigation?' Anytime I say no, he tells me I have to."

"And your dad?" Mamoo fixed Duck with her clear eyes. "Have you talked to him?"

"It's a little late for me to learn how to talk to my father, don't you think? There were so many things I wanted to share with him all those years he was busy at the office, busy at the jobsite, busy with his lover, who knows? Now all of a sudden he wants to 'open the lines of communication' "—Duck aped her father's slow, sober speech—"and there's nothing I want to hear from him anymore."

Mamoo dug a blunt nail into the age-silvered arm of her chair. "I think he used his architectural practice to hide from the problems in his marriage, Laura. Not from you."

"Well, while he was hiding, I invented a father for myself. Somebody smart and strong. Not this guy I've found out about from the papers. I don't want a father like that." Duck was surprised at the vehemence of her declaration. She cut herself off abruptly, feeling that she had gone over the line in excoriating Blake to his mother.

Mamoo reached for her hand and interlocked firm fingers between Duck's limp ones. "You know, the father you invented is closer to the truth than the man in the papers. The papers draw cartoons, Laura. They have no room for depth in a story like this one, or for understanding that even smart, strong people sometimes do stupid things."

"Well anyway, my father can't help me with the trial. Joey knows all the ins and outs over there. He says I've got to go. He says the judge won't let it last too long—I should just go on and cry, then rush home and watch myself on

T.V. He says the network artist will do me up great. It'll be the start of my modeling career."

Duck smiled through her tears. Her long lashes clumped together over blue-green eyes. Her cheekbones were emerging, Mamoo noticed; her mouth was widening. Mamoo switched off the eyes of a grandmother, which had always seen beauty, and tried a more objective view. The girl could be a model, she thought. And she was pleased that someone other than the facile Rick Wrigley was around to appreciate it. "Which one is Joey?" Mamoo asked. "I think of the Cristina boys as an Italian soccer team. So many of them, so much alike."

"Joey's the third oldest," Duck said, drying her eyes on her T-shirt. "He's twenty, tallish, real smart. Cute," she added as an afterthought.

"He sounds like a good friend," her grandmother remarked.

"He's always been like a big brother, mixing me in with Maria and Maggie. But he's not teasing me at all about the trial. He's been really professional, explaining all the pretrial maneuvering, describing the courtroom, letting me know what to expect."

"Has he told you that victims of crime and their families often break down in the courtroom? That it's commonplace for the folks who work there? That even if you do cry, it'll hardly be noticed?"

Duck nodded. She was grateful to Joey and Mamoo for realizing that performance anxiety was at the heart of her fear.

"Except when you're on the stand," Mamoo said, "I'm going to stick to you like glue. I reckon if I put on my little-old-lady disguise, the reporters will be less likely to push past me than an armed guard; they wouldn't want the mini-cam to catch them roughing up an old lady."

Duck was grateful for the offer, but the unbidden thought

assailed her, *I want my mother to go with me*. She forced herself into the realm of possibility and said, "If you want to avoid a brawl, you'd better not deliver any of your karate chops. Anyway, Joey promised a phalanx of deputies if I need them. If the press goes after Junior, Joey'll look after him, too."

The suggestion that Mr. Spencer would have to look out for himself hung in the air. Mamoo left it there. "It's a crime as heinous as the murders, the character assassination that woman and her lawyer are trying on Junior."

There had been several skirmishes between the prosecution and the defense over Junior. Junior had been home when Alexandra and Evelyn Spencer were shot. The police, the first to arrive after Duck, had not known to look for him. Duck had not thought to. It was Blake, Sr. who thought of his son first. He had acted as well as the circumstances allowed. He had circumnavigated the body of his wife at the door and the sight of Alexandra in an unnaturally graceless jumble on the stairs, and he had come directly to Duck, still gripping the phone and his secretary's voice repeating the mantra, "Your dad's coming, baby, he's on his way." He lifted his 120-pound daughter like the child she felt she was and carried her into the living room where there was nothing horrible to see. Without disentangling her, he had asked softly, "Where's Junior?"

Both of them had seized on the task of finding the boy, but Duck had remained attached to her father, too, as they searched through the other rooms of the house. Beyond the foyer, everything was undisturbed, unbloodied, and empty. She clung to the courage of her father, lifting bedskirts searching for his son or maybe his son's body; she clung to the safety of him, standing between her and any attacker who might leap from behind a door; she pressed her face into his chest where he held her as they passed back through the hideous foyer and out the front door; and she drew on the strength of his chest, vibrating with his sure, loud call *"Blake!"* into the gaggle of neighbors pressed against the yellow police tape around the fence.

Then, miraculously, Junior had sheepishly touched them from behind, saying, "Don't yell." They had all rejoiced, laughing, crying, and clinging to one another as if it had all been a bad dream.

Blake, Sr. roused them. "Where were you, Junior?"

"In the closet," Junior replied, gesturing vaguely behind his back in order not to turn or look in that direction.

A police sergeant had followed Junior out. "He was in the front hall closet, sir. We need to talk to him."

"All right." Blake, Sr. held both children across their shoulders and sheltered them back into the formal living room. Seated on the white linen sofa where hardly anyone ever sat, Duck concentrated on the pristine normalcy of the swags in the moiré silk drapes, the undimmed glint of the crystal obelisks on the mantel, the seamless polish of the dove-gray ceiling moldings.

"Let me ask him," Blake, Sr. instructed the sergeant, who acquiesced, pad in hand. "Why were you in the closet, son?"

"Momma told me to go," Junior answered, fighting back tears.

"Why?"

"I don't know. She told me to get in and not talk and not get out until she said, and she closed the door and it was dark. I couldn't see." The tears came freely, and Blake, Sr. held him close for a while before pressing further.

"When did she put you in the closet, Junior?"

"Before," Junior answered. The sergeant stirred at the sidelines, repressing his urge to intervene or raise his hand.

"How long before?" Blake, Sr. continued.

"I don't know. An hour?" Junior asked tentatively, questioning his own understanding of time.

"What was happening before she put you in the closet?"

"Nothing . . . You mean me? I was looking at my base-ball cards?" Junior struggled to give his father what he wanted.

"Not you, son," Blake, Sr. declined the offering gently. "Your mother, what was she doing? Was anyone else in the house?"

"Momma was cooking. She said don't bother her. Alexandra was in her room. Duck went out. Bahalia didn't come today."

"But what was Momma doing right before she sent you into the closet?"

"I don't know."

"Did you hear anybody speaking?" Blake, Sr., Duck, the sergeant, and five or six other officers leaned in, holding their breaths.

Junior hung his head and spoke earnestly to his hands, which were twisting in his lap. "I couldn't hear too good. Momma said, 'Not today, not today.' I think Alexandra came down and it went 'BANG!' and Momma screamed . . ."—Junior covered his ears with his hands—". . . and then 'BANG, BANG, BANG.' " Junior was bent over now and talking into his stomach. He choked on his sobs. Blake, Sr. held him tighter and whispered into his hair, "Then what, son? We have to know."

"I don't know. Momma told me don't come out so I didn't."

"Who shot them?"

"I don't know."

"Did you hear him speak at all?"

"No-o-o." Junior wailed, drew up his legs, and began rocking under his father's arm. Duck had also pulled up as tight as she could into him and against herself. The police officers maintained a respectful distance and silence while the surviving Spencer children cried. Then the sergeant stepped forward. "I have a few questions," he said kindly.

"Not now. Not today," Blake, Sr. replied.

"We have to talk to him while it's fresh in his mind, sir."

"It's going to be fresh in his mind forever. I'm not going to put him through any more of this today." Blake, Sr. rose with his attached children, drove them to the Point, and returned alone to deal with the police, the neighbors, and the funeral arrangements.

6

Most of my acquaintances only know three Finns: Papa, Elga, and me. From this they have deduced that Finns are the coldest, most dispassionate race of men on the planet. I cannot speak for Elga, but Papa certainly held a great passion for Katrina, and I have certainly had mine. But passion is a very private thing with us. Finland breeds the shyest people on earth. Travelers there are always struck by the way pedestrians walk with their eyes downcast. Passersby, even if they chance to see one another, never exchange a greeting; friends do not share intimacies; lovers do not say "I love you." And although I was raised in America, this Finnish phenomenon, when I first witnessed it in the mother country, seemed perfectly normal; it felt like Papa's household.

Papa developed a public face, and he was very adept at manipulating it. When he smiled, he smiled wide and pulled up his broad cheeks so that his eyes wrinkled; and he held the whole thing in place for a reasonable period of time. But if you looked into his eyes, you could see that they were dull and that his smiling features were only wooden puppets yanked by the strings of his will. I didn't find Papa's public face attractive and I never cultivated one.

The tender Eudora, who weeps daily over the newspaper,

had her second cry today as I was telling her my family history. (*She has not read* Memoirs.)

"No!" she shouted. "Hella is not your mama! I know that woman's black. She sings too good for a white woman."

"That's a slightly different spin on my grandfather's view. He was horrified that his Valkyrie daughter became the queen of soul. I guess you never saw a picture of her, then?"

"Yeah, but she was purple and her hair was snakes. I never knew she was white."

"She had the fairest skin, the palest blue eyes, ash-blond hair. She looked exactly like her mother. And I'm told she had Katrina's voice, too. Papa doted on my mother when she was young; he looked on her as a second Katrina."

"How did the first Katrina like that?"

"She was killed in an air raid during the Winter War. Hella was only a few months old."

"Oh!" Eudora cried.

"Katrina loved to sing. So Papa started voice lessons for Hella before she could talk in complete sentences. For as long as she sang Finnish ballads and opera, she was his darling; he gave her everything she ever asked for and lots that she didn't. I think he expected her to stand at his side and warble until he died. When she entered her hippie stage in the sixties and became the lead singer for Lockjaw . . ."

"Oooh . . ." Eudora threw her arms up in the air in appreciation. "I can remember what my daddy said about them: 'That's not singing; that's screaming.' "

"Exactly. Papa was bewildered that she could abuse her classical training, and still pull money in faster than he did. He was even more bewildered at how she spent it."

"Drugs, drugs, drugs, drugs, DRUGS."

"You're psychic, Eudora."

"*I been around the block a few times. I guess your papa didn't have much use for a stoned-out hippie daughter singing about drugs and sex.*"

"*It was worse than that. He deplored the drugs and sex. He deplored her relationship with my father—'that stringy-haired bass player' was all I ever heard Papa call him. But Papa tried to hold on. He said that Hella's failure to marry my father showed she hadn't taken leave of her senses entirely. But then Lockjaw came out with 'Bleached Crossbones.'* "

"*I love that album.*"

"*You remember 'Why Can't the People Choose?', about the right of the Vietnamese to determine their form of government?*"

"*Sure.*"

"*Well, you have to understand that after the Communists overran Finland, killed Papa's wife, and appropriated that part of the country that held his hometown and the family shipyards, Papa hated the Red Menace worse than sin. 'Hakkaa Päälle' was the battle cry of the Finnish troops during the Winter War; it means 'Cut them down.' I can remember Papa yelling 'Hakkaa Päälle' at boat launchings, political rallies, christenings. He saw his every endeavor as pitting the forces of capitalism against Communism. Hella's little polemic was heresy to him—a betrayal of everything he believed.*"

"*Whoa.*"

"*I'm getting all of this from Elga's book. She worked for Papa for fifty years, raising Hella, then me. According to her memoirs, Papa called Hella in New York right after he heard the song, told her she wasn't his daughter anymore, and hung up.*"

"*They never patched it up?*"

I shook my head. "It was only a few weeks later that she and the bass player headed in their private plane for a weekend getaway in Maine. Without me. They took so many Quaaludes, they were probably asleep when their plane dove into the Atlantic."

"Your poor papa."

"You are psychic, Eudora. He went to his death believing he had killed her. And he tried to fix it as best he could by raising me right. No singing lessons. No indulgence."

Eudora eyed me suspiciously. "Wait a minute here, how come I'm crying and you're not?"

"Because I'm bored with my story," I told her.

"Well, that's fine in here," she said, "but you get in front of that jury, you better turn on the faucets." Then Eudora explained her theory that most murder trials have less to do with guilt or innocence than the worth of the accused in the eyes of the jury. "So they got to know you. They got to love you," she summarized. "You gotta crack the ice, girl, and let 'em see the fire inside."

Eudora and Blake are the only two people who have ever discerned, on first meeting, that there was a fire inside me. Maybe that's why I loved them both immediately. I think of myself as a person of great passion—my art hints at it, Blake confirmed it—but it lies deep, deep beneath the ice.

"So, you gonna cry for the jury?" Eudora asked.

"I don't think so." I smiled coolly. So many layers of heredity and breeding, so few tears.

7

THERE HAD BEEN more interviews of Junior after that first miserable interview, but no more information had emerged. The Spencer household knew Junior for a forthright child who kept no secrets and believed that he had told all he knew.

Neither the prosecution nor the defense was satisfied. There were no signs of forcible entry into the house on the day of the murders. Nothing had been taken. The killer had access to the house or had been freely admitted, and the motive had probably been something other than greed. If Junior were telling the truth, he had been a few feet away in the closet during the entire encounter; if he were lying, who knew the extent of his involvement? One or the other opposing team of lawyers wanted him examined by doctors, hypnotized, polygraphed. Whatever one team wanted, the other objected to. Cedric Ernst, the lawyer hired by Blake, Sr. to protect his son's interests, opposed everything involving the boy. Nevertheless, the court ordered Junior examined by a panel of experts. Lengthy reports were prepared. Junior was found incompetent to serve as a witness. More hearings were held. Junior's statements were excluded as inadmissible hearsay; the reports of the examining physicians on his competency were ruled admissible; and Junior himself would not be allowed to testify. The appellate courts were petitioned by both sides to intervene and refused. The latest conflict, initiated by the defense, revolved around its motion to introduce Junior as a piece of "demonstrative" evidence. Demonstrative evidence usually referred to some physical object that could demonstrate something to the jury, something like a diagram, a photograph, or a murder weapon. In this case, Junior, the incompetent witness, was to serve as a deaf-mute object for the jury's inspection. The defense, presumably, would then call upon the jury to conclude from his shuffling gait, frightened eyes, and frozen smile that Junior was the killer.

The trial judge could not decide the demonstrative evidence issue, and the trial had been postponed once already while he wrestled with it. Duck had missed freshman orientation at Auburn, then missed registration and decided to sit out for a semester. The director of admissions wrote to say that in view of the tragic circumstances Duck's admission would be deferred until the beginning of the spring term in January. The case of *State v. Catherine Liem* was scheduled to begin on October 14, less than two weeks off, and still the judge had not decided the pending motions. He had stated, however, that the trial would go forward as planned and that he would make his ruling before the lawyers made their opening statements.

Duck and Mamoo leaned against the railing of the catamaran's deck and tested the defense's ludicrous theory of Junior's culpability against its subject. Junior had contrived some game with the waves, involving great flatfooted leaps, and much whooping and flapping of arms. For a Down Syndrome child, he was uncommonly tall; and the awkwardness that would have afflicted any teenager in a growth spurt was physically amplified in Junior, whose small head and stubby hands had not kept pace with the rest of his body. Still, he looked more gawky than threatening.

"It's a moral carcinogen," Mamoo declared.

"Huh?"

"Like calling someone a 'nigger' or dissecting cats in biology class—somebody's pet before they put it in fixative. That kind of conduct causes cancer of the spirit."

"So which carcinogenic agent are you talking about here? There are so many to choose from."

"Maybe they could've convinced me it was a crime of passion against your mother, that Alexandra got caught up in it by mistake—I don't know." Mamoo hesitated. "But denying that she did it: that's the act of a murderess, not a love-besotted mistress. And trying to pin it on Junior! It's completely unforgivable!" Mamoo exclaimed, as though the double murders could perhaps be overlooked if not for this added treachery.

Ignited by Mamoo's outburst, Duck exploded. "And what about my father? Why does he deserve everybody's forgiveness? Why doesn't he go on trial? Why doesn't he face any punishment?"

"Oh, Laura. Your father has been horribly punished. He lost his daughter. He lost his wife."

"He didn't want his wife!" Duck clenched the railing of the deck, her knuckles white as the hummocks of sand below.

"Whatever he wanted or didn't want of your mother, Laura, he didn't want her killed."

"How do you know? How do you know he didn't plan it with Liem?"

Mamoo's eyes gripped Duck's tight. "Because I know. And you must know it too. And you must know that every day is a punishment for him. Everyone knows his troubles. Nearly everyone condemns him. Your father has showed a great deal of strength and courage by holding his head up and going about his business. I'm very proud of him, Laura."

"Well, I'm not. I think he's getting off easy."

"I know, honey, and I suspect he does, too. He's on trial every day with you. And you have the power to punish him more than anyone else." The breeze ruffled her gray hair softly across her cheek.

Duck looked at Mamoo soberly, but felt something like a smile spreading inside of her. It felt good to know she could hurt the source of all her pain.

"Well, from what Joey says, Liem has her problems, too. Joey says the defense has been pretty vague about pinning it on Junior. It's a problem for them that he can't drive." What had led the police to Catherine Liem was her silver Volvo, parked around the corner from the Spencers' house that awful afternoon. In their exclusive neighborhood, interlopers were easily identified. No one had seen the murderess entering or leaving the house, but Mrs. Appleby had pointed out the strange car to the detectives. In short order, they had inspected it, found bloodstains on the trunk lid, and obtained a search warrant. The blood-spattered weapon was found in the trunk. By evening, when Catherine Liem called to report her car missing, the police were prepared. They figured she made the report because she knew they had found the car. And whatever suspicions Ms. Liem and her quick-talking lawyer could build around Junior's presence in the closet, they could not account for the stalled-out Volvo.

"It's a problem, all right," Mamoo concurred. "Making up a lie as big as her plea of not guilty is always a problem."

Duck and Mamoo sat on the nearest chair together, exhausted. The difficulty of holding themselves precariously on the narrow chaise was somehow reassuring; focusing on the concrete challenge helped them loose the hold of the dark thoughts they had shared.

When the pressure of the unyielding wooden armrest against her ribcage became unbearable, Mamoo sat up and reflected aloud, "You know, your mother and I had our differences. But she had her virtues." Mamoo paused, as if trying to remember one.

While Mamoo was thinking, Duck reflected on Mother's and Mamoo's difficult relationship. Mother refused to visit the Point or see Mamoo on any occasion when it could be decorously avoided. She had said once to Duck, "I cannot bring myself to begin a sentence with the word 'Mamoo'; it sounds like something a calf would call its mother's udder," as if this explained her failure to talk to her mother-in-law.

"But this Liem person," Mamoo continued, "I simply cannot understand how your father got himself tangled up with someone like that. Even if it was all sex, I don't see how it's possible to have good sex with someone so thoroughly despicable."

Up until recently, Duck had not considered that it was possible for someone over forty to have sex at all. And certainly not her parents. And certainly not in an extramarital relationship. The whole idea was revolting. "She's not even pretty," she said aloud. "I thought men were supposed to pick trashy-looking blond bombshells for their mistresses. Someone like Ivana Trump—oh no, she was the wife, wasn't she? Well then, the other one."

"She's the wife now, too," Mamoo said, a smile tugging at the corner of her mouth.

"I guess that was Liem's plan. Mistress to wife. No shame in that if you're rich enough." In her mind's eye, Duck held up the image of her ravishingly beautiful mother against the pictures she had seen of Catherine Liem. Duck saw no room for any fatal attraction in the thin, lusterless blond hair falling around the small gray eyes and pinched features.

"Maybe your mother put your dad off of good looks," Mamoo said enigmatically. "Your father was such a romantic in his youth. He honestly believed that 'beauty is truth, truth beauty.' Of course, the second part is an eternal verity, but only Keats, your father, and the so-called beautiful people place any trust in the first."

"Well, Mother sure didn't put him off of money, did she? He sure traded up there." Duck flung out the only explanation for the affair she could imagine; Catherine's cosmic riches. It was the explanation Mother would have given. Mother had placed a great deal of stock in money and in the role her wealth had played in her marriage. Her money was particularly precious, she said, because it was "old." When Duck was younger, she had thought of old money as some finely-crafted antique whose value increased with age; but Mother explained that the beauty of old money was simply that one didn't have to work for it. The only occupation Duck's maternal grandparents had ever pursued (apart from drinking, Blake, Sr. said) was shepherding their stocks and bonds. They had done this so aggressively that by their mid-sixties they were exhausted (or, according to Blake, Sr., their livers were), and they died within a few months of one another, transmitting to their only child Evelyn money even older than had been transmitted to them. Mother confided to Duck that it was the source of Blake, Sr.'s extraordinary success: paid by the job, not by the hour, he could afford his uncompromising standards in his architectural work because she was rich.

"Nonsense!" Mamoo exclaimed. "Your father never touched your mother's money, and I'm certain he wasn't interested in Catherine Liem's, either."

Could Mother have been wrong about her contribution to the family's good fortune? Surely Mother was in a better position to know their finances than Mamoo? And if Blake, Sr. hadn't been attracted by Catherine Liem's money, then it was all sex. Revolting.

"Come on, let's go for a walk," Mamoo directed rather

than asked, springing up from the chair as if rejuvenated by
their chat. Duck pulled herself up heavily and followed.
Junior galloped over to join them and they scrunched arm-
in-arm through the damp hard-packed sand left by the
ebbing tide. The rhythmic thump and flush of breaking
waves displaced conversation.

Mamoo would have strode past the marker. It had been
part of the landscape for so long she scarcely noticed it.
The Daughters of the Coastal Settlers had plunked the
marker here fifty years before, just above the tide's reach
on the spit of sand that had earned the Point its name. Atop
a squat concrete podium a bronze plaque, weathered to a
beautiful marine verdigris, still clearly proclaimed:

On January 27, 1699, Pierre LeMoyne d'Iberville anchored his frigate "Bodine" at this site which had previ-
ously been explored, but not settled, by the Spanish.
Iberville established a small colony, in an effort to re-
claim the area for France by peaceful means. When settlers from Canada arrived a year later, they found only
sixty skeletons. They named the island "Massacre Island," and abandoned the settlement.

One corner of the monument had sagged deeply into the
sand, and the angle of its ancient list seemed to Duck to
have sharpened dangerously.

Junior pulled up short, examining it. "Mamoo," he said,
"your history is falling over."

"An apt remark," Mamoo chuckled. "An apt remark."

Junior accepted this praise quietly and Mamoo seemed
prepared to move on.

Duck drew up short. "What do you mean? This is a
monument to the collapse of our family?"

"Why, no." Mamoo looked at her in surprise. "Surely
you know the joke?"

"Uh-uh."

Mamoo placed her hands on her hips and regarded the monument thoughtfully. "I've been waiting for the sea to take that monstrosity since it was planted there. Ozymandias should've built his empire of the same material: it's indestructible. And everything on that indelible plaque is a complete fabrication and a personal embarrassment to me. When I was a freshman at the Jefferson Davis High School, Miss Pratt assigned us the task of unearthing some little-known fact about the local area, and gave us three months to do it. Well, I was something of a procrastinator back then, and I'd planned to go to the library the weekend before the paper was due; but that weekend my little brother came down with a life-threatening case of whooping cough. I can still hear it—sounded like he would honk himself inside out. I couldn't do my research, and I didn't have the courage to test Miss Pratt's resolve against extensions . . . Are you *sure* you've never heard this story before?" Mamoo broke off.

"Positive," Duck said.

"I was certain your mother would've told you," Mamoo said, rather testily. "She probably took great pride in our fake history, though." Mother was the only person Duck had ever heard Mamoo speak of in this clipped tone, although Mother's death had suppressed it recently.

Duck fought her digression. "What *are* you talking about?"

"Well, don't you see? I made the whole thing up. About Iberville's landing on this site. Bibliography and all, I made it up so I'd have a report to turn in. At the time, I felt very clever and daring. I half-expected Miss Pratt to seek my expulsion for defiling History with such transparent tripe. But far from it. She loved it. She gave me an 'A-plus' and read my paper to the class. Then she read it at the next meeting of her chapter of the Daughters of the Coastal Settlers.

Then she took it to their landmarks subcommittee, on which she served. And they came to my father and asked if they could honor the spot. He was pleased and surprised; he'd never heard the story nor seen my paper. Now, there was the place I should've stopped it. He would've known what to do if I'd told him the truth. But it seemed to me already to have gone too far. So I kept my own counsel, and the rest, as they say, is history."

"Oh, Mamoo." Duck sighed over the triviality of this particular confession.

"It's a prime example of how things can get away from you. Poor Miss Pratt, she must've been in her dotage to rely on a high-school student's report without checking it. Actually, since we're truth-telling, she was just out of college, young and insouciant; she just made the mistake of trusting appearances."

"Me too," Duck said. "I was proud of our fake history, too."

"Oh, darling," Mamoo answered, "you have everything to be proud of in yourself. The landmark's only there to keep us modest." After a moment she added, "But I do wish the sea would wash it away. I won't be able to look Miss Pratt in the eye until it does."

"You still see her?"

"As seldom as I can. She married a man named Rodney Burke and moved away for many years. They moved from place to place, I heard, as he climbed the corporate ladder. And then, about fifteen years ago he died and she came back to live with her spinster half-sister, Jane Tipton. Next door to you."

B

They moved me to Block B last week, after our second motion to set bond was denied. Arnie made it clear that the amount could be as exorbitant as the judge liked—$100,000, $500,000, $1,000,000—so long as bond was allowed. However, it's an election year and Judge Porter is anxious to show that he does not employ dual standards for the rich and the poor. Besides, Arnie's investigator learned, Papa made substantial contributions to each of Judge Porter's unsuccessful challengers in the last two elections. What a powerful legacy my grandfather bought for himself.

I have been adjudged a risk to the surviving members of the Spencer family. Moreover, the judge found, working uncommonly hard against being reversed on appeal, my worldwide assets render even a million-dollar bond inadequate security against flight. On the judge's lips, I sounded like a member of the Medellín cartel. The inmates are impressed. Arnie is disgusted. He's applied for writs, but is pessimistic about our chances.

Emboldened by my legal losses, the guards moved me to B, the only unairconditioned block. They think they are hurting me; Papa's Finlandic lore obviously has not reached these beige-shirted Neanderthals. (How completely I have subscribed to the principles of us-against-them!

47

*Would the prisoners seem so much cleverer than the guards
if the latter were not my captors?)*

Even Eudora has a copy of Elga's Memoirs now, that
modest book whose readership I thought would be confined
to me and a few loyal employees of Liem Enterprises.
"Girl," Eudora tells me from her reading, "your grandfather was something else." Indeed.

Memoirs confirmed what I suspected, must have known
about my upbringing: that Papa was, from the time he took
custody of me, engaged in a pitched battle to eradicate any
gene that might have passed to me from my luckless, feck-
less father. No wonder Papa responded so enthusiastically
to my love of the sauna. My artistic and academic accomplishments were nothing to him by comparison. After all,
my mother's stellar accomplishments availed her nothing in
Papa's eyes; but then she never took to the sauna, that
Finnish passion for heat, that generation-skipping gene that
he thought had passed from him to me.

The sauna was his home's sole extravagance. He shipped
the huge stones from Finland to Country Club Estates and
brought the engineer with them. (Who in the sauna-like cli-
mate of Alabama would know how to build an artificial
one?) For the few months that the sauna wasn't made re-
dundant by natural forces, Papa and I would recline on our
slabs, and he would discourse on the evils of the cold, especially the Winter War of 1939 that stole his wife, my
sainted grandmother Katrina. Papa's acumen was never
dulled by age, but anyone looking in on our sauna sessions
would have thought him senile as he returned again and
again to his life in the "bicycle battalion" from 1939 to
1940. Papa thought the paradoxical name of his unit contributed to the Soviets' arrogant and mistaken belief that
their superior numbers and armament could crush the
Finns in a matter of weeks. In his telling, those brave
young men came alive again, charging from the deep

woods on their cross-country skis to attack the monstrous
tanks with no heavier weapons than Molotov cocktails and
their prodigious courage, or using themselves as bait to
lure the behemoths onto a lake concealed beneath ice and
snow where the tank might break through the ice or might
simply have an unimpeded shot at its prey. In Papa's telling, that cruel winter—the coldest in a hundred years—
came alive again, and we would shudder despite the
enveloping heat of the sauna.

Papa's fundamental tenet was frozen into place in those
few months: he could do anything if he could stay warm.

I don't think such a trait, born of such an experience, is
heritable, Papa. Anyway, my mother, your daughter, was
born before your battlefield epiphany. Truthfully, Papa, it
wasn't the heat that drew me to the sauna; I just wanted to
hear you talk. Doesn't that count for something, Papa, that
I loved you?

In any event, heat, of which there is an abundance in
Block B, has always comforted me. I am in my element
here. When the afternoon sun strikes our outer wall, I can
close my eyes and imagine myself in Papa's sauna. I drew
the scene for Eudora, who now joins me in occasionally la-
dling water onto the stones—in this case, our bare cement
floor—and making hissing noises of steam rising. The
guards hate us for our little joke. They are all too aware of
the subtle shift in power that occurs when we draw humor
from our environment, and they cannot control their stone-
age tempers even though they know it shifts the balance
more markedly. We hiss, and they clatter their billies along
our bars, sounding the alarm of our victory.

There is more hissing now, even among women who pre-
viously surrendered power by hurling obscenities that the
guards ignored. So invigorating, these small pleasures.

9

"How's your lovely grammaw?" Bahalia asked at dinner.

"Great," Junior answered briefly, too enthusiastic about his dinner to continue. Duck silently straightened and curled the moist red antenna sprouting from the boiled shrimp on her plate.

"How was the water?"

"Fine," Junior answered perfunctorily. Duck studied the small, perfectly round black eyes of the shrimp and marveled at their similarity to the coriander seeds Bahalia had used for seasoning. Blake, Sr. regarded the scene silently.

"Did you tell your grammaw I need some help around this here table at dinnertime, and for her to come on by?"

Junior looked up, puzzled. "Uh-uh."

Duck tested the spring of the tails, which pulled back into a C shape after she had extended them.

Bahalia muttered loudly, as if speaking to herself in the kitchen, "That's all right. They don't need to talk to each other if they don't want to. Lawd knows, there's nothin' to say. Jus' keep on 'til they all get ulcers an' got nothin' but oatmeal to play with at supper time. Nobody's askin' me, so I'm not sayin' nuthin'."

Blake, Sr. ventured into the silence Bahalia left behind. "I've been thinking," he began, too loud and too chipper. He paused and adjusted. "We're all anxious about the trial next week. We need something beyond it to look forward to."

"Ain't that the truth." Bahalia was encouraged.

"I'd like to take some time off and take a trip to Europe. All of us. You too, Bahalia. I haven't been to Spain for twenty years. I want to take Junior to the Prado, show him something more than baseball cards." Junior and Bahalia followed his words eagerly, warming him with their shining eyes. "And we can go to Paris to exercise Duck's French."

"Excuse me," Duck said, rising, folding her damask napkin, and breaking the spell as she left the table. She walked carefully from the room and up the back stairs, but as she closed the door to her room she let her body succumb to her grief. Her back slid down the door, her stomach heaved with silent sobs, and she cried until tears ran from her nose and covered the backs of her hands. Spent of tears, Duck smeared her hands across her swollen face and began chewing on her knee. "I hate him," she thought. Gaining strength, she mumbled into her knee, pushing her teeth painfully into her upper lip that was mashed against her kneecap, "I *hate* him!" There, it was out, said aloud.

Theatrically, her father's tread sounded on the back stairs at that moment. He was coming. Duck felt a rush of adrenaline, and held herself motionless at the base of the door, waiting for her prey. He would knock with his timid knock. She would startle him with her proximity and her fury. She would roar through the closed door, with all the force she could muster, "I HATE YOU!" And he would be shattered.

At the top of the stairs, Blake, Sr. hesitated but did not turn toward Duck's room. She heard his steps recede across the landing toward his room, and the quiet click of his door closing. *How dare he not come by to check on me?*

The phone rang and was answered on the second ring. Duck waited for a call. Maybe it was Rick. Nothing. She nestled her cheek against her knee and readied herself for a long cry. Tears slid sideways from the corner of her right eye across the bridge of her nose and into her left eye where they formed into a torrent. She could make them spurt out if she snapped her lashes together, but then her eyes ached more. She longed for her mother, who would have held her without intruding, who would have put a cool cloth over her eyes, and who, alive, would have erased the need for tears. Her father could go off with his mistress. They would be fine without him.

She heard her father's door open. "Laura," he called across the vast reaches of the landing.

"What?" she called back through the door with as much sullenness as she could muster.

"Telephone," he replied.

"Okay." Duck hummed a little to check her voice and cleared her throat before saying hello. Blake, Sr. politely hung up the extension as soon as she answered.

"Hi. It's Maria."

"Thank God. There's no one else I could talk to right now," Duck confided.

"Have you been crying?"

"Yeah, there's nothing else to do over here."

"Here either. Maggie just told Ma she's pregnant."

"Wah." There was a moment of silence.

Maggie, Maria's sister, was fifteen, Alexandra's age. She and Alexandra had been good friends and both sets of sisters had been frequent companions. Duck knew from both Maria and Alexandra that Maggie had been "doing it" for more than a year. Maria had been scandalized; Alexandra had been intrigued. Maggie had been the first of Alexandra's friends to become sexually active. Alexandra had begged for all the details, which Maggie had happily provided. There was a distinctive, throaty giggle that emanated from Alexandra's room when Maggie's sexual exploits were under discussion. Alexandra would later share the reports with Duck, and they would analyze them exhaustively, with interest that was more reverent than prurient. Duck knew from Alexandra what Maria did not know, that Maggie had had several partners.

"Maggie won't tell Ma who the father is," Maria added.

Duck wondered whether Maggie knew, and quickly reviewed the now-stale information she had on file for a clue to the mystery.

Maria's dramatic tone deepened. "She wants to have an abortion."

"Whaaah." This was momentous. The Cristinas were the most stolidly Catholic family Duck had ever met. Their parish priest regularly came to dinner. The only political activity Duck had ever known Mrs. Cristina to undertake was the right-to-life campaign. She had an ADOPTION NOT ABORTION bumper sticker on her van and thousands more in tilting stacks of boxes throughout the house. And it was no idle slogan for her. With nine children of her own, Betsy Cristina had taken in foster children as soon as Vinnie and Theo, her eldest, grew out of the house. Maggie, the rebellious one, had hit pay dirt.

"Can I come over?" Maria pleaded.

"No, we'd have to interact with my father."

"I like your father. I can interact while you sit out. It'll take some of the pressure off of you."

"Were you talking to him before I got on the line?" Duck asked, reflecting back on the delay before she was called.

"Ma did first. She wanted to know if he minded you coming over or me going there."

Duck was outraged. "What are we, eight years old?"

She could hear Maria choosing her words carefully. "Well, Ma's just worried about you, Duck. She doesn't want to drive a wedge between you and your dad."

"My dad did that." Duck wrapped the telephone cord

around her finger and watched it turn from red to purple to white.

"Ma thinks you need to spend time together to work it out." Maria raced ahead with trepidation. "She doesn't want you to hide from your dad at our house."

"Oh, nice. I need to make up with the adulterer so that I'll have a solid basis for a friendship with his murdering lover after she's acquitted, Junior's hauled off to prison, and she becomes my stepmother. What a pretty family portrait." Duck gained momentum. "Do you suppose my father can get his first marriage annulled so that he and Catherine—I think I'll call her Kitty—or should it be Pussy?—no, so he and *Kitty* can be married in the church?"

"Duck. He's a widower. He doesn't need an annulment." Maria was nothing if not practical.

Duck steamed past the technical nicety. "Do you think she'll wear white . . . or black? Maybe red. Hey, maybe she'll adopt Junior and me. Maybe she'll adopt Alexandra, too. Can you adopt a dead person?"

"Duck, please stop."

"*You* stop. Stop plotting with your mother and my father what's best for me. He won't let me move out and now your mom won't even let me sleep over. I'm trapped in this ghost house with a zombie and a moron." Duck stumbled over her own unkindness and fell. "Oh man, listen to me. I can't believe I said that. Junior. You know I don't feel that way about Junior."

"I know," Maria said quickly. "Look, I was trying to tell you, your dad said you could come whenever and as long as you liked. Ma said the same. I just wanted to get away from the Maggie thing for a while. But come on here; we'll just close the door. And bring Junior."

"Thanks, Maria. And thanks for putting up with me. Should we come tonight or tomorrow?"

"How 'bout tomorrow? I have all day off the day after."

Maria worked at the neighborhood Bee-Mart, a giant supermarket. She had begun as a part-time cashier at fourteen; she had been so punctual, industrious, and proficient, and the turnover of other employees so high, that she had quickly risen to head cashier. Now she was an assistant manager. "A check approver," Duck's mother had dismissed the news of Maria's promotion. "Bahalia's family is more upwardly mobile than the Cristinas." But Maria's position was much more worldly and weighty than Mother would acknowledge. Like Duck, Maria had always excelled academically; but to be capable in real life, *there* was a challenge. Maria seemed to have outstripped their friends who had gone off to college and came back for weekend visits looking stoop-shouldered from carrying lumpy backpacks. She had certainly outstripped Duck. It was intimidating, this sense that Maria had leapt ahead. And through no fault of Maria's, Duck found it harder to confide in her than the year before.

Duck felt out of place both with her friends in Mobile, who had gone to work right after graduation, and with her friends at college, who seemed distant and hurried in their brief encounters with her. Left idle on the sidelines, Duck regretted her decision to stay home. She had agonized over her choice of schools, and slid thoughtlessly into the far more important decision to skip the first semester. Evelyn Spencer had wanted her daughter to attend her alma mater, Wellesley; Vassar, Smith, or Radcliffe would have been fine; Hollins, Vanderbilt, or Duke would have been acceptable, although Evelyn believed that quality eroded as one moved south. Harsher winters, she felt, lent clarity and sharpness to northern intellects. However, Duck had not taken the graft of purpose and ambition that her mother had carefully nurtured.

Alexandra had broken the news to Mother one night at dinner. (Alexandra frequently served as Duck's emissary, not suffering the unease Duck felt in Mother's presence. Mother was so perfect. She didn't come out of her room in the morning until she was beautifully dressed and made up. She spoke in perfectly formed sentences, about matters of importance. Duck would begin some sloppy transmission, "Me and Alexandra . . ." "Alexandra and *I*," Mother would correct.) Alexandra dished up hard facts as smoothly as mashed potatoes. "Duck's applied to Auburn."

"Well, isn't that fine," Blake, Sr. said, addressing Duck. "What attracted you to Auburn?"

Mother gave her no time to answer. "Where else are you applying?"

"No place," Duck said timidly. "I'm pretty sure I'll be accepted."

"Of course you will. With your grades and test scores, you could have your pick of a number of schools better than Auburn."

"But I like Auburn."

"It's beneath your abilities," Mother persisted.

"It's a fine school, and you'll be close to home. We'll get to see more of you," Blake, Sr. said.

"If coming home is what you're worried about, we can afford to fly you back from anywhere you want to go." Now it was a full-fledged fight. This was how her parents usually did it, in genteel voices, without addressing one another directly.

"I want to go to Auburn."

"Why?" Mother pressed.

Duck could not take much more of this. She had been moved by no higher objective than to follow Rick to Auburn, where he planned to study engineering, and where she could stall for two years before choosing a major. She didn't know much about the school. Under Mother's withering examination, she could feel her application to Wellesley taking shape.

Blake, Sr. rescued her. "If you want to go to Auburn, that settles it."

"Don't they have guidance counselors at Wright?" Mother asked, and added tartly, "Because you certainly don't have any at home."

"It's settled," Blake, Sr. said, ending the conversation and the possibility of any other that night.

On further reflection, Mother was disappointed but brave, for she was more confident that Duck could wrest honors from Auburn's less rigorous curriculum.

But the murders in May had stripped Duck of all pretense of ambition. She had spent the summer sleeping, reading, and idly passing time with her friends. Most of them were college-bound, and they had tried to draw her into their excitement. Rick, Jenny, and Suzie, all of whom were going from the Wright School to Auburn, had included her in every college-preparatory plan. For Jenny Ainsworth, this involved careful consideration of the schedule of sorority rush parties and football games they would attend, and the sartorial requirements for each; Jenny shopped all summer long and accumulated a dizzying collection of clothes, shoes, and accessories. Suzie Daggett, who was to have been Duck's roommate, set herself on a disciplined course of self-study so that she would be ready for the pre-med curriculum she was tackling. Rick, working at a construction job over the summer, spent almost every evening and all day Sundays with Duck. Most of their dates ended in the Municipal Park, in the "Bomber Hotel," as Rick called his car on these occasions. His prescription for curing her grief was passion. Duck had stopped him just short of intercourse, and Rick ruminated on how blissfully happy they would be when she'd left home and they could sleep together.

Duck politely declined all of her friends' offers. They frightened and intimidated her with their dazzling energy.

She thought of their energy multiplied by that of tens of thousands of students, and felt that going to college would be like flying into a bug light. Exhausted by her fears, Duck needed more and more sleep. By the beginning of August, she often felt too tired to see her friends, to call them on the telephone, or even to take their calls. She hardly saw them in the month before they left, and on the morning in August that Suzie and Rick drove away together in the Bomber and Jenny's parents crowded into the station wagon with their daughter and her trunks, Duck slept late and missed saying good-bye.

After the college students left, Duck had needed even more sleep, which was just as well because there was little else to do. Rick had called once or twice a week, but could not afford to talk long. Apart from the expense of long distance, conversation generally wore down quickly because communication by voice alone had never interested Rick. After inquiring after Duck's health and well-being, and reporting that "nothing much" was happening on campus, Rick had expended his entire store of conversation and patience.

The coming October weekend was to be Rick's first trip home since school began. Earlier plans had been foiled by term paper deadlines and not-to-be-missed home football games. During their separation, Duck's affection for her steady boyfriend of two years had flared into a great passion. She flushed with excitement at the thought of their reunion. In an uncharacteristic departure from his taciturn telephone persona, Rick had said, "Reserve Friday, Saturday, and Sunday for me. One of those nights I'll have something to celebrate, but I can't tell yet when the surprise will come. Only that it's going to be great."

"Better than the Bomber Hotel?" Duck asked, considering whether she would enjoy any variation on their usual agenda. Rick's bracing kisses had gotten Duck through the summer. She thought of him holding her in the front seat of his car, parked at the edge of the lake. His arms had grown browner and stronger over a summer of hoisting and hammering lumber; and the feeling of his restrained strength was much more powerful than the crushing embraces she knew he could deliver. And his face. To die for. Duck had grown accustomed to her friends' frequent exclamations, "He's so adorable!" But she never tired of looking at Rick. Because it embarrassed him to be ogled directly, she usually consumed him in profile. Square jaw. Aquiline nose. High prominent cheekbones. Deep-set blue eyes. Gently curved brows like a pair of boldface swung dashes, the inner corners of which drew together when he was angry or worried and jumped when he was happy or surprised. An endearing slightly off-center cowlick that the sun had bleached a radiant white against the burnished blond of his crew cut. If there were any flaw to Rick's features it was that his wide mouth was disproportionately thin-lipped, lending a deceptively stern appearance to his face. Duck could not look at Rick's mouth, however, without remembering its sensuous mobility. She could, and had, kissed him for hours without thought of anything else.

"Okay," Rick said, "we'll work kissing into the surprise. I can't wait."

"Me either." Perhaps, Duck thought for the thousandth time, they would do more than kiss this weekend.

10

*Today Arnie brought me this lovely vellum paper and my
Mont Blanc fountain pen, with strict instructions not to
write anything of the circumstances that brought me here.*

*I am not to discuss Blake, my views on my innocence,
and certainly not my views on my guilt. But because I have
pleaded not guilty, Arnie, they must know I count myself
innocent—at least of the crime charged.*

*It took a formal motion to get me my pen. They've all seen
"Silence of the Lambs": they know I could use it to cut out
their hearts. They must not realize that this pen is called the
"Diplomat," this precious pen that Papa gave me when I
was seven. Every day for twenty years, I have wiped it carefully before putting it away. Fashion it into a sword, indeed!*

*I remember the first time I held it; it was fat and clumsy
in my short fingers. "You will write without erasures now,
my Katya," Papa instructed. "You must learn to think before you write, before you act. It is time you learned that
every thought you express is indelible."*

I know, Papa. I know.

*Thank God he missed reading this chapter in our family
history. He lived an extraordinary life—an exemplary life—
and his reward was that an angel snatched him out of it
just in time.*

From Elga's book I gained more understanding of the strictures of my upbringing than my nanny felt free to disclose to me alone. Why it was suitable to share these insights with the world I will never understand. Well, the truth is that I would prefer not to understand, but I do. Elga's first allegiance was to Papa. My significance for her was first as a link to him; I was the potential stepgranddaughter. But if she could not marry him, she was not willing to have more than a professional relationship with his ward. She was genuinely fond of me, I know; but she did not love me, as he did not love her.

Fifty years she gave to our family, and when Papa died, who was left to appreciate her lifelong dedication? Only I, from the proper distance she had instilled in me. And so Elga sought the world's approbation by writing her book.

I learned from that book what a personal failure it would have been for Papa to see me thus brought low. I would be the third in three generations of Liem women that Papa couldn't save with his love and his money. It started with my grandmother Katrina, my namesake. Papa saw the war coming, moved Katrina west from their border home to Helsinki, and marched off to the front to repel the Russian bear. He took all the risks, but she was the one struck by a stray shell when the Soviets mistook a library for a factory. Elga's memoirs shocked me with the revelation that Papa felt somehow responsible, that his uncanny safety at the corpse-littered front had been purchased with Katrina's life.

Then came my mother, Hella, whose meteoric rise to rock stardom vaporized in the drug-rich environment of the sixties. According to Elga, Papa fretted that there could only be so much fame and money in one family and that his uncanny successes canceled out Hella's success and her life as well.

Now it's my turn. What was it this time, Papa? An excess of love? Hardly.

11

From a distance, the Cristina house was magnificent. It was a huge house in a neighborhood of merely large houses. Situated on Government Street in one of Mobile's finest historic neighborhoods, it commanded attention from the front and side. Its most imposing feature was a rounded turret that rose above the three-storied structure, banded at each level with florid carved panels. At the ground level a wide verandah, hemmed with delicately turned spindles like the lace on a little girl's party dress, swept across the front of the house and tucked in behind the turret; slender columns supported a second-story balcony sporting the same railing like a sash, above a cornice draped with garlands. Every surface was crowded with decorative shingles, sunburst patterns, stained glass, and other ornaments to delight the eye.

Stavros Constantopoulis, importer of olive oil and smuggler of Greek antiquities, had built the house in 1896 for his sixteen-year-old bride. He himself had designed the stained-glass windows that were to shine propitiously on his master bedroom, featuring Demeter, the Greek goddess of agriculture, plenty, and, most importantly, fertility. But the imagery of abundance had failed for the Constantopoulises. Ruined by the Great Depression, Stavros and his barren wife had returned to their native Thessaloniki in 1930. The palatial house remained empty for more than a decade, until Betsy

Cristina's father, Everett McCall, bought it at a sheriff's sale.

The fecundity that Demeter had denied the devoted Constantopoulises she lavished on Everett and his progeny, who spurned the goddess. Everett and his wife Celeste raised six children as effortlessly as weeds; their daughter Betsy followed with nine; and now Demeter was shining on third-generation Maggie.

During the Cristinas' occupancy, the mansion had suffered intensive use and scarce maintenance. Money saved for porch repairs went for tuition or braces on someone's crooked teeth; paint jobs yielded to car repairs; and so on for more than twenty years, until the house took on an unkempt and rather shabby look. As Mother had predicted it would.

When Mother went house-hunting soon after Junior was born, she targeted the Constantopoulis mansion and approached Betsy, whom she had not met, with an offer. Betsy explained the sentimental value of the house and politely stated the obvious, that it was not for sale. Mother raised her offer, and just in case Betsy was serious on the point of sentiment, told Betsy that she could not possibly maintain the mansion properly, so that it would be kinder to the house to relinquish it to the Spencers. But Betsy could not be moved, and Mother had never quite forgiven her lèse-majesté.

Nevertheless, Junior and Mark Cristina, also a Down Syndrome child, had united the two families: the two little boys had been devoted to one another since the meeting arranged by their mutual pediatrician ten years ago. For Duck and Junior, the Cristinas' house was a second home. Maria and Duck were the same age; Maggie's and Alexandra's birthdays were only weeks apart; and Mark was only a year older than Junior. Considering the number of Cristina children, the age parallels to the Spencer family were not terribly surprising; the Cristinas had children close to the same age as those in every family in town, it seemed. More remarkable were the deep friendships between the Spencer children and each of their contemporary Cristinas.

Duck and Junior pushed through the front door without troubling the heavy brass ram's head knocker. They tossed their bags into a corner of the great hallway with the same disregard for its fine oak wainscotting and coffered ceilings that was displayed by the Cristinas, and moved into the final stage of the pre-dinnertime melee. In the first of the triple parlors that ran from the front of the house to the kitchen at the back, Simon Cristina and his best friend Duke were frantically trying to reach the next level of some Nintendo game. "GET THE CAPE!" Duke screamed over Simon's shoulder as if their lives depended on it.

"Can't we put it on pause?" Duke wailed. A simple command would have held the game in suspended animation until they finished supper.

"Naw, Ma gets philosophical about it," Simon answered. "She says life ain't like that; you gotta finish what you start."

Three-year-old Duane, dubbed "the foster child du jour" by Maggie, was entertaining himself with a roll of toilet paper. Nothing had escaped at least one looping white turn; even Simon and Duke, seemingly unaware, were bound at the neck by a double-layered figure eight.

Duck fell into place as porter with Maggie and Maria, which gave her an opportunity to inspect Maggie. The petite, lissome girl, wearing form-fitting spandex that concealed nothing, gave not the slightest outward sign of her pregnancy. What Evelyn had described as Maggie's "come hither look" seemed fairly accurate this evening. Her pink lace crop-top hugged smallish, rounded breasts, that may have grown (or swollen) a bit, Duck thought, but her black knit bandeau skirt stretched across a taut stomach. She had worked as a lifeguard at the Center pool all summer and into the warm October weekends; she was brown as a pecan, and showed as much worry. Against her dark skin, the effect of her lipstick was dramatic: it was an iridescent pink, the color of pulled taffy. Duck thought she detected a new gold stud in the line running up the rim of Maggie's right ear, a thought that was confirmed when Maggie's nineteen-year-old brother John glanced up from his studies and asked, "Why you wanna put braces on your ears when you just got 'em offa your teeth?" Maggie flashed a wide pink grin in reply.

"Aw, Jesus Christ," one of Peter's fifth-grade friends moaned, as the fortress they were moving from the table began to collapse. Before Peter's hand could reach the boy's mouth to cover it, Betsy was at the door.

"We do not take the Lord's name in vain in this house," she announced. "To the wall with ten Hail Marys." Betsy had a deep, hoarse voice that sounded as if she had just come from cheering one of her sons to victory on the Little League field.

"I don't know how," the boy whimpered.

"Not you," said Betsy, not unkindly. "Peter is responsible and will say them for you."

Peter was already at the wall making short work of his penance; he could do a Hail Mary in five seconds, and could say it intelligibly in twelve. Showing off for his friends, he did the five-second drill, as they silently circled him like wagons. Meanwhile, Junior and Mark slammed napkins and silverware down at each place in practiced rhythm. Maggie, Maria, and Duck, with the speed and agility of plate spinners, filled in with china and glassware.

At 6:30 p.m. on the dot, Betsy took her place beside Mawmaw Celeste at the head of the table, joined the circle of clasped hands, and presided over the blessing.

Duck never worried about having to push away a

hamburger at the Cristinas, because they had gone vegetarian long before she. Betsy ladled stewed okra and tomatoes from a steaming tureen onto Duane's plate. With a trilling yowlp of pride, Luigi, the Cristinas' sleek gray tabby, leapt onto the table and dropped a small wet lump beneath Betsy's elbow. The headless carcass of a mouse. Betsy froze, the spoon in one hand, the plate in the other.

"I'll get it," Maria volunteered, taking the thing by her fingertips. Duck followed her outdoors, stomach heaving, and leaned against the back of the house, gulping air. She thought of her mother's misshapen body, of the crime-scene detectives painting a white swastika around it on the floor. Maria stood wordlessly beside Duck, prising flakes of paint from the weatherboards with her fingernail.

When Duck regained her composure, they went back inside. The lively discussion Duck had dimly heard from outside hushed when the screen door banged behind them. Duck thought they had interrupted a conference about Maggie when she noticed that no one but Junior and Mark would look at her.

"What *is* it?" Maria asked.

Junior smiled sweetly. "Daddy's in the paper again."

"Have you seen today's *Daily Times*?" Betsy asked ominously.

Duck shook her head. Her stomach rocked again.

"Come sit by me and read it, baby. It's a red block," Betsy warned.

Duck felt the blood drain from her face, and approached the newspaper with foreboding. Not every article on the Spencer murders provoked this reaction. In fact, most of the information Duck had about the killings, her father's relationship with Catherine Liem, and the ongoing criminal proceedings had come from the newspaper. Duck searched them every day with a mixture of eagerness and dread. But this morning the *Daily Times* had been missing from the breakfast table, and Duck hadn't given it a second thought. A red box, which the *Daily Times* had invented for this case, would explain the disappearance. The highlighting signified, as the boldfaced print above and below the article warned, that the contents were "intended for mature readers and might prove offensive for some. Reader discretion advised." Put another way, a red block meant that the contents would appeal to salacious readers and that every newspaper in town would be sold quickly and circulated widely.

It was no consolation to Duck that Betsy pushed the paper toward her saying, "Lord, forgive me for showing this to this child, but she was going to see it anyway."

Within the red block the heading read, OBSCENE POEM DECLARES ARTIST'S INTENT TO KILL. After a brief report of the defense's efforts to suppress the poem on the grounds that it had been obtained in an illegal search of the defendant's home without a warrant, the *Daily Times* reprinted the evidence at issue in its entirety.

A NEW YEAR'S RESOLUTION—*a ditty by Kitty*

Duck paused in her reading. "Kitty?" she asked no one in particular. "Her name really is Kitty?" The name did not fit what Duck knew of Catherine Liem: one of the richest people in America, raised strictly in a convent-like setting, and taught a classical curriculum by her Finnish nanny, Elga. "Kitty" seemed a rather common nickname.

"I think it was probably a private joke between her and your father," Betsy replied.

"Ditto, the poem," John opined.

"It's not private anymo-ore," Maggie said in a sing-song voice.

Duck returned to the poem.

For Kitty the artist,
Who weaves thin and thick,
There's no greater challenge
Than architect's dick.

And Blakey the draftsman,
Who drafts best from twat,
Gets Kitty to lend him
Her brush and her pot.

In tandem they work out
Astride and astream
They build slow and steady,
Scale heights as a team.

Away from each other
They rue the sad lot
of Blakey's soft dick
And Kitty's dry twat.

Yet fear not, dear children,
For their satisfaction
Mere thought of reunion
Stirs organs to action.

When New Year arrives,
Announced by the bells,
K & B will again be
Awash and Aswell.

Now together they vow
That in this year at last
Blake and Evelyn will be
A thing of the past.

"That is ... the ... most ... disgusting thing I ever read," Duck enunciated slowly, reflecting on Catherine Liem's reputedly strict upbringing, which obviously had not taken hold.

"I can't believe they printed it," John observed.

"Loo-o-ok," Duane piped in, "they's raisins in my muffin. I *love* raisins," he mumbled through a mouthful of muffin.

"Blueberries," Betsy corrected.

Duane spat the whole thing out, wiped his tongue on his sleeve, and declared, "YUCK! I *hate* blueberries."

"It's raisins," Celeste falsely reassured him. Betsy shot her mother a chastening look over Duane's head, but let it go. Duane happily scooped the wet glob back into his mouth.

"I can't believe it," Duck repeated. The anticipated reactions of each person she knew began crowding into her mind, pushing out all other thoughts.

The telephone rang in the kitchen and Betsy rose to answer it.

"I think it's sort of cool," Maggie said comfortingly, with her mother out of the room. "I'm glad to know *somebody* was hot for your dad, since your mother sure wasn't."

"Maggie!" Maria exclaimed. "That's a terrible thing to say—and you don't know."

"Oh, come on," Maggie argued, "she never got closer than an ice tray to Mr. S., and you know how she hated anything 'dirty.' " Maggie wrinkled her nose.

"I don't see what's so bad about it," Peter said. "There's only two dirty words. 'Dick.' 'Twat.' Big deal."

"How many Hail Marys is that?" asked his friend.

"None," Peter replied, "it isn't profane. So what's the big deal?"

Betsy returned, holding the receiver on its twenty-foot

extension cord. "Wait, Joey, you tell her," she said into the phone, and passed it to Duck.

"Hello, Joey?"

"Hey. I'm at work. Listen, it's not official yet, but the word is, the judge's going to continue the trial for a couple of months. He hasn't decided what to do about Junior's testifying, or the new thing . . . the poem." Joey spoke quickly. Duck could almost see him holding his brown curls up off his forehead, an unconscious mannerism that accompanied hard news.

"Oh, that's terrific," Duck said, overcome with relief. "Thanks for calling," she said sincerely.

"Any time. I wish I could cancel it for you."

"Thanks, Joey. Thanks."

When Duck repeated the news, Simon said challengingly, "See? They can too put it on pause in real life."

Duck and Maria repaired upstairs to deliberate for several hours on the events of the last fifteen minutes. "They're prob'ly continuing the trial because Catherine Liem hasn't come up with a defense yet," Duck speculated.

Joey, who picked up an extraordinary amount of information from courthouse gossip, was their authority. He had expounded at length on the difficulties confronting the defense. There was Catherine's obvious motive, her car found at the scene with the gun in it, and the lack of any other suspect. Also, the police had quickly stripped Catherine of the possibility of an alibi. When she called to report her car stolen, the police, who already knew exactly where it was, took a keen interest in the theft. When had she first noticed the car was missing? they wanted to know. Just then, she told them. Where was she? they asked. At home, she told them. Where had she been all afternoon? they asked. At home, she told them. Was anyone with her? No, she had been alone all day. They got all of this on tape. Catherine's attorney tried to have the tape excluded from evidence because the police had questioned her without advising her of her rights before she answered their questions. There was a hearing on the defense motion, and the police officer who took Catherine's statement claimed that he had had no idea then that Catherine's car had been located at the scene of a murder. He was in the auto theft division of the police force, and he was simply making a thorough investigation of a reported theft. "Bullshit," Joey had commented, brown eyes flashing. "Since when did they do anything on auto thefts besides take down the license number and hang up?"

Judge Porter, however, was convinced, and he ruled that Catherine's statements were admissible. So she was stuck with her account that she had been home alone on the afternoon of the murders.

"From what Joey says, I don't think they're trying to do her any favors," Maria observed. "He thinks they're trying to squeeze a guilty plea out of her."

"What would she plead guilty to? Sexual misconduct, with a sentence of community service?"

"Uh-uh. Manslaughter, with a ten-year sentence," Maria said.

"Well, I hope she turns it down. They'd probably send her to one of those country clubs. My father would probably move in with her there. . . . On second thought, I hope she takes the deal, if it would get him out of the house."

"Duck." Maria was smiling an indulgently critical smile.

A few hours in close communion with Maria in her room distanced Duck from Liem's bad verse. She was able to say, with a touch of humor, "Well, thank God Mother didn't live to read it."

"Duck . . ." Maria hesitated. "Don't you think your mother must've known?"

"God, no," Duck answered without thinking. "If she had, she would've killed my father. Or Catherine Liem. Or both of them."

12

I had been suffering the loss of The New York Times *in the way that I suffered the loss of classical music, Chinese food, and all the other forms of cultural deprivation we (or maybe just I) suffer here. There are compensations. I had never before read the* Investigator's *reports of women impregnated by aliens, and I found them almost as intriguing as Eudora's belief that this is responsible journalism. For a prostitute, she seems remarkably credulous. At least, for my notion of the generic worldly-wise prostitute. Eudora is the first woman of the night I've ever met. Other than Elga. Oh dear. That was mean—and indelible.*

But I digress. We get the Daily Times, *which is treading a fine line of distinction between itself and the* Investigator. *I think the red blocks ought to be inked in the true colors of the* Daily Times' *journalism: yellow. The limit of the editor's discretion seems to be positioning the worst items below the fold, where all of his readers have learned to look first.*

I remember one of the rare occasions when Blake and I went out to dinner together. We were sitting side by side on the brocade bench of our private dining room at Pierre's. My skirt had crawled up a bit when I sat, revealing a round hole in my tight black lycra stockings, just above the knee.

*A button of white thigh-flesh protruded through the open-
ing. It was truly hideous against the smooth black background. I hadn't noticed until Blake playfully reached over
to press it. He was surprised when I pushed his hand away
and pulled my skirt over that little lump of nakedness. He
said, "That's a lovely part of you," and he laughed when I
told him it looked obscene. If I'd been wearing shorts or a
skirt without stockings, it would have been nothing. But it
was obscene because it wasn't supposed to show.*

*How much more obscene my little New Year's composi-
tion, exposed through the rent fabric of our relationship.
What was so funny in private is appallingly lewd in print.*

*I thought I was reconciled to having no privacy. Show-
ering and defecating in front of other women was nothing
to Eudora's boisterous appreciation of my bad verse. It is
unsettling to be valued for another indelible thing I deplore.*

9 October

*It seems that my right to a speedy trial is to be the price of
my Mont Blanc pen. In granting the prosecution's motion
for a continuance of the trial, Judge Porter told Arnie,
"Well, you won the last one," meaning the pen motion.*

*Papa had a name for successes like Arnie's. The only
thing my Commie-hating grandfather ever credited to the
Russians was the expression of one of their generals, describing the land taken from Finland in the Winter War at
the cost of one million Russian lives: "We have gained only
enough territory to bury our dead." That's what Papa
would have said of Arnie's Pyrrhic victory with the pen. I
have won the right to record my ruin.*

*Ever upbeat, Arnie says we can make good use of the ex-
tra time. Easy for him to say. The work of the Liem Foundation is drawing to a close for this year. Out of sentiment*

*as well as practicality I have continued most of Papa's pol-
icies: support for the public radio station is still contingent
upon the weekly airing of Sibelius's* Finlandia; *scholarships
are still merit-based; support for the A.C.L.U., the drug rehabilitation programs, and the public library continue unconditionally. A few policies are changing. I have embraced
for the first time this year the battered women's shelter and
animal welfare groups. And I am not using the money to
buy myself love. When I have finished dispensing money,
though, I will have nothing to do, an entirely novel experience for which my life's training has made me particularly
unsuited.*

I tried to fill in productively, but Arnie would not have it.

*He has put an end to my teaching career. The trustees
had allowed me to take over the 10:00 to 11:00 a.m. beginning reading class without any bureaucratic hassle—in fact,
without determining whether I know how to read myself—
such is the intensity of their interest in bettering the inmates. My first action was to revise our basic text to
something more relevant than "See Spot run." Short words
are no impediment to an active imagination, I found. Here
is a sample from my primer:*

The D.A. is a fat pig. He can eat shit and die.
I am a good lay. My old man is sad that I am gone.

*Enrollment in remedial reading had more than doubled
and participation within the classes was active. It was a
chorus of happy voices that read from my blackboard, with
noticeable improvement each day.*

*How Arnie got wind of this I don't know, but he put an
administrative stop to it, without even offering me a chance
at reforming my curriculum. He does not want me to make
good use of my extra time. I am under strict instructions to
watch soap operas and play cards.*

13

IN THE AFTERNOON, a cold front finally pushed through. The first sign was a palpable charge to the hot air, which began to stir as if moved by electrical currents. Then the wind picked up in force, whipping leaves from the trees and carrying them in a sideways stream past Duck's window. In the space of an hour, the outside temperature dropped twenty-five degrees, and the air-conditioning system shut down with a battle-weary WUFF!

Best of all, the banging of wind-tossed shutters and the house-rattling thunder brought noise back into the house. It took Duck a little while to realize why the hubbub was so invigorating: it was as if Alexandra and a horde of her friends were pounding up and down the stairs, banging doors and playing heavy metal music in her room again; it was as if the phones were jangling, the hairdryers thrumming, and laughter reverberating through the walls. The house felt *alive* again. Duck dug around in a drawer and found a Bruce Springsteen CD with a thumping beat. She put it on and, a minute later, turned it up loud.

Junior pushed her door open timidly. "Music?" he asked.

"It's finally fall, Junior. Isn't it great? A change of seasons, a change of mood. I'm tired of moping around. Besides, I can't mope, I'm going out with Rick tonight."

"You going to a Bulldogs game?" For Junior, Rick was synonymous with sports, which they always discussed; and

Junior had accompanied Rick and Duck to many a football game at Wright the year before.

"Sorry, Junior. No. I don't know what we're going to do."

"Then how do you know what to wear?"

"Wear! Oh shit!" Duck exclaimed. Days earlier, she had picked out a forties-style sundress, with a figure-flattering belted waist and a full skirt (easy to raise, Duck had thought). But the sudden onset of cool weather had ruled out the thin crepe fabric and short sleeves. Duck assaulted her closet, but as Bahalia had observed, most of her clothes were not in it. She began rummaging through the piles on her desk, her chair, her bed, and her floor.

"Maybe we could clean it up," Junior offered.

"You're a sweetheart." Duck heaped clothes on him to carry to the laundry room. His next load was several trash cans overflowing with old magazines, newspapers, and fast-food wrappers.

Bahalia followed him up on the next trip. "I got to see this here," she declared. When she found Duck lining up the shoes in her closet, she said, "Well, now. This startin' to look like a room instead of a Dumpster." She backed out and returned in a few minutes with rags, a duster, and the vacuum cleaner. "Get them shelves," she directed Junior. "Strip that bed," she ordered Duck. "Lawd knows how long it's been since we seen them sheets."

"Let's paint the walls," Junior suggested, fully in the spirit of the renovation.

"Yeah," said Duck, surveying the pale blue walls. "Let's get some spray cans and apply some graffiti."

"Cool," Junior responded, unsure whether Duck was serious.

"Ya'll go on ahead," Bahalia shouted over the vacuum. "And shave your heads while you at it. Paint your heads green, too. Then you'll never have to worry 'bout Rick comin' roun' here again, and you'll never have to clean again."

"Bahalia," Duck said, "Rick's got nothing to do with this. It's fall cleaning."

"Sure, girl. I know that. I been watchin' you turn your room inside out every fall since you was a baby," Bahalia laughed.

When Rick arrived a little after eight, Blake, Sr., observing a family tradition, showed him into the formal living room. For Rick, the screening was perfunctory. He had sat in the living room countless times waiting on Duck, and had developed a relaxed and comfortable but duly respectful manner toward Blake, Sr.

"Good evening, sir." They shook hands, and Rick led the way into the living room.

"It's good to see you again, Rick," replied Blake. "Did you have to drive through all the rain this afternoon?"

"It was pretty hairy; but nothing could've kept me from seeing Duck this weekend." Looking toward the empty hallway, Rick added, "I guess a few weeks' notice wasn't enough to get her ready on time. Maybe I would've had time to pull over, after all, for the half hour that I couldn't see the road."

"At least it's cleared out for you now," Blake observed. "It looks like a beautiful evening. Where are you two headed?"

"Just around," Rick answered easily. "We'll probably catch up with some of the old gang. Hey, speaking of the gang, where's Junior?"

Blake, Sr. started in his seat, then went quickly to the hall closet, as Rick looked on, perplexed. "Come on, son. Come on out." Blake, Sr. had to draw his son out because he had retreated not only into the dark musty coats but also into a trancelike state lulled by his headphones. Junior blinked sleepily in the light.

Rick mustered the bravado to call out, "Hey, Sport. How 'bout them Saints?"

Junior recovered at once, saying, "They'll make the playoffs this year for sure. If they make the Super Bowl, Dad said he'll take me."

At that moment, Duck made her entrance. She stopped at the doorway, and much as she wanted to be demure, she could not suppress a cheek-splitting grin at the sight of Rick. She wanted to fly into his arms, but she contained herself and leaned against the door frame blushing.

"You look great!" exclaimed Blake, Sr., Rick, and Junior.

And they all laughed because they had been simultaneously stricken and had all spoken at once. Duck had felt that she looked all right—for her. Her skin was clear, the shadows beneath her eyes were gone. She had pulled back and braided her hair in a loose style she knew Rick liked, and she had added just a touch of color to her lips, cheeks, and eyes. She had done the best she could and had thought that if her nose were a little narrower, her hair a little straighter, and the color of her eyes a little deeper, she might almost have been pretty. However, the spontaneous outpouring of admiration from her father, Rick, and Junior told her that they saw something more. Part of what struck them was the sight of Duck emerged from her chrysalis of depression; but the other, more striking fact was that she suddenly looked very womanly. And they were right, she looked great. Duck did not have the naturally ravishing beauty of her mother and Alexandra, but when the spark of joy lit her from within, she was beautiful in her own way.

Rick said, "This town's gotten too small for you, kid. I think we should go to New York."

"Wherever you go," Blake, Sr. threw in, "please remember to be home by one."

As Duck walked arm-in-arm with Rick to the gate, she thought, *Why? Are you worried I'll follow your immoral ex-*

ample? She wished she had thought of it sooner, and said it. Her best repartees came in this *esprit de l'escalier*, too late to do her any good.

Rick turned the corner onto McGregor Avenue, then screeched the Bomber to a halt in front of the Applebys' house, thudding against the curb. "What the . . . ?" Duck asked, laughing, in mid-ricochet from the sudden stop.

"I can't stand it another second," Rick explained, pulling her to him. "You . . ."—he kissed her cheek—"are . . ."—he walked his lips down to her throat—"the most . . ."—he traced the line of her cheekbone with his tongue, and nuzzled into her ear—". . . beautiful creature I've ever seen, and I've missed you so much it's unbearable." They kissed with desperate longing, and clung to one another with exploring hands. "What's this?" Rick asked, feeling the chain around her neck. "You haven't gone Catholic on me, have you?"

"No. It's Alexandra's." She pulled it out and showed him Alexandra's gold initial "A."

"That's nice," he remarked. "You can leave that on." Duck giggled and tilted her head to give Rick access to the side of her neck. She glanced upside-down out the window and caught the return gaze of Monica Appleby. Duck shot bolt upright, and used both hands to eject Rick's face, as though he were a volleyball. In the same fluid evasive movement she tucked her head down between her knees; and then, realizing that things had passed far beyond any chance of concealment, she began to laugh, an uncontrollable belly-laugh that pained her doubled-up abdomen.

"What *are* you doing?" Rick asked.

"It's . . . it's . . ." Duck tried to answer, but was racked by another spasm of giggling. Finally, she contained herself and said, "It's Mrs. Appleby. She's been sitting right there on her porch swing watching us." She ventured another sidelong glance and collapsed again. "She's *still* watching.

She's probably thinking, 'That brazen Spencer girl's going to do it right here at the curb. She won't care if I watch. The whole family's shameless.' " Duck was laughing so hard she had to gasp for breath.

"I bet she's not thinking like that," Rick countered, reassuringly. "I remember when her domestic problems were the neighborhood scandal." Monica Appleby had been pregnant with Jonathan, her first child, when her husband Richard, a well-respected dentist, left her for his oral hygienist. (His *new* oral hygienist; Monica had been his oral hygienist until he divorced his second wife and married her.) Maggie and Alexandra had had great fun role-playing as the dueling hygienists: "Oh, Richard, may I give you an oral high?" "No, darling, please, I need you for *my* cavities." And although the Spencer and Cristina girls tittered and shushed each other whenever they encountered her, Monica had remained stoically cordial.

"Boy, her scandal seems small-time now," Duck remarked, "since my dad went off the charts."

"C'mon," Rick said, starting the engine, "let's move on." Duck sneaked a look back, and was surprised to see Mrs. Appleby cheerfully waving good-bye.

"So is this the night for my surprise?" asked Duck, turning back to Rick.

"You're the surprise, baby," he said, taking a long appraising look at her. It was all the more exhilarating because he was doing forty miles per hour and neither slackened his speed nor gave any sign of attending to the road. "What I had in mind pales by comparison to the way you look tonight. But yes, this is the surprise party. Just be patient while I get us there. It's taken some careful figuring, and I just hope I've got it right." He slung one arm over her shoulder and draped his left hand over the steering wheel, driving with his wrist. They conversed desultorily, and Duck tried to find the pattern to the snaking route he took to their usual spot. He detoured to the right and to the left, took dizzying turns through parking lots, doubled back, and generally confounded her.

"If you're trying to lose a tail," Duck commented, "you're doing a terrible job. I think we've attracted the attention of everyone in town."

"Keep guessing," Rick responded, enigmatic as the Sphinx. "You're real cold."

It took well over an hour to reach Municipal Park, two miles from Duck's house by direct route. When they approached the turnoff Rick bypassed it, circled the small lake, past the Azalea City Golf Course and the old locomotive, looped several times through the parking lot of the Fine Arts Museum of the South, then made the turn on Flournoy, and pulled into their traditional necking spot with an exultant crow. He folded his hands behind his head and declared, "We did it!"

"Well, that was . . . surprising," Duck observed, thoroughly enjoying the entire meaningless exercise.

"You still don't get it, do you, dufus?" Rick smiled at her broadly. "C'mere." He dragged her by the arm into the driver's seat as he jumped out. Duck gazed over the lake and listened to the trickle of water over the low dam. Cool air wafted through the window carrying a faint smell of the paper mills north of town on the Mobile River. Rick was in the back seat now. She could hear him fumbling around in an ice chest but she remained entranced by the view. Then, as she reached down to shut off the headlights, she saw it. The odometer had just rolled over to 100,000. The five zeros were perfectly aligned.

"Ha!" she exclaimed. "Oh Rick. Oh Rick." He hugged her from behind and at the same time prised a cork out of a bottle of champagne. Shaken by the drive, the bottle gave an explosive pop and erupted with foam that soaked Duck's blouse.

"I'll clean that up later," Rick promised. "I've brought glasses for starters." He produced two of his mother's fluted crystal champagne glasses. "Do you remember when we made this date?"

"Of course. I'll never forget," Duck answered. She and Rick had been going out for about a month when his parents gave him the Bomber, an Oldsmobile they had driven for seven years. Rick and Duck were sitting in this same spot when she noticed that the car had gone exactly 50,000 miles.

"My parents thought I'd crack it up inside of a year." Rick patted the dashboard of the sturdy Oldsmobile lovingly. "But I told you that you and the Bomber and I would still be together when she made a hundred thousand. And here we are." He touched his glass to hers and they drained them. "This is the most wonderful night of my life," he said. They kissed, refilled the glasses, and drained them, again and again.

As Rick sucked the champagne from her shirt Duck felt as though she were one with the champagne, woozy and tingly. Somewhere deep into the second magnum, when Rick helped her out of her clothes, Duck was drifting away. She felt his weight bearing down on her uncomfortably; she heard him saying, "I love you. God, I love you," into her ear, over and over; but she was floating and could not understand why he was so moved.

Then Rick was bathing her face and neck in ice water. It was shockingly cold and she wanted him to stop, but she could not make her voice work. "Bluh," she finally managed to say.

"Good, baby. Wake up. We got to get you home," Rick said from far, far away. The cold drubbing continued inexorably. She was cold all over. And something smelled terrible. The act of raising her arms to protect her face woke her fully. They were parked in front of the Applebys' again, it was 12:45 a.m., and she was drenched in her own vomit, which had soaked under her as well.

"Aagh," she cried out in disgust.

"It's okay, baby, really," Rick consoled her while dabbing at her stinking chest with a wet paper towel. "We just got to get you cleaned up to go home."

"Oh Rick, your car. I'm sorry."

"Duck," he said, touching her cheek tenderly, "it's been a wonderful night. I can clean the car. Don't worry about it." They tidied her up as best they could, and drove the half block to her house.

"Listen," Rick said, "I've got to spend the day with my folks tomorrow. I'll see you tomorrow night, and we'll have all day Sunday. Now let's make a run for it." They raced to the door, where Rick gave her putrid lips a lingering kiss. "I love you," he told her again.

Mercifully, her father had not waited up.

Duck went wobblingly to bed. She lay between the crisp, clean sheets and tried to remember what had happened after she got drunk. She knew, more than she felt, that she was not a virgin anymore. There was a small, dull throb in her groin. "This," she wondered, "is what Mother and Alexandra died for?"

14

Along with the chilly weather came a visit from Elga today. She has traded in her matronly look for the garb of a Famous Writer: she was sporting a tweed jacket with suede patches on the elbows. Elga always knew how to play her part. She looked good, really, much younger than her sixties, and I told her so, which pleased her. She had to restrain herself, I know, from telling me to tuck my prison uniform shirt into my prison uniform pants. But no doubt she made careful note of that detail.

One of Elga's regular maxims was "Never do only one thing when you could be doing two." Embroider while you listen to music. Compose poetry while you swim laps. Research your next book, Elga, while you pay a social call.

I found her questions about the details of my daily prison life impolite. By her refined standards, they were downright boorish. But I answered them. It was good to talk to her. And if I must now have a biographer, she will be more sympathetic than most. But if Elga writes my biography, it will have to be fiction. We never talked intimately, my closest companion and I. We had such a peculiar relationship. There is genuine affection between us, bred of so many years of proximity. But Elga taught me long ago the difference between proximity and closeness—she was always one

84

for subtle distinctions. And I knew implicitly that she had acted on Papa's instructions. "You are not here to cosset her," Papa would have said. Mary Poppins would have been discharged from our household in a heartbeat. Elga's job was to educate me in affairs of the mind, not of the heart.

It seems to me that life began when I moved into my own house on Monterey, alone, at twenty-one. My sweet house of high ceilings and long windows. If not then, a few years later, when I met Blake. And even now, maybe especially now, I question my understanding of affairs of the heart.

Now I am the teenager I never was in my teens. I am flooded with hormones, desires, irrationality. Every man reminds me of Blake. Some women do, too. A dumpy, balding little man came into the visitors' room today wearing a pair of battered old sneakers like Blake's. Only the bulletproof glass kept me from throwing myself at him. Elga looked from me to his turnip-shaped face and back again, sensing but not understanding the attraction. I almost told her, "It's the shoes, check out his shoes," but I didn't think she would get it.

15

SHE DID NOT know how long she had slept. It felt like the headache woke her up. She had never experienced such a gripping pain in her temples. She held herself still, not wanting to jar any of the agony in her head into shards that might pierce her eyes or cheeks. She opened her eyes and clamped them shut again; the light was blinding. Gingerly, she rolled her tongue inside her mouth. It felt carpeted. She tried opening her eyes again, just a fraction this time. Better. Without turning her head she strained to read her bedside clock, focusing with difficulty on the slender hands: five after eleven or five to one, she could not tell which. "If I don't move," she thought, "I may make it." Then she became aware of a hair lodged in the back of her throat. She thought it was partway swallowed, and she imagined the gagging, pulling sensation it would cause if she drew it out; she imagined the length of it emerging from her stomach and fishing up mucusy gobbets of vomit.

She bolted from bed and made it to the toilet for the first heave. She heaved and heaved but there was nothing to bring up except a nauseating sweet smell. The retching seemed to have pushed her headache into a tighter, more concentrated space. Unable to rise, she lay down beside the toilet. The ceramic tile floor felt coolly refreshing on her cheek. Presently, however, the floor began to feel cold and clammy. It was a sickening color of pink. She dragged herself painfully into the shower in her T-shirt and underpants and feebly turned on the water. She sat on the floor in the blessedly warm and purifying spray until the hot water ran out. By then, she was able to stand upright. She brushed her teeth, stripped out of her sodden clothes, and went back to sleep.

When Duck opened her eyes again it was definitely 1:30 p.m., and she had definitely slept for two more hours, because she could turn her head and read the clock clearly, and she was famished. She sat up cautiously and felt only a dull throb in her head. Feeling miraculously recovered, she bounded from bed and started her day anew. She had another twenty-minute shower, upright this time, washed her hair, brushed her teeth, and dressed in her favorite jeans and sweater, which she had not worn since the winter before.

The only sign of last night's mischief that Duck could find in the mirror was a red chin, chapped from hours of kissing. It brought back a memory of Alexandra at twelve, at war with Mother over her right to wear makeup. "But Mom, it's an ice-breakers' party. We're *supposed* to act like teenagers. Even Maggie's wearing lipstick."

"Just because everyone else is doing it doesn't mean that you have to," came Mother's familiar reply, "and Maggie's no example."

"Oh, Mom. I'll look so stupid. I might as well wear a pinafore," Alexandra argued.

"If you wear a gunnysack, you'll still be the prettiest girl there," Mother said with conviction, "and the boys that have been following you around like puppies will still notice you, whether or not you get yourself up to look like you're in heat."

"*Mom.* A *little* blush. A *little* lip gloss. A *little* mascara. *Please*," Alexandra pleaded.

"Alexandra. A *little* respect. A *little* obedience, or you won't go at all."

"Oooph!" Exasperated, Alexandra turned on her heel and sought shelter in Duck's room.

"Don't worry about it, Alex," Duck consoled. "You'll probably make all the other girls feel overdressed and start a new fashion trend." It was true. Alexandra was so popular and had such an infectious enthusiasm for all of her ideas that her friends regularly emulated her. For months, Alexandra's room had been converted to a bead-making factory, where all her friends copied the jewelry she made. Or they practiced dance steps together until they could dance like clones. When Alexandra started a weekly discussion group on "women's issues," everyone joined. She was a natural leader, never proprietary about her ideas and never demanding credit for having thought of them first. She welcomed everyone into her circle, which was therefore large enough to provide a natural constituency for any trend she set, and to lend a party atmosphere to any group she convened. And she had an indomitable will, so that when she took something up she could be counted on to follow it through.

As in the case of the party makeup. "Want to go for a walk?" she asked Duck.

"Sure, but I thought you had to get ready for the party," Duck answered.

"I am getting ready," Alexandra said decisively, and bounded from the room.

Duck had to fly to catch up. "Where are we going?" she asked, panting.

"Pik-a-Pak. I've got a sudden craving for a cherry popsicle." They reached the convenience store six blocks away in as many minutes. Alexandra went straight for the freezer, selected two cherry popsicles, and lit into hers at once.

"Don't bite it," she directed Duck. "Suck. Like this." She showed Duck how to wrap her lips around the frozen shaft

instead of pursing them. "Lemme see," she said after a
minute, pulling the popsicle from Duck's mouth.

Duck looked at Alexandra's cherry lips in amazement.
"Perfect," she told her. "Cherries in the snow." How did
Alexandra *think* of these things?

"Well, I'll have to keep my tongue in my mouth," Alexandra commented, brandishing a ruby-red tongue to complement her cherry-red lips.

"And your teeth," Duck added, eyeing her sister's
bubble-gum-colored teeth.

"Uh-oh. Maybe I'll just keep my mouth shut."

"Fat chance," Duck remarked.

When they got home, Alexandra went to work on her
cheeks with an abrasive pad. She scoured them alternately,
broadening the "blush" as she tried to even up the two
sides.

She leaned into Duck's room from the bathroom. "How
do I look?"

"Like a little Dutch girl who's been eating cherries,"
Duck responded honestly.

"That's what I thought," Alexandra said. "I hope
Mother's satisfied."

Mother, naturally, was very put out. But only for a minute. Alexandra had toned down her flaming cheeks with a
fine dusting of baby powder, and toned up her lips with a
fine film of Vaseline. "It's not makeup," Alexandra pointed
out, flashing a wide pink-toothed smile. Mother could not
help but laugh. That's how it always was with Alexandra.
She got her way, but without belligerence. And, of course,
the next time she asked to wear makeup, Mother assented.

Duck smiled at the memory as she blended some cream
concealer over her chin. No good. It gathered ghoulishly
against the chapped skin. She tried pulling a tiny flake free
and drew blood. She rinsed and gently dried her chin,
which looked worse for her attentions. She reminded her-

self that pimples and such were hardly noticeable to others. It was going to have to be chin up and forget about it. Besides, the only opinion she cared about was Rick's, and he would be amused.

She started thinking about the evening and what they would do. She didn't know what she wanted to do, and the new possibilities were both exhilarating and anxiety-producing.

The weather, at least, appeared to be smiling on them. It was a glorious day. From Duck's window, she could see her backyard and several adjoining neighbors', all handsomely landscaped. Everything looked brilliant in the rain-washed air. The sun-scorched browns of yesterday seemed like the hues of autumn today. Junior and Mrs. Burke were weeding and pruning in the Spencers' garden, and an overflowing wheelbarrow showed that they had been at it for some time.

Duck picked up her nasty clothes and towels and headed for the laundry room, hoping that she could ease past Bahalia. "Morning," she greeted the indignantly-angled shoulder blades as she swept by.

"Afternoon," Bahalia retorted. "I hope you ain't expectin' to wash that stink in hot water. You done used up about a year's supply."

Catching a whiff of Duck's load, she exclaimed, "Whew! You sure had you a time last night. You feelin' all right now, sugar?" Bahalia came into the laundry room after her. When she caught sight of Duck's chin, her voice went up a few decibels. "Lawd! What did he do? Drag you behin' his car? No wonder you's feelin' sick." Bahalia helped her with the clothes and doused them with a variety of chemicals before banging down the lid on the washer. She took Duck by the arm like an invalid and led her to the kitchen table. "Sit yoursef down here, honey. I got some tomato soup on the stove'll settle your stomach an' contradick that chin." Bahalia chuckled to herself.

"Prince Charmin' called a little while ago. I told him Sleepin' Beauty was spendin' the day snoozin' and showerin'."

"What did he say?"

"He say, good, you'll be able to stay up late tonight. He's comin' by around six. And Maggie call, too. She wants you to call her back."

Duck was perplexed. Maggie usually relayed messages through Maria or waited until they saw one another. Duck dialed from her room. One of the boys, she could never tell which one, answered.

"Hey, Duck. It's John. Maggie's been waiting on your call all day, but she just left a minute ago. Mom dragged her to the obstetrician for an ultrasound. She wants her to see the fetus."

"Poor kid."

"Yeah. But they'll be back in a couple of hours. Maggie said to tell you she really needs to talk to you. She asked if you guys could get together around five-thirty or six this evening."

"Oh John, I can't, I'm going out with Rick. Would you tell her for me that Rick's leaving Sunday night and the rest of my life is free?"

"Why don't you come for dinner Monday? Dad'll be home," John said.

"Uh-oh. Does he know about Maggie?"

"Yep. He checked in last night from California and Ma told him. He's dropping his load and flying home tomorrow."

Vincent Cristina was a trucker. He owned his own rig, which he loved like another child. His name was emblazoned on the driver's door in lettering more ornate than the monogram on Mother's silver tea service. For him to abandon his beloved rig and fly home was the ultimate measure of the seriousness of the situation.

"I don't know, John. This might not be the best time for you to have company for dinner." Duck thought the stiff silence of the Spencers' table might be preferable to a stormy scene at the Cristinas'.

"You're not company. You're family," John urged. "And besides, it'd go easier on Maggie if you and Maria flanked her."

"Well, okay, if you think so. Tell Maggie I'll see her then," Duck agreed. She hung up, still unenlightened about what Maggie wanted.

Rick arrived a little after six, and Duck was at the door right behind her father. She felt uncomfortable about a parlor visit tonight. Would her father detect some sign of their sexual initiation in Rick or in her flaming chin? She was unwilling to risk it, and almost leapt out of the front door before Rick could come in. "Good night," she flung at her father over her shoulder.

"Good night," he returned. "Have fun. Be back by one."

Such an opportunity had never presented itself before. Last night's unuttered retort flashed into her mind, and she hurled it without thinking. "Why? Are you worried I'll follow your immoral example?" Somehow, the delivery was not as satisfying as she had expected. She felt Rick's hand tense, and then the lightning struck.

"Laura! Come back inside!" her father commanded in his old tone of authority. She had not heard it in a long time, and had forgotten how powerful it was. She momentarily considered bolting, but if Rick did not follow, her flight would be foolish. Rick stood frozen beside her. She turned back to the house, feeling helpless and shamed.

Her father said to Rick, "Why don't you wait in the kitchen. I need to speak to Laura alone."

Blake steered her into the living room, back to the white couch that had become an emblem of misery for her since the day the survivors huddled there after the murders. Duck

glared at her father's loafers, the cuffs of his chino pants.
He had lost weight, she noticed. The braided leather belt
she had given him for his birthday last year was cinched a
couple of notches tighter. But instead of looking appropri-
ately wasted, he only seemed fitter. He had no right to wear
the belt anymore, she thought; he had no right to wear the
plaid flannel shirt Alexandra had given him. The mood that
seized Duck was that of Cinderella's sisters, seeing the
beauty decked out in their castoffs on the way to the ball.
Duck wanted to rip her father's casual finery from his body.

"Laura," Blake said, in his "I'm disappointed in you"
tone of voice; and inexplicably, she began to cry.

"You don't care what I do," she snuffled. "Why do you
have to embarrass me in front of Rick?"

"Laura," he said, "I spend more time than you could
know worrying about what lessons you will take from my
example. And I don't worry nearly so much that you'll become licentious as that you'll have difficulty in a loving
and trusting relationship with a man. God knows, your
mother and I haven't had a good relationship since you
were too young to remember." *Licentious?* Was this the
way her father really talked—when he talked? This had the
sound of something he had been saving up to say for six
months. Duck was stunned at the content, but said nothing.

"And what you've seen of my relationship with Catherine is a grotesque cartoon of what it was. I had so many
plans—before—for your introduction to her, so many
dreams for your friendship. Right now—with all this—I
have no hope of explaining my love for Catherine to you."
His speech was halting, timid. He didn't sound like himself.
"I must tell you again and again that I do not believe she
killed your mother and Alexandra, or had any part in it."
Now he was pleading, another tone unfamiliar to Duck. "I
know it as surely as I know that Junior didn't. I think someday we'll find out who did, and then maybe we can talk

about Catherine." Duck wanted to run. She did not want to hear any of this, but she was transfixed. Her father had never spoken to her like this before. The gray walls of the room seemed to close in on her. She felt light-headed, insubstantial, like one of the pen-and-ink drawings Mother had hung over the couch.

Blake moved inexorably on. "You have reason to hate me for all the lies and the disloyalty to our family. I will suffer your anger, your sulking, and your silence because I think I deserve them. But no matter how much you hate me, I'm going to go on loving you; and I will not permit you to say that I don't, because saying has always been believing for you."

Duck wanted to insist again, "You don't love me," because then he would try to convince her that he did, and perhaps he would succeed. But then he would hold her while she cried, and she couldn't allow that to happen because she hated him. Even so, it wasn't as much fun hurting him as she had expected. He was wearing his belt. On display at his office was every scrawled, lumpen creation she had ever given him—the things Mother banned from the house after a week or two. Blake also let her chop his hair when she briefly considered becoming a beautician. He taught her how to dance in this very room, with Duck standing on his shoes in her sock feet.

Duck groped for something to say to him, but she couldn't think in sentences. She could not hold a coherent thought.

After what must have been five minutes but seemed an eternity, her father tossed aside the cushion he'd been holding, laid his hand on the couch beside her, and said, "If you ever want to talk to me, I'll be here." Then he stood and left the room. Duck felt somewhat comforted, but immeasurably sad as well.

Presently, Rick joined her. "Are you okay?" he asked, holding her secure against him.

She nodded. "Let's get out of here."

Duck was silent for a time in the car. She leaned against the door, enjoying the icy press of the window on her hot cheek. Finally, she asked Rick, "Do you think Catherine Liem could be innocent?"

"Are you kidding?"

"No. That's what my father was just telling me—that he really believes in her innocence . . . and it's not just him; so many people are talking about how sweet she is, how shocked they were about the shootings."

"It's the *mo-ney*." Rick accentuated each syllable. "Everybody in this town has a hand in the Liem pocket. Look at your own family. Your dad did the Liem Enterprises Building and the Pelican Building for the Center for Retarded Citizens, which Rudolf Liem funded. Betsy Cristina wanted him canonized for that, remember? And then Bahalia's got Brandon working at the Liem shipyard welding casino barges and Taneeka on a Liem scholarship to medical school. What are they supposed to make of all this?"

Duck sat stiffly, hands in her lap. "But they all say Catherine's sweet. Did you see the papers yesterday? The title of the article on Catherine was 'Still Waters Run Deep.' "

"What do they mean, 'still'? What's 'still' about murder with a submachine gun?" Rick asked shrilly. He glanced at Duck and saw the shine of tears in her eyes. "That's you, babe," he said softly, tucking a strand of hair behind her ear. "You're the still waters." His fingertips on her neck coaxed a small smile from her lips.

Rick dropped his hand to her knotted ones and shook them. "Just how sweet do you think she was to be sleeping with your father all those years?" he asked. "She tried to break up your family for a long time. I think that was pretty violent even before she brought in the gun. And all those people who thought Catherine and her money were so sweet didn't know what she was up to."

"Yes, but my father was just as guilty there. More, really, because we were all counting on him and trusting him. He had obligations to us that she didn't. . . . But what he did is awfully different from being a killer," Duck argued.

"All I'm saying," Rick said, "is that the people who're sticking up for Catherine Liem didn't really know her; and if they didn't know she could commit adultery, maybe they didn't know a lot of other things about her, as well. She was notoriously reclusive. I think only people who have things to hide live like that."

"Maybe," Duck conceded, taking note of their surroundings. They were on the I-10 heading west. "Where are we going?" she asked.

"Just driving," he said. He turned a mischievous smile toward her. "Foreplay."

Duck squinted against the bright lights of the interstate, relieved that Rick was at the wheel. All these people racing about in their cars, how did they hold to their lanes, obey the speed limits, remember their turn indicators, avoid massive pile-ups?

"What do you think, Duck? Do you think she's innocent?"

"I really don't know. I've never really thought about it before. I just accepted that she did it."

"Well, why shouldn't you? For God's sake, Duck, her car was parked around the corner from the Spencers' house with the murder weapon in the trunk. And not just some ordinary pawn-shop gun. No, a 1937 Suomi pistol used by the Finns in the Winter War. Rudolf Liem's gun!" Rick's voice rose, and he hammered each point with his fist on the dashboard.

"But she might've been framed," Duck said tentatively.

A billboard for the greyhound races floated past, crowned by a flat stretch of dog, running full out. Sleek. Overbred. Innocent.

"Right." He turned off the interstate with an aggressive cut of the wheels that tossed Duck upright. "Someone gets into her house, steals the gun, and steals her car. All this happens on her studio day when everybody knows she's home alone and not to be disturbed. Convenient day for her to plan a murder, maybe, but not so convenient for the cat burglar. But let's just say the guy slips by her, drives to your house in her car, and kills your mother and Alexandra. Then cat-man turns into master mechanic, gets to work on the car right there at the scene, and stalls it, but in a way that looks completely natural. Come on, it just doesn't make sense. I'm not saying her fancy New York lawyer can't sell it to a jury. Just that he can't sell it to me."

"But it could've been done like that," Duck insisted, wanting him to quell her doubts entirely. The piney woods were closing in around the narrow two-lane strip leading east back to town, and she felt bolder in the darkness.

"Oh, really? By *whom*?" Rick shouted. He was uncharacteristically heedless of the Bomber, pushing her over potholes that jounced his words. "Who else would've wanted your mother and Alexandra dead? Poor little Junior? That really burns me, her trying to pin it on him because he's retarded and can't defend himself. Do *you* think Junior might've done it?" Rick asked, almost accusingly.

"Of course I don't. I just . . . she just doesn't look like a murderer," Duck offered up her hardest kernel of doubt.

"Oh, Duck. That's just your Spring Hill bias talking. If she'd been some dyed-blond barmaid with a tattoo on her hip, you wouldn't have a doubt in your mind."

He was right. No wonder she loved him so much. He knew her so well, and he still loved her, biases and all.

"Look," Rick concluded, "Catherine Liem just got

caught up in something bad that pulled her in deeper and deeper. If her car hadn't broken down, she might've gotten away with it. Who knows? She still might."

"Why do you think my father still believes in her?" Duck asked.

"I think your dad's a decent man, Duck. I think he can't believe he started something that would end in the deaths of his wife and daughter. And he probably really loved her. He's still thinking with his dick. Which," Rick added, as his hand stroked deliciously up her thigh and gently gripped her groin, "is something you cannot emulate."

They were parked at the lake again. And this time, it was wonderful.

16

11 OCTOBER

*I have writer's block. I want only to write of Blake, and I
cannot. I came to my cell in the afternoon and found that
my journal was missing. Two hours later it was back. It
could have been read here easily enough. So. It's being
copied.*

*Because you will be reading this, Mr. District Attorney,
let me just offer a comment or two about your appearance.
Perhaps when you look in the mirror, you do not notice the
deformity of your nose. Head-on, it almost looks normal,
and both your handlers and the media have been very kind
in limiting themselves to frontal shots. In the side view, the
absence of any depression between your forehead and the
tip of your nose lends an air of—let me be blunt, like your
nose—utter stupidity to your face. I am looking forward to
hiring photographers to capture that angle for your next
campaign. I am looking forward to hiring researchers and
investigators who will demonstrate that your stupidity is
more than nose-deep. (Perhaps they will locate women you
have known, who will reveal that your penis projects—if it
ever does—from your groin at the same unnatural angle.) I
am looking forward to contributing vast sums to the war
chests of all your opponents so that they can disseminate
the photographs and the information to the voters.*

*I have never involved myself in politics before. I am mo-
tivated to do it now because I have learned that our district
attorney, a man sworn to uphold the law, has no regard for
the most fundamental precepts of our Constitution. You
knew when you sent to have these pages copied that the
Fourth Amendment prohibited such a search. You really
should not have read my private diary, Mr. Betkins. It was
unconstitutional—and it was nosy.*

But surely, Arnie, they have divined by now that I was
having an affair with Blake. What harm in my remem-
brances of our innocent meeting in Papa's conference
room, the three of us dwarfed by the forty-foot table; what
harm in recording my apprehension at unrolling the first
public display of my work to this brilliant architect I so admired, his body language all antagonism? Blake glanced at
the drawings out of politeness, and then with barely concealed surprise began studying them. He touched the lines,
traced them with his fingers, leaned into them as if he
could feel their contours. It was a laying on of hands that
brought my work alive. And watching those strong, capable, sensitive fingers on my work, I could feel them on my
skin, where no man had ever touched me. When he looked
up, held my eyes, and declared only moments after that first
sexual act, "They're splendid," I heard, "You're splendid,"
and fell in love.

Later that day, over coffee, Blake told me that I reminded
him of his mother. "It's a compliment," he said.

"Do you play the bass guitar?" I asked him.

"No."

"Then you don't remind me of my father. That's all I
know about him. You don't remind me of my grandfather,
either, although I can't say why, given your extraordinary
successes in your fields." I perceived the distinction later:
Blake didn't need a sauna to stay warm, warmth flowed
from his heart.

Can you really fault us for our love, Mr. Betkins? I had never had a man, and Blake, whose wife would not suffer his "diseased sperm" to enter her body, had not had a woman for fourteen years. I doubt you've heard that from him, have you? I didn't learn it for a year, until I sobbed out my jealousy that he was cheating on me with his wife. "Katya," he told me. "I couldn't make love to anyone but you." After that, it mattered less to me that he was married.

Is this strengthening their evidence of motive, Arnie?

17

ON SUNDAY, they honeymooned. Rick picked her up at 9:00 a.m. They drove to the island, holding hands and talking the whole way. They went to the east end, safely distant from Iberville Point and Mamoo. It was a perfect beach day. The cloudless sky was a rare, primary shade of blue, untinged by haze or humidity. There was no breeze, or need of any, in the dry, cool air. The water was still warm enough for swimming, and beautifully inviting.

Along the shores of Louisiana, Mississippi, and Alabama, west of Point Clear, the effluence of the Mississippi and other rivers muddied the coastal waters to an opaque brown. But on the seaward side of this barrier island the water was clear and shaded in jewel tones from aquamarine to dark jade. Today, the ocean was almost still, with low, gentle swells that never crested until they curled onto the shore. On this sublimely perfect day, the beach was nearly deserted, according to some unwritten rule that deflected beachgoers from Labor Day to May, regardless of the weather.

Apart from a fisherman a quarter mile away, two men strolling arm-in-arm behind their frolicsome sheltie, and a family encamped around an ice chest, Rick and Duck had the beach, which stretched for miles in either direction, to themselves. They walked barefooted in the wet sand, dodging the incoming waves, further east where only the other lovers had ventured. The pair ahead was searching through the sparse shells for the occasional thing of interest: whole sand dollars or purple-tinted clamshells. One gestured excitedly, attracting Duck's attention to the bright backs of dolphins just barely arching above the swells. There were perhaps ten in the school, breaking the surface with the flashing symmetry of a pinwheel. Watching their rolling approach, Duck confided in Rick, "I see them almost every time I come to the island, and they never lose their magic."

"I think you may be part dolphin, then," Rick replied, "because that's the way I feel about you, too."

"You've made me feel magical this weekend, Rick," Duck said, in a sudden outpouring of emotion. "It's the most amazing thing. I've been miserable for so long, I'd forgotten what it felt like to be truly happy. I've felt like a prisoner awaiting this trial; but it's finally registered that it's not my life on trial. I can walk away from it no matter how it turns out. It's such a simple realization, really, but it's set me freeEE!" Duck flung out her arms and ran across the hard-packed sand at the water's edge, Rick in hot pursuit.

When she flagged, Rick caught her around the waist and gasped, "I hope you'll never be free of me."

"Are you kidding?" she remarked. "You're my liberator. Part of feeling free is making plans for the future: coming to school next semester, spending nights with you . . ." Her voice trailed off. She was moved to say, "Getting married," but something held her back.

"Nights sound great, but don't forget '*carpe diem*'," Rick replied, and holding her by the waist he led her into the dunes that rose tall and broad as cottages, providing perfect shelter.

The day had dawned cold, but it had warmed steadily, as if to accommodate their nakedness. It was not a day for huddling together against the cold; it was a day for standing back admiringly and for wondering touches. At first Duck was shy to be so fully exposed in the revealing sunshine. But the feathering movements of Rick's fingertips over her breasts bent the back of her shyness into an arching readiness for whatever he wanted of her.

They lay spent, cradled between the dunes. Duck slept lightly, with her mouth unself-consciously agape. A cascade of sand onto her face and into her open mouth startled her awake. It was an avalanche caused by the dancing paws of the sheltie, frenziedly barking above them. Duck dove for her clothes, which defied easy access. Her jeans were turned one leg in, one out. It was the same with her shirt and sweater. Her white panties were lost in the camouflage of blinding white sand. Rick threw a clump of sand at the dog, who only yapped more furiously.

"Bette!" came the voice of the owner. The little animal persisted, bouncing straight up and down, without ostensibly flexing a muscle. "Bette, you come here right now. Right now!" On the second "right now," Bette wheeled in a flurry of sand and was gone. Thirty seconds later, a freshening breeze carried her owner's voice clearly over the dune. "You lascivious thing," he berated Bette fondly. "She can smell sex a mile away," he boasted to his friend. "She's more fun than a metal detector."

As their laughter receded, Duck's tension eased. She looked at Rick, who had obviously not experienced a moment's worry; he was smiling at her discomfiture.

"Rick," she accused, "I don't think you'd mind if your mother came tromping through with her whole birding club." Duck could picture Mrs. Wrigley's spindly stork-like legs perched on the ledge, her wide-eyed binoculars trained down on them. Duck looked up to chase the thought away. Beyond the comfortingly empty shelf of sand, she saw only a squarish solitary cloud. It looked like the bunk bed she and Alexandra had shared as children; and she remembered how often, going to sleep and waking up, Alex's heart-shaped face hanging over the edge was the last and first thing she would see. She thought of Alex peering over the mattress of cloud above, unwilling to miss anything. It was a sweet thought until the image of Mother slipped in beside Alexandra. Duck began working at her clothes again.

"Rick," she asked, "do you think there's a heaven?"

"Yep," he answered sleepily. "You."

"No, seriously." She jabbed at him with her foot.

"You mean with angels and harps?"

"With anything." Duck lay back down and lazily swept a one-winged snow angel in the sand with her right arm.

"Nope," he answered simply.

Duck waited for more, but when it became evident that Rick considered the subject exhausted, she tried again. "Do you suppose Mother and Alexandra are out there anywhere?"

"Oh, babe." He covered her in a sandy, body-length embrace that rubbed in a painful awareness of sunburn. She pushed him gently away.

"Well, what do you think?" she asked again.

"About what?"

"About an afterlife," she reminded him, a little peevishly.

"I think"—he rubbed the sand off the palm of her right hand—"that the only sure life is the life of the flesh." He cupped her palm and ran a hard tongue back and forth through the crevice of her life line. Then he pressed her back down into the sand.

The idea did not lie right with her. Rick felt heavy; and she was hot. The sand bit into her back. But she felt tenderly toward his desire for her, and yielded to it. She looked for Alexandra's cloud again. It was gone, and only a small pillow crept slowly past, marking the plodding passage of time until Rick slept heavily on top of her.

The sand, which had looked so soft and cushioning, was not. There was a hip-sized hump jabbing into her back. She could not shift it or depress it. She tried ignoring it. There were no clouds in the window of sky she could see past the dunes. For a while she watched the nodding shocks of sea oats, fragile-looking grasses that held in place the tons of sand beneath them. She tried letting them lull her into slumber. She was not tired. She was acutely uncomfortable. Perspiration, hers or Rick's, she did not know, trickled down her side. The hip of sand in her back grew sharper. Rick was crushingly heavy. He began to snore. It started as a polite, snuffling sound; then came rapid-fire chomps and loud liquid snorts. He sounded like a frenziedly rutting pig. A few gentle prods only served to rev him up.

Finally, she roused him enough to roll him off of her. He slept on, undisturbed. She pulled on her bathing suit and went for a swim. She swam long, slow laps parallel to the beach, luxuriating in the freedom from the concrete boundaries of a pool, the buoyancy of the salt water, and its cool astringent feel on her skin. When she emerged a half hour later, she felt wonderfully refreshed and ravenously hungry.

Rick was still sleeping, quietly now. He lay posed, Adonis-like, as if he were about to throw a spear. His beauty pierced her heart. Duck opened a warm beer, the only provision they had brought with them. She sipped it while watching her naked lover sleep, feeling voyeuristic. When the beer was gone, she took a leisurely walk a half mile up the beach and back. Rick had not stirred. She puzzled over whether and how to wake him, until the polite approach to arousal occurred to her. Crouching on her hands and knees, she straddled him and kissed his mouth deeply. His arms immediately encircled her and pulled her down. After a moment, though, in an extraordinary show of strength, he lifted her up and trudged over the hill with Duck clinging to him like a koala bear.

"Rick!" she exclaimed over his display of his naked self on the beach. "Put me down!"

"I can't. I'm wearing you."

"Oh come on, it's not your chest that needs to be covered." She struggled out of his grip and headed the few feet back to shelter. Rick, on the other hand, emitted a rebel yell and streaked across the beach into the ocean. Peering over the top of the hill, Duck could see the family hastily packing to leave. When they had gone, Duck joined Rick. They were alone, and they made love again in the water.

Hunger finally drove them back to the mainland. They went to the Dew Drop Inn, a Tudor-style family restaurant specializing in chili dogs that had been a favorite haunt in high school. Their usual waitress, Agnes, fussed over them like they were her long-lost children. She slapped them simultaneously on their shoulders with the backs of her hands. "Where you kids been?"

"Went to Auburn this year," Rick answered.

"Well idd'n that nice," Agnes commented, and asked Duck, "Whatcha gonna be, a rocket scientist?"

"Actually, I've been home," Duck told her meekly.

"Oh yeah." Agnes clasped her hands in the air above her towering bouffant hairdo. "Well, honey, you still gotta eat, so don't let that shit keep you away." She slapped Duck's arm again for emphasis, or maybe discipline, and bustled off to get their food.

It sounded so simple the way Agnes said it. Duck felt silly to have lain so low for so long. She was radiant as a debutante at her coming-out party. Agnes, in the spirit of the occasion, brought out a bottle of champagne with Duck's tomato sandwich and Rick's chili dogs. "It's on the house, kids. Welcome home. Where's the resta the gang?"

"Maria's working a lot of nights now," Duck told her.

"Jenny and Suzie are up there with me," Rick added.

"Well, I miss the noisy lotta you. We hadd'n had a good food fight in months. Y'all get time off for Thanksgiving, you better come round and sling some turkey at one another."

"It's a date," Rick said.

This broached a subject that had been very much on Duck's mind. "How much time do you get for Thanksgiving?" she ventured, when Agnes had returned to the kitchen.

"Not much," Rick answered, absorbed with his chili dogs. "Too close to finals. But then we've got three weeks over the holidays." He tapped her champagne glass with his. "And if you don't mind, I'll be coming home every weekend."

Duck's happiness was complete. "It's only two months before I come up."

"Suzie's made it okay without you this long. Why don't you just hang your hat in your dorm room and come stay in my apartment?" he asked.

"Oh, Rick, I'd love it." She took a deep breath. "I love you," she added.

"You too, baby," he responded.

"Maybe Jenny can room with Suzie."

"Yeah." Rick leaned back and stared out of the dark window for a minute. Duck's gaze followed his, but she saw nothing there. "Jenny might not be too happy about all this. I've been going out with her a little bit. Nothing heavy. It's not like you and me. We were just lonely without you."

"Well, we can all hang out together again, just like old times," Duck said.

"It's gonna be a blast," Rick agreed.

He had a long drive back to Auburn ahead of him that night, so he dropped her off at eight. Mrs. Burke, taking Fluffy to the corner on his "evening constitutional," witnessed their eminently proper leave-taking. Rick took Duck's hand, bowed over it, and delivered a courtly kiss to his own thumb, so as not to dampen her skin. Duck stood on the doorway watching until he had driven away.

"Such a nice boy," Mrs. Burke called out.

Smiling throughout, Duck raced for the phone in her room. "Maria," she announced momentously to her friend, "I am a *woman*."

"Aaah!" Maria squealed. Duck could hear a chorus of voices asking "What? What?" in the background. There were only two telephones in the Cristina household: one in Betsy's and Vincent's bedroom; and the other in the front parlor, where Maria was now, with no privacy.

"Can you switch to the other phone?" Duck asked.

"Uh-uh. Dad just got home and they're in there working Maggie over."

"How's she holding up?"

"Not too well. You know, Dad's never so much as looked cross-eyed at Maggie her whole life. When he got in this evening, there wasn't any 'How's my little darlin'!' He's really steamed. He told her, 'Put on some decent clothes and come to my room.' Maggie sort of crumbled. They've been in there for two hours."

"Maybe I really shouldn't come over tomorrow."

"Could I come over there, then?" Maria suggested.

"I hate this house. I don't want to defile my weekend by talking about it here," Duck said.

"Then you've *got* to come over. I've *got* to hear. And Maggie's been very mysterious about needing to see you too; but Dad's grounded her except for going to school. *Please*," Maria pleaded. "Mom and Dad would never make a scene over dinner. I'll be off at seven, and we can find someplace to hole up."

"Okay, if you're sure I won't be in the way."

"Positive. In fact, bring Junior, too. It'll distract Mark. He's pretty bewildered about the whole uproar."

"Junior would enjoy a little uproar. He's bored to death over here," Duck observed.

"You'll tell me everything?"

"Everything," Duck assured her. As she hung up, Duck heard a prying voice in the background ask, "Everything about what?"

Duck smiled at herself in the bathroom mirror. It made her happy to see herself looking so happy. Her face did not look like a face that ought to be smiling, though. It was only a shade or two shy of lobster red, and drawn so tight that it hurt to smile. She was thoroughly and evenly scorched, as if she had been turned on a rotisserie. The tenderest burns were on her breasts, which had never been exposed to the sun before. Yet the pain was mildly pleasurable. She felt that she had been seared from within by her newfound passion, which was still burning. As she removed Alexandra's chain for the night, she noticed the only skin on her body that had been shielded from the sun was the spot that lay under the initial charm: a small, distinct, white A was sharply defined on her scarlet chest.

18

Chapel is available for those who want it. Mr. Dalton, the nonsectarian minister, is a pasty-faced young man with thin hair and a genuine calling. He addressed us with respect, performed the service with untheatrical reverence, and delivered a simple, erudite, and eloquent sermon on obedience.

When Mr. Dalton announced his subject, I thought at once of Papa, of his dedication to rules, of the comfort he derived from those rules, and ultimately of the comfort I did not derive from them. Mr. Dalton sensed my rejection before it was formulated in my mind. He was not speaking of mere obedience to the law, he said. He was speaking of obedience stemming from the love of God, from the desire to please Him, and from faith in God's blessing; he was speaking of grace. I cannot say that I apprehended the full message, and I cannot record it here, much as I would like to. I have reflected upon it all day and I fear it has only become more muddled.

And yet, there was something in Mr. Dalton's sermon that touched on the heart of my rebellion against rules, rules, rules; I have been bound to rules, defied them, redrafted them, bound myself to them, and found no meaning or salvation in them. Mr. Dalton would say, simply, that Papa

111

could not give his blessing to me, nor me to myself, because we are not God.

Papa had faith, but he did not transmit it to me. I yearn for it, but I cannot find it within myself.

I would like to talk to Mr. Dalton again. I had a terrifying fantasy during the service that I would be sentenced to die and that Mr. Dalton would be my confessor. I have not allowed myself to think before of the death penalty I am facing. I suppose I shared Eudora's confidence that a good lawyer would place me beyond such jeopardy. Arnie, reputedly, is one of the country's best, and the $150,000 I have paid him thus far has given him no reason to stint on my defense. (How do they arrive at these fees, exactly? Why not $148,000 or $152,000? A novice salesman in any field knows that $19.99 has a better ring than $20. But Arnie seems to operate according to loftier principles: squeeze it until it squeals.) My high-priced Arnie hasn't succeeded in winning anything more than my pen.

My life. I could lose my life. And I went to chapel this morning only because Eudora was going. My God. Where is my God?

Mr. Betkins, you are making me self-conscious. I reread what I had written and I thought of your reaction: "How much time did Alexandra and Evelyn Spencer have for spiritual growth after they faced death?"

Do murder victims need time? Don't their souls fly straight to heaven if they remember to say Allah? And doesn't everyone call upon God when she confronts death?

19

JUNIOR HELD a small posy of lantana in his big hand. The little orange and yellow flowers, known in the South as "ham-and-eggs," were among the few things still blooming at this time of year. "I'm going to visit Mario," he said, as they pulled up at the Cristinas'.

Duck patted his knee. "He'd like that."

Mario and Luigi were littermates, named by Simon after the "Super Mario Brothers" of the Nintendo game because of their acrobatic gifts. To keep them off her curtains, Betsy had bought a water pistol, with which Simon had exercised the little animals until only a few drops would propel them three or four feet into the air. Mario's death had been a freak accident. Junior, sleeping over one night at the Cristinas', had been taking a bath in the old claw-foot tub in the boys' bathroom. Mario had curled up against the warm base of the tub to take a nap. As best they could put it together afterwards, Junior had stepped out of the tub and caught himself just before his foot came down on the sleeping kitten. But Junior must have dripped water on Mario, who launched himself at about the same time and on the same angle as Junior. Off-balance from trying to avoid Mario, Junior slipped and came crashing down on top of the kitten, killing him instantly.

Junior's grief and shame were heart-wrenching and sadly enduring. It had been a year since Mario died, and

113

everyone else might have forgotten him by now had it not been for Junior's tender vigil. Duck left him to visit the backyard gravesite alone.

The scene downstairs was routine. It was early. Boys were sprawled about, working on homework. Duane had climbed onto the sideboard and was singing a repetitive song, "Doon mah homork . . . Doon mah homork . . ." As she drew nearer, Duck saw that Duane had a sizable stack of mail that he was feeding into the toaster. Blue smoke wafted from the mail slots.

"Duane," she said in a chiding voice, withdrawing a handful of charred envelopes from the toaster. The smoke smell had brought Betsy from the kitchen.

"Oh no, Duane! Dangerous!" Betsy said, lifting him down. "You come in the kitchen with me and be my helper. You can butter the bread for dinner. Duck, can you go see Maggie in my room?"

"You sure you don't need another helper?"

"I need help with Maggie," Betsy said. "Go see what you can do."

It was forbiddingly quiet behind Betsy's closed door.

Duck felt a sense of dread as she entered the still room, which had a funereal air. Maggie was lying on her parents' bed staring at the ceiling, her hands clasped over her chest as if she had been laid out for her final rest. When Duck came in she sat up slowly. Maggie sat with her legs splayed, shoulders slumped, and head bowed. When she looked up, Duck could see that her face was pallid; the only color in it was the red of her puffy eyes. This side of Maggie was frightening.

Duck sat beside her and held her. She had not thought of Maggie's predicament as a tragedy until now. Maggie had always been so together, so strong. She had a wonderful, loving family; and they were all alive. But with Maggie leaning against her, Duck felt the full weight of her problem. Duck felt guilty about her self-absorption, about the way she had discounted the rest of the world's unhappiness, and particularly Maggie's. She remembered that Maggie had been looking for her for days and that she had not gone out of her way to respond. "Oh, Maggie," she apologized, "I'm so sorry."

Maggie pulled away and scooted over to the end of the bed. "Duck, you don't have anything to be sorry for. I'm so sorry for what I've got to say. I've gone around and around about it. I don't know whether I held back more to protect you or to keep you from hating me. I still don't know what's right. But Mom's always said that you've got to go with the truth. So here goes." Maggie rested her elbows on her knees and mashed her cheeks between her hands. A cluster of silver bangles jangled from her ears with incongruous jauntiness. There was little spark in Maggie herself. Behind her swollen lids, her brown eyes were dull. She seemed unable to go on.

"Maggie, I don't know what you're talking about, but I promise I would never hate you." Duck prepared for the worst. *She's been sleeping with my father,* she thought.

"It was Rick," Maggie said. "It happened at the end of August when you guys weren't seeing each other. It didn't start out as a date. We'd been out with a whole bunch of people, just driving around."

The color had drained from Duck's face. She felt faint. She wanted to put her fingers in her ears and cry "beebeebeebeebeebeebee" like Simon did when he didn't want to hear something. She wanted to put it on pause. But Maggie wasn't watching her, and kept going. "Then after we'd dropped everybody else off, Rick drove me to this beautiful spot in the park and he had a cooler and a bottle of champagne with these crystal glasses. And we just got real drunk. Rick said you guys were finished; I thought you were. And I was just so drunk, Duck. It never happened again."

She paused, waiting for Duck to speak. Duck rubbed at a bruise on her arm, as if she could erase it. She rubbed and rubbed.

"You know I've been with a lot of guys," Maggie continued. "It wasn't such a big deal for me. But the next day I realized it would be a big deal to you. And then I found out I was pregnant. And then Maria told me Rick was going to see you this weekend.

"He came down to take me for an abortion, but I really didn't know if that was what I wanted to do. I wanted us to tell you together about what happened. We spent all day Saturday arguing about everything. Finally, he just threw the money at me and said it was my choice about the baby, but I'd better not tell you. He said he'd just deny it if I did."

Duck couldn't look at her friend's face. She studied Maggie's knees, knobby as deflated soccer balls, and crept with her eyes up the smooth-shaved brown thighs, to the belly which, in Maggie's slumped position, protruded ever so slightly. With Rick's baby. Duck wanted to hate Maggie but she couldn't. She felt too weak to hold so strong an emotion. And she knew Maggie was telling the truth about all of it. Every detail.

But Rick. Rick should have told her. Of course, it had happened in August when she had withdrawn from everything, including him; *and it never happened again*. And everything was different now. But their special place. And the champagne. But that was August, and this was October. Everything was different now. He should have told her; she would have understood. She could understand, though, why he had not. It was all right.

Duck slid over and hugged Maggie, whose face was streaming with tears. "It's all right, Maggie. I mean, I know

it's not all right at all, but it's all right with me. I'm glad
you told me, and I love you to death."

"Duck, I haven't told anyone else and I won't. And . . .
and . . . I had the abortion today. I wanted to do what I
could to fix it for you and Rick. It was just too complicated. I couldn't see you coming over here with Rick's and
my baby toddling around. I played hooky from school today to go. My folks don't know yet, and they're going to
kill me. They don't believe in abortion, but they believe in
capital punishment."

"MAGGIE!" Vincent's voice reverberated in the hallway.
"Come help your mother get dinner!"

"I gotta go." Maggie gave Duck another squeeze.
"Thank you. I'm sorry. I love you." She gathered herself
together and was gone.

Duck sat alone in the fading light. The sun was setting,
and its dying rays angled down through Stavros Constantopoulis's westward-facing stained-glass windows. The goddess Demeter wore flowing robes of white folded into soft
blues, carried a sheaf of heavy-headed golden wheat in one
arm, and with the other arm half restrained and half ca-
ressed an impossible wealth of thickly gathered golden
tresses that escaped in sinuous tendrils flaring in every direction. In the window to the goddess's left, plump fruits
tumbled from an overflowing cornucopia; to her right three
fat babies were clumsily intertwined in indistinct play.

With Maggie gone, the light shone full on Duck, bathing
her in gold and amber. She watched the prismatic beam
from Demeter's jeweled crown travel across the bedspread.

When the wand of fertility touched Duck's thigh, a shock
ran through her as if she'd stuck her finger in a socket. "Oh
my God," she said aloud. She and Rick had made love . . .
how many times? Five, she thought—without any contra-
ceptives. She had not even thought of it until now. *How
could she not have thought of it?* Heart racing, she tried to

remember when she had had her last period. Two weeks
ago? No, please God, she begged, don't let it have been
two weeks ago. That would have put her at her peak fertility last weekend. She thought it had been longer. Three
weeks? Four? She had no idea. She never kept track. *How
could she not have thought of this before?*

She took stock of herself. She felt a little bloated. Her
breasts were a little tender. Either I'm about to start bleed-
ing, or I'm pregnant, she thought. Pregnant. Jesus. This was
what Maggie had been going through. Until today, at least.
Both of us knocked up by Rick.

But she would keep the baby. And marry Rick. They
would marry when she got up to school. Maria and Maggie
would come for the ceremony. They could bring Junior.
Jenny and Suzie would be there. Her father would not. She
wouldn't tell him until after they were married. And she
would never have to go home again. She would have her
own home with Rick. And the baby. A cherubic blond
curly-haired little darling. Boy or girl, it didn't matter; she
knew now how expectant mothers felt—she would love it
all the same.

The fantasy was considerably strengthened by Duck's
sudden memory of a fact she had put out of mind: she had
inherited all of Mother's money. Her father had reviewed
with her the substantial portfolio of stocks and bonds, and
had told her that he would manage it for her until she was
ready to take it over. This conversation had taken place a
month after the murders. To avoid any possibility of physical contact with her father, Duck had sat too far away to
see the figures he was discussing, and having closed her
ears to him also, she was uncertain how much money was
involved. But she knew it was a lot. Close to two million
dollars. It had made little impression on her earlier, but now
she felt ready to claim her inheritance. She began envi-
sioning the sort of wedding Mother would have wanted for

her: white canvas tents on a verdant lawn; a band; white-coated waiters bearing silver trays of canapes and champagne. She made a quick adjustment indoors, recognizing that this wedding would not wait for spring. If she hurried, she could wear a white satin gown. Her father still would not be invited.

"Du-uck. Dinner!" Maggie called. There was a healthy timber in her voice again. Duck wanted to pull her aside and confide in her, but the family was already settled at the table. Vincent was seated at the head, and there was a full complement of Cristinas for his homecoming. Only Maria was missing. When Duck arrived, Vincent, Vinnie, Theo, Joey, John, Peter, Mark, Junior, and Simon rose for her, southern-style. All cast from the Vincent Cristina template, with their dark, curly hair and heavy-lidded brown eyes, pulled down at the corners, melancholy as the eyes of saints. Vincent, Sr. came around to kiss Duck on the cheek.

"How you been, girl?" he inquired.

"Great," she answered genuinely, pecking him back.

"You look pretty in purple," he laughed, commenting on her sunburn. What a sweetheart he was. Maybe Vincent could give her away at the altar. Or maybe Joey, her handsome, attentive friend, who held her chair for her as she sat down.

Betsy came in. Duck noticed how lovely she looked, and marveled for the hundredth time at the transformation she underwent when Vincent came home. Normally, Betsy was a bit frumpy. She economized on her clothes, which were usually mismatched, and on her hair, which she colored herself. She had "frosted" or "tipped" it many times, using any product that was not tested on animals and not bothering overmuch with the hard-to-reach places that she couldn't see. The overall effect was much like the back of the house, which Vincent had been sanding for about a year, revealing many faded layers of color down to the bleached wood, in odd patterns depending on the placement of his ladder. Betsy's hair was usually bound up carelessly or tied into a bandana. But when Vincent came home—even for an occasion like Maggie's crisis—Betsy found time to set her hair, coordinate her outfit, and put on makeup.

It was so different from her parents' relationship. Duck had sometimes accompanied them to parties to which they would drive in silence (unless Alexandra were along); once inside, Evelyn would smile on her husband, attend to his stories, touch his arm; she might wave good-bye from the car; then it was face front again in stony silence.

As Betsy entered the dining room, the men and boys rose again, and Vincent remained standing to deliver the blessing. "Bless us, oh Lord, for these thy gifts, which we are about to receive from thy bounty, through Christ, our Lord. Amen."

"Amen!" resounded around the table, with the snap of a flag brought down to signal the beginning of a race.

"Wait!" Duane screamed; and before anyone could stop him, he jumped up and dashed into the kitchen on some urgent errand. For some reason, everyone obeyed Duane's command and silently awaited his return with building anticipation. Presently, Duane emerged from the kitchen, holding a large basket straight out in front of him, gripping the handle in both hands. Due to the seriousness of his mission, he was struggling to contain his smile, like a flower girl on the long trip down the aisle. His basket was loaded with envelopes and fliers, thickly smeared with butter on both sides, so that it was a struggle to pry some of them apart. He deposited one on each plate; and what he thought of the merriment that swirled around his presentation, no one could tell, for he maintained the same controlled flower-girl smile throughout.

Simon was prepared to eat his, but Betsy, wiping away tears, gasped, "No! That's the water bill!"

"Oh, otherwise it would've been okay?" asked Vinnie.

"And you thought *I* was dumb," said Mark.

"Mark!" Junior cried. "That's not nice."

Peter said to Mark, "You're handicapped. But Simon's a ree-tard."

"What about Duane?" asked Simon.

"What about Mom?" added Duane, setting off new peals of laughter.

Several conversations splintered off. "They've set a new trial date," Joey told Duck. His left hand swept the hair off his high forehead, accentuating the concern in his dark eyes.

"What is it?" she asked, hoping it would be a year off.

"December second," he replied matter-of-factly.

Betsy, Duck, and Maggie moaned collectively.

"What?" asked Joey, making another sweep across his hair.

"Alexandra's birthday," Maggie said.

She was among the select few who knew the actual day. Alexandra had so many friends in so many incompatible circles that she had concealed the date of her birthday and instead proclaimed December her "birth month." That way, she could be celebrated by everyone without offending those who didn't command *the* day. This arrangement suited everyone but Betsy, who noted, "There's another birthday in December, and if one day is good enough for Him it ought to serve for Alexandra too." But Alexandra's popularity outdistanced Betsy's objections.

"I'm sure the judge didn't know," Joey said. Now his long fingers were tangled in his hair.

"That drunken lout don't know much," Vinnie tossed out, and popped a whole roll into his mouth.

"The *judge*?" Duck asked in wonderment.

Vinnie nodded, his mouth full of bread. He mumbled through it, "He's an alkie from way back."

"Like my daddy!" Duane interjected, referring to his birth father.

Vinnie continued, "Prob'ly his disappointment over abolition drove him to it."

"He's not *that* old," Duck countered.

"When was it that the judge tried to make a slave outa Charlie Deed?" Vinnie asked his father.

Vincent consulted the air above him. "Sixty, sixty-one, I think."

"Bahalia's husband?" Duck asked in astonishment.

"You never heard about that?" Vinnie shot back, equally astonished.

"About *what*?"

Vinnie set aside his fork and settled into the authority that he enjoyed as the eldest son. "Judge Porter wanted him a house boy. Thought all our young blacks had gotten too uppity 'cause every now and then their eyes came up off the ground. He went to Jamaica and imported Charlie. Had him sign all these papers about working off his airfare and room and board. Nobody knew the deal until Charlie met Bahalia at church and they started talking about getting married. Judge Porter said fine, as long as she came to work for him too. Bahalia went to the Civil Rights Action League and your grandmother got all fired up about it."

"Mamoo?" Duck cried.

"Yeah." Vinnie scarcely paused at the interruption. "She had to take the case up to the State Supreme Court before they ruled in her favor. They said indentured servitude was banned by the Constitution. Sounds pretty obvious, but it was a big deal then."

"But Mamoo's not a lawyer!" Duck almost shouted at Vinnie.

"Was then," he said, returning to his food.

"What am I, a Martian? I've never heard anything about any of this," Duck wailed. But she knew why she hadn't been told. She wasn't a Martian, she was a Spencer. Her father didn't communicate much; her mother didn't communicate about Mamoo; and Mamoo lived in the present and seldom talked about her personal history.

"You're not from Mars," John said, "you're from Old Spring Hill. That's further out!"

Duck shot a grateful moue at him. Recently the Cristina boys had treated her with a peculiar and unwelcome sobriety, out of sympathy, she supposed; but John, thankfully, was an irrepressible tease. "So how does Vinnie know?" Duck asked. "He wasn't even born in 1961."

Theo joined in. At twenty-two, Theo was the second oldest of the Cristina children. His brown eyes brimmed with social conscience, magnified by his round wire-rimmed glasses. "It comes up again every time Judge Porter runs for office."

"How could somebody like that get reelected?" Duck queried.

"He wasn't elected for the first time until after *Deed v. Porter*. The black vote wasn't too strong then," Theo said.

"Wasn't too registered," Vinnie added.

"Later on," Theo continued, "Judge Porter said he'd lived and learned—like George Wallace. Some people believed him, and most of those who didn't voted for him because of it."

Duck shook her head at the whole tale. "I can't believe Mamoo is a lawyer."

"Was until Judge Porter took the bench. He ran her off," Betsy said, directing a freezing glance at Simon, who had shot a skittering bowl of mashed potatoes to Peter at the far end of the table.

Joey returned to the matter of the trial. An orderly thinker, he was not easily diverted, nor did he lose the significance of digressions. "That's why the defense tried to get Porter recused. They feel like he's gunning for Catherine Liem to get at your dad."

"What's he got against my father?" Duck asked.

"Your grandmother." Joey's gold badge winked from the chocolate-brown breast of his deputy's uniform.

"Jesus," she whispered.

"Now, Duck . . ." Betsy began.

"Sorry, sorry," Duck said hastily.

"Don't tell me, tell Him. These are trying times, dear, I know, but the Lord will help you through."

"Amen," Vincent said solemnly, "and He will provide for Maggie, too."

"Oh no," Maggie moaned, "not at the table."

The clatter of eating subsided. Forks clinked onto plates. Eyes dropped. Vincent went on, "Maggie, I asked everyone to be here tonight so that we could have a family conference about your situation." Duck's heart sank. She wanted no part of this.

"Daddy," protested Maggie, "it's *my* situation. It's *my* decision. This is not something for the whole family to get in on."

"You made one decision, Maggie," her father said sternly, "and the consequences of that decision are something we'll all have to cope with. We're going to make the rest of the decisions together."

"Well, that's great," Maggie tossed back. "We can all go through my junior year pregnant together. We can all have stretched-out bodies together. We can all stay home together for a year, and be branded for the rest of our lives."

"Maggie!" Vincent stopped her. "We're not talking about your inconvenience or discomfort. We're talking about a child."

"That's right. We're talking about *my* child. And I've already made the decision. I got rid of it today." Her voice

trailed off and she spoke the last in a whisper. It was received as a thunderclap. Everyone sat in stunned silence as
Maggie and Vincent glared at one another.

When he began again, his voice was awful to hear. "You
sit at this table and *DEFY* everything we have taught you!"
His fist came down with such force that the dishes clattered
all the way down the table. Duck had never thought of
Vincent as a physical laborer. Driving a truck had seemed
like a soft sedentary job. But now she noticed the ropy
muscles in his arms. She thought of Vincent bending tons
of truck to his will, and wondered how little Maggie could
withstand him. She felt Maggie cowering beside her, and
understood her physical fear of this new, enraged, strong-
bodied Vincent. "Have we taught you nothing of self-
respect? Have we taught you nothing of obedience? Have
we taught you nothing of honesty? Have we taught you
nothing of the *value of life*?" Vincent looked to be torn between jumping across the table at her and bursting into
tears. "Get to your room!" he shouted. "I can't stand to
look at you!" He sat down shakily.

Maggie, eyes brimming with tears, looked to Betsy for
help. Betsy's head was bent; she only reached over to hold
Vincent's arm. At that gesture of solidarity, Maggie climbed
clumsily back over the bench and ran stumbling from the
table.

It was Mawmaw Celeste who first spoke into the silence.
"I think you have also taught her something about families
coming together in times of crisis," she said simply.

Junior nudged Mark. "Tuck in your shirt," he murmured.

Betsy got up to go after Maggie. Duck excused herself
and went home.

20

This will please you, Mr. Betkins. Arnie was impressed with your offer of a plea bargain: I plead guilty to two counts of manslaughter; I receive a sentence of seven years on each count (Judge Porter can go no lower because a firearm was used in the killings); the sentences run concurrently; with good behavior, I will serve only about four more years.

Only four years. Better than life in prison, Arnie points out. To be sure. Better than a death sentence. Of this, I am not so sure. Four years in this brown mushroom of a building with its slitted windows and razor-wired exercise yard. I have been hanging on, one day at a time, the days stretching out impossibly long, to the trial. I cannot wrap my imagination around a period as long as four years beyond that. This morning, waiting for Arnie to come at 10, I looked at my watch. 8:35. I busied myself with quiet contemplation, and looked again. 8:42. I read a magazine. 8:59. It became an act of will not to check my watch more than every 10 minutes. More than half the time I failed. Starting at 10:00 I mostly just watched the second hand. It crept. Arnie was 23 minutes late. Flogging would have been less painful, I think. It would have been something to do. Only four years? I could do death more easily. At best it sounds momentarily exhilarating: a bungee jump without the bungee.

Arnie imagined for me a scenario in which, blinded by passion, I went to the Spencer house to kill Evelyn. Alexandra unexpectedly got in the way and I shot her too. Arnie did not ask me to confirm or deny this scenario. He "simply suggested" its logic in view of the evidence. He ran through all the conceivable alternative theories, and suggested the illogic of each in view of various items of evidence. As he reviewed the difficulties of our position, he spoke of the pressures of defending a capital case. The pressures on him—his fears, his anxieties, his doubts. All intensified by the public perception that a good lawyer never loses. A misperception he wants to be certain I do not entertain.

Arnie has never tried a capital case before. (He might have mentioned this sooner.) He has never tried a case of any sort in Alabama before. He wanted to know whether I have ever heard of home cooking—the process by which out-of-town lawyers are roasted by the local prosecutor, judge, and jury. I reminded him that I am local. The judge does not seem to like me either, he noted. However, Arnie is working on his accent. He tried his new elocution on me. It sounds less New York, more pompous.

I mentioned that Papa was the one who told me that I should call him if I ever needed a lawyer. Oh yes, Arnie confirmed, he had worked with Papa on many projects, international contract negotiations, securities work, lobbying efforts. He reminded me that he had recommended one of his partners specializing in criminal law and that I had insisted on his handling my case personally. I asked him point-blank whether I had made a bad choice. No, he is consulting with his criminal-law partners all the time. They all think I should take the plea. If I go to trial and am convicted of manslaughter, the sentence will be 15 to 20 years.

If I am convicted of murder, it will be life imprisonment or death.

The decision, of course, is mine. I am not to decide today. I am to "think about it."

I wanted Arnie to stay with me and think about it for six weeks until the trial begins. He had to go. He flew back to New York and will not return for three weeks. Griffin, his associate, will see me in a week. It was all I could do not to throw myself around his legs as he was leaving.

21

"No SCENES at dinner, eh?" Duck lightly chided Maria when she called later.

"Never before. I'm really sorry you got caught up in it. Did you get to talk to Maggie at least?"

"Mm-hmm."

"Well?" Maria asked.

"Well, what?"

"Agh!" Maria exploded. "You sound just like Maggie. I get the feeling there's an awful lot going on that I'm not being let in on."

Duck felt chastened, but unready to divulge anything more. Whose secret was the paternity of Maggie's baby? How would Maria react to the complication of Duck's own suspected pregnancy? She had never shut Maria out before, but she did it now. "No, there isn't," she lied. "There's just an awful lot going on. More than I can handle, Maria," she said truthfully, "and I don't want to talk."

"Can I help?" her friend asked, softening.

"No. I need some time to myself to sort things out." She hung up, feeling bone-weary, confused, and isolated. Her earlier conviction that everything would work out for the best had evaporated. So had her understanding of Rick and Maggie's brief liaison. The insistent thought of the two of them at Municipal Park was sickening. She wanted to push the Bomber into the lake with them in it.

129

She had thought Rick was a virgin, too. Looking back on his aplomb over the weekend, it seemed a foolish self-deception. It hurt her, too, that he had told Maggie they were finished in August. He knew how sad Duck had been in that awful month. Was he really prepared to drop her? Or was he only saying what Maggie needed to hear—and which was worse? For some reason, the champagne and crystal glasses hurt the most. She had felt so honored by Rick's grand gesture. How many other women had he lionized in the same way? And no matter how drunk she was, how could Maggie think it was "no big deal" to sleep with her friend's steady? What had she been doing with Rick in a dark, deserted corner of the park in the first place, if not hoping for just such an outcome?

The phone rang and she grabbed it on the first ring, hoping it was Rick so she could give him a piece of her mind. It was her roommate manqué.

"Suze!" Duck exclaimed, overjoyed to hear from a safe friend. "How are you?"

"I'm doing better than the last time we talked. I made out all right on my midterms." That meant straight A's, Duck knew. "And I'm loosening up a little bit. I'm learning my way around campus so I can be your guide when you get here."

"I could use a guide right here at home," Duck confided.

"How's everything going?" Suzie asked.

"I don't know. For months, it seemed like nothing was happening. Now it's moving faster than I can process."

"Did you see Rick last weekend?"

"Yeah." Duck searched for something noncommittal to say about seeing Rick.

"Did he tell you about Jenny?" Suzie asked.

"Yeah, he did," Duck answered, trying to remember what Rick had told her. *Jenny and I have been hanging around together, nothing heavy.*

"Thank goodness. I told him I'd tell you if he didn't, but I really didn't want to be the one to do it. How did you feel about it?"

Duck had a bad feeling that she didn't know everything.

"Well, she's there and I'm not, so I guess it makes sense," she equivocated.

"Duck, you're too nice. I think it stinks. Man, she was on him like a fly on honey. She moved in two weeks after we got here."

Moved in? Was that what Rick meant by "nothing heavy"? Duck grasped for her salvation. "I think that'll all change when I come up next semester."

"You still want him? Rick with a capital 'P'?" Suzie sounded incredulous.

"I don't know, Suze. I don't know what I want."

"Well, you're going to have your pick of a lot of nice guys. I've met someone."

Duck could hear the excitement in Suzie's voice, and forced herself to inquire further, although Suzie's budding romance held no real interest for her. She only half-listened to her friend's breathless account.

We've been hanging around together, nothing heavy. She could hear Suzie's disappointment in her lack of enthusiasm, but she could not muster anything more. *She moved in two weeks after we got here.*

"Suze, I gotta go," Duck said abruptly.

"Oh. Okay. Are you okay?"

"Yeah. It's just been a bad day. They set the trial for Alexandra's birthday."

"Oh Duck. I've been going on and on about Loomis and I didn't even ask about that. I'm such a dolt."

Loomis? Duck wondered if Suzie had mentioned his name before. "Please don't say that. It's good to hear some good news, but I'm just sunk in my own bad news. Birthdays used to be so happy around here."

"Remember your last birthday?"

"Yeah." Duck remembered her entire family crowded around her as she carefully peeled the paper from the small, rattling box, certain that her mother had gone back for the silver earrings she had pointedly admired the week before. When Duck saw the pair of keys on a bed of cotton, she had been bewildered at first, wondering how to thread through her ear the loop of wire holding the keys, and trying to hide her disappointment that her normally tasteful parents had strayed so far from the vogue. The extravagant reality had burst upon her as Alexandra, who had suppressed the secret as long as possible, erupted, "It's right out front! Come see!"

Duck could not have been more surprised. Sure, she had hinted broadly that she wanted a car, but hope had vanished the previous November when she'd had an accident. Duck had been driving herself and Alexandra home from the mall when a bright yellow butterfly had flitted in front of the windshield. With lightning reflexes, Duck mashed the brakes, sparing the butterfly and skidding the car sideways into a champagne-colored Mercedes. Apart from Duck's pride, no one was hurt. The repair bill, on the other hand, had been phenomenal, and considering the even greater impact she had wrought on the family's automobile insurance premium, Duck had not expected a car. Yet there it was.

Alexandra dragged Duck by the wrist toward the front door. "I helped pick it out. Daddy wanted sky blue and Mother thought white, but I told them it had to be red!"

And red it was. At the sight of it, Duck had stalled in the doorway, with Alexandra, Junior, and her parents pressing behind her, and burst into tears.

"Come *on*," Alexandra demanded. "You can't drive it from here." Alexandra danced ahead on the walkway. Duck circled the car in a daze, laughing and crying at the same time. It finally registered, when she saw the DUCK license plate: "This is mine."

On either side of the license plate were Alexandra's gifts, a pair of matching hand-painted bumper stickers. On the left side of one and on the right side of the other were two brilliant yellow swallowtails. Between these two emblems, like bookends, the first strip read CAUTION: and the second finished, I BRAKE FOR BUTTERFLIES!

Then they were off. By the time they reached Springhill Avenue, Alexandra had activated so many distracting gizmos that Duck pleaded, "Why don't you see if you can find the James Bond ejector for your seat so that I can drive in peace?"

"This is so incredible," Alexandra declared, cupping the cool April morning in her upstretched palms. "I'll do anything, anything for you, Duck, if you'll let me drive it. Need some help with your civics term paper? How about if I clear my stuff out of the bathroom?"

"How about if you learn to drive first?" Blake, Sr. offered sensibly.

"Me too!" Junior crowed.

"Not in *my* car," Duck said firmly, luxuriating in her newfound sense of proprietorship.

"I don't need driving lessons to do what you're doing. I could push this thing faster than we're moving," Alexandra replied, more fairly than Duck cared to admit. Alex's needling was always fun, never harsh.

On that brief tour through the tree-shaded streets of their neighborhood, Duck felt as if she were piloting a hydrofoil, buoyed on a cushion of privilege and love. That had been a month before the murders. Duck had meant to give Alex driving privileges on her birthday the following December. This December. The first day of her murderer's trial.

"Duck?" Suzie asked.

"You're a great friend, Suze. But I'm not up to talking tonight, okay?"

"Sure. I wish I could be more help. Call me whenever you feel like it."

Duck hung up and dialed Rick's apartment. The chirruping voice that answered was unmistakably Jenny's. "Hello, may I speak to Rick?" Duck asked, suppressing her urge to slam the phone down. Jenny's hand was clasped over the mouthpiece for a long, long time.

"Hello," Rick answered brightly.

"Rick." Duck's chest was tight. Her throat was clamping shut.

"Duck. Hey!" Rick said, even more brightly. He was walking with the phone, she could tell. She heard a door close; and Rick's end sounded suddenly empty.

"Rick?"

"Yeah. I'm glad you called, hon. I was going to call you."

"Who answered the phone?"

"Uh, Jenny. She came over with some friends," he said.

"To live?" Duck charged.

"Hey, don't go jealous on me, Duck. Please. It's going to take a little while to straighten things out. But I will. Jenny's not important, baby."

"Have you told her that? Have you told her about our weekend?"

"Duck, please. Calm down. I promise I'll get straight with Jenny."

"I think I'm pregnant," she blurted out.

"Oh shit!" he exclaimed. There was a long silence. "Didn't you use anything?"

"Didn't *I* use anything? Didn't *you*?"

"Duck, that's not fair. The woman's supposed to . . ."

"Is that what you told Maggie?" she asked coldly.

Another long silence. "So that's what this is all about.

Duck, the girl's a tramp. She got drunk one night with me and now she's trying to pin something on me that never happened."

Darkness spread in front of Duck's eyes. Darkness with bright floaters and Maggie's voice. *He said if I told you he'd just deny it.*

"Duck, nothing happened between me and Maggie."

"Why did you pay for her abortion, then?"

"Look, I don't know what she's been telling you, but it's all a lie," he said urgently.

"Save it for Jenny," she said, and hung up.

She stared at the phone. *Call me back,* she pleaded. *Call me back and explain.* She waited, willing the telephone to ring with all her might. It remained cruelly silent.

What if Maggie *was* lying, she thought with a start. Or what if Maggie thought she was telling the truth, but she was wrong, because she was too drunk to know that nothing happened. That was it, she thought with building excitement, Maggie was too drunk to remember.

Drunk on champagne. Poured into crystal glasses.

The image of the glasses shattered the fragile lie. All the golden happiness of the weekend spilled out, fizzing into nothingness.

22

Eudora is leaving. Her breach with her pimp is healed. He discovered that she had been pocketing sizable tips and moonlighting on the side, so he had stopped paying her protection money to the police. She was arrested. But he thinks she has suffered long enough and learned her lesson. Besides, her punishment is cutting into his profits. He has hired her a good lawyer. One of the best, he claims. She will be out within a week. We hugged and cried. She will visit.

I've suffered long enough, too. Set me free, Mr. Betkins. Come rescue me, Blake.

As far back as I can remember, there has always been a man to rely on. Who in Papa's ordered household could ever fear that the world might go awry? And before Papa passed on he walked me down the aisle, figuratively speaking, and handed me to Blake. I don't think that Papa arranged the match, but certainly he was perspicacious enough to have apprehended it. The closest he came to acknowledging our relationship was when he took a bead on his schnapps one night and said, to my utter amazement, "So many of society's rules are designed for youngsters and simpletons. You are neither. You have philosophy, morality, you are gaining in experience. Make your own rules, Katya, but make them at your peril." I held myself perfectly still, waiting for more, but Papa was done.

Blake thought I was imagining things, to read our relationship into that remark, but Blake didn't know Papa like I did. Blake shared Papa's views on rule-making, though. At our peril.

Papa cannot save me now, nor Blake. I have flagging confidence in Arnie. I have no experience in saving myself.

I asked for Eudora's lawyer's name. Alto Johnson. I want to remember that. It's too late to switch lawyers in midstream, but maybe Mr. Johnson would make a good candidate for District Attorney. Until we can inject some fairness into your office, Mr. Betkins, I must content myself with merely evening up the odds. Today I authorized the Liem Foundation to make a three-million-dollar endowment to the local indigent defender board.

By some trick of the light in the visiting room, the accountants' spread sheets, held up against the glass partition, looked like Mobile River when it catches the light of a white-hot summer's day. I had the strongest sense of déjà vu: that I was sitting in the Foundation office, doing Foundation work in the usual way, and could rock back in my chair and look out over the river, the docks, Water Street, the green roofs of the new convention center. My mind's eye rafted up the river, along the bright curve of the Cochran Bridge; and even the tufts of smoke from Scott Paper were lovely, so free in the broad sky.

Sadly, another window has closed on my tight little world. We finished the year's work of the Foundation today. The award of the annual Liem prize to the Cristina boy gave me the greatest pleasure. What a small town this is. Another year, another connection. Papa put the Center for Retarded Citizens on its feet and hired Blake to design its new building when I was still in my teens. I remember being struck, like so many others, by the sweeping roofline of the Center that earned it the popular name "The Pelican Building." Even then, the upreaching lines of the Center impressed me as a work of genius—the functional expression of lofty ambitions for the endeavors within. I stood at Blake's side at the ribbon-cutting ceremony, in awe of him. Of course, he doesn't remember my being there. I am never so memorable as the men around me.

23

IT WAS AUGUST again in her mind; and she was insatiably sleepy. Sleep was dreamless, heavy, and safe. The first few times that consciousness intruded she could draw sleep back over her, like holding her nose and sinking to the bottom of a deep, dark, quiet pool. Eventually, though, she had to surface. Pressure built painfully at the back of her head, pushing her into the glaring light of day. But she did not have to get up. She lay beached on her bed, unable to lift her sodden limbs. It was pleasant lying there. She pinch-pleated her sheet into a folding fan. When the tiny folds jumped out of her fingers, she started over again.

The intercom in her room squawked. "You gonna come eat or you want me to hook up an IV?"

"Thanks, Bahalia. I'm not hungry," Duck answered heavily.

"Fine. Your mouth's not hungry. Now lemme speak to your stomach. Tell it I got a nice Waldorf salad down here."

Duck adored Waldorf salad. In spite of herself, her mouth began to water. "Is Junior around? Would you ask him to bring up a tray?"

"Girl! How stupid you think I am? You think I'm gonna help you hide up there, you think again."

"You're tough, Bahalia! . . . Uh, did anyone call?"

"Nope. But maybe I'll let your dad and Junior know

you's receivin' on the phone." Bahalia cackled off, or maybe it was the static.

No one called and Duck did not get hungry enough to leave the safety of her room that day.

The next morning, she discovered in a warm rush that she was not pregnant. Against all reason, she felt terribly sad about it.

"You drivin' a hard bargain, girl," Bahalia squawked over the intercom. "You still livin'?"

"I'm fine."

"That's the new name for catatonic? Whoop! Never mind, nobody askin' me. You gonna let me feed you?"

"Yes, please," Duck answered weakly.

"Okay, I'll carry it up. But you got to promise you'll make supper with the family."

"Sure, as long as I don't have to talk."

"Lawd, you can't . . ." Bahalia, speaking angrily to herself, released the button that would have communicated her closing thoughts to Duck.

Call me, Duck concentrated at the telephone. *He doesn't even know I'm not pregnant.* She pitied herself pregnant, desolate, frightened, and helpless. She raged internally at Rick, who still thought, however wrongly, that he had abandoned her to face the travails of unwed motherhood alone. She pictured herself in the mall, haggard and unkempt, dragging a squalling toddler in search of some white high-top shoes. Rick and Jenny would stroll by on their way to the movies, arm-in-arm and heads bent toward each other. The screaming child would catch their attention. Rick would notice her with a start. "Hey, Duck," he would say breezily, "how's it goin'? And who's this little guy?" He would reach over to tousle his son's curly locks, but the boy would shrink against Duck, whose eyes would shoot daggers at Rick. "Well, gotta run or we'll be late for the show," he would say. And as the crowd swallowed them,

Duck would hear him tell Jenny, "You know she went crazy after the killings. No one knows whose kid that is." *What a self-centered jerk,* she thought. Then, *Please, please call me.*

Only Maria, Suzie, and Maggie phoned. Duck pleaded illness and would not talk to them. For days, Junior was the only person whose company she tolerated. Junior was dependably easy. He brought in *Sports Illustrated*, a few tapes for his headset, and an occasional bowl of popcorn. Junior would sit bolt upright at Duck's desk, clear a space for his magazine, and leave Duck to her bed and her silence. When he needed closer contact, he might say, "Close your mouth," or "Don't stare." Sometimes, and only if Duck signaled her willingness, they talked. Their conversations were always variations on the same theme.

"I miss Alexandra," Junior would open.

"Me too," Duck would answer, adding, "Mother, too." It was remarkable, really, how lifeless the family was without them. And it was not only grief that had immobilized the survivors. It was the loss of leadership. Duck was forced to the awareness that she, her father, and Junior had seldom planned anything. The dinner parties, trips to the theater, vacations, and Sunday drives were all Mother's initiatives. The quotidian outings and gatherings of friends at the Spencers' were orchestrated by Alexandra.

For Junior's sake, Duck sometimes tried to think of activities they had regularly shared and enjoyed.

"Wanna go out for some frozen yogurt?" she asked him listlessly.

"Uh-uh," he answered. "You?"

"Not really," she said gratefully, "unless you do."

"Too much trouble," Junior observed.

Every so often in these discussions Junior's insights surprised her. There was the day, for instance, when Junior opened, "I miss Alexandra."

"Mother, too," Duck recited. She sat spreadlegged on her bed, playing game after game of solitaire. Piles of cards slipped and merged on the uneven surface of her rumpled covers.

"Yeah, I guess her too," said Junior, departing from the script, "but I don't think she misses me."

"Why not?" Duck straightened her aching back and looked enviously at Junior, sitting carefully erect in her desk chair.

"Aw, she didn' like guys too much, especially not stupid guys like me." He lined his magazine up even with the edge of the desk, adjusting one corner, then the other.

"That's not true!" Duck protested indignantly.

Junior shrugged noncommittally and returned to shuffling the pages of his *Sports Illustrated*, as if he had come to terms with his mother's disaffection long ago.

Duck remembered when they had brought him home from the hospital. It was one of her earliest memories, and the first fight she remembered between her parents; it had been frighteningly loud and bitter. She was almost five and Alexandra was two. They had been primed for the new arrival, but Mother had come home joyless and tired, without the baby; she said only that he was being held for tests. By the time they went back for him a few days later, Duck was anxious to conduct her own tests. She and Alexandra waited at the front door for their first glimpse of their brother. Their parents made no proud display of the baby; they walked in deep in their quarrel and heedlessly continued it in front of the girls.

"I want to call him David," Mother shouted, with a tremor in her voice.

"We agreed that if it was a boy we'd name him Blake. It's already on the birth certificate," Blake, Sr. argued.

"We can change it."

"I don't want to change it. He's my firstborn son and I'm

proud of him." The object of his pride was loosely cradled in the crook of one arm, waving dangerously at Evelyn. "We can call the next one David."

"There aren't going to be any more," Evelyn declared, sweeping upstairs.

A nurse came to help with Blake, Jr. (The notion of "David" withdrew with Mother to her room.) He was agreeable from the start. He slept through his first night at home and every night afterwards. He seldom cried; if he felt some need to be held, changed, or fed, he kept it to himself and accepted what he was given happily. He smiled early, and readily. When he was a few weeks old, after Mother had gotten her figure back through rigorous exercise, she assumed his care in her brisk, competent way. She bought him rompers with trains and bears on the bibs and red piping on the collars, played pat-a-cake, sang lullabies. She never, never turned on him (or any other member of the family except Blake, Sr.) the sharp tongue she lashed at much of the rest of the world. Wasn't all of that love?

Duck thought of Mother's soothing backrubs, her strong fingertips massaging Duck's neck and shoulders, and Alexandra's, with never a nick from her manicured red nails. Had she ever done that for Junior? Duck thought of cool cloths on her forehead when she was feverish, of lotions gently applied to sunburnt skin, of her hair brushed with boar bristles, of Band-Aids tenderly laid over cuts, of hand-holding during inoculations.

"Did Mother ever give you backrubs?" she asked Junior. He was absorbed in his magazine, nose down, as if he could decipher the letters by smell. She had to repeat the question.

"She never touched me," he said. It would be much later before Duck realized the unintended irony in his simple statement.

"But she took you lots of places," Duck said.

"Yeah. But I never had a party." Junior went calmly back to his browsing.

Could that be true? She remembered so many parties, with clowns, ponies, and magicians, covered in the society page. For her and for Alexandra. But the only party she could remember for Junior had been hosted by Betsy Cristina at Constantopoulis Mansion.

Duck considered her inheritance again. Mother had written a new will two months before her death, leaving all of her property to Duck and Alexandra. Alexandra, of course, had renounced her share by dying. Blake, Sr. had not been named in Mother's will since Duck was born; Mother had mentioned from time to time that she was leaving everything to her children to avoid the added inheritance taxes that would result from passing part of her estate to them through Blake, Sr. Duck had never attended to such remarks, believing her mother immortal. Duck tried to remember what Mother had said. Had she mentioned leaving Junior out? What would be the sense of that? But maybe it was part of the estate plan that Mother would leave her money to the girls and Blake, Sr. would provide for his son. It was troubling, like so many of Duck's memories of Mother. It was one thing to harbor animosity toward a living mother; all of her friends did, even Maria. It was quite another to develop a growing dislike for a dead mother, which was what Duck, with a great sense of guilt, felt happening. Perhaps she was remembering Mother wrong, and it was doubly unfair because her mother could not defend herself. But no matter how much Duck drew on her pleasant memories of Mother or said "I miss her" to Junior, the fact remained that she did not really much like or miss her mother. And she excoriated herself for feeling that way.

One October afternoon about a week into Duck's hermitage, Maria dropped by, giving Duck no opportunity to refuse her. Maria was dressed for action in blue jeans, a sweatshirt, and new white sneakers. Her thick brown hair was pulled back in a ponytail, accentuating her cheeks, which glowed from the cold outdoors. At the sight of her, Duck shrank into her flannel nightgown. She reluctantly put aside the crossword puzzle she had been working on. Duck was good at puzzles. This one was half completed, and she had reached that critical mass of solution where she had not only the clues but a fair number of letters to guide her. The empty squares beckoned her from the unsolvable mystery of relating to Maria.

"How are you?" Maria asked in a meaningful voice that indicated she would not be satisfied with "fine."

"Fine."

"Then why are you holed up in your room?"

"I don't have anything else to do," Duck began, watching Maria's mouth set as she said it. "I don't feel like doing anything."

"Well, let's go do nothing together somewhere. I'm off today."

"Thanks, but I really don't feel like it." Duck reached for *The New York Times Magazine*. "What's a four-letter river in Italy starting with 'A'?"

"Asshole?"

"Won't fit." Duck smiled in spite of herself.

"What's the *matter*?"

Duck's thoughts ran horizontally across Rick and came against an impenetrable black square. She spun downwards past Alexandra's body on the stairs, and struck another black block. This one hit harder. *I should have been the one to die.* Alexandra was the better person, the beauty, the fighter, the survivor. How could she be dead and Duck alive? It was an accident, a mistake. *You got the wrong one,* her mind screamed at Catherine Liem. Another small black square yawned open: it was a three-dimensional cube centered in her chest, the seat of all her pain, lightless and private, and comforting. *I can die. I have that much control.*

A small voice said, *You can't do that to your father.* Then the voice was drawn into the black hole and became part of its density. *Sure I can. That's the best part. I have finally realized how to talk to my father.*

When she had toyed with the idea of suicide in the past, playfully, Duck saw now, she had thought of taking a handful of sleeping pills and slipping peacefully into oblivion, like Shelley sinking into the blue enfolding depths of the Adriatic Sea with his eyes fixed on the dancing light above. But she would do it violently, with a gun in her mouth. Yes. In front of her father in the foyer. Yes.

Maria laid a hand on Duck's knee. "Please talk to me." Duck shook her head. "I can't."

"I know all about it. Suzie called me. She was worried about you."

It took Duck a moment to orient herself to Maria's train of thought. *Oh that,* she considered dismissively. Maggie was right, *no big deal.* For that matter, Rick was right, too. *Nothing heavy.* But accepting the proffered justification for her mood, she told Maria, "The whole thing knocked me flat." To Duck's surprise, tears flooded from her eyes.

Maria hugged her, saying, "I know, I know," while she cried. When Duck finished, Maria brought her a wet washrag. Duck dabbed, then scrubbed at her face, then blew her nose into it with a honk. They both laughed.

Maria looked at her affectionately and said, "Well, I don't think I'm taking you out today."

"This was better, really. Thanks."

"Things have a way of working out," Maria counseled, sounding exactly like her mother. "If Rick's a creep, it's better you found out now. But I still want to hear about your weekend someday."

"Another day, okay?" Duck wondered whether her carry-

ing this secret to her grave would be added to Maria's list
of reasons to hate her for killing herself.

"Sure. And also on another day, maybe you'll notice
how Joey feels about you."

"Joey? He's my big brother."

"Right," Maria said sarcastically. "That's why he treats
us exactly alike."

"He does."

"Duck, for somebody so smart, you can be so dumb."

The conversation had turned delicate. The sort of no-
holds-barred discussion Duck and Maria would have had in
the past was constrained by the fact that this was Maria's
favorite brother.

"I never thought of him as anything but a brother," Duck
ventured cautiously.

"That's clear. But watch how he looks at you sometime.
Try sticking some french fries up your nose one night at
supper. I swear, the poor guy'll say, 'How daintily she
eats.' "

Duck guffawed.

"And how daintily she titters," Maria said, pressing her
fingertips against her mouth in a picture of Victorian
delicacy.

"Life is so complicated." Duck sighed.

"Oh, Joey'll live if you keep him on as your big brother.
Just give the poor guy a break and don't mope too hard
over Rick in front of him."

"It's a deal. I wouldn't hurt Joey for anything." *One
more thing I won't have to deal with,* Duck thought.

After Maria left, Duck felt well enough to shower and
dress. Well enough, in fact, to go out. She went to Woodrow's Pawn Shop in Creighton, a tiny, chartreuse-green
storefront so heavily barred that the merchandise arranged
in the window was invisible from the street. Duck bought
a little twenty-two-caliber derringer, with a mother-of-pearl

handle. It felt feather-light in her hand. Harmless. Pretty. Toylike. And it was so easy. Woodrow asked her if she knew how to use it. She said no. He showed her. He sold her bullets and loaded the gun. He emptied the chamber and put the bullets back in the case, so neat and compact, like a box of chocolates. He told her where she could go for target practice, writing the name on the back of one of his cards. She threw it away in the waste bin at the front door of the shop. She could find her target without practice.

24

When I was little and costumed for Halloween, I went as a hobo with a sooty face, a pumpkin with green leggings and green felt collar—never anything spooky. It was a night to stay up late until my throat ached from eating candy. There were no religious overtones.

This is my first real Halloween. My cell is peopled with ghosts. Alexandra and Evelyn flit in and out, shadowy figures whose shapes do not hold; I did not know them. Katrina, Hella, and Papa are my tormentors.

Lights are out. It must be near midnight. The glare from the spotlight over the parking lot outside casts an eerie greenish glow across the page. My hands are unsteady.

I awoke when a finger brushed across my cheek. It was probably a cockroach. Angelle is sleeping peacefully, unaware of the terrors in our cell. Her arm is flung over the side of the bunk, for any of the wraiths to tear at. I want to tuck that unsuspecting hand under her and draw her blanket over her; but I am afraid to leave my bed. If I put my feet on the floor, something will grab my ankles.

Papa, I do not think Katrina could have been the saint you remember, to haunt me so now. I see how she haunted my mother with the cruel perfection of her memory. I see my mother backing away from that blinding white light,

149

backing over the cliffs. And now the bloody image of my mother's failure walks stiff-legged towards me, arms out-stretched. I must not be touched by her. I must never be touched by my own mother. All my life, Papa, I shrank from my mother and embraced the light of Katrina. Your precious icon never hugged me back.

And you, Papa. You were obedient, loyal, steadfast, sure. But you did not love me. What an opportune camouflage, that you were Finnish and Finns do not speak the "L" word. I thought it was my squeaky voice, my pinched features, my lack of grace, intelligence, and will that held you from me. But Papa, your fear is a clutching presence in my cell tonight, and I know that if I had been Katrina, you would not have loved me. You lost more in her and my mother than you were willing to risk losing again. For anyone. You were weak, Papa; and that may be the one trait you have successfully transmitted to me.

I have seen my ghosts, and I fear that daylight will bring me no escape. I say to my shades, "Hakkaa Pääle!"

When they fade from my cell and leave me to clearer thoughts, I realize what summoned these visions to my side. It was my mother.

Earlier today, Angelle tuned the radio to K-BAY, the oldies channel. It made no difference to me. I was raised on Papa's preaching that music is the lowest form of the arts. I've always studied and listened to classical music, and never cultivated a real passion for it. Papa battered me into developing a frigid ear, Blake says; better that than a frigid———, he says. But there's nothing like being lovelorn to awaken you to music. Every song on K-BAY was written for me, it seems. And today, listening intently, I heard one that I think truly was written for me. My mother's voice, with none of the raw edge of her rock and roll numbers, filled the cell clearly and sweetly. "Lullabye, lullabye, baby mine . . ." she sang. When she faded out, the D.J. shouted at me, "From 1969, that was Lockjaw's 'Gift from Heaven.'" Written and performed for me by my mother. Who was also a Finn and who crooned the "L" word with such exquisite sweetness. The implications were horrifying.

I had not heard the lullaby in more than twenty years. I had no recollection of having heard it at all until I heard it again, and then, across time, the strains of my mother's voice blended in stereophonic sound with the radio. It broke my heart. I cried as I probably have not cried since my mother died and Papa told me that crying was not for Liems. Angelle regarded me as if I were having a bout of flatulence.

Papa, how could you have kept that beautiful love song from me? How could you have stolen my mother from me? And you, Elga, who professed to love her as your own; in those thousands of days we spent together, alone and unwatched, mightn't you have slipped me a word, a story, a picture of my mother, hummed me the song she wrote for me? And why did I never go in search of her myself?

Blake always encouraged it. He loved her music. I told him I wasn't interested. But that wasn't my disinterest. It was Papa's anger. At her, or at me too? Blake knew; I see now that he knew; but as in all things, he did not press, he waited for me to learn.

I think I miss my mother almost more than Blake, now that I have heard her song. Her siren's song. Calling me.

25

POSSESSION OF the gun was invigorating. On the afternoon and evening of its purchase, Duck returned to her dresser again and again, held her breath at the screech the bottom drawer made when she opened it, and reached to the back to touch the hard feel of power wrapped inside her scarf. The sharp contours of the weapon honed her thinking. She was a wizard at the crossword puzzle. The solutions came to her almost as quickly as she could fill in the squares. The Arno River, the answer that had eluded her earlier in the day, flowed through her mind with the full force it carried into the Ligurian Sea.

But there were still questions. Before or after the trial for her dramatic moment in the foyer? Before, she would miss seeing Liem brought to justice. After, she might lose her resolve. And it would be a long wait, trapped in this house with her father.

She heard muffled voices in the kitchen, right below her room. Her father's voice was easily recognizable. There was a softer second voice, a woman's. It sounded like Mamoo. But it couldn't be. Mamoo seldom visited this house, never arrived unannounced, and hated driving in the dark. "No matter how many carrots I eat," she had explained, "I'm still night blind."

The way the intercom system worked, any room could be signaled from another with a beep. The kitchen, however, housed the main terminal, and through some quirk in the wiring, it was possible to eavesdrop on the kitchen. Duck crept over to her speaker, depressed the TALK button with her trigger finger, and listened.

". . . that's not what Bahalia says." It *was* Mamoo. "You're closeted in your work. Duck's closeted in her room. And Junior's closeted in the closet. The situation is intolerable."

"I know it is, but there's nothing much to be done until we get this trial behind us. It's only a month away."

"The trial may be foremost in your mind, Blake, but I don't think that that's what's preying on the children. Junior isn't even aware of it. Duck's not so much interested in the trial as she is afraid of making a public appearance. And why? I think she feels disgraced. She doesn't want to be with her dearest friends, much less the target of a red block in the newspaper or a minicam. And who's supporting her through all of this? Her mother's dead. Her sister and constant companion is dead. Do you think they're going to come back after the trial?" Mamoo's voice had risen, but she was neither strident nor shrill. She was reasoning with her son. Like a lawyer. Like Duck's lawyer. A cheer rose in Duck's chest. She had lifted the magazine in her free hand and was almost inclined to pump it like a pom-pom, even though she did not know what Mamoo was advocating.

Blake, Sr. mumbled something feeble. Mamoo went on. "The loss of a mother and a sister would be traumatic enough under any circumstances. But these were murders. Both children saw the mutilated bodies. Then they were confronted with your mutilated marriage. How is Junior to understand your affair? How is Duck? She's too young to have come to terms with her mother. She's especially ill-equipped in view of the so-called 'protective' upbringing you and Evelyn provided." Mamoo was flying, and Duck could not process all she was saying. The clarity Duck had brought to the puzzle minutes before had retreated behind a dense fog.

"Mamoo, I protected them from things I thought children should not have to contend with. I thought when they were older there would be time enough to prepare them . . ."

"Oh, Blake. Listen to yourself! *After* they grow up. *After* the trial. All your life you've waited for things to work themselves out without your intervention. What about now? What about today? Why aren't these children in therapy? Come to think of it, why aren't you?"

"You know how I feel about all that psychobabble. I spent fifteen thousand dollars on Evelyn's biweekly sessions with Dr. Hoenecker. As far as I could tell, all they talked about was *his* marriage. I paid for his swimming pool, and got a little advice about the comforts of an asexual marriage in return. Evelyn wasn't just asexual. She had a positive loathing of sex. She wouldn't even watch an R-rated movie."

"Evelyn was a tall order for a psychiatrist."

"Mamoo, I don't think Dr. Hoenecker had any idea how sick Evelyn was. She was the consummate actress. She had her perfect public face, and she probably had a slightly modified face for the good doctor, but the guy thought she was a 'charming lady,' which tells me he never got to know her." Blake warmed to his subject. " 'She's all surface,' I told Hoenecker once, thinking, I guess, that it might be helpful if he knew what he was dealing with. You know what he said?" Blake's voice crackled with indignation.

"What?" Mamoo asked, impatient to get past it.

"He said, 'still water.' 'Still water,' like that was a real insight. Deep, eh?"

"But you and the children are not Evelyn," Mamoo argued, "and there are other doctors."

"I *hear* what you're saying, Mamoo, as Dr. Hoenecker

would say"—Blake, Sr.'s voice was heavy with sarcasm— "but I don't have any confidence in therapy. I know the kids are 'in crisis,' as Dr. Hoenecker would say—well, maybe he'd have some stronger term for their conditions since he diagnosed PMS as 'in crisis.' " Blake assumed a pleading tone. "It's because they're so vulnerable right now that I don't want some potential Hoenecker experimenting on them."

"What's your plan, then?"

"We all need some time, Mamoo."

"Aachh!" Mamoo reverted from lawyer to exasperated mother. "This is not a bug bite, Blake. If the children were both running fevers of a hundred and six, you wouldn't be saying 'Give it some time.' They're sick, son, and they need your help."

Blake, Sr. said nothing. Duck could almost see his elbows resting on the table, his head cradled in his hands.

Meanwhile, Duck's finger had gone white and numb from holding down the button. She let it go during the lull in the conversation, quickly shook out her hand, and reconnected with her left thumb.

"What do you think, Duck?" Mamoo asked.

Shit. Had she missed something in the conversation, or did Mamoo know she was listening? The thing about eavesdropping on the kitchen was that there was a tiny red light that came on when the speaker was activated from another room. If they were sitting at the breakfast table and Mamoo was facing the wall, she could see it. But would she know what it meant? And if she did, did she know how much Duck had heard? If Mamoo had watched the light with an understanding of its significance, Duck could not easily extricate herself, because if she disconnected now, the light would go off, betraying cowardice on top of sneakiness. As these thoughts rushed through Duck's mind, she heard her father shifting in his chair, probably to look at the intercom.

"Oh, for heaven's sake," her father moaned.

Duck said decisively, "I think I have a right to be a part of this conversation, and I have some ideas of ways to improve things. I'd like to come live with you, Mamoo."

There was a brief silence on the other end.

"What do you think, Blake?" asked Mamoo.

"It might not be a bad idea to get out of this house," Blake considered aloud. "But I don't want to split the family up. Junior and I would have to come, too. I'm willing to give it a try if you'll have us, Mamoo."

"I'd be delighted. When do you want to come? Duck?"

"Tomorrow."

"Do you want to come downstairs and talk about it?" Mamoo asked.

"No."

"All right then, I'll see you tomorrow, whenever you're ready. Good night."

"Good night," Duck said.

She sat down on the bed, shook out her hand, and reconsidered her options. It was one thing to commit suicide against her father. It was another to violate Mamoo, her home, and Junior with her anger. She couldn't do it at the Point. That left only tonight.

Her father had already seen Mamoo to her car and come upstairs. Could she call him down to the foyer and finish it now? It seemed a staged and graceless approach, lacking the fluid drama of her imagined scene. Besides, if she did it tonight, Mamoo might think she had provoked it somehow. No, it would have to wait. After the trial, then.

And she would have to testify.

A charge of adrenaline struck. Duck pictured herself in front of a sea of faces. *Look over their heads,* the debate coach used to say. *Find a point on the back wall. Now, just talk.* Duck closed her eyes. The desk lamp flared red behind her lids. *Blood,* she thought. *I have to talk about blood.* Nothing in her debate experience had prepared her for this. *The courtroom is not the auditorium at Wright. The audience will not be children. And my topic is not health care or famine in Africa.*

Duck crossed the room to her dresser and withdrew the derringer, swaddled in lilac silk. She carried it back to her bed and lay down. *I bought this gun. I've gotten myself out of this house. And I can get myself through the trial.* She closed her eyes, saw the blood again, and forced herself not to recoil. Then, for the first time, she saw the hideousness of her memories as a weapon, and saw herself as a weapon in the prosecution's case. *I'm going to spill Mother's and Alexandra's blood at Catherine Liem's feet the way she spilled it at mine. See if she can play the poor little rich girl victimized by love after the jury understands what she did.*

She unsheathed the barrel of the derringer from the gossamer folds and put it in her mouth. It felt remarkably hostile. There was no mistaking it for a carrot or a finger, or even something more foreign, like a fork or a pipe. It was unmistakably a gun, and her throat ached in anticipation of the bullet's bursting strike. She intended to fall asleep with it in her mouth, its lethal power as comforting as her thumb had been when she was a baby; but sleep offered a more comfortable oblivion, and as Duck drifted into it, the gun fell to the floor, making a sharp, unheard report.

26

My last romantic notions that I might salvage a life for myself in this place left with Eudora. Only one conversation is possible with Angelle: how the world has mistreated her. "And now this," she almost says, "imprisonment with you."

She tosses the paper at me. "For your scrapbook," she says.

Thank you, Angelle. God knows, I have nothing else for my scrapbook. I have no pictures of my surrogate parents, Elga and Papa, such is my emotional detachment from them. My real parents are strangers to me. Perhaps I could send out for an album cover or a promotional poster and become one of their groupies? And Blake. Mr. Betkins has seized my pictures of Blake. What I'd really like on my wall is a Spencer family portrait with Evelyn cut out. Wouldn't you have fun with that at trial, Mr. Betkins? Or maybe like Cissy down the hall, I could tape glossy 8 x 10s of myself around the cell. To preserve some sense of myself in the face of my lack of ancestors, descendants, legitimate lovers. Stripped of the forms, conventions, rules, and patterns that defined my life, I really don't have a clear picture of myself.

What melodrama in all these pages. What self-important drivel. Will you read them to the jury, Mr. Betkins? A jury might condemn me for nothing more than the vanity in this diary. But as we all know, there is much more.

Delia Wallis, the woman who bludgeoned her twins beyond the coroner's capacity to tell which corpse was which, has pleaded not guilty by reason of insanity. She was herself a battered child. She was scalded, cut, punched, and broken. One New Year's Eve she set off fireworks on the sidewalk and awakened her father from his drunken stupor. He bound her hands with a strand of two hundred firecrackers and lit them. Delia says she killed her children to protect them from such agony.

There must be a glimmer of madness in me to sustain the glimmer of understanding I have for her decision. More than a glimmer of madness. If she had administered lethal injections to her babies while they slept, I would champion her cause. Maybe.

I hold my pain up for comparison against hers and I am ashamed. My grandfather required me to wear my Mary Janes with my ankle socks neatly turned down. He would not allow me to go barefoot! He made me sit up straight beside him when he read to me in the evening. He never held me in his lap!

Oh Catherine. Please.

I wish, with an ineffable longing, that I could go look out over the ocean.

27

DUCK WAS BRACED for a pang of sadness on returning to the beach, where she thought that everything would remind her of Rick, or more properly, of the loss of Rick. But the coast had reinvented itself in the last two weeks: it was cold, gray, and windy. Each scudding wave bit angrily at the heels of its forerunner, churning up showers of salty spray. The ocean was so dark that when a particularly strong gust of wind sent stinging pellets against Duck's hand, she looked down half expecting to find flecks of obsidian.

Duck, Mamoo, and Junior were wrapped in old woolen blankets and huddled in deck chairs, their backs against the weathered wall of the house. Mamoo had fixed hot chocolate, which had turned cold before anyone could finish it; but three pairs of hands still gripped the vanished warmth of their mugs. The scratchy wool and the chafing cold, the creaking wooden chairs and the immense horizon were reminiscent of a transatlantic crossing Duck had made two years earlier on the QEII with Mother, Alexandra, and Junior. Mamoo must have had a similar thought, for she went inside and returned a minute later with two pairs of binoculars. "Let's look for whales," she proposed, offering Duck and Junior the ancient cracked leather cases.

"There aren't any whales here, are there?" Duck asked.

"You never know until you look," Mamoo replied. "It seems like a whale-watching day."

"What does a whale look like?" Junior asked.

"Oh, they're magnificent creatures, Junior," Mamoo said. She went back inside and returned with a sketch pad and charcoal. With a few deft strokes she had rendered the gloaming ocean; then a whale broke the surface, and then a gray mist exploded from her blowhole. Beneath the water, the dark shape of a calf appeared at her side, and shadowy outlines of others in the herd appeared from the depths.

"Cool," Junior murmured, as each form emerged.

About midway in the QEII voyage they had seen whales. It had created quite a stir: books, games of shuffleboard, letters, and maps were abandoned; the passengers crowded the rails to watch the great beasts, so distant as to be almost indistinguishable from the waves. Yet their remote presence was strongly moving.

The voyage had been filled with luxurious discoveries, whales and Beluga caviar, daily movies, bridge lessons, and massages. They had all felt pampered and grateful to Blake, Sr. for sending them ahead. He flew over on the Concorde and joined them in London. *He bought himself a week with his mistress,* Duck now realized. Was no happy memory safe from contamination?

"I remember when they met," she mused.

"What?" inquired Mamoo. "Who?"

"Dad and Catherine Liem."

"Were you there?"

"Uh-uh. I remember him talking about it. When was it that they finished the Liem Enterprises Building?"

"About three years ago, I think," Mamoo filled in.

"It was right before it opened. In the planning phase, Mr. Liem had gotten Dad to design a two-story atrium and gave him the drawings for those wavy steel rod partitions. You know how annoyed Dad gets when the owner tries to control the design—beyond saying what kind of space he needs."

"Mmm-hmm," Mamoo agreed, her lips pressed against the rim of her mug.

"Dad loved this stuff, and they designed those massive wrought-iron screens on the front doors to match the patterns of the partitions. And Mr. Liem told Dad that he had commissioned a twenty-foot floor-to-ceiling sculpture; he had the exact specs for the mounting and the pedestal, but he wouldn't show Dad the drawings. It was all very mysterious, and Dad was really nervous about what this centerpiece was going to do to his beautiful entrance.

"Then he came home one night and told us that the surprise sculpture was some atrocity Liem's granddaughter had designed in her sandbox. I remember the discussion so well because he had us all rolling with his description. He hadn't seen it yet. No one had seen Catherine Liem's work at that point, and Mr. Liem had described this particular piece only as a twenty-foot-high multimedia weaving. So Dad pictured this combination crocheted afghan, with macramé placemats and silver spoons dangling from it. I can't do it like he did, but it was a riot, he was so worked up. He said he was going to make it multi-multimedia by putting her name on it in neon so no one would think he was responsible.

"Then a day or two later, he did an about-face. He said he'd met Catherine Liem and seen the sculpture at her studio. It was amazing—a masterpiece of welding more than weaving; and it tied in with the partitions and the doors, which she had designed. He went on and on about how talented she was, how mature for her age.

"Later he stopped talking about her altogether, and I guess we know why."

"I guess so," Mamoo agreed.

"Why?" asked Junior.

"Because he was *seeing* her," Duck explained.

"Oh," Junior remarked, in a voice that feigned understanding.

"Mamoo . . . did you know?" Duck asked.

Mamoo squinted into the wind. "No."

"Do you think Mother knew?" Duck asked, bouncing Maria's question off Mamoo.

"No. I don't think she would have tolerated it," Mamoo said, a softer echo of Duck's own conclusion.

They fell silent and let the pounding of the surf take the place of conversation. Duck was shivering inside her blankets. Her fingertips were white and numb now, and her nails were blue. The trembling, though, seemed to be stemming less from the cold than from the tension in her muscles, which were drawn so tight that her neck and shoulders hurt. Duck clenched her jaws in an effort to still herself, and her teeth began to chatter.

"Why, you're half frozen!" Mamoo exclaimed.

"N-n-o I'm n-not," Duck answered, "I'm n-not c-cold at all."

"You're giving a pretty good imitation of it," Mamoo countered, jumping up. "Let's go inside and build a fire."

"Yeah!" Junior agreed. It took him several forward pitches to heave himself out of the chair. "I'll go down and get the wood."

"I th-think I'll s-stay here for a while," Duck chattered.

Mamoo did not argue. "Do you want another blanket?"

"N-no really. I'm not c-cold. I'm just scared." Duck waited for Mamoo to tell her there was nothing to fear.

Instead, her grandmother sat back down beside her and laid a hand on one of her trembling knees. "What are you afraid of, honey?"

"Ev-v-verything. I d-don't understand anything. N-nobody's who I thought they were—Catherine Liem, the artist. Daddy, the dependable man. Mother. I thought she was a w-wonderful mother, but now I'm seeing she was cold to Dad and to

Junior. I never knew you were a lawyer. R-r-ick. I thought we w-were in love, and he's such a jerk!" All of Duck's tremors coalesced into one cathartic jerk as she said it. *And then there's Maggie. And Jenny.*

Mamoo took a deep breath and let it out slowly. "One of the terrible lessons of age, Laura, is that we old folks are condemned to watch you stumble over the same stones that tripped us. All I can do is help dust you off after you fall." She mock-dusted the blanket over Duck's legs with firm strokes as she said it.

"Can't you explain *any* of it?" Duck importuned. "How do you know what to believe in?"

"I'll share one of my secrets with you," Mamoo offered. "I believe in the ocean."

"Oh, that's useful," Duck grumbled, more sarcastically than she intended.

"It's very useful to me. You can study on it some while you're here. Maybe it will become useful to you, too."

Duck made a quick study of the roiling, dark water. The waves had risen and the wind had strengthened, but the booming, chilling, salty pummeling of her senses carried no messages. She said, "The ocean would be terrific consolation if I could live at Iberville Point, hidden from the world like you are. But I can't exactly carry the Gulf of Mexico into the courtroom with me."

Mamoo sat up in her chair. "Is that what you think—that I'm hidden from the world?"

"Sorry, Mamoo. 'Hidden' was probably a bad choice of words. But you don't have to do too many things you don't want to here. You don't have to appear in front of Judge Porter in two weeks, for instance. And I don't see how believing in the ocean can be any help to me there."

A bit sharply, Mamoo said, "Everyone has to do things she doesn't want to do, Laura. We can make choices for ourselves, certainly—like my choice to abandon a legal career that wasn't right for me. That's not the same as retreating from life and life's problems altogether. And when I face my problems, Laura—as we all must—whatever they are and wherever I may be, I carry the beauty and tranquility of Iberville Point with me into the fight. When you come to believe in the ocean, you'll see the use of it."

Duck wanted answers, not methods. Still, it was reassuring to see that Mamoo, enigmatic though she might be, was not mired in confusion, and that there might be answers out there somewhere. As she looked out over the vast, heaving ocean, it was easy to believe that it might hold some wisdom. She was prepared to accept Mamoo's abstract response, when Mamoo offered something more concrete: "I also believe in my own feelings; I believe in honesty; and I believe in love that endures." With that, she gave Duck a strong hug.

They went inside together. A huge, neatly stacked pyramid of firewood greeted them. Junior, the sorcerer's apprentice, had been chugging up and down the back stairs throughout their discussion. He returned from what must have been his tenth trip, balancing a fifty-pound load that hid his head, and carefully shifted it onto the pile.

"Well!" Mamoo rubbed her hands together and looked very pleased over the towering mess in her den. "That should last us for quite some time!"

Blake, Sr. arrived a few minutes later, laden with sacks of Chinese food. He circled the wood pile and asked gamely, "What, are we having New Year's Eve early, and indoors?" It was a holiday tradition to build a giant pyre on the beach on New Year's Eve.

Mamoo kissed her son on the cheek and relieved him of his aromatic packages. "Not a bad idea," she responded. "I think we're all ready for a New Year."

"Amen. We've got Thanksgiving covered, too. Betsy Cristina called today and invited us all for dinner."

"How dear of her," Mamoo said.

"Do you think we could do up a couple of turkeys to bring?" Blake, Sr. asked.

"You can *be* the turkey," Duck threw at him. "They don't eat meat."

Her father refused to surrender his good cheer. "We'll sculpt one from tofu, then. I'd like to bring something. And they may have the only table in town big enough for both of us, Laura. You can sit twenty feet away from me."

And from Maggie, Maria, and Joey? Duck wondered. "I suppose you already accepted for all of us," she said, accusingly.

"Yes, Laura, I did. It was a kind invitation from a good friend to all of us. But if you don't want to go, you have only to call Betsy and tell her."

Duck was infuriated by his reasonable tone. "So I have to be rude to get out of the bad position you put me in?"

"Laura, I didn't know you would feel this way, I don't know why you do, and I can't make the call for you because I don't want to invent a reason for your not going."

Duck felt Mamoo's eyes on her. She hated her father all the more for making her look bad to Mamoo as well as Betsy. "You should've asked me first!" she spat.

"Yes, I should have. But I didn't, and I'm open to your ideas on the best way out. I'm not ready to fight to the death over this, Laura."

"I hate you!" she cried, feeling the disapproval of all of them as she stormed out of the room. It propelled her down the beach a half mile. Then self-disapproval overtook her. She had so many good reasons to hate him. Why did she have to undermine the strength of her position by fighting a trivial battle? And making an unstrategic retreat? It was cold. She had left her sweater inside, and as the heat of her anger dissipated she felt the chill of the wind.

She was far from the house. It was a moonless night and

clouds dimmed even the faint light of the stars. The darkness that engulfed her relented only enough to reveal the threatening shapes of the dunes to her right and the black, sucking ocean to her left. Nothing was audible above the roar of the wind and the waves. She stood stock still, gripped by fear. Someone could be out there, close at hand. What if Catherine Liem were innocent? Whoever had murdered Mother and Alexandra could still be out there. Hiding in the shadows. She forced herself to turn around, straining into the darkness. She could not see well enough to distinguish between a dune in the distance and the looming shape of a man nearby. There could be stalking movement in the shifting blackness. If she screamed, no one would hear her.

In the moment that she spun around and dug her toes into the sand, seeking purchase for her flight, she felt him lunge for her. She ran for her life. She sprinted over the uneven surface, dropping with heart-stopping clumsiness into unseen hollows, straying into the foot-dragging surf, and feeling him close the gap with every leaping step. She fought for balance and for breath and for courage. In games of freeze tag in the schoolyard, she had always been tagged early. She preferred being caught to the sensation of being pursued. But the fingers outstretched for her now were fingers of terror. She pulled away from them with all the strength she could pump into her flailing arms and legs.

The house grew from a pinpoint of light to a shining beacon. Then it was a bright band of windows. Then it had form and color and beckoning stairs lit by the glow of the porchlights. Duck veered from the water's edge into the soft, resisting hillside. She took it on all fours, scrambling and clawing until she made the first landing of the deck. She could hear music from inside. Handel's *Water Music*. She could hear nothing clattering on the steps behind her. In the apron of light thrown out by the house, the beach was empty, had been empty all along. Duck lay heaving on the stairs, her lungs burning.

She felt ridiculous, but her body's reaction lagged behind her mind's. Her legs shook uncontrollably. Her hands were fairly flapping. It was twenty minutes before she could slide open the glass door with an air of normalcy.

Junior was perched on a barstool at the kitchen island. He held a white carton out to her. "Chicken," he announced between mouthfuls.

Mamoo had laid out a place for her. "Rick called," she said.

Blake, Sr. was stretched out on the couch with a magazine. He looked up reluctantly from some item of interest. "Have a nice walk?"

28

(translated from the Finnish)

Arnie is back. He is displeased with my decision to reject the plea bargain. He told me of his family's traditional extended Thanksgiving weekend at his father's house on Cape Cod. He told me that he would miss it this year while working on my case. I told him that I would have to miss it, too. The slight narrowing of his eyes when I said this reminded me of you, Papa. Economy of movement; enormity of moment.

And after that tiny flex of Arnie's eyelid, I reminded myself of myself with you. I cowered by smiling . . . the simian signal of surrender. I told him prison jokes. I attended to his plans for the defense. This time, I approved his theories on Junior. Yes, he may suggest that Junior is as likely a suspect as I am—that is, we are equally unlikely. Arnie will keep it gentle, noninflammatory. What if I hadn't approved Arnie's strategy, and he had clenched his jaw?

Papa, how much simpler it all would have been if you had just told me, "My Katya, I cannot love you and you are not to blame." I do not think I would be here, writing in Finnish, still striving for the approval of a dead man, looking for the world to affirm me because I cannot affirm myself. Probably, Papa, I would have had more self-respect than to squander all my love on a married man. But what a happy mistake that was.

Well, Mr. Betkins, was it worth the cost to the taxpayers to have this translated? Or are you there, Elga, offering free assistance? What an attractive couple the two of you would make. You see how strange life is, in the matches it arranges?

29

THEY WERE part guest and part family at the beach house. They were free to come and go as they pleased, but their natural rhythms were interrupted. Duck felt uncomfortable lazing about in her room: it seemed an affront to Mamoo's industry. She made up her bed and came to breakfast at 7:00. She and Junior kept their clothes in the closets, their toiletries off the counters, and their magazines off the couch. They fell naturally into Mamoo's patterns, beginning with a long brisk walk every morning after breakfast. The first day, her frail-looking grandmother set the pace of a Panzer tank. After a quarter mile, Duck and Junior were sweating; at a half mile, they were gasping for breath. "Breathe in through the nose, out through the mouth!" Mamoo commanded. Junior kept up for about a mile, then plopped himself down in cross-legged rebellion. Grateful for the excuse, Duck fell out beside him. Mamoo acknowledged their unfitness with a backward salute and swerved into the dunes. She hardly broke her speed as she strode up the first steep bank and disappeared from view over the side. A moment later, she appeared at the crest of the next one.

"She's showing off," Duck said in awe.

"Yeah." Junior laughed. "I wish I could."

When Mamoo swept past their sandcastle on the return

route, she seemed to have built up speed. Junior and Duck had to jog to keep up.

Hearing Duck's ragged breath, Mamoo reminded her, "In through the nose; out through the mouth!"

"The next thing out through my mouth is going to be vomit," Duck panted.

Mamoo relented and led them in a cool-down stretch that was half exercise, half religion. Mamoo incorporated principles of yoga into a routine of exercises scientifically designed to release the tension from every muscle in their bodies. Here Mamoo demonstrated a limberness to match her strength and endurance. The backs of Duck's legs screamed when she held onto her flexed toes and tried to touch her forehead to her knees. Mamoo, bent double, laid her forehead on the ground as easily as if she were hinged with rubber bands.

"In answer to your question about why I do this every day," Mamoo said, while hugging one of her legs in an inimitable position, "I'm harvesting endorphins that elevate my mood for the rest of the day. On the rare occasions when it's too stormy for my walk, I can really feel the difference in my mood."

After a week or so at Iberville Point, Duck's spirits lifted, too. Whether it was the walks, the change of residence and routine, the ocean, or Mamoo's soothing presence, Duck could not tell. But after their walk and the good hot shower that followed, she could curl up in one of the deep-cushioned rattan chairs and read without the heaviness that settled on her at home. She even learned some hard truths without despair. "Mamoo," she asked one day when they were alone on the deck, "why were you and Mother so cool to one another? Why didn't you ever come over to our house?"

"I wondered when you would get around to asking me that." Mamoo drew a deep breath. "Junior was the end of our relationship, such as it was. You've heard me speak of my second son, Stewart. The umbilicus wrapped around his neck during the delivery and he suffered brain damage from the oxygen deprivation. He was a lovely boy, a lot like Junior, but not as strong. He contracted pneumonia when he was six years old and died." She stopped for a moment, her eyes searching sorrowfully out to sea.

"When Junior was diagnosed with Down Syndrome—right after he was born—I went to the hospital thinking I could comfort your mother and help her see the joys of a retarded child. Your mother told me that she held me responsible for Junior's congenital defect, which she thought he'd inherited from me. There was no telling her that Junior's problem was completely unrelated to Stewart's. Not only did your mother refuse my help, she said she never wanted to see me again. I hoped that her statements grew out of temporary shock and grief; but she never let up. Perhaps I could've helped to smooth things over, but I was angry, too. Your mother's distaste for my Stewart, and poor newborn Junior, was a moral carcinogen for me."

Mamoo turned her foot sideways and dragged the sole of her sandal stuttering across the rough boards of the deck. "That was the end of your parents' relationship, too. In your mother's eyes, your father was culpable, as well. And the situation was only made worse because your father refused to feel any guilt. He had loved Stewart and he loved Junior."

Another stunning revelation. "Mamoo, why didn't anybody tell me?" Even as she said it, she had a vague sense of having had the pieces without putting them together. Stewart had been dead for so much longer than he had lived, his life and his death had seemed unimportant.

Mamoo seemed to read her thoughts. "I'm sure I've spoken about Stewart to you; he's never far from my mind. But you have to reach a certain age before you experience

any real curiosity about your ancestors; that comes at a time
when you start realizing the interconnectedness of things, of
families."

"But nobody told me about Mother and Stewart, or about
you and Mother," Duck persisted.

"Some questions aren't ripe to be answered until they're
asked, Duck." The older woman settled into a wooden
chaise in the shade of an overhang. Her head was tipped
back, eyes closed, palms upturned at her sides in the posture of a sunbather. She seemed perfectly comfortable with
disclosure.

"Why did my parents stay together?" Duck asked.

"I'm not sure I have all the answers," Mamoo said, without opening her eyes, "but I think I can give you some.
Your mother was very keen on propriety, and part of what
that meant was staying married. She also enjoyed your father's fame and position in the community, and I suspect
that in her own way, she loved him. In any event, they long
ago worked out an accommodation to one another. For your
father's part, I think he stayed mostly for the sake of his
children; and like many men in unhappy marriages, he re-
placed his wife with his career so that their estrangement
became less important to him over time. Perhaps in Blake's
way, he loved Evelyn, too, but it seemed to me that they
were leading very separate lives under the same roof."

"Mother was a . . ." Duck started to say "bitch," but it
frightened her to blaspheme against her dead mother. "She
was awful."

Mamoo raised herself up on one elbow and regarded her
granddaughter tenderly. "Duck, everyone is a mixed bag.
You're just beginning to see your mother's faults; that's a
natural part of growing up. But you can't carry it too far.
I can't give you much help in bringing things into balance,
because I was cut off from your mother, and I don't have
a balanced view. You'll have to draw on your own recollec-

tions for perspective. I know this much: your mother raised three beautiful children; she couldn't have produced the three of you without some goodness in her."

"We were raised by Bahalia."

"Laura, I don't think you're being fair. But if you believe that's true, then thank your mother for providing you with Bahalia."

Poor Junior, Duck thought. He was right. Mother had hated him. Duck reflected sadly that Mother's death may have been a blessing for Junior. If only he would come out of the closet.

One day Mamoo and Junior pulled Blake, Sr.'s trunk of blocks out of the loft. For Duck it was like bringing the manger scene down from the attic at Christmas and becoming reacquainted with the precious porcelain features of the wise men or the tiny, curled-up lamb in her hand. She had not seen the blocks for many years, but as they unboxed each one, its details clicked into their grooves in her memory and ran cleanly back to her grandfather. She remembered his rough, gnarled hands rubbing, rubbing each piece with a rag soaked in tung oil. Arthur Spencer—Pop to his grandchildren—had made each one of the blocks from driftwood. Many of them were the standard geometric shapes to be found in any comprehensive set. Then there were blocks keyed for Romanesque arches and for Gothic vaults, domes, Doric and Corinthian columns, dentate cornices, and much more. Pop had started the set when his son Blake was three years old, and had added to it until his death. Duck's favorite pieces were the later ones, on which Pop left ocean-wrought ornamentation. A perfect column would end in a spiraled unicorn's horn, or a cube would be satiny smooth on three sides and rippled with fretwork on the fourth. Of these fanciful pieces, the best were what Pop called the gargoyle series, blocks from whose clean-cut planes twisted forms struggled to life. While Duck, Alexandra, Junior, and Mamoo cursed at a thousand-piece jigsaw puzzle, Pop and Blake, Sr. would work endlessly with their jigsaw blocks, building magnificent Gaudí-esque constructions. It was a game they had enjoyed since Blake, Sr.'s childhood; it was the game by which Arthur had hewn his son into an architect; and the adult playing of it was a redolent rag soaked in tung oil that seasoned and preserved them both.

It was difficult to work with the blocks at all without making something splendid. Junior and Duck thought they were building a fort, but the blocks drew themselves into a cloistered courtyard hemmed by a cathedral-like building on one side and monastic quarters on the others. Duck and Junior were barring the windows with tiny grills when their father came home from work. He sat beside them on the floor, fondling first one piece and then another. He was rubbing his thumb under the dewlaps of one of the gargoyles when he asked Duck, "Is Pop going to make an architect of you, too, then?"

Duck had been reflecting rather kindly on her father. Playing with his childhood toys, she thought of him as a child in this nurturing setting. So different from his troubled marriage. But she wasn't ready to be modeled after him. "No," she answered crisply.

"What would you like to do, Laura? Are you going to school in January?"

Duck didn't want to have any conversation with her father, particularly not this one. She had been wondering herself what she would do after the trial. Her only firm plan was to kill herself. But other options kept presenting themselves anyway. Staying home was boring—an endless summer vacation without so much as a reading list to occupy her. The idea of college beckoned; but the only school that had admitted her was Auburn, and the thought of sharing a campus with Rick was sickening. It was probably too late to apply anywhere else, even if she got onto it immediately, and she didn't have the energy. Maybe, she had thought, a small bookstore somewhere would take her in with only a high-school diploma. They wouldn't have to pay her ... No, her plans were not ripe for discussion with her father.

He backed off. "Come over here," he said. "I want to show you what I'll be doing in January."

He led her back to the small alcove behind the kitchen, never seeming to question that she would follow. To Duck's surprise, her father had set up a drafting table overlaid with drawings weighted down at their curled corners. It was his newest project, a large-scale beach-front development. The design was nearing completion, the only stage at which Duck could visualize the finished product. In the distant past, her father had sometimes spoken excitedly to her about floor plans and elevations. She would nod dumbly; she might as well be examining the pattern for a tile floor. But these were the finished drawings of landscaped facades, courtyards, and sample interiors. Duck looked over her father's shoulder as he reviewed the project for her. It was a small-scale village, with offices, apartments, hotel rooms, shops, and an abundance of sports facilities. The buildings were scattered about with seeming haphazardness, except that there was a harmonious interaction among them. Studying the simple, graceful lines, and knowing the attention that had been given to every detail, Duck felt a faint stirring of the pride she used to take in her father's accomplishments. He was a great architect; everyone said so, and his success had demonstrated it. It was impossible to examine his work without seeing both the natural gift and the hard work that underlay his achievements. And there was always some very personal mark on the work, like the gargoyles in the block set, but less obtrusive. On these buildings, the mark was a subtle, irregular scoring of all the walls that fronted on the water, as if the wind had eroded them. From the land side, the structures would appear elegantly tidy and civilized. From the beach they would be vaguely disturbing, in harmony with wild elements at work there. Duck was drawn to these, as to some window on the unruly and unknown planes of her father.

He was describing the layout. "This central building is the lodge. There's a boardwalk, here, to the apartments, and on the other side, here, to this grouping of cottages." His fingers traced a path around the buildings. "But look at the stonework here on this terrace, and here, here, and here." He swiftly tapped out the locations. "It comes to almost eighty thousand square feet on the whole project. Arnold Watson's the general, and I've convinced him to sub the terracing, masonry, and stonework to Charlie Deed."

Mamoo called from the kitchen. "You think he can handle it?"

"I know he can, and once he gets this in his portfolio, he'll be made. There's a growing demand for minority contractors, especially on city and state projects. Charlie's going to be pulling them in as fast as he can line up his crews."

"That's wonderful!" Mamoo exclaimed.

"Except that I'm going to lose a very good cook," Blake said, without a hint of remorse in his tone.

"But I think you'll be keeping a very good friend," Mamoo added.

"I'm considering taking Duck on as my cook, and having Bahalia and her family over to dinner every night. It seems like a more congenial arrangement than we have now." He sent a playful nudge backward into Duck's belly, his first acknowledgment that she was there. It had not escaped anyone's notice that this was also the first time he had called her by her nickname in months. He looked over his shoulder at her and smiled. It was as warming as it was embarrassing.

Duck averted her eyes from his to the drawing board. "It's nice," she nodded at the plans.

Her father turned and gripped her in a crushing embrace. She had to fight to hold back her tears.

Blessedly, the phone rang. "I'm frying eggplant," Mamoo called out. "Can someone get that, please?"

Blake, Sr. went. "Hello, Rick. Yes, she's right here. Hold on, one second." He extended the receiver to Duck.

"Hello," she said woodenly.

"How are you?" he asked, in a voice heavy with awkward concern.

"Fine," she answered woodenly.

"Duck, talk to me, please. I've been real worried and real scared. I know I haven't done a very good job of showing it, but I care a lot about you. Please talk to me."

"I can't."

"Can you answer questions?" he asked.

"Yes."

"Are you pregnant?"

"No."

"Were you never, or just not anymore?" Relief lifted his voice.

"Never." This was awful. Duck was not sure what else she would say to Rick if she were not surrounded by her family; but communication under these circumstances was impossible. Junior, dependably incurious usually, was staring at her quizzically. Mamoo was busy at the stove and her father had discreetly raised his newspaper, but they were within unavoidable earshot of this unnaturally strained conversation.

"Can I come down next weekend to see you? There's so much I want to say."

"No."

"Duck, I'm sorry. I'm really sorry. I want to talk to you. Over Thanksgiving?"

"No."

"Will you ever give me another chance?" He sounded small and boyish.

Duck squeezed the receiver tight. Tears spilled from her eyes. She wanted to say something between yes and no, but she did not know what it was, and she was not free to talk anyway. "No," she said, because it was the easiest.

"I'm sorry," he said thickly. "Good-bye." And he was gone.

Duck wordlessly left the living-room side of the house and crossed the breezeway to her bedroom. No one tried to stop her. She lay on her bed in the dark, listening to the muffled booming of the surf. She tried to take from the sounds of the ocean the wisdom Mamoo said it had to offer. But the background din could not drum Rick's voice out of her head. She replayed their conversation countless times, steering it down different paths; even in the privacy of her own thoughts, she could not find her answer to Rick's question whether she wanted to see him again. What she wanted was to see him as she had envisioned him a month ago, full of golden promise. Not even the apology he had offered could reinstate that vanished image. She still loved him for his beauty, strength, intelligence, and humor. But those sterling qualities were tarnished by his lies. Duck considered whether the circumstances explained or excused the lies he had told. In the end, the ocean soothed her to sleep, unresolved.

30

Arnie has somehow commanded a workroom, which he calls a war room. Because it's in the center of this ugly building, my trip there did not take me outside. Nevertheless, the sheriff's policies for the handling of dangerous prisoners required that I wear handcuffs and leg irons connected by a 14″ steel chain. The ankle cuffs were designed for slightly larger dangerous prisoners; I could easily have slipped my feet through the thick bands. But that was beside the point. The point was humiliation. They might as well have collared my neck and run another short chain down to my ankles, forcing my head down. You cannot raise your head if you must walk in clanking baby steps.

I trotted noisily through the halls between two deputies who made mighty sounds: thunk of heavy shoes on linoleum, creak of leather gunbelts.

Elga's voice whispered inside my head, Mind over circumstance. *All right. I am a geisha-in-training, I thought.* Stronger. *A parade horse with weighted fetlocks.* Stronger. *An experiment in sexual bondage.* You can do better than that. *A punk rocker, then. My green hair is spiked. I'm wearing a studded collar. There's a tattoo on my cheek:* mom, *in jagged blue letters.* Oh, Hella would be proud of you.

181

A shadow of a smile lingered on my face as the door opened on our destination. The guard removed the handcuffs, left the ankle cuffs. A precaution, they said. Theater, I reminded myself.

I had an image in my mind of what our war room would look like. A map of the area from Viipuri to Petsamo, thousands of lakes colored in pale blue, the positions of Russia's 200,000 troops marked in red-beaded pins. Diagrams of tanks. And of course, a disassembled Suomi machine pistol. Short-range, light, rapid-firing.

The room was bare. A stubby conference table capped with plastic wood laminate. Six mismatched wooden chairs that must have come from the old jail. Mint-green walls crowding in. And Arnie. And a woman, with long, thick, blue-black hair, a broad smile, and a big white bow at her throat.

"This is Ms. Tripe," Arnie said, "the psychologist authorized by the court to treat you for stress."

"Ginger," she said, extending a long-nailed hand. Matching bright red lips spread wide.

"Does she look like a psychologist?" Arnie asked.

A test of my psychological makeup, I thought, and didn't answer.

"I'm an actress," Ginger said in a deep stage whisper. "An acting coach."

Arnie leaned into my ear and said, "She's hear to teach you how to look fearful. Upset. Innocent."

I have already been a geisha, a horse, and a punk rocker, I thought. Enough theater for one day.

"Arnie," I said, as patiently as I could, "I need someone for stress."

31

DURING THE morning walk, Rick diminished in importance from a consuming interest to a merely obsessive interest. This enabled Duck to take in her surroundings, which were splendid. The sky was a deep, pure blue, with a few wispy clouds trailed along the shoreline horizon. The deep water reflected the cerulean tone, shading to a crystalline aquamarine in the shallows. It was still cold, and her laboring breath foamed onto the air in rhythm with the low surf foaming gently onto the sand. It had warmed over the past few days, and the warmth of the rising sun on their backs promised a mild afternoon. The gray light of morning lent sharpness to the towering ranks of dunes and softness to the dipping, tassled heads of the sea oats. Duck and Junior had built up enough wind to make conversation possible; but it seemed unnecessary. There was a warm communion in their metronomic steps, their swinging arms, and their lusty breathing of the salt air, in through the nose, out through the mouth. They walked in single file so that each could tread on the narrow band of firm sand above the wave wash. They overtook skittering flocks of sandpipers, which circled around and settled down behind them. Hermit crabs ducked into their shells and tentatively hooked their slender legs back out. Pelicans glided past intermittently, broad-winged and timeless as pterodactyls. Duck felt timeless, too, and strangely, comfortably disembodied.

By the time they finished stretching, Rick had receded behind thoughts of Maria and Suzie and what-was-his-name, Louie? She couldn't believe she hadn't asked how old he was, where he was from, what year he was in, how he looked, *anything*. A few more neck rolls and she would call Suzie.

Mamoo leaned against a railing of the deck. "There's been another development in the trial," she said softly.

Duck's neck tensed, mid-roll.

"It's going to be broadcast on Court TV."

Duck let her head flop forward, her chin touching her chest. "Why am I not surprised?"

"It'll just be one more camera, Laura. They'll keep it as unintrusive as possible."

"We're going to be humiliated on national television," she whimpered.

"Humiliated how?"

"Oh, Mamoo. Now it's a full-fledged Hollywood celebrity trial. When I'm feeling nervous about testifying in front of a couple hundred people, I can think to myself, 'What's a couple hundred? *Millions* are watching.' Millions of people getting their entertainment kicks off of our family's sleazy misery."

"I can't pretend I don't think it's terrible, Laura. But there's nothing we can do about it, so we'll just have to rise above it."

"How did this happen?" Duck took off her running shoe and shook the sand onto the deck. Angrily, she swept sand between the broad cracks of the deck, heedless of splinters.

Mamoo sat down, with her legs out straight and her back against a silver-gray post of the railing. Bluntly, she said, "Money. Sex. Murder. It's great for TV."

"But Judge Porter's supposed to run such a tight ship."

"The deal was cut over his objection. The network's going to pay two hundred thousand dollars into the court fund. The rest of the bench overruled Judge Porter's objection."

"So now what? Are they going to play Lockjaw tunes in the background? Have Finnish subtitles so they can call it an art film?"

"We've been assured, Laura, that this will not turn the trial into a travesty."

"Oh, yeah? By whom?" Duck's voice rose to a shout. "Nobody seems to even remember that Catherine Liem is the defendant. The press keeps running stories on her mother, her grandfather. The radio's playing Hella's songs like they were top-ten new releases. Elga's stupid book is getting snatched off the racks." Duck pitched her voice high and recited the opening lines with her hands clasped to her chest: " 'I knew Rudolf Liem was destined for greatness when I first met him; but I could not have guessed how far he would have to travel to fulfill that destiny, nor how much pain he would suffer along the way.' " Her arms dropped. "Give me a *break*."

"Court TV can't interfere with anything. All they can do is broadcast."

"Oh, yeah? The jury will know it's on national TV, too. Think about it, Mamoo. How many defendants have you seen convicted on Court TV? Juries can't do it. I bet Liem put up the two hundred thousand dollars for the broadcast." She stood and threw her shoe as hard as she could, out of sight over the railing. "She's gonna walk." One shoe on, one off, Duck stormed off the porch at a thudding limp.

32

20 NOVEMBER

*There are so many things I cannot remember. Arnie has
been asking, asking, asking about everything. And I remember so little. It isn't only dates, times, and sequences, although those are the worst. Whole events are also lost to
my recall. They come back only when Arnie confronts me
with what he already knows. "Oh," I tell him then, "now I
remember that." And he gives me one of those sidelong
looks and says, "That's why we're going through it now, so
you won't be stumbling and incredible in front of the jury."
"Thank you," I tell him tartly.*

*Part of the problem with my memory is that there are so
few external signposts to mark the passage of my relationship with Blake. No births, deaths (until the end), few outings, fewer trips. Almost all of our time was spent in my
bedroom, our talk as intimate and passionate as sex; we
were in the third year of our honeymoon when Evelyn burst
in on us by dying.*

*Another problem with my memory is that the details it
has stored most faithfully Arnie considers irrelevant.
"Evelyn told Blake that if he ever left her, she would—this
is verbatim—'expend all of my considerable resources in
turning your children against you.' "*

Arnie speaks slowly for me, and loudly, as if I just came

186

off the boat from Finland, "Unless we're trying to prove why you killed her, I can't use it."

Another problem with my memory is that I have shut the door on so many painful memories that I have closed myself into fairly cramped quarters from which I cannot escape.

I could recite for Arnie endless trivia from fillers in the Investigator to impress him with my steel-trap memory. "Did you know that Finland has the highest percentage of suicides per capita in the world?" I asked Arnie today.

"The point?" he asked back.

I could also tell Arnie everything about my favorite new program, "Love in the Afternoon," but I don't think he has any more interest in soap operas than in the evil and manipulative wiles of Evelyn Spencer or Finnish suicides. But parts of "Love in the Afternoon" positively resonate with my own story. It has converted me to daytime TV. With a box of bonbons and a glass of whiskey, television could be Nirvana. Elga will be so pleased to discover that I've found a new vocation, and less pleased, perhaps, that it is vagrancy.

What a rehabilitation this is.

33

A GLOWERING SKY lay over Thanksgiving morning, and a misting rain seemed to hang in the air rather than fall. Mamoo had risen early, built a fire, and gotten several cooking projects under way by the time the rest of the family rose. Duck was unwilling to leave the fragrant warmth of the house for a cold, wet walk. Surprisingly, Blake, Sr. chose this uninviting day for his initiation to the morning ritual, and set off in unsuspecting good cheer with his mother and his son for what he thought would be a stroll on the beach. Duck stayed behind to watch over the apple tarts in the oven and to stuff forty orange halves with brandied sweet potatoes. She was capping the last few with miniature marshmallows when the hikers returned, Blake, Sr. leaning heavily on his son's broad shoulders.

Duck joined them for stretches on the living-room floor. Blake, Sr. lay spreadeagled and unmoving.

"You'll feel better if you unwind a bit," Mamoo told her son.

"I barely have the strength left to breathe," he said, almost inaudibly.

"You didn't have to do the climbing on the first day," Mamoo chided.

"He did the dunes?" Duck asked in amazement.

"Yes," her father answered weakly. "It was carcinogenic."

"Whining is, but walking isn't," Mamoo grunted from a spectacular back bend.

"I couldn't let my septuagenarian mother leave me in the dust," Blake, Sr. whined.

"Unbridled male pride is carcinogenic, too," Mamoo said, twisting herself into a pretzel.

"Okay, Mamoo," Blake conceded, heaving himself up. "Well, I think I'll go have an ice-cold shower and slip into a loincloth for dinner."

They arrived at the Cristinas' a little after noon, fully dressed and heavily laden with food and wine. Maggie opened the door and greeted them with a little curtsy and an exaggerated bow of her head (her chin appeared to be cemented to her left collarbone). She was wearing mock-pilgrim's garb. A long-sleeved beige linen blouse was not buttoned but tied at the high-necked ruffled collar and at the flounced ruffles at the wrist. Over this Maggie wore a short-sleeved brown wool pinafore that fell to her ankles from a tucked yoke. A matching brown cloche was drawn down over Maggie's ears, and a pair of Mawmaw Celeste's black orthopedic shoes completed the look.

"Mamoo, you remember Maggie," Duck coached. Mamoo had met all of the Cristinas but had difficulty keeping them all straight. Duck had promised to help her and Blake, Sr. with the many names.

"If I didn't before, I certainly will now."

"It's Margaret," Maggie corrected, dipping another curtsy, her head still locked into place. "May I take one of those for you, ma'am?"

"Yes, thank you, Margaret." Mamoo handed over one of the apple tarts, still warm inside its rain-spattered plastic bag.

The front parlor was crowded with Cristinas and a number of displaced friends. Duck and Junior headed back to the kitchen, which was no less crowded than the parlor.

Betsy was besieged by offers of help as newcomers arrived and people swirled in and out of the other rooms. "It's all done. It's all done," she said repeatedly.

Joey appeared at Duck's side with a ginger ale for her. Not a brotherly gesture at all. And suddenly she felt tongue-tied.

She worked at wrapping the napkin more securely around the plastic cup. "Thanks," she said belatedly. It sounded to her like she'd said, "Aw shucks," with her toes turning in. *This is ridiculous,* she thought. *It's Joey.* "So," she cleared her throat, "what's the latest from the courthouse?"

Joey was wearing a blue shirt and khaki pants. He looked preppie out of uniform, and taller than the few inches he had on Duck. And those melancholy eyes, downturned at the corners . . . Before he could answer, she asked, "Do you mind me always hitting you up for news?"

He raised up on his toes. "Not at all. I think the courthouse gossip is terrific. I'm just sorry it's about your family."

"Yeah." She played with her napkin.

Joey ran his hand through his hair. "Cheltam's team is doing mock trials this week."

"What's the point of that?"

"They've got a jury psychologist. They've hired dozens of locals at a hundred dollars a day. They're running through the high points of the case to see how people react to it, and to get a profile of the sympathetic juror." Joey's hands were active, his eyes alight.

"How do you know all this?"

Joey squared his shoulders proudly. "It's a small town. They hired one of the deputies' sister."

Duck shook her head and began shredding her soggy napkin. "It doesn't seem fair to bring all this big-city technique to Mobile. What are the D.A.s doing to get ready? Watching the Macy's parade?"

Joey's smile dimpled his cheek. "Patsy Burdock's good, Duck. She already knows the locals; she doesn't have to pay people to tell her how they think."

"Why isn't the D.A. trying this case himself? Does Liem own him, too?"

"No, no, no." He waved both hands in her face, a time-out gesture. "Burdock's the first assistant, the brains behind Betkins. He assigns to her the cases he really wants to win. When Judge Porter steps down, Betkins plans to deliver her his seat on the Circuit Court."

"Cozy," Duck said, disgusted with the tangle of connections.

"It's good," Joey insisted. "The system's on your side."

"And what about the locals?" Duck asked. "How did the mock trial turn out?"

Joey's face dipped. "Well . . ."

"Shit!" Duck hissed.

Joey waved at her again, one-handed this time. "That doesn't count. Cheltam didn't have an opponent, Duck. It was a pep rally, that's all. Look, this is a family town. A law-enforcement town."

"Like when the D.A. was arrested for drunk driving and the arresting officer was fired for 'conduct unbecoming'?"

"That was politics," he said.

"And who's got more clout in this town than the Liems?" Duck shot back.

Joey took her arm, as if to steady her. "Murder's different, Duck. I really think it's going to be okay."

"I wish I did," she whispered.

Shaken, Duck went to help Maria lay the food out on the sideboard and on the card tables set up to accommodate the overflow. "What's with Maggie?" she asked, wanting to steer away from the trial.

"You mean modest Margaret?" Maria countered. "She thinks it's a joke, but Mom and Dad are eating it up."

"How long's she been like this?"

"She's been in the clothes since Sunday, when she finished making them. But the stiff neck just started this morning. It's okay, though, she lapses into normalcy when the grown-ups aren't around."

"How's she doing?" Duck asked.

"It's been rough. She felt physically sick for a while, and she didn't get the usual vegetable-soup-on-the-bed-tray routine. She's lost all her privileges. No driving. She gets ten minutes on the phone a day."

Duck groaned in sympathy, knowing what a hardship such a restriction would impose on the garrulous Maggie.

"She's grounded during the week and has an eight o'clock curfew on the weekends. They purged her closet. She's down to oxford-cloth shirts, pleated skirts, and cardigan sweaters. She's get to spend twenty hours a month at USA Medical Center working with babies hospitalized with AIDS—she chose that out of a half a dozen awful options Mom came up with. Maggie's kind of in shock from it all. But she's not fighting it, and both the restrictions and the mood around here are starting to lighten up.

"Anyway, that's enough about Maggie. How are you?"

"Mamoo's got me on a program that sounds pretty much like your parents', except that she didn't lay it down as law, it just worked out that way."

"I've missed you," Maria said, with a friendly bump against Duck's arm.

"You, too," Duck responded. "And I really need you. We're moving back to town tonight. The trial's starting next Thursday."

"I know. Listen, I've got some vacation time. You want me to take a few days off so I can stay by you?"

"Thanks, but no. Just talk to me every night, okay?"

"Sure. I'll even listen if you ever decide to talk to me again." Maria said it lightly, but Duck felt stung by the slight rebuke. It was a physical sensation, like a nettle lodged under her collar. It drew her eyes down, and bent her head. She had a sudden insight into the crick in Maggie's neck, and realized that she was one of the nettles under Maggie's flounced collar. On her next trip from the kitchen, she deposited a ten-pound green bean and almond casserole on the table and went in search of Maggie. She found her in the parlor, silently passing a bowl of roasted nuts among the throng of guests. Duck took the bowl from her, tucked her own chin against her chest, and asked, "Like this?" Maggie smiled a beautiful smile without raising her head. They linked arms and held the dish together with their free outer hands.

As they worked their way through the crowd, hands reached out of lively conversations and groped for the nuts, spilling a few onto the threadbare Aubusson rug. Duane dove for these as though he were the half-starved family dog. He was bare-chested, had two parallel slashes of lipstick across each cheek, and wore a red paper band around his head, from which three pigeon feathers waggled at the back.

Blake, Sr. gestured at Maggie and Duane with his Bloody Mary glass and said to Mamoo, "I didn't know it was going to be a costume party or I would've worn my breechcloth after all."

Betsy announced that dinner was ready, a cheer went up, and a funnel-shaped line formed quickly around the buffet. It was an orderly mob, but for Duane, who whacked at Betsy's kidneys with his rubber tomahawk, screaming, "I hate you, I hate you!"

Betsy swept him up in a restraining bear hug and asserted to him, "That's too bad, because I love you. I'll always love you, Duane." By way of explanation, she told

Mamoo, "He's going home next week. It's a pretty confusing time for the little guy."

It took about twenty minutes for the diners to fill their plates and settle down. Vincent looked out over the assembly proudly. The dining-room table, which he had built in the shape of a giant capital I, spanned the two back parlors and comfortably seated forty. Today it was almost full.

Vincent delivered the blessing. "Thank you, Lord, for your bounteous gifts over the past year. Thank you for our wonderful family and our fine friends, and for our togetherness on this day of Thanks. Today we remember those who were parted from our company; we ask that you embrace them at your heavenly table and give us the strength and wisdom to embrace your holy plan that bestows such sorrows upon us along with your many blessings. In the name of the Father and of the Son and of the Holy Spirit. Amen."

"Amen," the table chorused, some choking on their feelings. Duck had looked up at Vincent when he remembered Mother and Alexandra. To her surprise, she found his gaze fixed on Maggie, whose somber mien registered the reference to Vincent's first and lost grandchild. Mrs. Spears, a recently widowed neighbor of the Cristinas, signaled with ferociously clasped hands that for her the reference was to her departed Bennie. Duck was seized with sorrow for Alexandra, who would have been, or perhaps was, sorely aggrieved at this dilution of the sadness meant for her.

Vincent had hardly sat down before Betsy clinked her glass with a knife for attention and prodded her husband to rise again. He needed no further prompting. "I am proud to announce what you will all read in the paper on Sunday. The winner of the ten-thousand-dollar Liem Foundation prize—Joseph Anthony Cristina!" The table erupted with whistles and applause.

"Now you can buy a Super Nintendo," Simon suggested.

"I'm 'Bama bound," Joey declared. "I'm turning in my sheriff's badge and gettin' outa Dodge. I'll be enrolling full-time in January."

"How'dja do it?" Vinnie wanted to know.

"I kind of pandered to Catherine Liem's situational interests. I wrote about the development of Finland's criminal justice system. It wasn't too hard. The main library has the largest collection of Finnish materials outside Finland. I really got into it."

"I don't know how you found the time between work and night school," Mawmaw said proudly.

"He's in pre-law," Betsy announced to the table.

"And now I may be able to get my J.D. degree in less than the ten years I was looking at," Joey said, poised between pride and embarrassment. He stole a look at Duck. She caught his glance and tried to give him a sisterly smile, but felt the heat in her ears that told her she was blushing. Modest Margaret caught their silent exchange and kneed Duck immodestly under the table. Duck kneed her back and averted her gaze. Her eyes landed on her father, who was also glowing. It struck Duck that he was pleased about the uncritical mention of Catherine Liem and about her part in Joey's good fortune. Anger welled up inside of her at the thought that the condemnation this woman so richly deserved could be so cheaply diverted. And with the anger came a darker sentiment. This was too much of a coincidence. Suppose her father and his lover had plotted this conversion of the Cristinas together? Did her father already know about the $10,000 award when he finagled the invitation to Thanksgiving dinner? If Liem had influenced Court TV's decision to broadcast the trial, had her father conspired in that action, too? Once you start telling lies, he had told Duck when she was young, people don't know what to believe anymore. *Well, he's told some whoppers, and he's earned my mistrust. And if Catherine's going to get off, I'm going back to hating him.*

"He did it for you, you know," Maria whispered from her right.

"What?" Duck hissed back, questioning how her father could have believed his schemes would benefit her.

"Joey was determined to win that prize. He didn't say so, but I know he wanted to impress you. And his paper was really terrific. You ought to read it. He's going to make a great lawyer."

"Sure. I'd love to read it," Duck answered out of politeness. Her thoughts churned. Had Joey been used or had he won on his own merits? And how had she gotten involved? Confusion and bile intermingled to produce a fierce, appetite-killing headache.

Maggie threw off her Puritan traces and hollered across the din of a dozen conversations, "Joey! Duck wants to read your paper!"

"Do you really? It's awfully dry." Joey smiled sheepishly.

"I'd love to," Duck felt forced to answer, thinking, *I'll be home with my gun tonight.*

"I'd like to read it, too," Mamoo said.

"Me too," Blake, Sr. added.

"It's going to be printed in the paper on Sunday," Vincent told them. "I hope Judge Porter reads it. Justice à la Porter does not compare too well with the Finnish system."

How convenient, Duck thought, *right before the trial begins. Maybe they'll offer $10,000 awards to the best jurors on her case.* She resolved to do her part to see that justice was done, American-style, before she offed herself.

Duane's tomahawk flew across the length of the table, turning end over end, and bounced dully off Blake, Sr.'s chest. "I hate you!" the boy cried.

You tell him, Duck applauded inwardly, as Betsy dragged the wild Indian screaming from the table.

34

I believe it was an act of genuine charity that assembled 231 turkey dinners with cornbread dressing, petits pois peas, and canned candied yams. Yet the cruelty it worked on all of us was pathetic to see. If we had had chicken and string beans, we could have complained about the food. To have the traditional meal was to be fed awareness of all that the holiday really means and all that we lack. A woman who can bench-press 250 pounds pushed aside her tray and wept for her family. She said over and over again, "My ole man can't cook for shit! I know they misses me now." Once it began, there was no stopping it. So many trays were sent back to the kitchen that I suggested to one of the trustees that they deliver them to the Daughters of the Coastal Settlers with compliments from the Prison Ladies' Auxiliary.

I tried to see Mr. Dalton. I was informed that he was not the prison chaplain. There is no prison chaplain. We have rotating ministers so that no faith is slighted or denied the opportunities that abound in this den of misery.

I also tried to get Angelle to a doctor. She has been rubbing herself up and down against the wall. It is a vaguely masturbatory gesture, except that she does it with her shoulder. She has terrible lesions on both sides. I pointed

197

this out to Mrs. Stuckey, whom I mistook for humane be-cause I had never seen her strike or shove anyone. "She prob'ly just needs a nice sauna," she said, and hissed at me through bad teeth.

It is almost impossible to read or write or think in the presence of that small rubbing sound, no louder than breathing. From across the room, I smell the spreading bloodstains on the wall.

35

BAHALIA MADE Thanksgiving dinner over again on Friday. "What's the point of Thanksgivin' if you ain't got any leftovers?" She was mashing sweet potatoes like a jackhammer.

"Here, let me do that," Duck offered.

She and Junior had risen like clockwork for the morning walk and arrived in the kitchen in their jogging suits at 6:30 a.m.

To Duck's surprise, there was a fair amount of activity on the streets. They first encountered Mrs. Burke, who was walking Fluffy. Fluffy was a white toy poodle who only lived up to her name during the winter. Beginning in May, she was tormented by a flea allergy that caused her to chew away all the hair on her back end, which had the gray, rippled hide of an elephant. At about the time the bright green rye grass sprouted on lawns across the neighborhood, Fluffy sprouted too. Today her bare patches were bristling with new white growth. "She looks beautiful," Duck lied.

"I wish this cold weather were the tonic for my scalp, too," Mrs. Burke said in her high, thin voice, patting a bald spot on the crown of her head.

"It's so shiny," Junior remarked.

"Yes, it is, and my sister fusses at me so for not wearing a wig," Mrs. Burke confided. "We're such a pair. All she thinks about is appearances, and I scarcely give a care.

Except, of course, in the garden. I couldn't find you last week, Junior, and I came over and deadheaded all your mother's roses. You should have one last set of blooms if this beautiful English weather holds. The roses love it, you know."

"We were at Mamoo's," Junior informed her.

"Oh, how nice," Mrs. Burke piped. "I love your grandmother, you know, and I never see her. I just don't understand it. Did you children know that I taught your grandmother a half a century ago? She was a wonderful student, a wonderful student."

Duck nodded and backed away, fearing that Mrs. Burke might drift into the historic marker at Iberville Point.

"Tell your grandmother I'd love to see her," Mrs. Burke called.

"I will," Duck promised.

They weaved through winding lanes all the way to the top of the hill. En route, Duck tried to confront her fears about testifying next week. She used a reliable crutch. *What would Alexandra do in this circumstance?* The answer came to her at once. Alexandra would hold a moot court, just as the defense was doing. She would impress friends into service as judge and jury. The captains of the debate teams would play the parts of prosecutor and defense counsel. They would script out and rehearse it. It would be a great time for all.

Duck had to throw the crutch away, as usual. It was too tall for her. "Junior," she said, "ask me my name."

"Your name is Duck," he said.

"I know, I know, but it's a game. Ask me."

"Ask me my name."

"Laura Davidson Spencer," she began. Then she adjusted her voice and said more loudly and firmly, "Laura Davidson Spencer."

"Is it?" Junior asked.

"Yes."

"*That's* why Dad calls you Laura," he exclaimed.

"Yes. Say, 'Where do you live?'"

"Where do you live?" Junior asked with real interest.

Duck gave their address in her firm, self-assured voice.

"I knew that," Junior said proudly.

There it stopped. Duck could not tell Junior to ask her what happened on the afternoon of May 7, nor could she clomp along the sidewalk under the ancient oaks describing the bloody scene she had discovered. But she would remember it. And she was resolved to tell it when the time came. Later.

By the time they made it back to the house, Blake, Sr. had left for work and Bahalia was elbow-deep in after-Thanksgiving dinner.

Joining in to mash the sweet potatoes, Duck wrinkled her nose and asked, "Does anyone like these things or are they just sentimental, like that revolting candy corn they put out for Halloween?"

"I *love* candy corn," Junior said.

"There you go," Bahalia mumbled at Duck.

"I *hate* sweet potatoes," Junior added.

"There you go," Duck tossed back at Bahalia.

"You know," Bahalia responded, "I was reading about all of them refugee camps over in Somalia." Duck was braced for the children-in-Africa-are-starving lecture, but it did not follow. "When they first gets there, they's so happy to have something to eat, they don't even notice it's mush. They say it's a real good sign when those poor people start complainin' about the food. So I guess I'd rather hear your jawin' than see you pourin' food down your gullet without even tastin' it."

"Thanks, Bahalia, I guess," Duck replied.

"Nobody's askin' me what I think, so I won't say how much better you and my boy look after a few weeks with your grammaw. The main thing is gettin' outa this big ol'

empty house. This here never was your daddy's house anyway." A dozen puff pastries were stuffed and rolled during
this tirade. Duck's potatoes were still littered with lumps. In
fact, lumps seemed to be congealing while she mashed. Her
biceps ached and she was developing stronger and stronger
resentments against the sticky orange glob. It was the color
of the velveteen chairs Mother had had custom-made for
the den, to accentuate the warm tones of the Spanish cedar
paneling. Like everything else in the house, Mother had
chosen them without Blake, Sr.'s input.

The family had moved to Old Spring Hill twelve years
ago, from a country house Duck only hazily recalled. She remembered open spaces filled with light, and a meadow that
swept down to a perfectly round brown pond, like a giant
Reese's peanut butter cup singing with frogs. She remembered very well the day that Alexandra had been bitten by the
cottonmouth. It was a smallish gray-brown snake, about the
circumference of Mother's middle finger. It probably would
have shot into the tall grass as the girls pounded toward it,
but it had just swallowed a pocketwatch-sized frog that still
wriggled inside it. The weighted snake most certainly would
not have had the leverage to strike at Alexandra, except that
Alexandra, mistaking it for a stick, had stepped right on it
and then frozen at the soft writhing feel of it underneath.

The snake must have expended all its venom on the frog.
Alexandra's foot never even swelled. The two tiny fang
marks looked like the prick of a staple. Duck remembered
the race up to the house, Mother's blanched face as they
told her the exciting news, and the tire-squealing dash to
the hospital, Mother flapping her white handkerchief out of
the driver's window. In the last few miles they picked up a
police escort that muscled traffic out of their way with
flashing lights and sirens. Alexandra was having the time of
her life. She never showed the slightest distress until the
doctor gave her a shot.

At home that evening, her foot elevated on a plump satin pillow like a diamond on display, Alexandra extended her arms wide and told her father, "It was *this* big," overshooting Duck's recollection by about three feet.

"She could have been killed," Mother added. "And even with a police escort, it took us thirty minutes to get to the hospital. I'm not risking my children's lives for one more day in this house."

She didn't. She found them an apartment the next morning and had their beds and a few other essentials moved into it by evening. And so they vacated the award-winning house that Blake, Sr. had designed and Mother hated. The next house was all hers, at least in terms of design. She selected it (after the Cristinas spurned her offer for Constantopoulis Mansion), decorated it, and furnished it; and Blake, Sr. paid the bills without any complaint that Duck could recall. (Mother invaded her nest egg only for frivolous items, not for the basic elements of support to which she felt entitled by marriage.) She did all the decorating beautifully; the house was periodically featured in magazines and occasionally put on tour. Duck had enjoyed her friends' admiring reactions to their elegant home. But she thought now how odd it was that her talented mother had contributed nothing to their first house and her talented father had contributed nothing to the second.

Her reverie on the significance of her parents' separation of tastes was interrupted by a startling pounding on the back door. Bahalia's hands were encrusted with dough and she rushed to the sink to wash them, calling over her shoulder in alarm, "Don't open that, kids."

Her warning came too late; Junior had already thrown open the door. A strapping young black man, wearing a wide toothy smile, walked in. "Heyyy, Momma."

Duck had trouble placing him at first. She thought with a shudder that this might be the unaccounted-for bad seed of Bahalia's family; but as he stood on the threshold bouncing on the balls of his feet, Duck recognized him as Charles, the eldest son. He had thrown her off by shaving his Rastafarian mop of hair. His scalp was glossy as an eggplant up to a three-inch-high lozenge of hair perched at the top. It was the only part of his body that did not jitter.

Bahalia had abandoned her washing up, and she faced him with arms extended, dripping, gluey palms up, pushing on the air in front of her as though it were Charles. "Boy, I told you *never* to come to this house!"

Charles's smile widened. "Guess what B.J. told me, Momma? He said Daddy hired him on a big job. Daddy's got him a big, big job for Miss-tah Spensah." Charles pushed his face forward at this last and shook it rapidly. The smile looked menacing now.

"You get on outa here or I'm gonna call the police, Charles. You know I will," Bahalia said firmly.

"Now why you gonna call the police on your own flesh and blood when Daddy's passin' out money to everybody else? *I need some money, Momma.*" His empty outstretched hands jangled his missing coins and his entire body kept time.

"We would give ev'ry las' dime to put you in that treatment place. But not one more cent goes up your nose or in your veins, boy."

"It's not for *that*, Momma," Charles wheedled, smiling again. "I got an opportunity. I need me a new suit, Momma, so's I can look presentable. Hundred dollars is all." He mock-hooked his thumbs behind his nonexistent lapels and rolled back on his heels, bouncing.

Bahalia's eyes blazed at him. She picked up a dishtowel and began wiping her hands. "No."

Charles exploded. "Fuck you! Fuck you! Fuck you! You don't want me to succeed!" he screamed, advancing across the floor jabbing at his mother with his finger. "You want me to be a good lil' nigger like you and Daddy!" He bent his head so that he was screaming into her face. Duck could see flecks of his spittle glistening on her cheeks and forehead. Junior had cowered against the wall since Charles walked in. Now he stood, arms splayed, palms pressed backward like a mounted insect. Duck sat frozen, wondering whether she should dial 911.

Bahalia, lips pursed in fury, swatted at Charles's face, chest, and arms with her dishtowel. Next to her son, she was a tiny mosquito of a woman, yet she backed him all the way to the door with her flailing rag. When his shoulder touched the doorjamb, he stopped shielding himself from her blows; the smile returned and he stood almost still, taking it.

"You are one *bad* mothah!" Charles beamed at his mother, bouncing on his toes again. The bouncing shook loose a deep chuckle. Then his hands shot out and he seized her by the throat. He lifted her up easily by the neck and as her fingers worked frantically and helplessly against his, he said into her purpling face, "A hundred dollars, Momma. Can't you give your boy one . . . hundred . . . dollars." His fingers squeezed, almost gently. Duck had leapt up, overturning her chair, and was on the phone now waiting for 911 to answer. The rings were drawn out into individual blips, and went on and on. She should be attacking Charles, she knew. She, Junior, and Bahalia together could probably overpower him. Bahalia would be dead before the emergency line answered. But she was terrified even to be in the same room with him; she felt the brittleness of her bones. It took all of her strength to hold onto the phone.

Then Charles set Bahalia down and laid his fluttering hands on her shoulders. "Please, Momma. Give your baby boy a hundred dollars," he cajoled.

Bahalia planted her hands in his chest and shoved him backward out of the door. "You do not *exist*!" she rasped.

Charles fell down the two shallow steps and sat on the patio chuckling up at his mother. "Oh yes I do, Momma. Yes I do."

It was Duck who ended the conversation by slamming and bolting the door. Moments later, while Duck was still embracing Bahalia, the police arrived. The 911 operator had dispatched them immediately to the computer-registered address when there was no answer on the line. Calls from Old Spring Hill were processed like lightning. The officers had already stopped Charles, who bolted when their patrol car wheeled around the corner. Bahalia pressed assault charges. She and Duck both gave statements.

Junior was back in the closet and could not be forced or coaxed out. They called Blake, Sr., who got Dr. Goldberg to come to the house and give the child a sedative. Even then, Junior remained wedged in the corner until a second sedative knocked him out.

Charlie Deed came over to check on his wife. He sat at the kitchen table with her, patting the back of her hand while they spoke in low voices. Bahalia refused to go home, though. "I got a dinner to put on here," she cried. Blake, Sr. could not prevail upon her to put it aside, but he did succeed in inviting Charlie and Dumplin', whose name turned out to be Louis, to share their repast. Blake and Charlie talked about the beach project. Duck, Bahalia, and Louis were quiet as rocks, except that every so often Bahalia reached over to stroke her son's cheek and tell him, "Don' you never touch any drugs," to which he solemnly murmured that he would not. Duck did not doubt it. The boy exchanged a few shy smiles with her across the table; he had soft eyes and a sweet smile completely unlike his brother's.

Two more days until the trial. The Liem trial, that is. Then, Duck noted, we'll have the Charles Deed trial. The cases are piling up faster than the courts can process them.

36

It's here. As long as I have waited, filled with impatience, I am suddenly not quite ready. It's that feeling right before a piano recital or an opening, magnified 1,000 times. Perhaps brides feel this way on their wedding days, if they are sensible enough to know what they are undertaking. More likely, their parents feel this way and the brides don't, or there would be many fewer weddings.

Although I have been yearning for the trial, now that I am upon it I realize it is not the trial I have wanted at all. I want to skip straight to that magical moment when the judge says, "The envelope, please," and opens it to announce that I have won the Oscar—a trip home.

There is a long, long way to go between now and then. I do not think the state's case will hold any surprises. We are all more worried about how I will do. I am often uncomfortable talking to just one other person. I am usually uncomfortable talking to two—so many subtle currents to follow. How will I be in this crowd scene from Coriolanus?

37

THEY SPENT the first two days selecting a jury, broke for the weekend, and went into a third day empaneling the jury. The possibility of capital punishment lengthened the voir dire, as each juror was questioned about his feelings on the death penalty, and his ability to impose it if the facts warranted.

Mamoo arrived at the Spencer house before dawn on the third day, even though they had been assured that Duck would not be called until late in the afternoon, if at all that day. They all went for the walk, including Blake, Sr., who was staying home against Duck's wishes that he disappear into the woodwork of his office. Even for a workaholic like him, she allowed, this might be a difficult time to work. Neither she nor her father would be allowed into the courtroom until it was time for their testimony. They were "sequestered," or hidden from the proceedings, to avoid any contamination of their testimony by the other witnesses. The assistant district attorney, Patricia Burdock, had told them they were not to discuss the case between themselves once the trial began. "Don't worry," Duck had promised. *We don't talk about anything.*

The rule of sequestration had rescued Blake, Sr. from a certain dilemma. On whose side would he sit: that of the prosecution or of the defense? In their final interview with

Ms. Burdock on Sunday, she had asked Blake, Sr., "Whose side are you on?"

"I'm on the side of the truth," he equivocated. "I'm going to answer both sides' questions as truthfully as I can."

"You may find," Ms. Burdock lectured, "that it's not so simple. It's not only what you say, but how you say it. Unless you're certain that Ms. Liem is innocent—against all the evidence—you might want to think hard about conveying to the jury your trust in her. For your daughter's sake, if not your wife's." She stared him down hard. Duck realized that Ms. Burdock had deliberately provoked this confrontation in her presence. Had she said "your daughter's sake" or "your daughters' sake"? It may have been purposely ambiguous. Ms. Burdock was a few years younger than Blake, Sr., Duck guessed. She had a distinctively southern look that was framed by her distinctively southern hair: just-below-the-shoulder length, blond, highlighted, layered and curled, with a swept-back fringe of bangs. It was the look Betsy Cristina tried for and seldom achieved. It was a soft pretty look, with big blue eyes to match; but when those eyes penetrated and held, you could see that this was not a soft woman.

It was evident that Ms. Burdock did not like Blake, Sr., and that she was wrestling with the question of how to handle him. He was an important witness for the prosecution because he would establish the extramarital affair between himself and Catherine Liem, which developed both the motive for the murder and the deceitful nature of the defendant. He would testify that he usually spent Thursday afternoons with Ms. Liem, but had not done so on the day of the killings because Evelyn had scheduled a 4:30 appointment at his office to review the Spencers' tax records. Blake would say that he knew Evelyn was at home at 3:00 getting ready, and, through him, so did Catherine. All of this was critical to the state's case. On the other hand,

Blake, Sr.'s irrepressible sympathy and concern for his lover made him a mixed bag for the prosecution. Ms. Burdock had not decided exactly when she would call him. Duck was still definitely first.

Ms. Burdock had picked the clothes Duck would wear to court: a navy blue skirt, a softer blue blouse, and a gray blazer, with black flats, not heels. As Ms. Burdock explained her choices of color (for understated bereavement) and style (for youth but with maturity), Duck considered the many levels of manipulation at work here. She felt more frightened than ever, which she thought was probably the reaction Ms. Burdock had manipulated.

The morning passed with excruciating slowness, despite Mamoo's and Bahalia's best chattering efforts to draw them into mindless activities. Mamoo started Junior on hand-building with clay at the kitchen table. Duck pulled up a chair and watched. Occasionally overcome by the anxiety of waiting, she made stabbing, jabbing, mashing attacks on a stray mound of clay. Junior began by forming little houses with bulging walls and sagging eaves. His crabbed style and imperfect creations were a source of tension and frustration to him, and his tongue prodded his lips as energetically as his mudcaked fingers prodded the clay.

Mamoo sat down beside him, humming, and rolled out a few coils, sliced a few thick slabs with a wire, and twisted some irregular hunks off the twenty-pound block at the center of the table. Within minutes she assembled these elements into a fanciful, dancing sculpture. Then she smoothed some of its surfaces with a sponge and mottled others with a wooden tool.

Before the children could stop her, Mamoo laid the heels of her palms on the uppermost plane of her beautiful creature and slowly squashed it.

Junior balled up his fist and joyfully pounded his shantytown flat. Mamoo gathered up the pancakes, laid them overlapping one another, and with only a few additions crafted an armadillo. Junior threw himself across it protectively. "Please can I keep it?" he implored.

"You can, but it's so thick it's going to crack apart as it dries. You sure you want to watch that happen?"

Junior raised his fist and, hesitating only briefly, pummeled the armadillo formless.

Duck punched at it with him. "I can't stand it!" she cried.

"It wasn't very good," Junior agreed.

"Not your work, Junior. The waiting."

At 2:00 the call finally came: twelve jurors and two alternates had been chosen and the trial was in a brief recess. After that they would have the attorneys' opening statements, followed by Duck's testimony. They wanted her there for 3:00; but they expected she would take the stand at 4:00. Joey had warned her that Judge Porter was at his worst in the afternoon, by which time he needed his whiskey badly. As the afternoon wore on, he would be irascible at best, and if he had started drinking at lunch, he could be uncontrollably abusive. Joey said that the judge's temper was more likely to be unleashed on the attorneys than on witnesses, but that she should be very careful not to appear disrespectful.

"I'll be crying, remember?" Duck said.

"Good strategy," Joey told her. "Anyway, watch out for the judge's nose. The worse off he is, the redder it gets. If the red spreads into his cheeks, just put your head down and cover it with your hands."

"This is really reassuring," Duck told him.

"Well, I've only got a month to go in the Sheriff's Department. If he treats you too badly, I'll just shoot him." Joey patted the gunbelt that draped his slender hips.

Duck cringed. "No, please. Then I'd have to be a witness again. And who would kill the judge for me then?"

Mamoo accompanied Duck to court. Blake, Sr. stayed home, knowing that he would only serve as a magnet for reporters. Duck got in easily. Joey met them in the parking lot with a few of his buddies, who, it seemed to her, studied her more carefully than circumstances warranted. And she made a sidelong study of them, too. Joey, she noticed, was the only member of his group who had not affected a short, wispy moustache. And his brown hair curled slightly over his collar, while the others looked like they had shaved their necks that morning. He didn't swagger to make his presence felt, but he still exuded strength and confidence. Joey's hand, held lightly under Duck's elbow, made him a somewhat proprietary escort. But she knew he was acting out of protective concern for her and she trusted him to steer her safely to the courtroom. Also, she had to admit, he looked dashing in his beige and brown uniform, which complemented his dark hair and eyes. There was something about knowing that this was not a permanent position for Joey that made the easy grace with which he wore his gun all the more attractive. Duck was ashamed of herself. Joey was the same person today that he had been before he won the Liem prize and declared his intention to go to law school. She hoped that the loss of Rick and her new awareness of Joey's interest in her had played the bigger part in her looking at him differently. There was no time for these thoughts.

Joey called over his shoulder as they trotted up the stairs to the second floor, "They've moved the trial to Courtroom Number One. It's the biggest they've got."

The stairs let them out at the heavy wooden doorway of the courtroom. The halls were empty, the reporters having piled inside to hear the opening statements.

Joey led Duck around the corner to the makeshift witness room, actually a tiny anteroom of the sheriff's offices. Until this trial, witnesses had been sequestered in the hallways, but the press siege had necessitated more protective arrangements for witnesses in the Liem trial. Joey and Mamoo crowded with Duck into the tiny room, where one other witness waited, a policeman who had photographed the crime scene. After an hour of looking at the bare paneled walls under the glare of naked fluorescent rods in the ceiling, Duck was almost ready to go. Almost.

When she was called, Joey and Mamoo walked her to the side doors of the courtroom. Before pushing them open, Joey combed his fingers through his hair and said, "There's a big crowd in there. Just don't look at 'em."

When he opened the door for her, Duck immediately forgot his advice and surveyed the room. It was huge, packed like a high-school assembly, but infinitely more still and solemn. People were lined up against the walls. To her horror, all eyes were fixed on her. As she crossed the room, she skirted a Court TV camera and felt it swivel to follow her. "Take a seat over here, Ms. Spencer." The gruff voice came through speakers all around the courtroom. It was the audio equivalent of a house of mirrors. She did not know who had spoken, or from where. "Over *here*," the enveloping voice repeated, with a sharper edge of impatience. A member of the courtroom staff directed her to the witness chair, which she reached shakily. It was tall, square, and straight-backed, her image of the electric chair.

"Administer the oath," commanded the gruff voice, hurrying things along. She looked up and saw that it was Judge Porter speaking. His bulbous, dark-veined nose was definitely rubicund, but it had not reached the danger level on Joey's color chart.

"Ms. Spencer, would you state your name and address for the record?" asked Ms. Burdock.

"Laura Davidson Spencer," Duck whispered.

Gently, Ms. Burdock suggested, "Could you pull that microphone in a little bit and repeat that?"

Duck swiveled the microphone closer to her mouth, and

made the mistake of looking up. Catherine Liem was sitting directly in her line of vision. The defendant was erect and attentive; her gaze seemed benevolent. Duck averted her eyes, and looked straight into the searching black lens of the television camera. A second camera, she saw, was focused on Liem.

When Duck spoke again, the microphone whistled and screamed on its own, an amplified sound of fingernails on chalkboard. Everyone in the courtroom clapped his hands over his ears.

"Push the mike back and speak up," the judge ordered.

Duck got through her name, address, and family relationships with cheeks and ears much redder than Judge Porter's nose.

"Where were you at about three o'clock on the afternoon of May seventh, this year?" Ms. Burdock asked softly.

"I was at the dressmaker's. My graduation from high school was three weeks away. I went to pick up my dress."

"Where were your mother, sister, and brother?"

"They were at home. Alexandra was supposed to go with me, but she came down with a sore throat and went to bed."

"How old was Alexandra?"

"Fifteen. She would have been sixteen now. The first day of trial was her birthday—would have been," Duck's voice quavered.

Ms. Burdock's eyebrow lifted. This was news to her, as was Duck's ability to speak. "Were you close to your sister, Laura?"

Ms. Liem's attorney rose to make an objection on grounds of relevancy, which the judge understood and sustained, but the rustling jury obviously did not. *As Ms. Burdock intended,* Duck thought.

"About what time did you get home?" Ms. Burdock continued with no loss of composure.

"Around three, I think."

"How did you enter the house?"

"Through the front door, with my key," Duck answered, her voice growing weak. She thought, *It's almost over*. Joey had told her, "When you start to cry, don't fight it; just lower your head and cry. They'll offer you some water and send you home."

"What did you see when you opened the door?"

Duck took a deep breath. *Please let me do this for Mother and Alexandra,* she prayed to no one in particular. She fixed her eyes on the wooden railing in front of her. It had a dark, tight grain, and she felt that if she held onto the concrete sharpness of it, she would not faint. She took another deep breath, in through the nose, and the tiniest particle of scent reached her.

It came from one of the jurors, Roselle Lupon, seated in the box to Duck's right. Mrs. Lupon was a wealthy woman, widowed the year before. That morning she had dressed carefully for the trial, believing that she would be selected to serve on this case, where, on her first meaningful outing in months, she would have a significant part to play. Before leaving her house, she drew a single drop of perfume across the fine webbing of wrinkles beneath each ear. It was an expensive perfume, complex and delicate, like the role she envisioned for herself. The scent was extracted from crushed blossoms that grew only in Madagascar, where the perfumiers know something of subtle and far-reaching aromas. It reached out to Duck when she took her deep calming breath, and the memories unfurled in her mind like a hideous flower. Duck shivered against the smells that had assaulted her when she opened the front door.

"I know this is terribly hard. Would you like a glass of water?" Ms. Burdock asked, waiting for Duck's tears.

"No, thank you ... I want to get this over. The first thing wasn't a sight; it was a smell. Mother raised orchids. All spring she kept one with open, fragrant blooms on the table in the foyer ..." Duck pictured the broad-petaled phalaenopsis orchids that floated like stingrays in the gloom of the hallway. Ms. Burdock had never heard this, and had not expected any extended testimony from Duck; but it was the humanizing touch she wanted. It was disarmingly natural, and she let the narrative take its own course.

Duck's voice gained strength as she spoke. "Coming in from the bright sunshine, my eyes didn't adjust to the dim light right away. I smelled the orchid scent, but it was all wrong. I thought my mother had made a mistake and picked some carnivorous plant with a rancid smell to attract flies." Something in Duck's voice conveyed the dread that had overpowered her before her brain unscrambled the message. Her tears were flowing freely now but she pressed on. "It was blood, so much blood ... my mother's was spread all across the marble floor, and Alexandra's was dripping down the stairs. Mother's back was opened up ..." She did not relate the gruesome details: the raw-meat look of the exit wound, with the sheen of white gristle exposed in her purpling flesh.

"What did you do?" Ms. Burdock prompted.

"I stood looking at them for the longest time. I was holding my long white formal up high out of the blood." *You were thinking,* Duck remembered with self-loathing, *that this meant you wouldn't get to go to the graduation dance with Rick. And you didn't want to get it dirty, just in case.* "Finally, my arm went numb and I had to move. I circled all the way around the house so I wouldn't step in their blood, and I came back to the phone in the hall. And when I started dialing I thought, 'The killer could still be in the house.' I began shaking so badly I couldn't dial and I kept dropping the receiver."

"Who were you trying to call?" Ms. Burdock asked.

"I called my father's office, and as soon as the secretary answered, I started screaming 'Daddy, Daddy, Daddy' into the phone. Even after he got on the line, that was all I could say; even after he told me he was coming and the police were coming, I couldn't let go of the phone. My father's secretary stayed on with me, and I kept on crying 'Daddy.' "

A new thought welled up with Duck's tears, and she spoke it softly, reflectively, to the railing. "It was as if I knew it would be the last day I could call him by that name."

With a hint of triumph in her voice, Ms. Burdock declared, "No further questions. Laura, do you need a minute, or can you answer Mr. Cheltam's questions now?"

"I'd like to finish, please."

The defense attorney rose and stood before her. He clasped his hands behind his back, drawing open the lapels of his expensive-looking navy blue suit. "Ms. Spencer, I have only a few questions," Arnold Cheltam assured her in a twangy, nasal tone. "You did not see anyone leave the house as you were arriving home, did you?"

"No."

"And you did not see anyone else in the house when you discovered your mother and sister, did you?"

"No."

"But there was someone else in the house, wasn't there?"

"Yes," she answered warily.

"Who was that?"

"My brother, Blake."

"And where was Blake?"

"In the closet."

"In the closet right off the hall where you found the bodies, right?"

"Yes."

"Your brother Blake is handicapped, isn't he?"

"Yes." She was angry now, but kept her tone straightforward. "He has Down Syndrome."

"For the benefit of the jury, Ms. Spencer, that means he's retarded, doesn't it?"

"Yes, but it doesn't mean he's a killer," she said with an edge to her voice.

"Ms. Spencer," Mr. Cheltam asked reasonably, "you were not at home when your mother and sister were shot, were you?"

"No."

"You didn't see who pulled the trigger, did you?"

"No, but I still know it wasn't Junior because I know Junior."

"Did you ever know Blake to spend any time in the closet before May seventh?"

"No."

"But he does now, doesn't he?"

"Yes."

"He spends a good bit of his time in the closet now, doesn't he?"

"Yes."

"Thank you, Ms. Spencer. I have nothing further."

Duck looked to Ms. Burdock for the question that would let her explain. *He's a sweetheart*, she wanted to shout. *He's a sweetheart who gives all his effort to being nice to people.*

"Nothing further," Ms. Burdock said.

Then Joey and Mamoo flanked Duck and walked her to the hallway, where they were surrounded by the phalanx of deputies Joey had promised. Beyond their perimeter a horde of reporters flashed cameras, fished at her with microphones on long poles, and shouted over one another, "Did you know then your father was having an affair with Catherine Liem?" "Do you think she did it?" "Is your brother still refusing to talk?"

38

My darling Blake,

When I saw you last summer, it was so easy to agree that we would not talk or write until after the trial. Looking in your eyes, I could not doubt the constancy of your feeling for me, and a few months seemed a short test of our great love.

But these months have been so long, Blake. I miss you every moment of every day; my distractions are few. I cannot imagine how your life has been. Worse, I cannot capture the memory of the light in your eyes when we parted.

Listening to Laura testify today was much more painful than I was prepared for. I was filled with anger toward whoever had done this to your family; and I saw that some of the jurors were directing such anger toward me. It was deeply unsettling.

You are the fairest judge of people I have ever known, and certainly the kindest judge of me. Yet, you were not there. You cannot *know* that I am innocent; you can only *believe* . . . As I believed from all you had told me that Junior was innocent. Yet I find myself thinking, he doesn't *know*, it *could* have been Junior. And I have another thought, a new and worse one, which I will not

share with Arnie the Exhibitionist unless you find sub-
stantiation for it. Consider, Blake, how the Winter War
began; and contact Arnie if you think that history may
have repeated itself.

I wonder if you are entertaining the same extraordinary doubts about me. And I realize that in posing that
question to myself, I am entertaining doubts about you.
And if I am doubting you, how can you be so sure of
me? How can you afford to believe in me, over the
most niggling suspicion, considering what is at risk;
how can you take a chance on loving the murderer of
your family?

You see how I am tormenting myself.

I must know how you feel, although we cannot speak.
I have devised a simple code. When you come to court,
please wear white if you still believe in me, and red if
you doubt me—somewhere other than your shirt and tie,
please, or I won't know for certain that you have received this letter.

Even under these appalling circumstances, I can hardly
wait to see you. If you arrive wrapped in a red bow, it
will still be the most joyous day of these many months.

I love you with all my heart.

K.

39

ANXIETY HUNG IN the air acrid as chlorine gas. They wanted to know what was happening at court, and the reports came far too infrequently. Duck felt currents of agitation radiating from the silent television set. Behind its deadened gray screen, Court TV throbbed like a living presence. She could turn it on and see everything; she wanted to, and she was sure the screen beckoned to her father, as well. On principle—that this broadcast which had so rudely invaded their lives would not also invade their house—the television stayed off until the evening news.

From Joey, the *Daily Times*, and the local television news, Duck obtained a near-complete report of the fourth, fifth, and sixth days of the trial. Innumerable prosecution experts had gleaned information from various sources which they related to the jury. Duck learned some troubling new facts. Alexandra had been shot four times, and she had been shot first. They knew this because some of her blood and tissue had splattered Mother, who, shot once through the heart, fell on top of the scraps of Alexandra. There was no question that they had both been shot with a 1937 Suomi pistol. It was a rare weapon; the Finns had used them during the Winter War, and Catherine Liem had inherited hers from Rudolf Liem. The gun had been found in the trunk of Catherine's 1990 silver Volvo, which was parked around the corner from the Spencers' house. The prosecution theorized that Catherine had deposited the gun there before she discovered that the car would not start.

Some of the liveliest debate in the trial revolved around the Volvo's mechanical difficulties. Both the district attorneys and the defense experts had been over every millimeter of the car. They agreed that the car had stalled because of a short circuit in the fuel pump relay. The relay was a safety device on most fuel injection engines. When it was disabled, the engine got no fuel and could not run. It was the sort of motorist's nightmare, the D.A.'s expert explained, that could happen without warning at any time. In this case, he said, it was apparent that it had happened naturally: sensitive tests had revealed that the coil inside the fuel pump relay had been exposed to only twelve volts of current, which was the normal voltage. There was no evidence that the car or engine had been tampered with in any way. In fact, Catherine Liem's keys were found under the driver's seat—and not just her car keys but her house keys, keys to the Liem Enterprises Building, etc.—a hefty chain of keys on a silver hoop with her initials dangling from it.

Joey reported that Cheltam's cross-examination of the state's mechanical engineer had not scored any points for the defense. Cheltam's suggestion that the fuel pump relay coil on Liem's Volvo had been purposely disabled to strand the car struck Joey as far-fetched and unconvincing. On redirect, Ms. Burdock had established that if such a thing could conceivably be done at all, it would have involved partial disassembly of the engine, and running an electrical current from some external source to specific terminals on the fuel pump relay. It would have been a cumbersome, time-consuming, precise, and extremely difficult operation. It went without saying that it would not be a prudent project for someone fleeing the scene of a double murder. Junior could not have accomplished it in any amount of time.

Ms. Liem had not reported her car stolen until late that evening, long after it had been discovered by the police. And when she did make the report, she did not mention that her keys and gun were missing, too.

The murders had been committed on a Thursday, which was both Bahalia's day off and Ms. Liem's "studio day"—a day of secluded work when her maid was off duty, calls were not answered, and visitors (other than Blake, Sr.) were not seen. This was no coincidence, according to Ms. Burdock. Ms. Liem's studio day had been on Wednesdays until a month before the shootings.

That was it, then, Duck thought. She was guilty. The motive was obvious and the evidence, although circumstantial, was overwhelming. She might buy her way out with Mr. Cheltam's expensively cut suits and snooty New England voice, but she was guilty. Duck was equally certain that her father knew nothing about Liem's involvement, before or after the killings. She remembered the night two months ago when he had told her of his faith in Catherine Liem, based solely on his knowledge of her character. How foolishly credulous he was! No one could understand anyone else, much less know a person's dark capabilities. It was as Rick had said, her father was shielding himself from the awareness that he had indirectly brought death and ruin upon his family. In the past, Blake's unreasoning denial of his lover's guilt had infuriated her. Now she realized that his ignorance had only heightened his loss: he couldn't rage against Catherine, as Duck could; for him, she was one more victim to be mourned.

The ruin of the family was not confined to Mother's and Alexandra's deaths. After sedation and persuasion failed, Blake commissioned a locksmith to bar the closet. Junior then stationed himself outside the locked door, whimpering and clawing to get in. He could not be moved. Blake, Sr. was on standby in court that day and could not help. Dr.

Goldberg was called again, and he came to the house again, canceling the balance of his morning's appointments. Dr. Goldberg was a short, squat, silver-haired man with incongruously long fingers. He had been the Spencers' pediatrician since Duck was born, and his watery, faded blue eyes showed his concern. "Why do you want to go in there, son?"

"Momma said to go in the closet and don't come out."

"Your momma's dead, Junior," Dr. Goldberg said simply. "She wouldn't want you to be in there now."

"She wanted me safe. She wanted me safe," Junior cried insistently. He said it unintelligibly a dozen times before they could understand him.

Duck explained. "He was in there when Mother and Alexandra were murdered. Mother told him to get in and stay there. She must have seen Catherine Liem coming up the sidewalk and wanted to spare him from a scene. He's been going back in there every few days, but he always came out when we asked him to. But after Charles Deed attacked Bahalia in front of him, he got so scared he wouldn't come out anymore. You saw."

Junior was wailing throughout Duck's explanation. Dr. Goldberg gave Junior another shot and they helped him to bed.

After he fell asleep, Duck asked Dr. Goldberg, "Should we let him back in the closet? It seems cruel to shut him out. Should we go back to my grandmother's? He seemed fine there."

"I'm not sure what should be done, Laura. We most certainly cannot continue to handle it like this." He gestured with the empty syringe. "I'm going to give you a prescription for something milder. And I think he needs someone to work with him on a daily basis. There's a very capable young social worker named Nancy Voss, who has some experience working with Down Syndrome patients. I'm going to call her, and I want your father to call me as soon as possible."

When Blake, Sr. called from court and heard what had happened, he came home at once; Joey later advised that this was over the strenuous objection of Ms. Burdock, who wanted to sandwich Blake, Sr. into the middle of her case, rather than taking a chance that he would slow her momentum at the end.

Nancy Voss came over early that afternoon. She was a petite, red-haired, freckle-faced young woman, not much older than Duck. Duck admitted her, and was a bit put off by the bubbly enthusiasm Ms. Voss brought to this sober task. "So good to meet chooooo!" Ms. Voss pumped Duck's hand up and down. She did the same thing to Blake, Sr., who looked similarly skeptical. Duck felt that if they brought her up to see the sleeping Junior, she would flop his flaccid hand.

"Good!" she said when she learned Junior was asleep, clapping her hands together as if she had just won a trip to Disneyworld. "Then I'll have some time to take his history from you before he wakes up! Dr. Goldberg gave me some, but there's so much more I want to know!"

They moved into the den, and Duck and Blake, Sr. answered her questions for well over an hour, while she took copious notes and chirped little "ohs" and "oohs" when something particularly struck her, as it often did. But her questions were fairly penetrating. "How was Junior's relationship with his mother?"

"Formal," Blake, Sr. answered.

Duck and her father sat on opposite ends of the couch, with Nancy Voss facing them in an armchair. Nancy saw Duck's eyes roll at Blake's response, and questioningly lifted her eyebrows at Duck.

"Their relationship was awful," Duck said, and she related Junior's statements that Mother hadn't touched him, that he felt rejected for his limitations. "Junior shows his affection for people by correcting them. That's the warmest thing Mother ever did for him."

Her father added, "There was definitely a lot of tension in the last year or so. I think Evelyn knew what was going on between Catherine and me."

Duck looked at him, surprised. She remembered Mamoo's observation. *Your mother would not have tolerated it.* "What do you mean, you *think* she knew?" she asked her father.

Blake, Sr. turned sideways to meet her hard stare. "Just that. I certainly didn't tell her; and she didn't ask. Our communications were masterfully indirect. There was a week, about two months before Evelyn died, when she left suddenly to go to a health spa in Arizona. The first notice I had of the trip was when I came home from work and found a note saying that she had gone and I would have to look after the family in her absence—'better than you have been,' she wrote."

Duck remembered the odd departure. Mother hadn't even said good-bye, leaving the girls a separate note saying she was feeling tired and was going to "refresh" herself. She didn't call once during the week she was away, but she came back looking refreshed, and Duck hadn't given it another thought.

Blake told Nancy, "I guessed she'd just found out about Catherine; nothing else would've distorted her public face for an entire week. She was only down for a day after each of her parents died."

"How could she have suppressed her feelings about something like that?" Nancy asked.

"Feelings?" Blake replied bitterly. "That's a term that doesn't apply to Evelyn, at least not in the usual sense. She had her constant pride; she had her constant anger; and she had her constant schemes. The first was always in evidence; the second almost never; and the third you caught sight of only if you were lucky."

Duck tried to imagine her mother living with such a secret. Lying in her satin peignoir beside a man who had just come from another woman's bed. Why would she tolerate it?

Nancy Voss had a variation on the same question. "Why wouldn't your wife have just left?"

Blake gave a bitter laugh. "Evelyn was very old-fashioned. She needed a husband in the portrait she had painted of her life. She wouldn't have wanted the public declaration of failure that a divorce would have meant to her; and she wouldn't have wanted to retrain a new husband, either. Evelyn's reaction to an affair would have been to end it and then use it against me for the rest of my life.

"And I couldn't leave her without losing the children. You tell me, Ms. Voss, how could I leave Junior with Evelyn when I was the only person in the world, besides her, who knew or would believe that she hated him? We were trapped with one another."

"Well," Nancy said, uncommonly subdued, "let me go see what I can do about Junior."

By the time Junior woke up, Nancy, as they were to call her, had decided to open up the closet. For starters, she thought Junior should remain in the house while they tried to understand and relieve his anxieties. Duck, her father, Bahalia, and Nancy carried all the musty coats, umbrellas, and other closet clutter to the den. When they had finished, the closet was a fairly capacious room.

Nancy met Junior in his room, without pumping his arm. She told him she was there to try to help him feel better. After a time, she asked what he wanted to do.

"Go downstairs," Junior answered.

"Where downstairs?"

Junior did not answer. "Show me," Nancy suggested.

He went straight for the back corner of the closet. "May I come in?" she asked. Junior looked down and did not answer. She went. "Do you mind if we bring a couple of chairs in here to make it more comfortable?" Junior remained silent and Nancy moved three stools in from the kitchen. A few minutes later she invited Blake, Sr. in also.

When Duck looked in on them later, Junior was staring into space as Nancy and Blake, Sr. talked quietly on their adjoining stools. "Want something to do?" she asked.

"Sure!" Nancy exclaimed sunnily.

"I'll get Junior's baseball cards."

"That's a great idea!" Nancy cried. Blake, Sr.'s eyes were beginning to look a little glazed.

Duck raced upstairs, got a box of cards, and sped back down.

"Look at all of these!" Nancy fingered the collection excitedly. "I don't know *anything* about baseball. What's this one, Junior?" She held it in front of Junior's face.

Junior came alive. "That's Tony LaRussa."

"Oh, yeah? Who's that?"

"Manager of the Oakland A's."

"You're kidding! Do you know *all* of these?" Nancy flipped through the stacks and pulled one off the bottom.

"Deion Sanders. Atlanta Braves, Atlanta Falcons."

"Aren't the Falcons a football team?" Nancy asked.

"Uh-huh," Junior smiled. "Pretty neat, huh?"

"This is fascinating!"

Duck rushed back upstairs to get Junior's headset. Halfway back down the stairs with it, she pivoted and ran to Junior's room for his boom box so that the music would not isolate him. She took the tape out of the Walkman and inserted it into the portable stereo. Bunny Wailer. *Gumption*. Again. Was that all he was listening to these days?

She ran back downstairs. "Want some music?"

"Thanks!" Nancy exclaimed from deep in the cards.

Duck put the box at Junior's feet and turned it on. After only a few notes, Junior slouched back into his trance. Nancy reached over quickly and punched the music off. "Does that bother you, honey?"

Junior stared silently at the wall.

"Well, look, it's starting to feel a little cramped in here. Could we go spread these out on the table?" Nancy gathered up the cards. Junior followed her to the kitchen. She left soon after, promising to return the next day.

An hour later, Junior was back in the closet. Blake turned on the light and sat beside him on a stool, reading a magazine.

Duck went to get the mail. It was mostly catalogs, still mostly for Mother; the companies that had sent her so many plants, clothes, and linens were having as hard a time as the Spencers letting go. Flipping through the bulk mail, Duck came across a large, cream-colored envelope addressed to her father. Somehow, she knew at once what it was from the heavy paper, the perfect, scrolling letters, the blue fountain-pen ink, and the absence of a return address. *How dare she write him at his home—at this time!* Duck slipped the letter into a catalog and carried it up to her room. Blake didn't even look up as she walked past the closet. Duck spent fifteen minutes trying to steam the envelope open over a sinkful of hot water. She had only read about such a trick, and had no idea how it was supposed to be done. The paper grew limp and puckered, but the seal remained firm. In the end, she ripped it open.

She read it four or five times, more slowly and more angrily each time.

The woman was evil and devious. She knew just the right tone to take with Duck's father. *"You see how I torment myself?" EXCUSE ME? What about US?* There was no way Liem was going to get to him with this smarmy appeal, Duck vowed. Thank God she had intercepted the letter; no telling what effect it would have had on her father. She folded it back into the catalog and shoved it into her dresser drawer, on top of the derringer. At that moment, hiding the letter was as far as she meant to go with it, truly.

Poor Dad, she thought. *Poor, poor Dad, to be in the grasp of such a twisted, clever creature.* Duck startled herself with the bang she gave to her drawer, closing it. She was fired with adrenaline.

40

10 DECEMBER

Griffin, will you please relay a message to Arnie for me? During Blake's cross-examination, I would appreciate it if Arnie could remain seated at the defense table instead of pacing about the room, so that I will have some means of communicating with him while the questioning is under way. Please remind Arnie that I have given him free rein in everything else, but this segment is particularly important to me.

231

41

WHENEVER THE phone rang, the tremor of jarred nerves shook the house. On the morning of the seventh day of trial, Blake was called to court. He had an hour to shower, dress, and get downtown. He had not permitted Ms. Burdock to select his clothes. She wanted to know what he was wearing. "Something neutral," he told her.

Duck, feeling claustrophobic from the closet, went out to the patio for some fresh air. It was cool and sweet-smelling in the garden. The rosebushes Mrs. Burke had pruned two weeks before had burst into bloom. The bushes were loaded with flowers. Duck was drawn to the vibrant reds. They pulsed with color and beckoned to her as the flashing red light of an ambulance draws the eye of a passing motorist.

She had not thought before of what she must do; the thought positively assailed her. It seemed to come from outside of her, because she was implementing the plan before she fully comprehended what it was. Perhaps it was Mother and Alexandra who propelled her back into the house for the pruning shears. What had Mamoo said? *I trust my own feelings.* She selected a perfect crimson bud, its outer petals just beginning to curl open.

Her father was coming down the steps as she entered the hallway. He had not chosen a neutral-colored suit: it was navy blue; he looked like one of the lawyers. The suit even had a buttonhole in the lapel. It was meant to be.

"I'll be thinking of you, Dad," she said. With trembling fingers she slipped the flower into the buttonhole, which held it tightly. "This is to remember us by. I want you to know that I'm there with you in spirit. I think Mother and Alexandra will be, too."

He held her close, crushing the flower between them. "That means more to me than you can know. I love you, Laura."

"I love you too, Dad." She patted the bud on his lapel. It was still securely in place. The petals had opened a fraction further. The rose was now the shape of a heart, beating outside of his chest.

Duck stood at the picture window overlooking the patio and watched him go. She smeared a line down the glass with her fingertip. And another. She formed an oily grid that blurred the view of the rose garden. Worry shimmered over the bright flowers. Not that Catherine Liem did not deserve to have a red flag waved in her face. But Duck's father had been so touched by her action, and she knew that she had betrayed him. In addition to counseling trust in one's feelings, Mamoo had also told her, "I believe in honesty." But everything she had said to her father was true: she really was thinking about him; she really did want him to carry a token of her love and support into battle with him. It could be anything, though—so long as it were neither red nor white. She rushed to her room. How about a handkerchief? No, that was white, and he might slip it into his breast pocket, giving an unconsidered signal of faith to Catherine. What then?

Time was chasing her. As soon as she heard its heavy breath behind her, she froze up, just like playing tag in the schoolyard. *Don't do this,* she commanded herself. *Think.* What she thought, when she forced herself to it, was what she had realized to begin with. It didn't matter what she substituted for the rose. *Just get down there and do it.* She

stopped searching for chivalric tokens, grabbed her purse
and her keys, and ran down the back stairs. In those few
seconds of action, the solution presented itself: Alexandra's
chain, which was already hanging around her neck. It
would give her something to say, too. *"Here, Dad. Alexandra wants to be in your pocket, too."* She would slip it in
as she plucked the rose from his lapel. *"This is a bit gay
for the occasion,"* she would say, tsk-tsking at her un-
seemly first choice. It was clumsy, but it would work. She
rushed after him.

At the foot of the stairs she was intercepted by Nancy
Voss. "You know, I've been thinking and thinking about
Junior's thing with the music yesterday. I tried a coupla different tapes on him today and didn't get any reaction. Do
you think he might be associating Bunny Wailer's reggae
music with Bahalia's son who scared him so badly? Didn't
you tell me Charles used to have a Jamaican Rastafarian
look?"

"I don't think Junior knows that reggae music is Jamaican." Duck backed away from the conversation, impatient
to chase after her father.

Nancy was undeterred by Duck's rudeness, and held her
smile. "Well, has Charles ever played music in front of
Junior—maybe when he used to hang out around the
house?"

"I don't know. I don't think so, but you could ask
Bahalia." Duck steered Nancy into the kitchen, where
Bahalia was fixing supper. "I'm going out for a little
while," she told them.

Bahalia waggled her index finger in the air like a windshield wiper. "Uh-uh-uh-uh-uh-*uh.* You know your daddy
don' want you sneakin' off down there. That poor man
don' need any more trouble than he got."

"I need to tell him something, Bahalia."

Bahalia put her hands on her hips and cocked her head

at Duck. "Now how you gone talk to him at court?" She pulled out a chair at the table and ordered, "You sit down right here and don' you move 'til your daddy gets home."

Duck kept moving toward the door. "I'll be right back, I promise."

"Mmmm-mm!" Bahalia hummed in disgust. As she hurried away, Duck heard Bahalia telling Nancy, "You get that boy outa that closet quick. We gone hafta start lockin' the girl in." Duck smiled at the thought of Nancy Voss trying to sort through everything they had thrown at her in the last twenty-four hours.

Duck drove quickly to the courthouse, but because she was not expected, there was no red carpet treatment this time. The parking lot was full. There were no metered spaces open in front of the courthouse on Royal Street. She turned right on Church Street and encountered a traffic jam caused by construction. She dove into the first opening she found—an illegal one—and ran all the way from her car to the courthouse, her purse thumping against her hip as if it were goading her to go faster. Duck took the stairs to the second floor at a gallop and burst out of the stairwell, almost toppling her neighbor, Miss Tipton. The old woman was wearing a blue-gray suit that matched her hair, with white gloves, a little pillbox hat, and a pair of Minnie Mouse shoes that was almost fashionable. The question of what she was doing here at all, and outside the courtroom and witness room, brushed across Duck's consciousness. She had no time for idle thoughts, and asked hurriedly, "Have you seen my dad?"

Miss Tipton shrank back. "He just went in down there somewhere." Miss Tipton pointed vaguely down the hall, as if she did not know where the courtroom was.

"Thanks." Duck ignored the old lady's directions and rushed to the door in front of her, pushing it softly into the back of the deputy standing on the other side.

She saw details she hadn't noticed as a frightened witness. The paneled walls of Courtroom #1 were ringed with the sober pictures of former circuit judges. Over the dais occupied by the living judge, a brown stele depicted Hammurabi, sideways and two-dimensional—Egyptian-style—engaging in some indecipherable pursuit described in hieroglyphics. The spectators were less numerous than she recalled, disposed on three sections of benches, seven rows deep. Just as at a wedding, Catherine Liem's supporters had aligned themselves (to the extent the overcrowding permitted) behind the defense table on the left-hand side—the bride's side—while her detractors sat in the right-hand pews behind the prosecutor's table.

Blake was already on the stand, wearing his boutonniere. Duck could see only Catherine Liem's back. It was enough. Catherine's posture was not erect as it had been two days before. Her head and shoulders were bent. She had slumped down in her chair. A small white-knuckled hand gripped the edge of the counsel table. She was not looking at Blake. She had definitely seen him already.

42

STATE OF ALABAMA
V.
CATHERINE LIEM

(Excerpt from transcript of the proceedings, December 10)
CROSS-EXAMINATION OF BLAKE SPENCER, SR.
BY ARNOLD CHELTAM, ESQUIRE

Q. Mr. Spencer, your son Blake is fifteen years old now, is that correct?

A. Yes.

Q. At the time of the killings, he was fourteen?

A. Yes.

Q. Blake is afflicted with Down Syndrome, isn't he?

A. That's right.

Q. Your son Blake has the mental capacity of a six- to eight-year-old child, doesn't he?

A. Well, it's not that simple. You can't compare a Down Syndrome child to a normal child of any age because . . .

Q. That's right, it's not that simple because a young man like Blake doesn't think like a normal child, does he?

A. He understands ethics like a normal child, if that's what you're driving at, and he . . .

Q. Mr. Spencer, you're not . . .

BY MS. BURDOCK: Objection, Your Honor, Mr. Cheltam is not permitting the witness to complete his answer.

BY THE COURT: Sustained. Mr. Spencer, you may complete your answer.

BY MR. SPENCER: I was going to say that Junior is much more gentle than any of the children I know. I've never seen him harm a living thing.

BY MR. CHELTAM:

Q. Mr. Spencer, you've never seen Catherine Liem harm a living thing, either, have you?

A. No.

Q. You've never even seen her strike out at anyone, have you?

A. No.

Q. You spend, what, about one to three hours of waking time with Blake on the average working day?

A. It's been more than that lately.

Q. He's been especially troubled lately, hasn't he?

A. The entire family has been troubled, Mr. Cheltam.

Q. The entire family has not been hiding in the front hall closet, has it?

A. Well, as a matter of fact, the last couple of days, we've been sitting in there with Blake.

Q. Only because Blake won't come out, right?

A. Yes.

Q. Even with doctors, and sedatives, and social workers, you're having difficulty getting Blake out of the front hall closet?

A. Yes.

Q. And this problem developed right after the killings, didn't it?

A. Yes. Junior was in the closet when Evelyn and Alexandra were shot.

Q. Of course, you didn't see the shooting, did you?

A. No.

Q. So all you know from your own knowledge is that Blake was in the closet *after* the shootings.

A. I know that he was there during the shootings because he told me so.

BY THE COURT: Mr. Spencer, you have been instructed not to repeat what anyone told you.

BY MR. SPENCER: Yes, sir.

BY MR. CHELTAM:

Q. You want to believe Blake was in the closet during the killings.

A. Yes, I believe that.

Q. You don't want to believe he's lying to cover up, do you?

BY MS. BURDOCK: Objection, Your Honor.

BY MR. CHELTAM: I withdraw the question. Mr. Spencer, after Laura, you, and the police arrived, you found Blake in the closet, right?

A. Yes.

Q. Now, Mr. Spencer, you've taken your son fishing before, haven't you?

A. Yes.

Q. He can handle a rod and reel?

A. With some help.

Q. And he regularly goes to the workshop at the Center for Retarded Citizens, doesn't he?

A. Yes, three or four days a week.

Q. He does carpentry and other kinds of woodwork there?

A. Yes.

Q. He uses hammers, drills, saws, and many other tools, doesn't he?

A. Yes, other than power saws and things that might be dangerous.

Q. As far as you know?

A. Yes, and I know that it is a carefully supervised program. All of my son's activities are carefully supervised.

Q. That is, at your home and at the workshop?

A. Everywhere that he goes.

Q. Mr. Spencer, you don't go everywhere with Blake, do you?

A. No, but I'm very careful where he goes.

Q. One of the places that he goes is to the home of Elizabeth and Vincent Cristina, right?

A. Yes, they have a boy about Junior's age with Down Syndrome.

Q. Mark Cristina?

A. Yes.

Q. And Mark Cristina has several older brothers, doesn't he?

A. Yes.

Q. How many?

A. I'm not sure of the number. It's a very large family.

Q. Excuse me, you don't know who is around when your son is at the Cristinas?

A. Yes, I do. Family and friends are around.

Q. But you're not sure who or how many?

A. That's right.

Q. And you're not sure what Blake knows about guns, are you?

A. He doesn't know anything about them.

Q. At least one of the Cristinas' sons uses a gun regularly, doesn't he?

A. Joey Cristina is a deputy sheriff, and yes, I believe he wears a gun at work.

Q. Just how old is Joseph Cristina?

A. I don't know exactly. I'd say he's in his early twenties.

Q. Your Honor, I would ask that Deputy Cristina step forward for identification by the witness.

BY THE COURT: Please come forward, Deputy.
(Deputy Joseph A. Cristina complies)

BY MR. CHELTAM:

Q. Is this Mark Cristina's older brother?

A. Yes.

Q. Do you see that thirty-eight-caliber pistol on his hip?

A. Yes.

Q. Have you ever seen Deputy Cristina come home from work?

A. Yes.

Q. He wears that weapon home, doesn't he?

A. Yes, but I'm sure he handles it carefully.

Q. But you don't know, do you, because you're not there, are you?

A. No, but I trust him to handle the gun carefully. He's a very responsible young man and his parents are very responsible.

Q. You're going on trust, not knowledge, because you aren't there to supervise, right?

A. Right.

Q. And you weren't there to supervise when your son stomped the Cristinas' cat to death, were you?

A. He slipped and fell on him.

Q. He fell on him with his foot, didn't he?

A. Yes.

Q. While he and the cat were alone in the bathroom?

A. Yes.

Q. And the cat was killed before anyone else could get into the room, wasn't it?

A. Yes.

Q. And you weren't there to supervise when your son sexually assaulted your neighbor, Mrs. Burke, were you?

A. It was not a sexual assault. He complimented her breasts.

Q. Now let's be fair, Mr. Spencer, he commented on her tits, didn't he?

A. Yes, but he didn't mean anything by it.

Q. That was his word, wasn't it, "tits"?

A. Yes.

Q. And Mrs. Burke is eighty-one years old, isn't she?

BY MS. LIEM: Stop it!

BY THE COURT: Ms. Liem, sit down immediately!

BY MR. CHELTAM: Your Honor, may we take a brief recess?

BY THE COURT: Ms. Liem, sit down now or I will have you restrained.

BY MS. LIEM: I need to speak to my attorney.

BY THE COURT: You will speak only through your attorney and you will not disrupt these proceedings. Mr. Cheltam, continue your examination.

BY MS. LIEM: No, please. I want to talk to him.

BY THE COURT: Take the jury out.
(Jury removed; proceedings continued out of the presence of the jury)

BY THE COURT: Ms. Liem, you are in contempt of court. I will reserve ruling on your punishment until the conclusion of the trial. If you attempt any further disruption of these proceedings, I will have you gagged, do you understand?

BY MS. LIEM: Yes, Your Honor. But I must speak with my attorney.

BY THE COURT: You have had six months to speak with your attorney. This is neither the time nor the place. I will give you five minutes, and you will not address me again except through counsel. Court will stand in recess five minutes.
(A fifteen-minute recess was taken)

BY THE COURT: Is the prosecution ready?

BY MS. BURDOCK: Yes, Your Honor.

BY MR. CHELTAM: Your Honor, Ms. Liem and I have developed irreconcilable difficulties as to the conduct of her defense. She has dismissed me as her counsel of record and wishes at this time to undertake her own representation. Her right to be represented by the counsel of her choice is guaranteed by the Sixth Amendment of the Constitution, as is the right to self-representation. This right is particularly precious in a capital murder trial. Ms. Liem has assured me that she will not disrupt the proceedings, and I believe her to be capable of self-representation. Accordingly, I move to withdraw.

BY THE COURT: The motion is denied. We are in the middle of this trial. There is no way Ms. Liem can assume her defense at this point without disruption. She has already caused a disturbance and been guilty of contempt of court. As you well know, Mr. Cheltam, the Sixth Amendment right to counsel of the defendant's choosing cannot be exercised at such a time and in such a way. Mr. Marshall, bring in the jury. Mr. Cheltam, sit down. Your objection is noted.

BY MS. LIEM: Your Honor.

BY THE COURT: Sit down, Ms. Liem! Deputy Coltrane, gag Ms. Liem's mouth. Ms. Liem, if you rise again, I will have you shackled to your seat. Mr. Marshall, bring in the jury.

43

WHEN DUCK ENTERED the courtroom there were no seats left, nor even an inch of standing room against the walls. However, one of the courtroom deputies, whom she thought she recognized as a friend of Joey's, silently acknowledged her and directed an already tightly packed row of people to crush themselves so that she could squeeze into one of the benches on the prosecutor's side of the room. In this crowd, it was no wonder the white-gloved Miss Tipton had opted for the empty hall.

It was just as well that Duck scarcely had room to breathe, because her father's testimony seemed to draw all the air out of the room. Ms. Burdock led him through his relationship with Catherine Liem, which, as Duck had surmised, began during their collaboration on the Liem Enterprises Building three years before. He had seen Catherine as much as five days a week since. Most of those late nights at the office, the business trips he took, the family vacations he missed were spent with her. If Duck had not been wedged into her seat, she would have fallen out of it.

Yes, her father told Ms. Burdock, they had spoken of marriage many times. He had felt bound to Evelyn for the sake of the children, but the situation had become increasingly difficult and unhappy for him and Catherine. However, at the time of the killings, he was not prepared to leave Evelyn and had told Catherine as much. She cried often and sometimes appeared depressed. They both lied regularly to protect and continue their relationship.

Duck's father struggled to portray his romance with Catherine Liem as loving and positive, but it sounded miserably sordid to Duck, and, she thought, to those around her.

Ms. Burdock's examination probably only took about a half hour, although it seemed endless to Duck. When the prosecutor had finished, Duck thought the worst was over. She was wrong. Mr. Cheltam started right in on Junior. Listening to his cross-examination, Duck wanted to attack the man physically.

Her father occasionally sparred with Cheltam, but he gave her father no quarter, and Blake, Sr. steadily lost ground, both for himself and for his son. The defense attorney had no need of the podium, of the sheaf of notes he had left there, or of the microphone. He paced back and forth in front of Blake, Sr., drilling him in a powerful, clipped voice, and pausing only for emphasis. At one point he ground to a halt over her dad's uncertainty about the number of children in the Cristina household. In the face of such false drama, Duck was afraid that the point Cheltam was trying to make—that her dad was so inattentive to Junior's activities that he'd been left time for unsupervised gunplay—appeared less ridiculous to the jury than it was in fact.

Then Cheltam made the absurd suggestion that Junior could have gained access to a gun through Joey, of all people; and Deputy Cristina was called before the jury to display his sidearm. Duck noted his manly composure in striding to the front of the courtroom; but she could see rage in the set of his face and in his stiff-legged walk. Remembering Joey's offer to shoot Judge Porter if he came down on her when she testified, Duck daydreamed that her slender gunslinger would draw on Cheltam and take him out. Joey looked to be wound tight enough to do it. However, help, when it came, arrived from an unexpected direction.

Duck saw Catherine Liem trying to whisper to Cheltam's associate, who was seated beside her at the counsel table; he was obviously unresponsive and made shushing gestures at her. She then began writing notes to him with such furious slashes of her pen that it attracted the attention of everyone in the courtroom. The associate slunk over with one of her papers to Cheltam, who peremptorily waved him away. Without breaking stride, Cheltam moved from Junior's "stomping" attack on the Cristinas' kitten to his "sexual assault" on Mrs. Burke. It was unbearable to Duck. And it was apparently unbearable to Catherine Liem, also, who finally—and quite properly, Duck thought—put a stop to it.

Judge Porter, however, was operating under a different sense of propriety. Duck had noticed as soon as she sat down that the color of the judge's nose was in the danger zone. By the time Catherine Liem interceded in the interests of justice, the judge's nose was bloodred, the shade of her father's corsage, and the color had spread into his cheeks. His reaction to Catherine Liem's outburst was shocking. She could hardly understand what the judge was saying, for the manner in which he said it. He leaned over the bench and screamed at the defendant and her lawyer at the top of his lungs. It reminded her of Charles Deed's crazed confrontation of Bahalia. Duck feared he would throttle one of them next.

The jury was not removed until after the judge had vilified the defense. Wherever the jurors were taken, if it were anywhere in the building, it could not have been far enough away to place them beyond earshot of Judge Porter's rage. He held the defendant in contempt of court and had her gagged for her efforts to dismiss her attorney, which seemed a reasonable enough plea to Duck. Duck half-expected Cheltam to be shackled and gagged, too.

The court reporter's transcript could never capture the pandemonium. The judge ordered the reporter not to record a good ten minutes of argument by Mr. Cheltam. Judge Porter screamed at Cheltam for silence and ruled that he was in contempt of court, too, while Cheltam shouted back, with what impressed Duck as life-threatening courage, that the contempt citation could not stick without a transcript.

A shaken and cowed jury was finally returned for a few more minutes of subdued questioning of her father by Cheltam. When Cheltam said he was done, the judge stormed from the bench without another word.

Ms. Burdock raised a ripple of laughter by addressing the judge's empty chair. "I guess I have no further questions either, Your Honor."

That was another episode the court reporter did not appear to have recorded.

Much as Duck wanted to see Catherine Liem convicted, this was not the lofty and decorous means by which she had expected it would be done. She had felt sympathy for the woman when the judge and her attorney overwhelmed her. Equally troubling, she had felt guilty about the possibility that the crimson rosebud had undermined Catherine's ability to support her own defense. This was absurd, Duck remonstrated with herself, that *she* should feel guilty about derailing this killer's attack on her brother! Catherine's break with her hired-gun lawyer was the first moral step Duck had seen her take. If the rose had forced her to it, good! It was a fortuitous development. Perhaps Catherine would be driven to confess.

And yet, and yet . . . her father's ignorant complicity in his lover's collapse was more complicated. And the means by which Duck had co-opted him was even more complicated. And his reaction to Duck's buttonholing him with her treacherous token of love was more complicated still. The fragile peace between them would be broken if she told him the truth. He would see only the betrayal in it, not the equally true resurgence of her love for him. She wanted so much to preserve the spirit of the embrace they had shared, without the damnable flower between them! She wished she had never seen Catherine's horrid epistle.

Wait. Suppose she had never seen it? Might she not have acted in precisely the same way, with precisely the same consequence? Yes. She might very well have sent her father to court with a token of her love, just as she had said. All that stood in the way of her reconciliation with her father was guilt over an intent that might never have existed, and could therefore be abolished. Maybe she could slip the letter into tomorrow's mail. Blake would read it and do whatever he liked with it. Remembering the mangled envelope, Duck discarded this idea. Maybe the letter could just have been lost in the mail. That was it. It happened all the time.

The Spencers' house had taken on the feel of a refugee camp, filled with people who didn't quite belong and relief agencies there to minister to the needs of the war-ravaged survivors. Bahalia no longer kept regular hours but stayed late into the night scrubbing vigorously at the countertops, as if to remove moral impurities from the already gleaming white surfaces. Nancy Voss was in constant attendance on Junior, and Mamoo attended everyone. When Duck returned from court a few minutes behind her father, the entire assembly was gathered, as around a campfire, to hear Bahalia's war stories. Duck's entrance did nothing to slow her down. "She stay home all year, then when she need to be home, she go out, can't nobody say nuthin'!"

Blake smiled wanly. "I'm sure you said something."

"I told her I was gone lock her in that closet," Bahalia

related. "Don' look at me like that! Y'all got you a nice little sittin' room fixed up in there. Might as well use it."

Mamoo tried to change the subject. "Well, how did it
go?"

Blake, Sr. shook his head at her, nodding in the direction
of Junior, who was still looking at Bahalia.

Bahalia answered her. "Don't think you gone get nuthin'
outa these two! Go turn on the TV if you want some news.
Come on, dinner's ready. You can come listen to 'em eat.
That's the most noise they makes." Bahalia led the way into
the dining room; but after depositing the last serving platter,
she headed back for the kitchen.

"Aren't you eating tonight, Bahalia?" Blake, Sr. called
after her.

"You got your momma. I'll stay back here," Bahalia responded.

"If you're eating, Bahalia, I'd really like for you to join
us," he told her.

And she did, which was a good thing, because Blake and
Duck were incapable of conversation. Duck's father's face
seemed to have fallen in the space of a day. Or maybe it
was in the space of time since she had last really looked at
him. There were bags under his eyes, the beginnings of
jowls sagging beneath his jaw, and a slight drop of the flesh
under his chin. All of a sudden, he looked old.

"How's your family, Bahalia?" Mamoo inquired.

"They doin' fine, Ms. Spensah—all but Charles. Taneeka'll be finishing medical school this May. She gone be
obsatrician." Duck thought of Taneeka delivering babies
with no other instruments besides her surgical-steel eyes,
and shuddered. "She got so many offers for next year, she
don' know what to do. And I guess you heard about Charlie's big job with Mr. Spensah."

"Yes, I did. By the time Louis goes to medical school,
you won't have to worry about scholarships."

"Not Dumplin'!" Bahalia hooted. "That boy can't stand to put a Band-Aid on hisself. And he don' truck none with the books neither. But you should hear him play the piano. Taught hisself on my momma's upright. He's got a real gift."

"Bahalia, you've got more talent in your family than most small towns. You've done an incredible job with those kids."

"I sure am proud of 'em. All but Charles. Look like he's tryin' to be bad enough to make up for all the others." Bahalia's hands went up to her neck, which showed black bruises on her dark skin.

"Is he still in jail?"

Bahalia nodded. "Charlie's tore up about it. This is the worst yet. You know Charles had his little things with thievin' and schemin', but he never *hurt* anybody before. He's a mess, but he's still our boy, and nobody's ever laid a hand on him and he never laid a hand on anybody outside of some little street humbug."

Duck was amazed that Bahalia should be so concerned, after what Charles had done to her.

Mother to mother, Mamoo said stoutly, "No child of yours could ever go past saving." Mamoo was another who loved her son unconditionally.

"This time, I don't know, Ms. Spensah," Bahalia said. "Looks like he just bent on ruinin' hisself. Looks like he just can't live with hisself no more. Charles calls his daddy twice a day cryin' to get out. But we been through this so many times. Soon as he's out, he go straight for the drugs. He gone have to dry out in the jail this time." Bahalia cut at Junior's food until everything on his plate looked like a rice dish.

"There's nothing you can do until he's ready to help himself," Mamoo said. She could have been talking about Blake, Sr., Duck thought. Perhaps she was.

"That's what Nancy Boss say and that's what I know. Don' make it no easier."

"Amen to that."

Bahalia couldn't let go of the subject. "Charles used to work aroun' here, do little jobs all aroun'. Then last summer he got hisself into some money some kinda way and he been wild ever since. Charlie thinks he got goin' on that crack cocaine." Now Bahalia was sawing at her own food. She hadn't taken a bite yet.

"Maybe we can move him straight into a treatment program from the prison," Mamoo suggested.

"I'm gone try," Bahalia resolved. "Just pray he don't come up in front of Judge Porter. That man'd hang him."

So would Duck, given the opportunity. But not Bahalia, she marveled—the party most injured by Charles's transgressions was the consummate parent. Mother's relationship with Junior came into ugly counterposition. If Bahalia could love Charles, how could Mother reject Junior? And for a genetic condition that was as much a source of sweetness as limitation? Duck fought down her anger. Perhaps she was no better, rejecting her own dead mother for things Duck did not understand.

Maria called after dinner. "Joey told us all about court today. What a circus! Has your dad told you anything?"

"I was there," Duck said.

"Wah. What did you think?"

Duck told her about everything but the flower. Maria added the information she had learned from Joey. "You know where they got all that garbage on Junior?"

"Where?"

"That mean old bag, Miss Tipton."

Duck thought of the genteel white gloves overlaying her neighbor's venom. *All she cares about is appearances,* Mrs. Burke had said of her sister. "How could she!"

"Joey thinks she's lined up as a prosecution witness, but he doesn't know if they'll use her now."

"Maybe Junior and I can go trim her and her hedges with a chainsaw tomorrow."

"She'll prob'ly be at court."

"On Saturday?" Duck asked.

"Yep. Patsy Burdock ran the judge down and told him they couldn't let the jury stew in this evening's juices all weekend. She was furious with the judge. She thought the case against Catherine Liem was going great. Now she's scared the jury'll feel sorry for Catherine because the judge was so hard on her."

"It was awful, Maria. Even I felt sorry for her."

"Uh-oh. No wonder the prosecutor's worried."

"If she gets off, I'll die." *I'll really, really die,* she thought, her eyes flicking to the dresser drawer where her gun was stored.

"Why do you think she canceled her lawyer's examination? Apart from the fact that it was full of shit? Joey can't figure it. Patsy Burdock can't figure it. Did it seem to you like she was just admitting she knew the Junior thing was a lie and she wanted your dad cut loose from it?"

"I don't know," Duck said, the uneasy feeling rising like vomit from the pit of her stomach. *She smelled the roses.*

"Well, Joey said they might finish tomorrow."

"The whole thing?"

"The guilt phase. If she's convicted, they have like another trial with the same jury to decide whether she gets life in prison or the electric chair."

"I don't see how they can get through the first part in one more day," Duck said, feeling she needed more time to prepare for a verdict, any verdict.

It was, however, all over in one more day. Duck and her father stayed home. The prosecution called two brief witnesses, and Catherine Liem was the only witness for the defense. She claimed she loved Blake Spencer too much to do him harm by harming his family. She claimed she had tried to live her life in such a way as not to hurt anyone. She claimed she had been in her studio working on the afternoon of the killings. She had not seen or spoken to anyone, as was her custom on her studio days. She claimed she had a craving for ice cream that evening and discovered her keys and her car missing. She reported the car stolen. She claimed she did not report the keys stolen because she thought she might simply have mislaid them, and they seemed less important than the car. Then she looked directly at the jury and swore she had not killed Evelyn or Alexandra Spencer.

Ms. Burdock did not touch her story. She ran Catherine Liem through all the lies she had told in the three years since she had started seeing Blake Spencer. She had lied to acquaintances, to friends, to her grandfather. She had lied and lied and lied.

Joey said the cross-examination was very effective.

The jury thought so, too. After two and a half hours of deliberation, it unanimously convicted Catherine Liem of two counts of murder.

The Spencer family was congregated at the kitchen table, magnetized by the normalcy of Junior's clay work with Mamoo. They were modeling pieces of fruit. Bahalia was cooking feverishly. Blake and Duck were up and down. Put on a jazz piano CD. Fetch the newspaper. Eat a carrot from Bahalia's provender. Switch the music to classical cello. Every trip took them past the phone, hovering for a moment, as if they were in a game of musical chairs. Duck was closest when it rang. She jumped backward, and still caught the receiver before the first ring died.

"It's over," Joey said quickly.

Blake came to her side. "She was convicted, wasn't she?" he asked, looking gray as someone experiencing a heart attack.

Duck nodded, feeling miserably awkward relaying this report.

"Murder?" Blake asked.

She nodded, knowing that manslaughter had been a possibility that would have allowed for lighter sentences. She spoke over Joey's words, relating them to her father with the speed of a translator at a summit meeting. "They're not going for the death penalty. The prosecution wasn't really seeking it, apparently. They just wanted to keep her in jail and get the tougher jury that comes of being death-qualified on voir dire. She got life." She added weakly, "Without possibility of parole." Then for reasons she herself did not understand, she said, "She's probably got a good chance of reversing it on appeal, after yesterday." This did not come from Joey.

Her father looked at her oddly, but said nothing. He sat down heavily at the kitchen table, staring into space. In this aspect, his resemblance to Junior was uncanny. Duck wondered what Nancy Voss would think if she returned on Monday to find the three of them lined up in the closet wearing the same vacant expressions. Duck could picture them taking this family act out on the streets, lining up behind a banner that said WILL WORK 4 FOOD. They would be a contemporary existential version of the Trapp Family Singers.

Blake, Sr. interrupted her fantasy by lifting himself, with difficulty, from the table. "I think I'll pass on supper tonight," he said dully, and trudged upstairs. Duck redrafted the banner. WILL WORK 4 NOTHING. It was the first time, she realized, that her father had missed the family dinner since Mother and Alexandra died. He had sat patiently through months of her glowering at the table. For that matter, he had sat patiently through years of Mother's captious quips. He had held things together for so long. And perhaps, Duck thought uneasily, Catherine Liem had helped him do it.

On Sunday morning, Blake, Sr. went out early, saying he was going to work. Duck's ears were now attuned to her father's false notes; she knew he was going to see Catherine Liem. It didn't upset her. The woman was in prison; it would be a chaste visit; and she would tell Blake, Sr. about the letter, erasing the last trace of Duck's deceit. All Duck had to do was not look guilty when her father said he'd seen Catherine, or asked whether anyone had noticed a white envelope addressed to him. Just thinking of it made the blood rush to her face. She would have to think of it several times a day, until the color faded from the rose.

44

STATE OF ALABAMA
V.
CATHERINE LIEM

(Excerpt from transcript of the proceedings, December 15)

BY MR. CHELTAM: Your Honor, we have moved for a new trial based on our discovery that the foreperson of the jury, Mrs. Richard Lupon, was not impartial. We learned from interviews with the other jurors that Mrs. Lupon was an outspoken advocate for Ms. Liem's conviction. We have also learned from an independent investigation that Mr. Lupon was formerly Vice-President of Bethlehem Steel's Shipbuilding Division. His operation dwindled and he was discharged because of the success of Liem Enterprises. His animosity toward the Liems has been well known in this community and is well documented in the affidavits we have attached to our motion. Ms. Liem could not receive a fair hearing from Mrs. Lupon, and did not. Moreover, the entire jury was prejudiced by this Court's handling of Ms. Liem's dispute with me during the cross-examination of Mr. Spencer. For the reasons set forth in our brief on these issues, we urge that the verdict be set aside and that a new trial be ordered.

BY MS. BURDOCK: If Your Honor please . . .

BY THE COURT: Sit down, Ms. Burdock. I don't need to hear from you. The motion for new trial is denied. Mrs. Lupon was asked during the voir dire whether she was aware of any circumstance that would impair her ability to render a verdict based solely on the evidence. She answered no to that question. You have produced not a scintilla of evidence indicating that her answer was untruthful. I am not persuaded that a thirty-year-old business setback involving Mrs. Lupon's deceased husband and Ms. Liem's deceased grandfather has had any impact whatsoever on this trial. There is no evidence that Mrs. Lupon ever met Catherine Liem or harbored any ill will toward her. There was, on the other hand, ample evidence introduced in this trial that could have led Mrs. Lupon to argue for Ms. Liem's conviction.

Ms. Liem, do you have anything to say before sentence is imposed?

BY MS. LIEM: Yes, Your Honor, I do.

I'm not certain to whom I am addressing my remarks or why . . .

BY THE COURT: You are addressing them to me, Ms. Liem.

BY MS. LIEM: My lawyer has already explained that a sentence of life imprisonment without parole is mandatory, but he has counseled me to use this opportunity to reiterate my innocence.

I was going to quote *The Kalevala* to you, "Never, you children of mankind, never, never, forever never, put the blame upon the blameless, never hurt the innocent!" But I cannot hold myself out as blameless.

At this juncture, I would prefer to talk about my guilt. My

confession is a very personal one; I am probably the only person in this courtroom certain that I have never killed anyone, and without that predicate, my confession loses some of its poignancy.

Nevertheless, I want to make the most heartfelt apology for my arrogance. My grandfather instilled in me the belief that the American government, the American system of justice, and the American people made his phenomenal success possible and offered the same possibility to every hard-working and freedom-loving individual. I always knew that there were people ground down by the system, but I believed they were inevitable and acceptable losses, and probably at least partly responsible for their misfortunes. Certainly I am partly responsible for my predicament, having defied certain social conventions. I do regret the secrecy and dishonesty of my relationship with Blake Spencer; but now more than ever I cherish our love as the signal achievement of my life. I do not count it among my failings.

My failings would not have been enough to convict me had they not combined with the failings of a prosecutor motivated to malice by petty political grudges, a juror motivated to malice by a petty financial grudge, a judge whose failings I am not permitted to enumerate, and God knows what other frailties have shaken this ignoble tribunal.

With the wisdom born of my conviction for crimes I did not commit, I acknowledge the arrogance of my belief in this flawed system, of my belief that I was above it, and of my belief that all really innocent people were above it. And if my wealth, education, and status could not protect me, what hope does it offer for the poor and uneducated and classless?

I accept this Court's punishment for my sin in believing in a besotted fool like you, Judge, and in all . . .

BY THE COURT: Silence!

BY MS. LIEM: . . . you represent.
I have nothing more to say.

BY THE COURT: You stand convicted of two counts of murder.
The jury has recommended a sentence of life imprisonment.
I hereby sentence you to serve two terms of life imprisonment without benefit of parole, and I order that those sentences run concurrently. I further find you guilty of another
count of contempt of court, and I will refer that matter to
Judge Donovan for sentencing.

Court stands adjourned.

45

DUCK WENT BACK to court on a bitingly cold day for the imposition of sentence on Catherine Liem. The county court was festooned with faded plastic Christmas greenery that made the gray building drearier than the gray sky. A moth-eaten Santa, who had pushed his moustache and beard under his stubbled chin, shook a bell on the front steps of the courthouse. The cheerless sound pursued Duck inside.

Joey had forewarned her that the defense was moving for a new trial because of trial errors and because of the newly discovered bias of one of the jurors. Duck remembered noticing the impeccably dressed older woman during her father's testimony; Mrs. Lupon had kept a hard stare fixed on Catherine throughout. According to Joey, the Lupons had made no secret of their hatred, but he did not believe this would have any effect on Judge Porter, nor apparently did Mr. Cheltam, who presented only a brief and lackluster oral argument to the court. It was just one more thing for the appeal.

Catherine then created another scene, to the great delight of the army of reporters, by her "confession" to a naive belief in the criminal justice system. Duck sensed that Judge Porter's reaction would have been less restrained if it had been later in his drinking day or if the courtroom had not been packed with people. Her own reaction was uneasy also. She felt again the stirrings of sympathy and doubt she had experienced during Catherine's outburst the week before. Her discomfort was aggravated at the sight of her father attempting to pass a note to Catherine via one of the deputies. The defendant glanced at it, and pushed it aside. She never turned to look at Blake, Sr.

In the overheated courtroom, Duck, still wearing her overcoat, broke into a sick sweat. She felt none of the satisfaction she had expected when a deputy briskly snapped the defendant's slender wrists into handcuffs and led her through the dark-paneled walnut doors at the front of the courtroom.

As the reporters rushed to reattach themselves to their umbilicus of communication wires, Blake, Sr. walked through the swinging gates that separated the business end of the courtroom from the spectators' gallery, retrieved the note Catherine had left on the table, and tried to press it upon Mr. Cheltam, who shook his head and passed it back.

Duck intercepted her father on his way out. "Can't you talk to her?" she asked.

Blake, Sr. looked older than ever. Were those liver spots developing on the hand that held the rejected envelope? "She won't see me," he said.

"Since when?"

"I haven't seen her in months. Laura, could we have this conversation somewhere else?" There were people milling about on all sides.

"Sure."

If the conversation had continued, she might have said, "There's something I need to tell you."

But they did not continue it, even at home. The end of the trial did not usher in the new day Duck had expected. Life seemed disjointed. Night collided with morning, morning with afternoon. The Spencer family shunted from the Mobile house, where Nancy Voss wanted Junior to have access to the closet, to Iberville Point, where the mood was slightly more relaxed. Mamoo bumped back and forth with them for a week. While at the Point, Duck conceived of activities that could only be pursued in town, and vice versa. She was not ready to confront her derringer, nor was she motivated to get ready for college.

Blake, Sr. spent most of the week at the beach development, where they had broken ground. The project was on an expedited schedule; they were working night crews; and Blake stayed there or in his office eighteen hours a day. When in Mobile, Duck sometimes encountered her father in the kitchen, already settled with a cup of coffee and the newspaper by the time Mamoo and Duck met there for their predawn warm-up exercises. He could not be prevailed upon to join them. "I'm not in the mood to scale any buildings this morning," he said to his mother curtly on the morning she invited him. She did not ask again.

Duck warned Mamoo that eventually they must encounter Mrs. Burke. It happened late in the week, on Friday. Mrs. Burke, out walking her dog, recognized Mamoo at once, without any introductions. "Why, Eleanor!" she exclaimed. "How delightful to see you. Won't you all come in for some coffee?"

Mamoo smiled pleasantly and continued walking in place, her legs working like pistons. Duck and Junior followed her example. "We'd love to another time. We've got to go stretch out, right now."

Mrs. Burke began lifting her feet also, quickly and awkwardly high. "It's my sister, isn't it?" she spluttered, rocking from side to side and looking as if she might tip over. "I don't blame you if you don't want to come over after what she did. I can hardly look at her myself."

"No, it isn't that at all," Mamoo began, still pumping. "Well, it might be a little uncomfortable," she corrected herself, "but I think we can manage. Right now, though, we really do have to go stretch or we might kink up. Would you like to come by later, Mrs. Burke?"

"Please, call me Eloise. And yes, I'd love to."

* * *

At 2:00 p.m., the appointed time, Mrs. Burke, who usually let herself in through the kitchen, rang the front doorbell. She had changed into an emerald-green wool dress, the waist of which had searched out a fold right beneath her bosom to tuck into, hiking up the hemline above knee-high stockings that bit into her dimpled knees as though they were tying off sausages. She held a small plate of her homemade gingersnap cookies in her white-gloved hands. Duck wondered whether she and Miss Tipton shared the same pair. And whether these would serve the same function as her sister's, of keeping the Spencers' blood off her hands.

Mamoo took those gloved hands in hers without hesitation and drew Mrs. Burke back into the kitchen where Junior was carefully pouring coffee to within a millimeter of the rim of each of their cups. A silver tray of Mamoo's famous cheese straws and apple tarts graced the table.

"I've missed seeing you all these years, Eloise, and I must tell you it's entirely my fault. I've been avoiding you for the vainest, silliest reason." Mamoo went right for it in her direct way.

Mrs. Burke's gloved hand flew to her pearls. "Oh my. I certainly didn't mean to embarrass you," she said, looking terribly embarrassed.

"Not at all. I'm so grateful you've given me the chance to set the record straight. I'm sure you won't remember, but more than fifty years ago I wrote a little essay for your class about Iberville's landing at the Point."

"Of course I remember it. What an imagination you had! It was clear then that you'd be an artist, although I really thought you'd write."

"You mean you knew it was made up?" Mamoo exclaimed. Her delight seemed almost girlish. Her blue chambray dress deepened the color of her eyes. She was trim and pert, and in spite of her sculpted face and gray hair, she looked every inch the high-school student.

"Well, of course I did. I was an historian. You mean you thought I believed Iberville's frigate was named after your boyfriend?" Mrs. Burke laughed a rolling laugh.

"Oh goodness, did I do that?"

"That and much more. Delightful revisionist history. I wish I could remember all the details. Do you have a copy of it?"

"No, I'm sure I burned it. But, if you knew it was a forgery, how did you let the Daughters of the Coastal Settlers bronze it?"

"Oh, that bunch of old fuddy-duddies never saw your story. The landmark we erected is based on the facts."

"But I invented the whole thing!" Mamoo protested.

"Most of it, you did. Even your sources, if I remember correctly." Mrs. Burke's eyes twinkled as she wrote in the air above her head, "*L'Histoire de la Voyage*, par Jean-Pierre de François de Jacques d'Etienne. But one or two fundamental facts you had right, whether by osmosis from one of my lectures while you were playing tic-tac-toe with that O'Bannon girl or by lucky guess, I don't know."

"You remember more about it than I do!" Mamoo was laughing uproariously.

"Well, I am an historian." Mrs. Burke drew herself up in mock indignation.

"I declare," Mamoo said, wiping her eyes. "All these years I've worried about that bronzed lie. Isn't that something?" she said to Duck. Then she dipped her head pensively to slurp a little coffee from her overfilled cup. "Sometimes things are exactly as they seem. Sometimes we invent the truth."

And sometimes we don't, Duck thought. And who could tell the difference? She was living in a thicket of statements, charges, versions, and allegations, whose thorny branches were interlocking over her head and blocking out the light. Almost accusingly, she asked the two older women, "What difference does it make whether we invent the truth or lies? No one ever really knows. Most people don't really care. And truth or lie, if it's big enough, Court TV will be there for the entertainment value."

Mamoo held a cheese straw midair. Her girlishness vanished. "It makes all the difference in who we are," she said sternly. "And whether the world knows or cares, Laura, we must fashion ourselves into people we ourselves can admire."

Mrs. Burke commended her student with a blunt, magisterial nod. Duck, suddenly under suspicion, capitulated to Mamoo's position with a forced smile of assent. Presently, she excused herself.

As she climbed the back stairs, coffee cup in hand, she heard the ladies' mood of levity rising behind her. For Duck, it was not so simple to abandon the subject of falsehood. Her deception with the rose seemed to be fastened to her chest with a hatpin. Guilt and uncertainty throbbed from the wound, on a pulse quickened by caffeine. Her thoughts buzzed for an hour, then dropped. She refilled her cup a half dozen times over the course of the evening, and carried an electric charge into the still, dark hours of the night. Duck lay stiffly on top of her covers. Whether her eyes were open or shut, she saw the same shimmering gray shadows, which finally, after a sleep almost indistinguishable from waking, heralded dawn. Duck heard quiet movements in the kitchen, the sounds of her father moving through life with an effort not to stir so much as the air around him. Duck dug the letter out of her drawer, her fingers glancing against the hard shape of the gun. She carried it downstairs, and found her father sitting in the tenebrous gray of the formal living room.

"I need to talk to you," she said in his direction. She could not see him. He was a darker place in the darkness, like the fading bruises on Bahalia's neck.

"What is it," he said in a hoarse whisper.

She sat stiffly and told him the whole thing. Catherine's letter. Her reaction to it. Her feeling of protectiveness toward him. The appearance of the rosebud like a *deus ex machina*. Her sensation that Mother and Alexandra were guiding her. Her genuine desire to send him into battle with a token of her favor. Her tardy pursuit of him to undo her act. Her sense of having betrayed him. Her fear that she would lose him by coming clean. Her worry that she had influenced Catherine Liem's conduct in court when he sat in the witness chair brandishing his false sign of doubt. Her hope that Catherine would tell him about the letter. Her struggle to reveal the truth. "I've been thinking," she concluded, "about how hard I've been on you all these months, mostly because you lied to us. And here I did the same kind of thing. I finally understand how you can do something really wrong without meaning to hurt anybody. I'm so sorry, Daddy. I really love you. I'm sorry for all these months I've been down on you. You've been having an awful time, too, and I haven't done anything to help. I was just so angry. I didn't understand; but now I do." She stopped. She was crying hard. She waited for him to come across to her and hold her.

He did not move for a long time. It was frightening. At last he stood. He said in that same hoarse whisper, "Your understanding has come at a high price."

Duck realized he must have been crying when she came in. She had only seen him cry once before, after they got home from the funerals in May, when Junior patted him on the shoulder and said comfortingly, "Alexandra will come home soon. Nobody could kill Alexandra." Blake, Sr. had held his son and cried against him, scaring him badly. But he did not hold Duck and cry against her now. Instead, he left the room and left the house. This was going as badly as Duck had feared it might go.

She stood up and turned on a table lamp. She looked over at the couch. Next to the depression her father had left in the sofa cushion was the morning paper. Centered on the top half of the front page was the bold outline of a red block.

Duck would say afterwards that she had known immediately what it was. But she must not have, or she would have fainted then instead of later. She walked across the room and picked it up. She looked at the red-blocked photograph first. It was a giant web, stretched from the bars at the front of the cell to the bars at the window and anchored on the bed frame. Catherine Liem must have ripped up her sheets, blankets, and clothes to make it. And true to her multimedia style, she had included another element in the sculpture— herself. A ragged hole gaped at the center where Catherine had been cut loose from the strangling bonds. The angle of the photograph was odd. You could tell that the photographer had had to take it from outside the cell to get it all in.

Duck read the headline, JAILHOUSE CONFESSION?, and the subheading, *Liem Attempts Suicide in Cell.* The brief report stated that Mobile's most famous inmate had been found suspended in her sculpture by a midnight patrol, and rushed to the public hospital, USA Medical Center, where she remained in a deep coma brought on by oxygen deprivation. Ms. Liem's cellmate, Angelle Bascom, had slept through the incident. Prognosis for recovery was uncertain. Ms. Liem's doctor was unavailable for comment. The *Daily Times'* own medical consultant opined that even were Ms. Liem to survive, "further damage to an already diseased mind is probable. Ms. Liem may serve out her life sentence as a vegetable." This crude commentary reminded Duck of Maxine's long-forgotten, silly, and prophetic comment in the gallery, "Unless she can make a loom from her jail bars!"

The caffeine, the sleeplessness, and the shock wrapped a stranglehold around Duck's neck, and she fainted. Softly, onto the down cushions of the couch.

46

My darling Blake,

Arnie reminds me regularly that in losing my trial I have won the right of appeal, which he has generously offered to undertake at a reduced rate of $100,000. Papa had a saying for these sorts of successes: "We have gained only enough territory to bury our dead."

I wish now that I had spoken to you as I was going down so I could have assured you in person that this has nothing to do with you. I thought at first that it did, that you were one of the forces bringing me down. It was in that mood that I refused your visits and letters. But I see now that it wasn't you or the trial or the conviction or the life sentence. I was holding onto you for all the love I was denied as a child, attaching more weight to your lifeline than you could possibly have pulled. The impossibility of it has nothing to do with your limitations, and everything to do with mine. I do not love myself; you could not make up for that. Nor could a reversal of my conviction nor an acquittal. I have no use for freedom.

That I am prepared to cause you so much pain to free myself from the intolerable burden of myself is only one more reason for self-loathing. I hope that you will be more angry than sad.

In my pitifully limited way, I love you more than I can say. You are the most beautiful person I have ever seen. Our love is the most beautiful thing I have ever known. I believe that something of it must endure to give you comfort.

My undying love,
K.

47

WHEN MAMOO CAME downstairs a little before 7:00 a.m., Duck was sitting on the couch as her father had sat. Mamoo jogged into the living room on the tail end of saying perkily, "You're up mighty early." The bounce went out of her when she saw Duck. She sat on the sofa beside her granddaughter and studied the newspaper. "Has your father seen this?"

Duck nodded. She could not raise her head to look at her grandmother.

"Did he say anything to you about it?" Mamoo asked.

"Not exactly."

Mamoo sat quietly for a long moment before continuing. "It's sad, of course; witnessing another person's despair is always sad. But I'm trying to understand why this particular case is so upsetting to you."

Duck was beyond self-protection. "I killed her."

"She's not dead."

"But she will be. And I killed her."

"I don't understand," Mamoo commented, in a tone that said, "Nonsense!"

So Duck told her, much as she had told her father a few minutes earlier. But Mamoo did not get up and leave. She held Duck tight and rocked her back and forth, saying, "Oh, honey. Oh, honey."

Finally, Mamoo asked her, "What did your father say?"

"He said my understanding had come at a high price."

271

"Where did he go?"

"I don't know. I probably killed him, too." The thought had not crossed her mind until she said it, but once she had, a tiny shudder that began at the edges of her mouth reverberated convulsively along the length of her body, the way a wet dog shakes from head to tail.

Mamoo knelt in front of her on the floor, gripped her by the shoulders, and bent way down so that she could look up into Duck's eyes. "Listen to me, Laura. The fact that your mother and sister died doesn't mean that everyone in peril dies. We're just going to have to wait this one out. And even if Catherine Liem does die, no one is responsible for another person's suicide. You haven't killed your father and you didn't kill Catherine Liem. She had plenty of things to despair about besides your rose—not least of which is the fact that she killed Evelyn and Alexandra. That's as good a motive for suicide as I can think of. But whatever provocations she had, the despair was her own, and the decision to die was her own, do you understand me?"

Duck nodded to please her grandmother, but she did not understand at all. She wondered whether Catherine might have blundered into the murders as foolishly as Duck had blundered into destroying Catherine.

"Now," Mamoo said, "I'm going to look for your father. Will you be all right until I get back?"

Duck did not want Mamoo to go. She wanted her to stay and be the strong, sheltering grandmother Duck needed. It seldom entered her mind that Mamoo was also Blake, Sr.'s mother; but she thought of it now. Her father needed Mamoo more than she did. Duck nodded her approval of Mamoo's departure, feeling brave and generous.

"You promise?"

Duck nodded again.

"Good girl. I'll be home soon."

Junior came down as she was leaving. Mamoo instructed

him to circle the block ten times alone. "Duck's not feeling well," she told him, leading him by the shoulders away from the sickroom.

Duck laboriously climbed the stairs to her room, feeling older and more tired than even her father had looked. She closed her door against the imminent arrival of Bahalia and sat on the edge of her bed. *Put it on pause,* she prayed. *No, back it up. Back it up to last April, and let none of this happen. Let Dad and Catherine be married, with my blessing. Or let me stay home on May 7 and be shot, too. I didn't need my long formal, as it turned out. I might as well have stayed home and died.*

What would Alexandra do? It was an unanswerable question. Alexandra would never, never, *never* have gotten herself into such a position. Once in a position like this, there was no way out. Duck could not walk backwards through time and pluck the rose from her father's jacket; she could not untie Catherine Liem's strangling knots. Well, as Mamoo had said, Catherine Liem had her reasons for despair; but so did Duck. Some of the same reasons: they were both killers. Maybe. But maybe—the thought had to be confronted—maybe Catherine wasn't. The evidence against her, powerful as it was, was all circumstantial. Nobody close to Catherine believed her guilty. The possibility of her innocence squeezed the breath out of Duck.

Well. As Catherine Liem had made the decision to die, so could Duck. She retrieved the little derringer from her drawer and loaded it. She remembered the lethal feel of the gun when she had handled it before. Funny. It felt friendly now.

She also remembered the scenario she had envisioned, in which she was to shoot herself in front of her father in the foyer where Mother and Alexandra had died—the ultimate expression of her colossal anger toward him. What a cruelly misguided gesture that would have been. On the order of her flower stunt. Of course, if she had killed herself then, she wouldn't have been around to kill Catherine with the flower. And if she killed herself now, just think of all the future pain she could spare herself and everyone around her.

Except her father. As deeply as she had hurt him already, she knew that she retained the capacity to hurt him at least that much again by dying. And Mamoo, whom she had promised she would be all right. And Junior. She fondled the little gun in her lap. She couldn't do it. She didn't deserve so easy an out.

What about a convent? Did they still have those? Somewhere dark, cool, and quiet where she could live out her life harmlessly. Betsy Cristina would know if such a place still existed. Would she qualify as a novitiate after her experiences with Rick two months ago? Only two months ago? It seemed like a lifetime. Duck practiced at the monastic life by sitting still and watching golden motes of dust circling dizzily in the sunlight. They reminded her of the glitter floating inside the glass ball that encased a manger scene and played "Silent Night." It was one of her favorite Christmas decorations. Normally, it would be out by now, with the velvet bows, the pine cone wreath, the gold candles, the greens, the manger scene, and the Christmas tree with the handblown ornaments from Germany. All those things must still be boxed up in the attic. Motes of dust were as festive as this holiday season would get.

Bahalia popped her head inside Duck's door. "Junior say you sick." Her eyes went straight to the gun in Duck's lap and opened wide. Duck hastily drew a fold of her nightgown over the derringer, knowing it was too late.

Bahalia strode across the room. "Unh-unh. Unh-unh. Unh-unh." The sounds exploded from her like the blasts of a cannon. She held her hand out. "Give that here right now."

Duck unwrapped it from her gown and held it in the palm of her hand. "I wasn't going to use it, Bahalia, I promise. I'll put it away."

Bahalia lunged for it and Duck instinctively pulled back, trying to protect herself and Bahalia from an accidental discharge. Untrusting, Bahalia wrestled her for the gun.

"Let go! It's loaded!" she screamed at Bahalia.

"Give it to me!" Bahalia screamed back.

Finally, Duck wrenched free, flipped open the chamber, and let the bullets clatter to the floor. Bahalia scrambled after them as if they might detonate by rolling. They sat down opposite one another, panting from their exertions.

"What was you thinkin', child?" Bahalia cried. "Ain't we got enough dead bodies aroun' here?"

"Bahalia, I swear to you, I wasn't going to use it."

"Girl, you oughta know as well as anybody that thing is no toy. Now give it to me."

"I'm putting it away," Duck promised.

"For what you puttin' it away?" Bahalia exclaimed indignantly. "For what? You got no need for it. How I'm gonna rest thinkin' about you sittin' up here playin' with a gun? Please give it to me, baby."

"I'll give it to you if you promise not to say anything about it to my dad or Mamoo," Duck negotiated.

Bahalia pulled herself up to her full four feet eleven inches and placed her arms akimbo. "Oh yes I am, too, gonna tell 'em. Only thing we's bargainin' for right now is whether I'm gone get that gun without gettin' shot. But I sure is gonna tell your daddy."

"Bahalia, please. It'll only worry and upset them."

"Well, it look like they needs to be worried, don' it? I been keepin' my mouth shut about too many things around here and I'm not doin' it this time, no sir. You and your daddy both, you think you can avoid trouble by keepin' quiet about it. Look like you'd figure out by now that ain't workin' too good."

Bahalia struck the raw nerve leading to Duck's fatal silence about the rose. Duck threw herself onto her pillow and cried for all she was worth. Bahalia sat beside her and patted her back. "You need to be talkin' to your daddy, baby. That man loves you, girl."

Not anymore, Duck cried into her pillow. When the tears had started she felt they would come forever; but after a few minutes, she was worn out with crying. Bahalia got a wet washrag for her and a towel in which to wrap the derringer.

Duck tried one last time. "Please, Bahalia, don't tell them about the gun. Some things have to be private."

"That's right. But this ain't one. Now lemme go make sure your brother's alive in the closet and your daddy ain't snuck into his room with a semiautomatic. Then I'll be back check on you. You need me, call." On her way out the door, Bahalia turned and pointed a finger at her. "You hurt yourself, I gone come after you and wup you like you're one a mines, you understand?"

"I won't."

Bahalia was gone, but the finger flickered back into the room. "Don'."

Duck called the Cristinas' looking for Maria. Betsy answered the phone. "Duck, is that you?"

"Mm-hmh."

"We saw the paper. How is everyone over there?"

She means my dad. How is he doing with the news that his lover, who murdered his wife and daughter, has now murdered herself? If only Betsy knew the real question: How is your father doing with the news that his daughter murdered his lover who murdered his wife and other daughter? Jesus.

"Duck?"

"Oh. I'm sorry. We're not doing too well. Is Maria home?"

"No, sweetie, she's not, but let me give you her number at work. Call her there, okay? Is there anything I can do?"

"No. Thanks."

Duck called the Bee-Mart. An official-sounding woman answered. Duck asked timidly, "May I please speak to Maria Cristina?"

"Duck!" It was Maria.

"Maria, can you come over?"

Maria didn't hesitate an instant. "I'll be there in fifteen minutes."

She was still wearing her orange smock when she came into Duck's room. She sat in the armchair across from Duck's bed, a rising cartoon sun against the blue backdrop of Duck's wall. She listened to everything Duck had not told her before, beginning with Rick, and on through Maggie, the gun, the letter, the rose, and Duck's confrontations with her father and Bahalia that morning.

"You've been carrying so much by yourself," Maria said sympathetically.

"It's hard to open up so much ugliness."

"It all sounds much more scary than ugly to me. Like watching a horror film all by yourself in a dark house," Maria said.

"But this was no movie, Maria. Catherine Liem's really in a coma. And I really pushed her over the edge."

Maria harrumphed.

Duck was exasperated. "You can't help me if you won't face facts. I destroyed her."

"Well, Duck, there's a lot of competition out there for that slot," Maria said, as she lined up a row of stuffed animals across Duck's dresser. "Everybody who thinks Duck was the straw that broke Catherine Liem's back, raise your hand," she instructed them. She held her hand out to the unresponsive jury. "You see?"

"C'mon, Maria."

"Okay. Everyone who thinks Liem's parents ruined Catherine Liem by drowning themselves, raise your hand."

Maria gave the jury a moment to register their votes before continuing on. "No? Okay. Everyone who thinks Elga ruined her by being as bad a nanny as she was an author?

"No? Who thinks it was Grandpa Rudolf, by being too good to be true?

"No? Who thinks it was Mr. Spencer, by stealing her love and giving nothing in return?

"While we're on it, who thinks it was Rick?" Maria dove onto a dog and twisted one of his paws heavenward. She had the animal speak in a squeaky, singsong voice. "She was sleeping with Rick and he sued her for palimony so that he could afford to maintain the rest of his harem. It killed her to learn she'd have to foot the bill for all of Jenny's shoes."

Duck could not help laughing. "How can you make me laugh about this?"

"Shhh! This is serious. Order in the court!" Maria wielded a giraffe from the jury as a gavel. "Who thinks it was her asshole lawyer, who had the effrontery to attack Junior *and* Joey, two of the best brothers in the world?" Maria sat on several of the plump jurors and raised her own hand.

"Who thinks it was Judge Porter?" Maria paused, and added seriously, "Joey says the word around the prison is that she was wearing a gag in her mouth."

"She was? That's creepy."

"I think people are in a creepy frame of mind when they attempt suicide. Anyway, it supports a verdict against Judge Porter."

"You've made your point, Maria. But I still think I may have pushed her over the edge."

Maria accosted the stuffed animals again. "Who thinks Catherine Liem is responsible for her own actions because she just couldn't take it?" Maria bounced the jurors excitedly up and down, raising their hooves and paws.

"I think she might have felt exactly the way I did this

morning and just didn't have any friends around to help her through it."

"C'mon, Duck. She's got a lot more on her conscience than you do," Maria argued.

"I'm not so sure she does. That's part of what's been preying on me, the idea that I shoved an innocent person over the edge."

"Even if she's innocent of killing your mom and Alexandra, she sure isn't innocent of her own suicide effort. Joey thinks she had rotten representation from her lawyer; that's the consensus at court. That's occasion for hiring a new lawyer and taking an appeal, not committing suicide. It was a stupid choice, a coward's choice. What you did with the letter was wrong, but you didn't kill her. And you sure can't fix it by killing yourself." Maria's condemnation of Catherine's choice hung in the air; it would be a stupid choice, a coward's choice for Duck, too.

"I know."

"You promise you'll call me right away if you ever feel like that again?"

"Yes. And maybe if I call you a little sooner to tell you what's going on, I never will feel like that again."

"I love you, Duck."

"I love you, too. And you know what? I think I'm ready to be called Laura now."

"Oh, man. You sound just like Maggie. I mean, Margaret."

"I'm not sure that'll stick. I mean, Maggie *is* Maggie. But I've never really felt like a 'Duck.' I just got tagged with it. And the only down side of shucking the name is that it feels a little disrespectful of Alex, who gave it to me."

They talked about Alexandra, Maggie, Rick, and even Joey all day. Duck laid up in bed like an invalid and drank the hot soup of her friend's affection. Bahalia checked in on her periodically and fussed over both her and Maria. Mamoo returned after a few hours, and reported that Blake, Sr. was safely, if despondently, ensconced at the construction site.

"Didn't he go visit Catherine?" Duck asked.

"He couldn't get in to see her."

"How is she?"

"The same."

Duck thought she detected deeper lines of worry in Mamoo's forehead, signaling that Bahalia had told her about the gun; but Mamoo, like Bahalia, obviously considered Maria the best tonic.

Duck was certain Bahalia had been exercising the story of the derringer when Nancy Voss dropped into her room an hour before Junior's regular session. "Hi!" Nancy beamed from Duck's doorway.

"Hi, Nancy," Duck radiated back. She waved Nancy and Maria at one another. "Nancy Voss. Maria Cristina. Nancy, I'm not suicidal, really, and I've made it a practice never to kill myself in front of Maria."

"Great! I'm glad to hear it. Nice to meet you, Maria. You look like just the right sort of therapist. Would you mind if I talked with Duck alone for a minute?"

"Sure. No problem. I understand. I'll go hang out in the kitchen with Bahalia for a little while." Maria jumped up, her awkward eagerness betraying the burden of her concern for her friend.

When she was gone, Nancy asked Duck, "Do you want to talk about what happened earlier with the gun?" She stood by the door, declaring her intention not to intrude without an invitation.

Duck left her there. "There really isn't anything to talk about. I know how it looked to Bahalia and I feel really bad about upsetting her like that, but I wasn't even seriously thinking about suicide."

"What were you doing with the gun?"

"Not killing myself, Nancy." An edge of impatience had

pricked Duck's voice. "I really don't want to talk about it anymore."

"I believe what you say, and I'm glad you weren't in that kind of trouble." Nancy paused and considered for a moment. "Look, I know we haven't known each other long and you're not my patient, but I feel I've gotten to know you a little bit, and I like you a lot so I hope you don't mind if I yammer at you for a minute."

"Okay," Duck shrugged.

"When somebody makes a public display of self-destructive behavior—it doesn't have to be a real suicide attempt; just the appearance of it is enough—that person is usually making a plea for help. It may not even be a conscious gesture. Sometimes—especially in families like yours where people are having trouble talking about their feelings—the subconscious sends out that plea without the person understanding what's happening." Nancy headed off the objection Duck was poised to utter. "I can't say for sure that that's what you did this morning. All I can say is that that's how the people around you are reacting to it. Because they love you, Duck. You're surrounded by people who really love you. And that's something you can draw comfort and strength from whether or not you meant to ask them for help.

"So." Nancy punched the doorjamb with light finality. "We'll all be around if you do need us. Want me to send Maria back up?"

"Please . . . and thanks. I know people are trying to help and I appreciate it. But I'm okay. I wish you would just tell Bahalia and my grandmother that."

"It's a deal. Will you agree to tell them when you're not okay?"

"Sure."

"Thanks," Nancy said sincerely.

Maria returned looking more relaxed than when she left,

and she stayed with Duck for the rest of the day. Cloistered in Duck's room, the girls were unaware of the strong winds gathering around them. Betsy phoned and spoke to Mamoo. Mamoo talked to Bahalia. Bahalia went after her husband Charlie and brought him back to the Spencers'. Mamoo called Blake, Sr.'s office and had someone go in search of him with an urgent message to come home. Junior was removed to the Cristinas' house for the night.

Duck and Maria emerged into a grim atmosphere of silent activity that reminded Duck of preparations for a hurricane, when candles are brought out, batteries are checked, bottles and bathtubs are filled with water, shutters are bolted closed, and unshuttered glass is taped to prevent shattered fragments from deadly flight. The damage control Duck and Maria encountered was of a completely different nature, but suggested equally ominous possibilities.

"Mamoo?" Duck asked.

Mamoo said tensely to Maria, "Would you wait here in the kitchen while I talk to Duck? Your mother and Joey are on their way over."

Maria sat down at the table, looking frightened.

Duck followed her grandmother into the den. Before Mamoo could turn to face her, Duck blurted out, "Catherine's dead."

Mamoo shook her head, tight-lipped.

Duck guessed again. "Daddy's dead." She held her breath, fearful of the answer.

Mamoo shook her head in a disquieting way. It was not one of those shakes that said "Oh, nothing so awful as that." Mamoo spoke slowly. "Bahalia's son Charles has confessed to killing your mother and Alexandra."

48

P.S. I find myself more and more drawn to *The Kalevala*, searching for roots. Like all great epics, it has a prescription for every ailment. I found mine; not having been administered at the proper time, it places me beyond redemption:

> *Do not you, O future people,*
> *Bring up children crookedly*
> *In the care of stupid cradlers*
> *With a stranger as a rocker.*
> *Children brought up crookedly,*
> *Any infant cradled wrongly,*
> *Never learns the way of things,*
> *Never acquires a mind mature*
> *However old he grows to be*
> *Or however strong in body.*

Please take good care of Duck and Junior for me.

K.

49

MAMOO'S NEWS MADE Duck's ears ring. Charles's confession had come one day too late to save Catherine Liem. But Duck could hardly blame Charles for that. She was the one who had driven the poor woman to suicide, and she had done it in spite of Catherine's protestations of innocence, her father's declarations of support, and her own misgivings. Even as she had rushed to undo one wrong to Catherine—the rose—she had committed another—blundering past Nancy Voss's all-too-justified suspicions of Charles. The gains from Duck's day-long session with Maria ebbed away, and guilt and remorse flooded in, threatening to overwhelm her.

"Why did he do it?" Duck asked, not really caring.

Mamoo spoke in a monotone, her eyes fixed on the wall to Duck's left. "He's been going through withdrawals from cocaine and other drugs in prison. He was desperate to get out. He tried to work out an exchange of information about the killings for immunity from prosecution on his assault charge. He thought he could do it cleverly so that the D.A. would give a grant of immunity broad enough to protect him from prosecution for the murders. It doesn't work that way, and he won't be immune from prosecution."

Duck had wanted to know why Charles shot up her family, not why he confessed; but Mamoo's befuddled response was as significant as any. Duck stared at the wall with her grandmother, as the story droned on.

"The problem now is that the D.A. is embarrassed over the conviction of Catherine Liem, which, if she dies, will be beyond correction. Charles's confession is going to be a political bombshell for Betkins, Burdock, and Porter. Joey copied the videotape of the confession because he's afraid they're going to spare themselves the embarrassment by ignoring it."

Duck's eyes snapped back to Mamoo's face. "How could they do that?" she exclaimed.

"They probably can't, because several people know about it already. Joey's theft ensures that they won't. He's bringing it over to show to us. Betsy's seen it. She says it's horrible." Mamoo's face stayed glued to the wall, as though the videotape were playing there.

Naturally it was going to be horrible. This was what Duck's life had become, a daily progression from the horrible to the more horrible: from betrayed to betrayer; from victim to murderess. She said only part of what she was feeling. "It's horrible, all right. I killed an innocent person."

"Duck. She isn't dead and she hurt herself," Mamoo said firmly. "Betsy says the tape explains why Charles did it. She was so upset about it she couldn't tell me. We'll just have to see it for ourselves."

A somber-faced Maria walked in with Betsy and Joey, who had the frightening black box in his hand. Joey carried it into the den like a pallbearer. After he had gingerly buried it in the VCR, he turned to Duck. "Has anyone told you what's on here?"

She nodded.

Betsy interjected, "She knows about Charles. They'll have to see the rest. I don't know what to believe."

Joey stood between Duck and the television, shielding her from the blank screen. His face was drawn, his brown eyes filled with compassion. "Duck, you don't have to watch this now. Maybe it'd be better to let your dad get more information . . ."

She shook her head. She didn't care what was on the tape, and she didn't have the strength to move.

Duck lowered herself to the floor between Betsy and Maria. They waited for Blake, Sr., scarcely talking. Bahalia, crying quietly, joined them with Charlie; she sat hunched under her husband's arm in a wide orange chair. When Duck's father arrived, he went straight to the place Mamoo had reserved for him on the sofa without looking at Duck; but then, he was preoccupied. Joey dimmed the lights and started the tape.

Charles was seated at a table with two examiners, a uniformed policeman, and an older man in baggy street clothes. The camera, Joey explained, was behind a one-way window. The film was sharp and clear. It began with a lengthy explication of Charles's rights and his negotiation for immunity for his assault of Bahalia or related offenses, which was given. Charles's cliff of hair was askew on his head and the shaved sides of his scalp bristled with unkempt new growth. His hands jumped around on the table. It also appeared from the jiggling of his torso that he was furiously tapping one or both feet.

In answer to questions, Charles explained that he had known the Spencers all his life, through his mother's employment and his own odd jobs around the house.

"When did you arrive there on the afternoon of May seventh?"

"Doncha wanna know about the car? You guys had one piece-a-shit mechanic at that trial. When I get out, I'm comin' to work as an expert witness for you guys so you'll have somebody *knows* somethin'!"

"Yes, tell us about the car," the older man said.

Charles explained how easily he had burglarized

Catherine Liem's house on Monterey Street. He had been inside several times, usually on her studio days. "She get in that big side room, turn up her shit music real loud, I could be playin' the drums, she don' hear it, she don' come out for nuthin'." He had found the gun without difficulty and left it in place until the day of the murders. He had also discovered that she routinely left her keys hanging on a hook by the back door. He had checked out her car in the garage. He examined the fuel pump relay in her Volvo and then bought an identical part. "I fried the coil at my home, man. Didn' have to run no electrical line out to the car on the street like your 'expert' say. Did that in my kitchen." Charles drew a diagram of the fuel pump relay, and showed how he had disabled the coil by applying a twelve-volt current to the wrong terminals. "Then all's I had to do was pop the bad coil into her car. Thirty seconds, man." He shook his head over the stupidity of the experts.

"Why did you use Catherine Liem's car?"

"Well, that was the whole point, man. To make it look like she did it."

"Why?"

"That's how Miz Spensah wanted it done." Charles straightened up, smiling, in the posture of a proud pupil who had successfully completed his recital.

Duck half-croaked, half-whispered, "Oh, please, put it on pause."

She was only dimly aware of having spoken aloud, but the vigilant Joey immediately punched the pause button. Charles's cheerful image was frozen on the screen, still jittering from the horizontal lines of static that floated from bottom to top. Maria had clenched Duck's hand so hard that it hurt. Betsy held her by one shoulder and one bent knee. Thus anchored, Duck nevertheless felt as though she were floating free of her body. It was like an after-death experience. Without turning, she could see Bahalia burrowing into

Charlie's shoulder, her tiny hands folded inside his, and Mamoo and Blake huddled together on the couch, their eyes fixed on Charles's glaring, jumping face. Joey was watching Duck (her empty body, not her hovering spirit).

"This is probably a good place to stop," Joey said.

Duck had been speaking figuratively, not literally, when she asked for the pause. She meant that she wanted a break in the family's deepening misery. She wanted her mother not to have commissioned her own death. But she recognized that stopping the tape was an ineffectual remedy. "We need to finish. Would you put it back on, Joey?"

He hesitated. "It gets worse."

Naturally, she thought. *Things get worse and worse.* "Let's get it over with."

Joey touched the play button, and Charles jumped back into ebullient life. The older officer asked, "What was it that Mrs. Spencer wanted done?"

"Hunh!" The sound came from deep in Charles's throat. "Miz Spensah always knew just what she wanted." He stared past the officer, lost in some private reverie.

"What did she want?" The interrogator asked. He leaned sideways into Charles's line of vision, brought his portly face close to Charles. "What?"

"First," Charles said dreamily, tipping his face to the ceiling, "she gave me a hundred dollars. Just *gave* it to me, man. And a week later, she gave me another hundred. And a week after that, another hundred. Like she *knew* what I was gonna do with it.

"So then I had me a pretty good little habit going, you know. So the next week I asked her for another hundred. And she said I already owed her three, but if I'd do a little job for her, she'd give me two more. So I followed Mistah Spensah for her and gave her the dates and the times when he went over to the girl's house."

Charles pulled his gaze from the ceiling with an effort,

and looked the detective in the eye. "But you wanna know what Miz Spensah wanted. She wanted *more*, man. Bad as I wanted the coke, she always wanted more."

"What?" The question was soft, curious.

"She pay me five hundred dollars to take a video of her husband with the artist. She just wanted a picture of the two of them together, like goin' into the house, comin' out. But I got 'em, you know, really *together*." Charles laughed and slapped his knee. "They was at it so long the tape ran out."

"They were having sex?"

"What you think? Yeah, they was goin' at it like crazy . . ."

"Oh my God," Blake, Sr. whispered behind Duck.

Duck could not have spoken. She only vaguely intimated—and that was enough to send a paralyzing bolt of horror through her—what her mother, who had commissioned a PG-rated video she could "use" against her husband (how well Daddy knew her), would have felt when she viewed the feature-length, X-rated film of her husband in bed with Catherine Liem.

Charles's statement moved inexorably on. ". . . A week after I gave her the porn was when Miz Spensah decided to do this other."

That would have been right after Mother returned, "refreshed," from her week at the spa, Duck thought. Oh, God. Oh, God.

"What?" the detective asked. He was cleaning his fingernails, as if Charles's statement were of no consequence. The second officer sat stiller than a table leg at his corner of the frame.

"She asked me could I steal the car, an' I said, 'Can I steal a car?'" Charles pointed at himself with an expression of mock incredulity. "She sure got her money's worth. The stealin' was the easiest part. It was my idea to make the car look like it stalled out. Your big ol' experts couldn' even figure it out." Charles laughed proudly. "An' the gun, man. That dumb bitch had the gun out in this pretty little case jus' beggin' to be used." Charles wiped tears of happiness from his eyes. "Miz Spensah was so happy when I tol' her we could use the bitch's own gun."

"Mrs. Spencer wanted you to kill her with Catherine Liem's gun?"

"That's what I'm tellin' you. She paid me five thousand dollars to do her and the kid, and five thousand dollars never to talk about it. But I guess she ain' gone be collectin' no refund, is she?" Charles chuckled. He gave details of when and how he had been paid that Duck could not hear over the roaring in her ears.

"When did you and Mrs. Spencer make the plan?"

"About two months before I pulled it off. It didn't take me no time to get it ready, but she say she want some time to enjoy the idea since it's the last thing she's gonna enjoy. Then she call me and say she's got everybody lined up for May seventh, so I went."

"Lined up how?"

"Two kids out shoppin' and Mr. Spensah sittin' tight in his office so his girlfriend couldn't use him for an alibi."

"Tell me what happened when you got to the Spencer house that day."

Duck couldn't believe there would be more, that the officers could continue without a break, that Charles had breath left to speak.

But Charles looked rested and eager to tell his story. "Miz Spensah comes to the door all excited and says, 'Not today,' which I found out in a minute is because the little bitch is at home. She wasn't s'pose to be there."

"I thought you told us she paid you to kill them both."

"Not the girl. I was s'pose to do her and the boy. When we set it up she say, 'I will be remembered by my home and my girls. Junior is not my legacy.'" Charles had drawn himself up straight in his chair, and was speaking in a high, reedy, arrogant voice. He sounded uncannily like Mother.

"What happened after Mrs. Spencer said, 'Not today'?"

"This is good. This is good. Lemme tell you how it comes down. See, the little bitch comes out to see what all the excitement's about and Miz Spensah's hollerin' to stop. But she the one pick that day and I already done fix the car so it's gotta go. So I tell the little bitch, 'This your momma's idea,' and I pop her a few times. Then Miz Spensah goes over and pulls open the closet and there's the big stupid standin' in there like this." Charles pulled his hands up to his chest and blinked at his examiners like a frightened mouse. "An' the bitch starts hollerin', 'Kill him! Kill him!' An' I tells her, so business-like, 'But Miz Spensah, you only paid for two, so who's it gone be, him or you? An' she runs at me, so I do her. Then I close the door on the dummy an' I go on out."

"Didn't you think the boy might identify you?"

"He didn', did he? That boy don' know shit."

"You didn't want to kill anyone more than you'd been paid to kill?" the detective asked with a touch of annoyance, the most emotion he'd demonstrated during the interview.

Charles shed his chatty style like a husk and emerged raw, enraged, and wild. He leapt from his chair and waved his shackled hands in the air as he screamed, "It was enough killin'! Enough! I did enough! I never killed nobody before! I had enough!"

It was the madman who had attacked Bahalia, all over again. The uniformed officer was tensed and ready, his gun half drawn. But Charles made no move at them. He stayed planted like a tree whipped about in a storm.

When the tempest had subsided, Charles sat down in his chair and spoke in a calm, quiet voice. "Anyway, I had a talk with Junior before I shut him in. I tole him I'd give him his life for mine. He had to promise me, *promise* not to talk. And if he did, I would kill him. He was always good to me. I figured I could trust him. An' I was right." He looked into the detective's eye and told him conversationally, "An' you know what else? Him and me had something in common: I'm not my momma's legacy either. I didn't want to kill him."

They questioned Charles about all the details and then asked, "Does that conclude your statement?" Charles lifted his chair and turned sideways to face the camera behind the mirrored glass. "Well, Momma," he said with a big smile, "do I exist now?"

The keening that came from Bahalia was as terrible as anything on the tape.

50

THE VERDICT ON CATHERINE LIEM
AN EXCLUSIVE INTERVIEW WITH HER CELLMATE

Angelle Bascom, Catherine Liem's cellmate for the past two months, slept through the suicide attempt that crisscrossed the cell and must have been hours in the preparation. Asked how she missed the sound of tearing sheets and the anchoring of the web of doom to her own bunk, Ms. Bascom replied, "Living with somebody like her, you got to shut yourself off."

Ms. Bascom reported that there was no unusual activity before the two women retired for the evening, "depending," she said, "on what you want to call unusual. The ice lady did her usual scribbling, scribbling, scribbling." When asked about Ms. Liem's mood, Ms. Bascom answered, "The usual. She was the gloomiest person I ever met. The place is a lot livelier now with her dead."*

*Ms. Liem is not dead. She remains in a coma at USA Medical Center. (See related story.)

Ms. Bascom is awaiting trial on a charge of armed robbery.

Ms. Liem's suicide attempt also escaped notice on the Metro Jail's surveillance cameras, designed to monitor each cell 24 hours a day.

51

BLAKE, SR. WAS the only viewer of the videotape capable of action when it was over. He thanked Joey and sent the Cristinas home. On her way out, Maria silently ran a finger across Duck's back, as if checking her for dust. Blake called Ms. Burdock at home, asking whether she had disclosed Charles's confession to the press. He told her that he wanted Catherine's name cleared in the morning edition of the paper. If he were not called by a reporter seeking his comment within the next thirty minutes, he would notify the newspaper himself. No, he said, he would not identify the source of his information.

In twenty minutes, a reporter called from the *Daily Times*. Blake, Sr. refused to comment. He called Nancy Voss and asked her to come over, right then, to see the tape. She came, and the Deeds, unable to watch it again, left. Bahalia walked out bent over and shuffling her feet, supported by Charlie. He left her at the kitchen door and came back to ask Blake, who was rewinding the tape, "My wife wants to know, can she come back tomorrow?"

Mamoo's head snapped up.

Blake answered for all of them. "Of course she can. If she wants to. No one holds her responsible for what Charles did. But if she needs some time off, we'll all understand."

Charlie nodded his thanks and left.

Duck and Mamoo went up to Duck's room to miss the second showing of the confession. The stuffed animals were still lined up on the dresser, where Maria had left them. *Anyone who thinks Charles Deed drove Catherine over the edge, raise your hand.* Not one of the jurors stirred.

Duck could not cry. Her sorrow lay deeper than the seat of her tears. She and Mamoo sat on the bed, shoulder to shoulder, leaning against the wall. Mamoo massaged Duck's right hand methodically, kneading her palm, then pulling on her fingers, as if trying to milk the pain from them.

Mother had not tolerated Blake, Sr.'s affair, after all. And she had not tolerated Junior, either. No wonder she left her entire estate to Duck and Alexandra; she thought they would be her only living successors. *Oh, Mother.* There must have been so many signs of her monstrous rage, all missed by the family she had taught to tiptoe around her. And the Deeds had done a similar thing with Charles. His parents had rightly guessed that he came into some money in May. But even if he'd put Mother's entire five-thousand-dollar payment into his veins, Duck thought it would not have explained his degeneration from a jittery miscreant to the fiend he had become. She held the picture she had of Charles before the murders—the jumpy but capable Rastafarian who came by on weekends to repair the lawnmower (and who had carefully planned the Spencer murders)—against the grinning live wire who had attacked Bahalia and bounced happily through his gruesome confession. Duck thought the murders themselves were the psychic jolt that explained the change in Charles. She wished that someone had recognized it for what it was in time to help Catherine; she had no concern for what happened to Charles now, except that he be locked away forever.

Blake, Sr. came to the doorway. "I think we should sell the house. I've called a real estate agent."

His mother asked wryly, "Are you going to buy a new one tonight?"

Duck giggled.

"I need to keep doing things," Blake explained.

Duck kept on laughing. They were looking at her. She had to tell them what was so funny. "Alexandra," she cried, choking on laughter, "Alexandra's been snake-bit again so we have to move. And Mother was the snake, just like the last time."

Duck's laughter became sobs. Blake turned to leave, and Mamoo signaled to him that she wanted to talk out in the hallway. He waited impatiently and began walking downstairs as soon as she exited Duck's room.

Mamoo stood at the top of the stairs. "Where are you going?"

"To the office." His words grew muffled as he descended.

"You're needed here, Blake." It was a command.

Duck stayed hunched in her bed. She couldn't see, but from the clarity her father's voice regained, she could sense his turn, his rise up a few steps. "I need to go dig out our bank statements and see if I can trace the money Evelyn paid Charles."

"You don't need to do that tonight, Blake. They've got the confession to prove Catherine's innocence. It's Laura who needs you tonight." Mamoo fought to keep her voice low and reasonable.

"The best I can do for her right now is to stay away from her, Mother. And I think you ought to stay out of this one." The words faded again. He was turning away.

"It would be better for you to have it out with her than to pretend she doesn't exist." Mamoo turned the volume up so high that Duck, a few feet away, could not help but overhear. She was no longer an eavesdropper; she was a participant. Whatever response her father made would have to be made to Duck as well as Mamoo. And Mamoo was not finished. "Do you want to repeat Bahalia's mistake with Charles? Do you know Laura had a loaded gun in her bedroom this afternoon? Can you afford to lose another child, Blake?" Duck flinched.

Blake said, "I'm trying to protect her from my anger! It's the best I can do." His anger drew closer and Duck shrunk against her headboard.

"It is not!" his mother shouted. "If you confront her, at least she'll know you care about her."

Blake loomed in Duck's doorway, breathing heavily. "Do you know how the Winter War began, Laura?"

With a will, she sat up straight and faced him, shaking her head and trembling all over.

Coldly, he recited the history lesson. "The Soviets massed two hundred thousand troops along the Russo-Finnish border, although there was a neutrality pact. Then the Communists shelled one of their own border villages. They claimed Finland did it, and they overran the country without ever declaring war.

"Do you get it, Laura? Do you get what Catherine was trying to tell me in her letter?"

Duck bent her head and nodded, splashing fresh tears onto her lap. She knew the letter by heart. *Consider, Blake, how the Winter War began; and contact Arnie if you think that history may have repeated itself.* Duck had accomplished more by hiding Catherine's letter than she'd realized.

Blake pushed past Duck's guilty acknowledgment, and hammered her with her wrong. "She was saying she suspected Evelyn. Before the trial, Laura, when we might have found the evidence to acquit her."

"Well, why didn't she just say so?" Mamoo asked, annoyance tingeing her question. "Why all the obscure intrigue?"

With a heavy dose of irony, Blake said, "I guess she was worried about her letter falling into the wrong hands." He slammed Duck's door and left.

Mamoo held Duck's shaking body until she fell asleep. When Duck woke the next morning, Mamoo was still holding her. She loosed herself carefully from her grandmother's embrace. It was a testament to Mamoo's exhaustion that she did not stir. Duck went downstairs wearing yesterday's clothes, in which she had slept. Her father sat at the kitchen table wearing yesterday's clothes, and did not appear to have slept at all. A cream-colored envelope lay across the salver of his hands like a calling card from the grave.

Recognizing the stationery, Duck was swept with joy. "She's better! She wrote you!"

Blake glowered at her. "This is from before. It's a suicide note." He folded it carefully into his pocket, and rested his face in his hands.

"Daddy, I'm so sorry. This is all my fault." It was lame, she knew. She wanted to say something momentous to him, something that would leap the chasm between them, but she didn't know what that might be.

Her father looked at her stonily, not arguing, and returned his face to its cradle.

"Why can't you go see her?" she asked. "She's not in jail, and they know she's innocent, so they can't lock her up."

"You've done quite enough already, Laura. Stay out of it."

Anger snaked up past her guilt. "You're not going to just sit there, are you? Not this time, Dad! You can't just sit and wait for her to get better. She'll die!"

The force of her blast reeled Blake backwards from his

shielding hands. Fury stoked his cheeks, but he spoke quietly. "She's still in custody, Laura. Sheriff Katzlow is determined not to have any more mishaps. There's an armed guard positioned outside of her room. The doctor, in response to my last efforts to get in, has left express instructions at all entrances to the hospital and at all nurses' stations that I am not to be admitted. He thinks that seeing me might kill her. I have no choice but to abide by his instructions."

"Bullshit! What about Catherine's instructions? Don't you understand what you have in your pocket there?" Duck's finger stabbed at the envelope. "Don't you understand that a suicide attempt is nothing but a plea for help? She's begging you, Dad. She's got nobody else to turn to. Please don't ignore her."

Duck collapsed into the chair across from him, unable to read his stunned reaction. Something on the wall caught her eye. A blinking red eavesdropper had taken a page from Duck's book. She smiled and asked, "What do you think, Mamoo?"

Déjà vu. Duck could see in the flesh now what she had only seen in her mind's eye before. Her father rocked back in his chair, startled, and twisted to view the offending intercom. "Oh, for God's sake."

Mamoo's voice came through clear and strong. "I think you're absolutely right, Laura, but I don't know how to do it."

"I think I do," Duck said, "but we're going to need Dad's cooperation." She eyed him questioningly.

He rose unsteadily to his feet and rounded the table to hold her. "I can't bear to lose anything more. I can't bear to lose you."

He was holding nothing back, and Duck was moved to bring forth the yet unspoken apology that had tormented her for months. "I'm sorry it was Alexandra and not me, Dad."

"Oh, Laura." He held her back and looked into her eyes.

"She was the best of us," Duck said.

"She was wonderful, beautiful, smart, talented, charismatic, big-hearted. I loved her past saying. And if she had lived, I would never have said what I'm going to say now." He took a deep breath and fixed his blue eyes on Duck's. "You were always my favorite. The most sensitive; the most like me. And we will not speak of it again, because it feels disloyal to Alexandra."

52

A FORTUNE IN THE BALANCE
AN EXCLUSIVE LOOK AT THE LIEM WILL

A lot of people have new reason to wish Catherine Liem
dead. Among the possessions left in Ms. Liem's cell was
a copy of her will, apparently executed on the night of
her unsuccessful (thus far) suicide attempt. The remarkably simple document by which the heiress intended to
dispose of several billion dollars in assets is printed below in its entirety:

16 DECEMBER

I, Catherine Liem, being sound of mind and body, although unsound of spirit, do hereby declare this to be my
last will and testament, revoking all prior wills.

I direct that Liem Enterprises, Inc., a closely held corporation of which I am the sole shareholder, be converted
to a publicly traded corporation. I direct that my estate
retain one-half of all the shares issued to be sold on a
timetable determined by my executors. I bequeath the
other half of Liem Enterprises, Inc., to the individuals
employed by the corporation on the date of my death or
participating on the date of my death in the Liem Enter-

prises pension plan. Their shares in the corporation are to be prorated according to the attached schedules.

Should any employee or former employee of Liem Enterprises, Inc., challenge any portion of this will in court, my bequest to that individual is revoked.

I leave the sum of ten million ($10,000,000.00) dollars to each of the following:

Elga, to whom I also leave my journals

The Laura Davidson Spencer Trust, see attached provisions

The Blake Sarduth Spencer, Jr. Trust, see attached provisions

Rev. Everett Dalton, individually

I leave the remainder of my estate to the Liem Foundation. I appoint the following Board of Directors of the Liem Foundation:

Elizabeth McCall Cristina, Managing Director, as a life appointee.

Blake Sarduth Spencer, Sr., as a life appointee.

Laura Davidson Spencer, as a life appointee.

Eleanor Carl Spencer, as a life appointee.

Taneeka Deed, for a term of two years. It is my recommendation that former recipients of Liem Foundation prizes, scholarships, or grants be appointed to fill the rotating fifth seat on the Board of Directors.

The compensation, if any, of the Board members is to be fixed by the Board. It is my recommendation that Elizabeth Cristina, as managing director, be paid an annual salary at a beginning rate of $75,000. Her appointment to the Board is not to be construed as a conflict of interest prohibiting the payment of prize moneys to Joseph Anthony Cristina, nor to his consideration, as a prize winner, for three annual scholarships in the amount of $10,000 apiece, should he choose to further his education.

I name the firm of Derbes and Waldrup as executors, without bond, to be paid the customary fees for such service.

CATHERINE LIEM

Ms. Liem is hospitalized at USA Medical Center and her condition is listed as critical. She has remained in a coma since her attempt to hang herself in her prison cell last week. The suicide attempt came two days before Ms. Liem was exonerated in the Spencer murder case, for which she had been convicted. (See separate story.) Sheriff Katzlow's office has doubled security at the hospital to diminish the risk of foul play.

53

WHILE DUCK ENGINEERED her plan for an incursion into the hospital, Nancy Voss came over to work with Junior. She recommended that the Spencer house not be sold until Junior had remembered his entire experience in the closet. She thought it was a good idea that they move out, but she wanted Junior to have access to the closet to help jar his memory.

"Why does he have to remember? Isn't it better forgotten?" Blake, Sr. wanted to know. Duck, looking on, had the same instinct.

"If he could truly forget, it would be wonderful," Nancy explained. "The problem is, he knows what happened at some level. He's just blocked it out. And until he confronts it and deals with it, he's going to be haunted by it."

"But what he says, when he goes in there, is, 'Momma wanted me to be safe,'" Blake, Sr. pointed out.

"That's what's so sad. He's clinging to the memory of his mother sending him in there to protect him. And the reason it's so important, I think, is that he's using it as a shield against the memory of his mother screaming for him to be killed."

A flimsy shield, as it turned out. Between phone calls, Duck checked on Junior's progress. About an hour into his session, Nancy brought out his clay and tools. "Have you ever tried a likeness of a person?" Nancy asked him.

"No."

"Would you try something for me?"

"Okay."

"Would you make your mother's face the way you saw her the last time?"

Junior cringed, and pushed his chair back. Everyone could see that he was heading for the closet.

Nancy supported him. "That's a good idea, Junior. We'll take the modeling stuff in the closet. It might help you picture her."

"She wanted me safe," Junior whimpered.

"Most of the time, I'm sure she did, honey."

Junior spent a few minutes fussing the clay into a roughly round shape. Then he dug a deep hole for the mouth, and made spiky teeth; he laid on two coils of lips, drawn back over the teeth. He was finished.

"It looks scary," Nancy said.

"It was."

Duck shuddered all over at the sight of the murderous visage, trying to imagine what it would have been like to stand pressed against the back wall of the closet with Mother standing outside screaming "Kill him!" to Charles, who would've been brandishing the gun he had just used on Alexandra.

Into the silence that followed his last remark, Junior whispered hoarsely, "He gave me something."

"Who?" Nancy asked.

"Him."

"Charles?" Nancy prompted.

Junior nodded.

"What did he give you?"

"His tape."

"Gumption?"

Junior nodded again, and an echo of the nod remained as a bobbing motion that intensified and rocked Junior's body back and forth. Speaking only on the forward thrusts, Junior said, "He told me . . ." Rock. ". . . it would block . . ." Rock. ". . . it out for me . . ." Rock. ". . . like it did for him." Junior hurled himself farther forward on each rock and began pounding his head on the wall. "But it didn't. It didn't. It didn't."

Blake, Sr. had come up beside Duck. He pushed past her now to become the cushion for Junior's blows. "There, son. You don't have to block it out any longer. My brave, brave boy."

Maggie met them at a rear service entrance to USA Medical. She had been serving her penance at the hospital for weeks, and no one would challenge her right to dispose of the diapers and other wastes from her small AIDS patients. It was a job nobody else wanted. She admitted Duck, Blake, and Bahalia into a cavernous room where biohazardous waste was stored for disposal. It was 9:00 p.m., a quiet time in this part of the hospital, and they were alone. For Blake, Maggie had a green paper hospital gown and cap, and for Duck, a pink and white volunteer's jacket that matched her own. She had commandeered a gurney, and Blake climbed aboard. He allowed Maggie to tuck a white paper sheet around him, but vetoed her move to douse him in fake blood that she extracted from a Halloween vampire kit.

"Spoilsport," Maggie whispered, and opened the door to the hallway a crack. "Ready," she told Joey, who was waiting in uniform on the other side.

Bahalia slipped into the hall with Joey, and before they parted he reminded her, "When those doors open on the eighth floor, all hell's going to break loose. Remember, if anybody goes ballistic and draws on you, you hit the floor and leave it to me."

"Get on." Bahalia shoved at him. "I've had more

experience with guns around the Spensah house than you ever had on the police department."

They headed out in opposite directions. Bahalia returned to the lobby and obtained a visitor's pass for an old patient on the eighth floor. Maggie had learned that the man had no family. "He's in my church," Bahalia lied gratuitously to the attendant. Armed with her pass, she mounted the wide stairs to the mezzanine to give Joey a minute's lead time.

Maggie, Duck, and Blake waited anxiously in the storage room while Joey sprinted for the nearby staff elevators. There the plan encountered its first mishap. For what seemed a lifetime, Joey stood mashing the buttons with no results and with increasing desperation. Bahalia, taking the passenger elevators from the center of the hospital, arrived at the eighth floor on time. The metal doors swished open on a quiet hallway, at the end of which Catherine Liem's guards leaned comfortably against the wall. Bahalia resourcefully ducked back inside and went for a ride.

Joey found some stairs, climbed the eight flights at a run, and emerged a few feet from Catherine's room, authentically out of breath. He banged out of the stairwell, and ran the thirty feet to Catherine's door, shattering the quiet of the hallway by shouting into his unactivated walkie-talkie, "No, there's only two guys up here. We're going to need more than that. Send us some backup!"

The two deputies on guard duty jumped to attention. Joey knew one of them, but not well. "They've got some trouble downstairs," he panted, holding his side. "Mrs. Deed. The mother of the guy who really killed the Spencers. She says she's gotta see Ms. Liem. She got past security at the front desk. They called me in from the emergency room."

This worked too well. Both deputies had unsnapped their holsters, and one was preparing to draw.

Joey moderated. "I know this lady."

Both guns were out of their holsters, aimed at the elevator, which had just dinged its impending arrival.

"She's harmless," Joey pleaded. "We just need to settle her down and send her on her way."

This also worked too well. The doors thumped open, and Bahalia, careful not to act prematurely, peeked out tentatively. Then, seeing Joey in place down the hall, and a much closer nurses' station that she wanted to circumvent without incident, Bahalia almost tiptoed toward Joey and company. The tiny, hesitant old woman made so unthreatening an approach that the guards, weapons holstered, employed smiles to disarm her of her purpose, whatever it might be. The duty nurse came officiously from behind her counter to investigate.

As Joey was groaning inwardly, Bahalia went wild. She charged the deputies, screaming, "I'll get her! You can't keep me out! I'll kill her!"

And for a few minutes, things went like clockwork. Bahalia was subdued quickly and without injury. Joey persuaded his colleagues to take her to the station for booking while he remained on duty with the backup he had pretended to summon. When the guards had departed with Bahalia and the nurse had returned to her station, Duck and Maggie rounded the corner with the stretcher bearing Blake. They parked him at Catherine's door and he slipped easily into the room while the others stood guard in the hallway.

Duck, Joey, and Maggie suppressed their nervousness by chattering in whispers, as if they were stealing a moment between classes at Wright.

"How did Bahalia do?" Duck asked.

"She was brilliant," Joey said.

"Too bad her performance'll prob'ly land her in jail for the rest of her life," Maggie said.

"No way," Joey replied. "I've still got the attempted con-

cealment of Charles's confession in my back pocket. It's a
great trading card. We can work out a deal that will keep
Bahalia from getting charged with anything."

"Unless," Maggie said soberly, "Catherine drops dead
when her prince bends over to kiss her. Then they'll put us
all away for life. They'll say we did it for the money in her
will."

"Maggie!" Duck and Joey elbowed her in the ribs from
opposite sides.

"Can you hear anything?" Joey leaned toward the closed
door of Catherine's room.

Duck moved to block him. "I don't think we should
listen."

"Sure. Right," he agreed sheepishly, backing off. After a
moment of respectful silence, he asked Duck, "Could you
use a little distraction when all this is over? Would you like
to go to a movie?"

Duck's first thought was, *It's too soon for distraction. I
want to know how this is going to end.* She shook her head,
and Joey silently took her hand. His quiet understanding
changed her mind. This was someone she'd like to be with
no matter what the circumstances were. She looked at him
and smiled. "Can Maria and Maggie come, too?"

"Absolutely. The whole family. But you have to understand that in Italian that makes it a courtship."

"Okay." She blushed furiously.

From within Catherine's room, Duck heard a voice raised
in anger. A woman's voice. Signaling with a backturned
palm that her friends should stay in the hall, Duck pushed
the door open and stepped into the darkened room. At a
glance, she took in the surreal scene. Catherine was impris-
oned between metal rails on the high bed, her pale face lu-
minous beneath a dim night light. Clear tubes snaked over
her, seeming to siphon off her life force. A bank of ma-

chines framed the bed; green lights blipped out the patient's slow rhythms.

The scene was clean, bloodless, orderly. But the machines were clearly not in control of the figure on the bed. Duck had prepared herself to see Catherine prone, with her eyes closed. This was not Catherine. Not the tense, alert woman who had faced Duck in the courtroom. Not even the woman who had slumped before Blake's testimony or shuffled out after her sentencing. The still, shrunken figure in the bed was spectral, not-Catherine. The sight spun Duck back in time to May, standing in the doorway of her home, her eyes fixed on not-Alexandra, not-Mother. *Please,* a voice within her had cried at her sister's clotted hair, *no.* The same childlike voice was making the same foolish plea now. Hope drained from Duck's skull, dizzyingly.

Blake stood with his back to Duck, his hospital gown flapped open like stunted wings. Beyond him, a moon-faced woman was planted on thick legs. Duck recognized her from photographs, from her thin mouth curled with disapproval. Elga.

She was mid-rant, and did not slow down at Duck's arrival but lowered her voice to a hiss. "You were forbidden to come here. On doctor's orders. You are trespassing and creating a disturbance that threatens this girl's life." Elga seemed to swell, blocking Blake's access to the bed.

"Elga," he said softly. "We're on the same side. Catherine's side."

"If you do not leave this instant," she said grimly, "I shall have you arrested."

Duck moved to her father's side. She thought to touch his arm, to tell him, "There's nothing we can do here," to lead him away.

Elga's voice strengthened to a near-shout, directed at Duck. "Get out."

Blake stood firm and held an arm protectively across

Duck's chest. "Please, Elga. I'm here to give her what Rudolf denied her—what he denied you. I love her. Let me go to her."

Elga shifted her gaze from Duck to him, a shimmering, wavering movement. The air seemed electrified by her hesitancy—and by something else. Duck turned slowly to Catherine.

Who was watching them. And smiling.